The Baleful Owl

by

Virgil Alexander

Aakenbaaken & Kent

The Baleful Owl

2nd edition. Copyright 2018, all rights reserved.

No part of this book may be used or reproduced in any manner whatsoever without written permission except in the case of brief quotations for use in articles and reviews.

Aakenbaakeneditor@gmail.com

This book is a work of fiction. Names, characters, places and incidents are either the product of the author's imagination or are used fictitiously. Any resemblance of the fictional characters to actual persons living or dead is entirely coincidental.

ISBN: 978-1-938436-56-7

Dedication

Much of this story is close to my heart because I treasure the diverse Native American culture, both living and ancient, that exists in the Southwest. I dedicate this book to my friend and coworker, Harold Victor (1947-2013), Viet Nam veteran, instrumentation technician, San Carlos Apache, and all around good guy.

Chapter 1

Do'ag Da'ivundam Pueblo – 1449 AD. In the season of the late harvest I, the shaman Ne'ee Sihki (Deer Singer), went to the sacred place and with great respect set out the ceremonial vessels made by the Old One, a potter, weaver, and most powerful shaman. I am the Old One's great-grandson. When the Old One had given his knowledge to grandfather, he died and took the form of the owl and watched over this place of the bubbling spring, and we prospered. The owl was a benevolent and wise protector, carrying good messages to the Creator. But the people have turned from the way taught by the Old One; his countenance has become baleful, and our blessings have diminished.

I softly sang the prayer song as I prepared each vessel for the sunset ceremony. Into the earth-mother vessel I put the sacred pollen and the spring water. I scooped meals of corn, amaranth, and mesquite into the basin, added a handful of red salt from cliffs above the salty river, and covered the Baleful Owl with the white doeskin cover. In the olla, I had the eagle feathers for blessing and the owl feather fan for healing. The bear contained steamed acorns. In the lion, I put a handful of pine nuts. This was done in the manner of all shamans before me.

I prepared myself while sitting on the upper plaza above the sacred place. I was wearing the fine woven tunic and kilt made for these ceremonials by the Old One. I watched as the elders, a short distance away in the pass, lit the fire and prepared the cooking stones. There I would perform what might be the last harvest rite in *Do'ag Da'ivundam* (Mountain Spring), the home my people had known for uncounted generations. For several years we had not held the traditional harvest feast. Our stores were spare, so the food was carefully used; instead of feasting, we now share only the small ceremonial cakes.

I reviewed in my mind the songs and prayers. Spotted Flat Top Mountain seemed to glow in the golden rays of the setting sun. I gazed at the rugged desert buttes, valleys, and layered ranges in tones of purple and blue stretching below the pass—a scene of beauty that now touched my soul with sadness.

I reflected on the plight of the people. For all time, since the people emerged from center earth, they had been people of peace and beauty, living in harmony with the river people and the other pueblos. Long forgotten was the art of warfare, and we became master artisans and merchants.

Our goods were valued from the great southern sea to the far white-topped mountains and the endless plateaus. Here in this mountain pueblo we grew only a few crops and gathered the natural bounty. We had always richly supplemented our primary supply by trading fine textiles, ceramics, jewelry, and baskets. Times had changed in a way none had expected. Now even the river people barely feed themselves. There are few crops for them to trade.

But the seasons still came and went, and the sun mark in the plaza said the cold season was near. The nights were already brisk and soon the dead time would arrive; no crops would grow, and the berries would all be gone; the nuts and the acorns would be gone; the bubbling water would turn white and solid; and the game would become lean and few in number.

This harvest was spare; for once again little rain had come. Now the fearsome raiders, the *ob* (Apache), had migrated from the north and east and were destroying pueblos, taking their food, and driving them to the land of the River Growers. Even our people fight amongst themselves — pueblo against pueblo for water, food, and wood.

The Baleful Owl, the spirit messenger, was still cursing us. To appease him I attached two matched sacred turquoise disks with deer-hoof glue into the depressions that were the owl's eyes, and using the warm doeskin cloak I made, I covered the messenger owl from the growing cold. Surely he would not block our prayers now.

I summoned the elders, each painted in the symbol of one of the earth forces: the sun, the wind, the rain, the lightning, the plants, the animals, and the bubbling earth water. The people were painted as I was with large white spots covering their limbs and torsos. To music of drums and flutes, the people assembled and, led by the sacred effigies, paraded through the Pueblo and up the slight incline to the mountain saddle.

There, facing the familiar scene of beauty made more glorious by the setting sun, we offered the prayers and songs. We mixed the pollen water, the meal, the pine nuts, and the acorns and formed little cakes, placing them with a dollop of deer suet on the heated stones to sizzle and cook until both sides were browned.

All the people came and ate the cakes and joined the songs. Finally, the doeskin cover was lifted off the Baleful Owl, and he saw the people; he saw the setting sun; he felt the cold. Then I sang to him: "Your eyes in beauty see our people. We give you the beautiful eyes. We give you the soft, warm coat. Now give up our prayers and songs, so the spirits will carry them to the Creator and we can continue to live."

We performed the remaining ancient songs and prayers as the golden glow turned to red. Finally re-shrouding the Baleful Owl, we sang as we walked in procession back to the pueblo, there setting the hallowed ceramics back in their place of honor. As the last crimson light retreated from the onslaught of night, we retired to our beds.

~

Upper dig, Queen Creek headwaters, present-day Arizona. At an ancient Salado pueblo a short distance from where Pump Station Spring produced its bubbling water, Jack Hager, third-year anthropology major, was digging up pot after pot in a most unprofessional way.

Earlier in the day, he and his boss Mike Fulton had found the first of the colorful and skillfully crafted polychromes, a large bear effigy with an arrow lifeline. Jack immediately recognized this might be the most valuable stuff yet and felt in his bones that there would be more of the same in this excavation. Fortunately for him, Mike would not risk the integrity of the dig or compromise the context of the artifacts by continuing after dark.

Earlier, owners Mike and Jill, and another third year student assembled at the dig to make a photo record of the event. After they had taken publicity photos against a background of Kings Crown Peak and Stoneman's Pass glowing in a spectacular Arizona sunset, Mike took the find and packed it in bubble wrap in a plastic storage container and strapped it onto his ATV. Before he and the others left to look at another site further down Queen Creek, Mike instructed Jack to finish up his field notes, then backfill over the hot area, to be reopened tomorrow.

As soon as the rest of the team dropped out of site, Jack grabbed his cell phone and called Dr. Middleman. "I think we hit the jackpot at the top ruin. Bring some light and packing material. We have to get it tonight before the others see the stuff in the morning."

By the time Dr. Middleman had reached the site, it was too dark to work without light, but Jack was holding his pin light in his mouth and continuing to dig. He had uncovered four polychromes, one of which was an owl effigy pot with hardened hide adhering to the face. Without speaking, Dr. Middleman hooked up a powerful flood light and began packing the artifacts.

Jack carefully removed earth from around a fifth pot. "This corner is too compacted, so this will be all we get out tonight. There may be more in the dig, but we can't get it tonight. As soon as I finish extracting it, you can pack it and take off."

Dr. Middleman nodded. "This is the best quality I've seen in a Salado dig. How much did Mike take out?"

"Only one pot was removed . . . a very nice bear effigy."

"Did they take photos? Do you think they will hold a press conference?"

"Of course. They also filmed us digging it out."

"Good. That will help drive up the price."

The roar of a speeding ATV interrupted them, and Middleman quickly swung the powerful light to focus on the driver. With his right hand he drew a pisto and fired. There was a spray of red from the helmet, and the driver flew from the ATV as it flipped and crashed into the shallow canyon.

Shocked, the trowel dropped from Jack's hand as he gasped, "That was Lester! Why did you shoot him?"

"He was a witness."

"You just murdered my friend! Are you crazy?"

"Now don't lose your nerve, just when things are starting to get good; you'll be rich beyond your wildest dreams."

"I don't want anything to do with this!!"

Jack was still kneeling in the hole. Middleman slammed the butt of the gun into Jack's right temple, and he slumped forward against the wall, unconscious. After thoroughly wiping the gun with his bandana, and then using it to hold the barrel, Middleman placed the gun in Jack's hand, pressed the muzzle against the injured temple, and squeezed Jack's finger against the trigger.

Middleman looked longingly at the partially uncovered pot that remained in the hole and thought, "It will be better to leave it in place; investigators will conclude Jack got caught digging by Lester and impulsively shot him before feeling remorse and shooting himself. Case closed. People who think with feelings rather than logic are doomed to utter failure." He gathered the pots and his belongings, except the gun, which Jack could keep.

~

Lester and Jack had begun this tragic day like any of their other days working for a small archeological survey company. Arizona is rich in archeological heritage. But, especially in Arizona, most modern archeology is a compromise between science and expediency. The key to archeology is funding, and very little of that funding goes to pure scientific investigation. Development is the primary driver of the vast majority of the work: a new highway, a new housing development, a new reservoir, a new gravel pit, a new hospital.

Each of these projects has a schedule that must be met, so the archeological survey and any subsequent excavation are also required to meet the timeline. Many archeologists resent this state of affairs, but those of a more entrepreneurial bent have found it to be a great opportunity.

EcoAnthro LLC, of Tempe, Arizona was one of these enterprises. Mike and Jill Fulton completed their master's degrees a year apart at the University of Arizona. Mike earned a BS in geology, a BS in anthropology, and an MS in archeology, and Jill a BS in history and an MS in anthropology, with courses and fieldwork heavy in archeology. They were married during Jill's last year of school while Mike was working as an instructor and a field supervisor for the Anthropology Department. After that they worked together on a six-month project with the National Park Service excavating a large kiva in a small ruin at Chaco Canyon.

During that project, they realized they were not going to eat very well, much less get rich, working in pure science, so they became a "trowel and brush for hire" company. After twelve years in the business, they had learned to do archeology according to a production schedule.

Their initial vision was to be a full-service, pre-construction, environmental-cultural impact study provider with plans to add biologists, hydrologists, and surface water experts to their staff. These dreams were bigger than their budget, so they fell into a niche doing low-cost, high-quality surveys and digs, often as a sub-contractor for general contractors or larger impact study companies.

Before 2007, the Arizona "population wildfire" was spreading in all directions, consuming the desert in great flames of suburban expansion. They, and several companies like theirs, were constantly in demand. With the 2008 economic crash, growth stopped abruptly and many of these companies went under. But EcoAnthro, one of the smallest, had survived because they had a great reputation, very little overhead, and were classified as a woman-owned business.

They mostly employed students from the local universities and community colleges to work their digs, catalog and pack the artifacts for transport, and keep track of human remains and funerary objects to be turned over to Indian tribes for reburial.

This job, one of three they had going, was a survey of the "Segment A" right-of-way for the new alignment of US Highway 60 through the Pinal Mountains between the towns of Superior and Miami. It was more interesting than some jobs, because the area the route passes through included the sites of 1870's Camp Pinal and Camp Infantry, a historic mining area, and four known but unexcavated Salado pueblo sites.

Lester Kenton was a third-year anthropology student at Arizona State University and had been working part time for EcoAnthro for two years. He became skilled enough that he served the company as a site supervisor. He enjoyed the irony of his new assignment: he was leading the dig of the old Fortuna Mine settlement where the proposed highway would follow Peachville Canyon through the site. This time the Indians were digging up the white man's history. Lester is full-blood Apache.

Lester had six students working the ruins of the first two of seven buildings they located. In addition to the houses, privies, wells, corrals, and outbuildings, they also found a trash dump from the 1880s settlement. There were several other historic mine sites that would have to be surveyed to determine if there was any reason to excavate. Lester was overseeing the uncovering of a crockery jug and two bottles by the two new employees, students from Mesa Community College, when Jill drove up on a quad ATV.

"Good afternoon, Lester. It looks like your team is making good progress." She smiled and nodded a greeting to the two new employees. Both students stared and muttered an incoherent greeting, struck by how gorgeous their new boss was.

"Yes," Lester answered, "but we had to redo the grid on one of the middle home sites. Some idiot drove an ATV through the middle of it last night, dragging away the lines and knocking over most of the flags. You weren't out in that thing throwing brodies in my site were you?"

"Ah, you got me! The sheriff was supposed to keep a close watch until we were finished here. I'll give him a call."

Lester grabbed a rock hammer out of the hand of one of the students. "No, no, no! Don't do that. Next time you think you need to use a pick, use a paint brush instead. You don't know what might be underneath or next to that rock. Something important could be damaged. Archeology is all about patience. Moving dirt is secondary to recovering an intact artifact."

Jill added, "That's a very important lesson. A couple of years ago we had a young anthro student working a dig on highway 87, and he used his rock pick to move what looked like a buried flagstone. The 'flagstone' shattered and it turned out to be a lovely Salado stone hoe which had survived 600 years intact until our fledgling archeologist smacked it, breaking it into seven pieces."

"Wow, did you fire him?" asked a student.

"If he had not already proven that he was a hard worker and had pretty good instincts, I would have fired him. But he still works for us, and he has not broken a single thing since then."

"All right, Jill, you've had your fun. At least I learned from my mistake."

"And now, so have they," she replied with a wry smile. "Let Greg oversee these guys for a while. I need you to see something at the site by Pump Station Spring."

Walking to their ATVs, Jill told him they were uncovering what looked like an undamaged polychrome effigy olla at the Salado site just above the spring. "It's a fine looking specimen!"

"I'm glad you're letting me see it come out, but why do you need me there?"

"I don't, but I thought you would like to be part of the find and publicity. What I really want you to see is about a mile downstream, below the spring. It's a small site—one I took to be a possible outlying pit house. We found a nice pinched-clay, pointed-bottom jug."

"Pinched-clay, pointed-bottom? That's not Salado . . ."

"Right. That's why we want you to take a look at the site. It's probably an Apache camp, but it seems more permanent than most."

The pair stopped at the Salado dig and watched as Mike and Jack gently extracted a beautiful nineteen-inch white, black, and red bear effigy olla. The diggers passed it out of the trench to Jill and Lester. They filmed the excavation and afterward posed for a group photo with the pot. Jill did this with nicer finds to use for marketing and to give the students a nice photo for their portfolio. For political and PR reasons, she liked having her Native American archeologist in the photos.

After the photo opportunity, Jill, Mike, and Lester each drove their ATVs down the canyon to the suspected Apache site. The jar was indeed an Apache artifact, though the dwelling site appeared atypical of an Apache wickiup, having low-stacked stone walls. Lester did a slow visual survey and identified four more possible dwelling sites. The manzanita was too thick to find more.

Mike told Lester, "Come up tomorrow with one of the students and continue the excavation. I told Jack to finish shutting down for the day and to drive your pickup back home. You can ride in with us."

"I'm not going in tonight. I set up a camp down by the mine. I'm going to spend the weekend nights here to discourage more vandalism."

"But you won't have a truck."

"I won't need one. I've got the quad and everything I need in my camp. The rest of the crew is riding back in the Tahoe. In the meantime, I'm going to explore that little side wash. With the cottonwoods around that seep, maybe there were more dwellings to take advantage of the shade."

"Good idea. You probably only have about fifteen minutes before you need to start back. I don't want you going down the trail in hard dark."

"Ok, boss. Will do."

The Fultons drove their ATVs up the dirt berm that had been made for the purpose of easily driving them into the truck, and in ten minutes they were heading west on US 60. Before the light was gone they were at the rented house that served as their home when they didn't want to drive back to Tempe. An unnoticed silver Chevy 4x4 pickup had passed them eastbound on US 60, turning off on the dirt road heading to the dig sites.

Lester drove his ATV up the side wash, stopping briefly to mark a spot here and there he thought might be promising. He heard a vehicle travel back up the road and thought that Mike must have forgotten something at the upper site. He finished his scout of the wash, made his way back to the jeep trail, and headed up it to return to his camp site off the mountain. In the rapidly-increasing dusk, he saw a bright glow of artificial light from the direction of the upper ruin.

"That's not right," he thought. "Somebody is messing around with the ruin." He sped up as the road left the creek and went over the little ridge below the ruin. As he topped out, he saw a silver truck and two men. The flood light was focused on Jack excavating the dig. The other man swung the light toward him, blinding him. Then he must have hit a limb because he was knocked from the ATV and felt himself falling into the wash before the world went black.

~

Mike and Jill left for work at about seven the next morning. They were on Highway 60 driving through Superior when Mike's cell phone rang.

"This is Mike."

"Mike, Greg here. When I got here this morning there was no sign that Jack or Lester were here last night, neither ATV is here, and the tent has not been slept in."

"Jack was taking the pickup home from the upper dig. I was worried about Lester driving the trail after dark. Drive your ATV to the top of the saddle. Take it slow and look for any sign of an accident. We're entering the canyon now, so we will probably get there about the same time you do. Wait for us there at the summit."

They checked the Apache site and saw the ATV tracks going into the side canyon and back out, so they continued following its tracks up the road. As they topped the little point Jill gasped, "Oh no, there's the ATV! Wrecked!"

Mike skidded to a stop, and they both jumped out of the truck and ran toward the wreck. They ran past Lester without seeing him, but he managed to croak, "Jill!"

At first they were too stunned at the bruised and bloody appearance of their friend to act. After a few seconds, Mike said, "I'll get the first aid kit. See if you can help him."

As Mike reached the truck he heard the sound of Greg's ATV approaching the summit. Mike picked up the two way radio and said, "This is Mike. Come in Greg."

Greg stopped the ATV and answered the radio. "Go ahead Mike."

"Stay on the summit and use your cell phone to call 911. Lester had an accident on his ATV he is badly hurt, but he is conscious. We need an ambulance. Tell them to come to the Queen Creek upper ruin. The sheriff's office can lead them to it. Stay where you are. In case a deputy isn't available, you can relay directions to the ambulance."

Mike ran back to Lester with the first aid kit and a blanket. Jill had checked Lester over and determined that there were no broken bones other than maybe a fractured skull. "He says his head really hurts on the left side . . . that it was bleeding a lot, so he took off his shirt and tied it tightly over the wound." Jill wrapped the blanket around him. "He says he has a bad headache, blurred vision, and is too dizzy to stand up. The bandage he applied seems to have stopped the bleeding, so let's leave it alone."

Mike said, "Lester, can you hear me?"

"Yeah, I'm awake. Spinning too much to open my eyes. Blanket feels good . . . I was freezing."

"Can you tell us what happened?"

"I guess I was knocked out. I woke up in the night and was bleeding, so I made a bandage with my shirt. I tried to go to Jack, but when I stood up I fainted. When I woke up, the sun was hitting this hill, so I crawled here to get warm. Then you guys showed up. Jack saw me wreck. I don't know why he didn't help me . . ."

"Why weren't you wearing your helmet?"

"I was. It broke. It hurt when I took it off. Maybe the helmet is what cut my head."

"You say Jack was with you?"

"No. It was almost dark . . . I was trying to get down the trail while there was light. When I came over the point, I saw some guy holding a light. Jack was in the hole digging. They were startled . . . the guy shined the light in my face. It must have blinded me, because I ran into the tree branch and ended up in the wash."

"Who was with Jack? Was it one of our team?"

"No . . . I don't think so. I don't know who it was. He had a silver-colored pickup truck. The light was on Jack. I thought they might be pot diggers, but it was Jack for sure."

Pinal County Sheriff's Deputy Dan Tomkins and the EMTs arrived. Jill met them at the ambulance and repeated what Lester had told her as they were getting the wheeled trail stretcher and their gear out.

The EMTs removed the shirt-bandage, cleaned the wound, and applied a sterile bandage. After they loaded Lester into the ambulance, one paramedic started an IV, and another called them over. "This guy did not hit a tree. He was shot. He's lucky to be alive."

Mike said, "Shot! Are you sure?"

"I know gunshot wounds. I served two years as a corpsman in Iraq. The bullet grooved his skull, another eighth-inch and he would be a goner."

Deputy Tomkins said, "That makes this is a crime scene."

"Either that or an accidental shooting . . ." The EMT said as he closed the back of the ambulance and left for the hospital.

Deputy Tomkins asked Mike and Jill to tell him everything from the beginning, which they did.

The deputy said, "So what I think is that the bad guy was either in cahoots with your man, or he was stealing the pots at gunpoint. He shined the light on the victim, blinding him, and what the victim thought was a tree branch was the blow from the bullet. Too bad he didn't get a better look at the shooter."

With a startled look, Jill cried, "Jack! Where's Jack?"

Mike said, "That's a good question. He might have gone with the suspect, because his ATV is still parked where it was when we left him. He could be a hostage, another victim, or a criminal . . ."

"Mike, this is Greg," squawked the radio.

"I'm sorry, Greg. We got so distracted here that we forgot about you."

"That's understandable. How is Lester?"

The deputy shook his head at Mike, saying, "Don't mention the shooting."

Mike keyed his radio, "Thanks for getting help here. Lester's badly injured, but not life threatening. He'll be out for a few days. Go take control of the job and let the others know what happened."

"Will do."

"Jacks still missing; call if he shows up."

"I can see his ATV parked at main the ruin."

"Yeah, we see it, but no sign of him."

Deputy Tomkins scanned the canyon. "So nobody has been to that ruin this morning, the one where Jack was last seen?"

"No, this was as far as we came, and the saddle from the west was as far as Greg came."

"Then most likely the last tire tracks on that section of road were made by the suspect's truck. Go park your truck across the road at that cut, so nobody can get in. I'm going to walk the road and get some photos of the tire tracks, maybe there will be some footprints or other evidence at the ruin. You folks wait in your truck; we don't want the crime scene anymore disturbed than it already is."

The deputy walked the edge of the road and took several photos as he went. For some, he laid a pocket ruler across the track to provide a size reference. He did find a number of shoe tracks as he neared the excavation and photographed each of those. When he was circling around the area near the excavation, he saw red spray paint on the side of the ditch and wondered if that is how they marked where something was found. When he was north of the excavation, looking down the trench he realized the red "paint" was blood from the person in the hole.

Using the zoom on the camera he took photos of everything in and surrounding the dig. Then being careful to avoid tramping on other prints he carefully moved to the body, where from the visible wound in the temple he knew that he would find no pulse, though he proved that by checking. He had met Jack: a nice young man, a college student. This shouldn't happen to young people. More photos, then he walked back to his truck and radioed for a detective and a crime scene team to investigate two scenes—a homicide or suicide and a separate attempted murder.

He walked to the truck where Mike and Jill sat with the windows open and told them the bad news. Both Mike and Jill broke into tears, obviously stunned at the news. He was glad to see that reaction from them, because he liked them both, and they would of necessity be suspects.

"Please don't talk about what you know about these crimes. I know your employees will want to know the details, but at this point everyone on your staff is a potential suspect or a potential witness. We don't want them tipped off if they are accomplices, and we don't need them prejudiced if they are witnesses."

"So what can we tell them?"

"Tell them that Lester was hurt in an accident and will recover, but it looks like Jack committed suicide, although we don't know why or how. Beyond that, just be your normal selves. There is a possibility that you know the person who did this, so be most careful of anything you say to anybody."

"That's an awful thought."

"We know for a fact that the shooter was trying to kill Lester, and at this point, thinks he did so. The only reason he would have to do this is to cover up some criminal activity, most likely theft of artifacts for sale on the black market."

Bitter contempt spilled from Mike. "The things they probably took out of that hole would be extremely valuable on the legitimate market. European or Asian museums for example, would pay tens of thousands for each piece. No telling how much higher they would be priced for rich illicit collectors. The filthy bloodsuckers don't care what science is lost or even if lives are lost, as long as they can own something that nobody else can own."

The deputy added, "Another example of what people call 'victimless' crimes causing harm. There is, as you said, the loss of science, but it is also theft of what should be public domain, and the harm to the innocent bystanders."

He glanced through his notes, then continued,"Well, I have the statements recorded that you gave me. I'll have them transcribed, and then you will need to review them, make any corrections, then sign them. I'll let you know when they are ready. You two should probably let your team members know about Lester and Jack. Remember, you know only those few bare facts and no hint of foul play or murder in relation to Jack."

"What about getting hold of their families? Normally with an on-the-job injury or death we would notify the family."

"You can contact Lester's family once you know which hospital he was taken to, but we will contact Jack's parents first; I'll let you know when we've done that."

"Thanks, Dan. I'm glad you're working on this; you know these guys and you care," said Jill, as they started the truck.

Mike said, "We'll be back up here in an hour or so. We'll talk to our people in Fortuna and come back. If you don't need Lester's ATV, we'll load it and take it for repair."

"That will be fine, but not until the crime scene is clear. That will probably take two to four hours; when the techs finish you can start work again."

The deputy walked up the side of the mountain a couple hundred yards, then traveled at that level cross-country to the saddle that the archeologists were calling the summit. He placed a call to Sergeant Al Victor of the San Carlos Apache Tribal Police.

"This is Al Victor."

"Sergeant Victor, this is Dan Tomkins."

"Yes, Dan, how are you doing?"

"I'm doing okay. I have a case that I would like your help with."

"What can I do for you?"

"I need your tracking skills to help us understand some evidence, foot prints, tire tracks, and such. It is a new, pretty much undisturbed, crime scene near Superior. I know it is a real imposition, Al, but I could use you here on the scene before the crime scene people show up and we lose some of the story in the dirt."

"You know I'll help any way I can, but a cooperative investigation, requires a tribal member be either the suspect or the victim. Otherwise it takes a formal request to both the Chief and Tribal Council for approval, which I'm sure we will get, but it might take a couple of weeks."

"One of the victims is an Apache. He's a student at ASU, a good kid named Lester Kenton."

"I know Lester very well! You say he is a victim? Of what?"

"Attempted murder. He was shot in the head, but it looks like he is going to be all right. Another archaeology student was murdered or committed suicide."

"I'll be there as soon as I can. It'll probably take a while. Where do I go in Superior?"

"It's actually at an archeological site off Highway 60 about ten miles east of Superior."

"Would that be at Top of the World?"

"No, it is west of Devil's Canyon. Turn to the north near Oak Flats. Shortly after the turn the dirt road forks, take the left fork and travel about five miles. You will see me and maybe a bunch of others there."

"Okay, I know exactly where the turnoff is. We used to go up there in the autumn to pick acorns. It's at the truck safety pull out, and the right fork goes to a power substation, the left to Kings Crown Peak."

"Yep, you got it. You go almost to the marble quarry. Your squad car might drag in a couple of places. It would be better with a high-clearance vehicle."

"I have an SUV now. See you as soon as I can get there."

"Could you run with the lights? It'll get you hear half hour faster."

"I was planning on it."

Chapter 2

San Carlos Tribal Police Sergeant Al Victor became known in eastern Arizona as an expert tracker and had been instrumental in providing evidence that solved several crimes in various jurisdictions. He was six-feet-four inches tall and weighed 270 pounds, with no fat. He had the broad face, high cheeks, strong chin and brow, black hair, dark eyes, and copper skin typical of his tribe. He was born in his parents' reservation home on Ranch Creek and attended Globe and then Miami High School from which he graduated.

After school he joined the Army and became a scout/sniper, was selected for tracker training, and ended up serving as an investigator with Army Intelligence. Following the first Gulf War, he was hired as a Police Officer for the Globe Police Department, where he went through the required police academy and became a certified Arizona Law Officer. He has worked for the Tribal Police for about six years, quite happy to work in his familiar mountain and desert home.

As he sped with lights and siren east on Highway 70 toward Globe, he called his boss, Chief of Police Walker, who authorized him to assist with the investigation into the attack on Lester Kenton.

He switched to the Globe-Miami dispatch frequency and warned them that he would be traveling east on US 60 code 10-39 to assist with an investigation in Pinal County. Dispatch asked if he wanted a local escort, but he said no, he just wanted to let them know he was passing through. As he reached Globe, officers were at most of the traffic lights, stopping traffic as he approached. This continued through Miami. He saluted each as he passed, and as he got out of the towns, he radioed dispatch with thanks for the assistance.

In less than an hour he reached the dig and was introduced to the Fultons by Deputy Tompkins. He was given a short briefing and crime scenes were pointed out.

The deputy said, "Things are pretty tracked up where Lester was, because of the rescue, but I have been the only person near the murder scene."

"So Lester was riding the wrecked ATV?"

"Yes."

About twenty feet from the wreck Al noticed a lot of blood on the ground and asked, "Is this where you found him?"

Jill answered, "No. He was in that little clearing on the side of the hill. He was cold and used the heat of the sun to warm up."

"Okay, so these tennis shoe prints are Lester's. It looks like he stood once and fell, then crawled after that. Jill's tracks are the smaller set of hiking shoes, and Mike's are the larger ones. Dan, you must be wearing the smooth-soled boots. So whose prints are these by the bicycle tire track?"

"They belong to the two EMTs who treated Lester and took him to the hospital. The bike tire was on the single-wheel trail stretcher."

"Well, it is pretty obvious what happened here. The ATV went out of control, right about here, and the blood spatter on the rocks and brush indicate that it is also the point where Lester was shot. He probably laid in the wash where the blood is for quite some time—that's a lot of blood. You can see that he seems to have pretty much stopped bleeding by the time he crawled to the place where you found him, because there is not much blood there."

Jill said, "He made a bandage with his shirt when he came to, then didn't move until the sun came up. So that's probably why he wasn't bleeding much when we found him."

Al nodded and continued, "Mike and Jill ran past him, going toward the ATV, then turned back and ran over to him. Then the others showed up and took him away. There was nobody at all at this scene except the people we can identify, so the bad guy never came over here."

Mike said, "Thank God for that! The killer probably would have finished him off if he had known he was only wounded."

Deputy Tompkins said, "We don't know that at all, because there were two people in the dig—Jack and the unknown person holding the light. Maybe Jack shot Lester because he had been caught stealing artifacts, then when he realized what he had done, turned the gun on himself. From what I have seen at the dig, it sure looks like Jack shot himself. The unknown man—probably a pottery thief—might not have had anything to do with the attack on Lester, and just decided to get away as fast as possible."

Jill looked incredulous. "I can't imagine Jack shooting anybody, much less a good friend . . . and he and Lester were good friends."

The deputy asked, "But can you imagine Jack stealing artifacts from a dig he was responsible for?"

"No, not really."

"There you go. We don't always know people as well as we think. And even when we do, they sometimes do strange things."

Mike shook his head, "I just don't buy it. Jack was a gentle kid; he was not at all violent. He wasn't interested in guns . . . he had never hunted. I doubt he would even know how to shoot a gun. Maybe he had nothing to do with the theft . . . maybe he was being forced at gunpoint to dig up the pots."

The deputy nodded. "In a way you're right. We don't really know what happened here. I'm hoping Al will be able to find some facts from the scene. Al, are you ready to examine the dig site?"

"Yes, just a couple more questions. Did you photograph all the scene evidence both here and at the dig? And do we know who has been to the dig?"

"I got pictures of everything. If you find anything I didn't see, we'll get a shot of that too. As far as who has been to the dig, Mike can best answer that."

Mike said, "The only ones that have been at the dig are me, Jill, the deputy, Jack, Lester, and our mystery person. It was a new excavation we just started yesterday, so none of our other employees were ever there."

Al looked and Dan. "Okay, so the only tracks that should be at the dig that I haven't seen are Jack's and the suspect's?"

"Yes," Dan said, then pointing to the gap above them added, "One other employee, Greg, was on the saddle a quarter mile above the dig, but he was never at the actual excavation site. He was there to provide communication with dispatch and the ambulance."

"Let's go take a look, Dan."

"I'll lead you up the way I went in originally, so we don't mess up anything else. Mike, why don't you and Jill go on home? We'll get hold of you later."

Jill said, her voice breaking, "Can't we wait here until they take Jack out? I don't want to desert him."

"Yes, you two can wait here."

Mike put his arm around her, and they went to sit in their truck.

By the time the coroner and the crime scene technician arrived, Sergeant Victor was finished with his examination of the scene. The deputies met with the coroner and the technician and briefed them on what they knew and what they had observed at the scene. The technician took samples of the two spatters, the pooled blood, and various tissues and fibers found at the scene. Then the body was bagged, and the law officers helped move it into the coroner's van.

The coroner wanted to clarify a few things with the Fultons, so they all stopped to talk with Mike and Jill. After getting the information he wanted, the coroner told them that Jack's body would be taken to the medical examiner's office. When finished, the body would be released to the family.

Mike suggested that the Fultons should go home for the night. He told them the scene work will be finished in an hour, so work could resume in the morning. The Fulton's followed the van out.

When the sad little caravan left, the two policemen discussed the crimes as they went to each scene and cleaned it up by digging out the blood, burying it away from the excavation, and throwing dirt over the remaining scattered droplets. They bagged the crime tape and debris that had been left by the EMT's and investigators. When they were finished the only remaining evidence that anything had happened were foot prints.

Sergeant Victor said, "Dan, I think that Jack was murdered."

"What makes you think that?"

"To start with, Lester said that he could clearly see Jack in the dig because the bright light was focused on him, but he couldn't see the other guy very well because he was behind the light, not in it. The tracks confirm that the unknown guy moved back and forth from the rear of the truck four or five times. He was receiving the stuff that Jack dug up and carrying it to his truck. The light was on some kind of a tripod or three-legged stand."

Al paused and thought for a few seconds. "So that guy should not have been in the hole at all . . . besides, it is pretty cramped space. Yet he did get in the hole and back out one time, behind and to the right side of Jack. The guy grabbed the light and shined it on Lester just before he wrecked, which we know means just before he was shot. How far is it from the dig to the point where Lester was shot?"

"A hundred feet, give or take a few."

"Think about that. What kind of a marksman does it take to make what would be a quick-draw headshot with a handgun at one-hundred feet at a man on a speeding ATV?"

"He would have to be very good."

"Now imagine the guy was on his knees in a hole with only his head sticking out."

"Impossible."

"The gun is a .45 automatic. When fired, it ejects the casing up and to the right. We found only one brass . . . in the hole to the right of Jack. Where was the other one? I looked the area over thoroughly, and it's not there. It could have been picked up by the shooter, but I doubt it, or he would have taken both."

Dan said, "So why would one be missing?"

"My bet is it's in the back of the truck, because the guy was standing holding the light with his left hand and shooting with his right hand, across the back of the pickup. Then there is the gun itself. Jack did not have a holster, so he would have had to have the gun in the hole with him or lying up on the edge with his tools. His brushes and spatulas were lying in the loose dirt, but there is no impression of a gun anywhere, and it is a lot heavier than those tools. And those who knew Jack say he had nothing to do with guns."

"Okay, that's pretty convincing," Dan agreed.

"There's more . . . did you notice that the tools were all lying on the left side of the hole? If you were going to dig those pots out, where would you put your tools?"

"Probably in front of me or on the right side."

"Why?"

"So I could reach them more conveniently."

"Why would that be more convenient?"

"Because I use my right hand."

"Yeah, because you and I are right-handed. So why did Jack have them on the left?"

"Maybe he was left-handed?"

"Maybe he was. In fact I'd bet you dollars for trade beads that he was left-handed. That's important because he's shot in the right temple. Why would a left-handed guy commit suicide by shooting himself with his right hand? We need to find out for sure if he was left-handed or not.

"The last thing that is not consistent with suicide is that Jack was slumped forward in the hole, and the exit spatter and bullet hole are aligned with his slumped position. He wouldn't slump and then shoot himself; he would shoot himself, and then consequently slump forward because he's dead. I think you have ample reason to assume that Jack was murdered."

Frowning Dan asked, "What would make him slump before he was shot? Was he drugged? I didn't see any trauma where he might have been hit and knocked out."

"Drugged doesn't make sense. I don't know, but we need to ask the medical examiner to look for any sign of blunt force trauma to the head, other than that done by a .45 . . . which is pretty traumatic."

"Maybe he got punched in the temple and stunned, then shot in the same spot?"

"Yeah, Dan, that would probably disguise the blow too. Anyway, discuss our suspicions with the medical examiner and ask him to look for that evidence."

Al continued, "I think we can also have a fair estimate of how much the suspect weighs. His shoe sole has a tread pattern very similar to mine. His shoe size is about three sizes smaller. I weigh 270 and, comparing our two prints side-by-side, his was a shallower depression, so I estimate that he probably weighs about 170 to 190 pounds."

"I'll discuss the wound question with the ME, and I'll include the weight estimate in my report."

Al said, "Let's check out a few more things before we go. Let's go have a look at the prints up on the summit and get a photo of the shoeprint of the guy that was handling the communication up there."

"You think Greg was involved in this?"

"I have no idea, but if nothing else, it will rule him out. I also want to look at the Apache site downstream to be sure the sign there validates that part of the story. Then I would like to go to the other dig sites below the mountain and get shots of the footprints there."

"That makes sense. We can walk up to the summit, then each drive our trucks to the other sites."

They examined the prints at the summit thoroughly. Then Al turned and looked at the view from the pass. There were probably two hours of sun left. The shadows were heavy in the canyons and crags of the mountains, and the view of Picketpost Mountain seemed accented by the slanting light.

He said thoughtfully, "I can feel history and the spirit of the old people here. Pump Station Spring was known by Indians as Mountain Spring. The Spanish called that mountain Tordillo, which means dappled or spotted. Before them the O'odham called it Spotted Flat Top Mountain. The people that lived in that pueblo may have been ancestors of the O'odham.

"Those old Puebloans were driven from the Mountains to the valleys by my immigrant ancestors, the first Western Apaches. We in turn were driven from them after General Stoneman built this trail. Stoneman changed the name of Spotted Flat Top to Picketpost, as it's known today.

"So much life and death. So much history and change, and yet it still looks much the same as a thousand years ago." Dan felt the feeling Al described. After a moment they turned and returned to their cars without another word and headed for the Apache and Fortuna sites.

After they had taken the photos of the EcoAnthro dig sites and camps, Al said, "Now I need to go see Lester. Can you tell me where they took him?"

As they got in their trucks, Dan said, "I don't know, but I'll find out and radio you."

~

Lester Kenton was in a room on the third floor of Banner Desert Hospital in Mesa, the largest hospital in the state.

Al knew the young man because Lester had been in the Police Explorer post when Al was the Post Leader. There were nine kids in the post, and Lester was one of only two boys—all the rest were girls. That was a typical ratio on the reservation in almost anything of educational or moral value: college classes, scouting, church, it didn't matter; the young men viewed it as trying to be white, and there was a lot of peer pressure to not participate.

Lester was different. He had always been eager to learn new things and was stubborn about doing what he wanted to do, so it was no surprise when he took classes through Globe's Gila Pueblo College and then enrolled in Arizona State University. Nor was it a surprise that Lester was doing quite well there studying to be an archeologist. Al was relieved to see the young man alert, and even smiling.

Lester was surprised to see Al Victor come into the room, "Hello, Officer Victor! What are you doing down here? I didn't think you got to come off the rez."

"Ah, you know how we Apaches are . . . always trying to bolt the reservation. How are you doing Lester?"

"I'm doing great . . . now. They cleaned me up, warmed me up, gave me a transfusion, fed me, and are shooting pain reliever into my arteries. I still feel dizzy. They said that I have a slight concussion, and they are keeping me in the hospital overnight to make sure there are no problems."

"That's good news," Al grinned, "It's a good thing you're such a hard head…"

"Al, I'm worried about something."

"What's that?"

"The transfusion . . . it's probably white blood," Lester laughed. "Does that mean I'm not a full Apache now?"

"Good question. Do you have a craving for English kidney pie?"

"Not so far, anyway."

Turning on his tiny digital recorder, Al said, "If you are feeling up to it, I would like to interview you and record our conversation. Is that okay?"

"Sure."

"I'll share the interview with the Pinal County Sheriff's Department, the County Attorney, and any other law organization that gets involved in your case. Do you agree with that?"

"Yes."

"I'm investigating the attack on you. The Sheriff will also probably question you about other matters associated with the case that are outside my responsibility. I would like to start with what happened prior to the incident in which you were injured. I understand that you had been helping with the dig on upper Queen Creek. Is that correct?"

"Well, not really. I'm responsible for the Fortuna Canyon work over the saddle to the northwest of that excavation. Jill or Mike normally stops by my area a few times a week. Jill came down and said she wanted me to see something on the upper survey area, so I followed her up the trail to the upper dig."

"You were on the ATVs?"

"Yes. When we got to the dig, they had a video camera set up filming Jack excavating a really nice polychrome pot. Mike was there observing. They had me receive the artifact from Jack on video, then switch to still and took photos of the four of us posing with the pot. Jill has a very good sense of public relations and advertising, so she captures a lot of special things in this way.

"She also makes a point of including me as a Native American in the pictures; diversity sells. It goes a long way to making the government agencies want to use them because they have to have contracts with minority or female owned businesses."

"So you are used as a poster child for Indian archeologists, to the advantage of their company?"

"I guess you could say that, yeah."

"How do you feel about that?"

"I don't mind. I think it is really good business, and it is good for my career. I have documentation of my involvement in all the spectacular finds. It will look good in a portfolio with my curriculum vitae."

"What the heck is that?"

"It's kind of a detailed résumé. Anyway, Mike has told me that they want me to stay with them when I get my degree, that they would give me a salary, benefits, and make me a junior partner in the business, with a share of the profits. They would also help me with tuition and books to get my masters. It would pretty well guarantee that we would be in every 'A' group of contractors for government work. Having an Indian owner would also give them preference for work by the various reservations, opening up many more opportunities all over the country."

"It does sound like they are good business people."

"They are just good people. They are very ethical and accurate in all their work. They respect their employees, pay fairly, and spend a lot of time teaching and working with the students. They really care about the science of the work, and not just the business, which *is* very successful. It's really important that the business be successful, or all these opportunities dry up for guys like me and dozens of others. I think of Mike and Jill as more like family than friends—that's the kind of people they are."

"So you don't think they would be involved in anything illegal, like the illicit artifact trade?"

"No, absolutely not! They are highly ethical and have real respect for the cultures they are disturbing. Their digs have an air of reverence about them. Jill has been known to cry when the grave a child has been opened. They have a wonderful relationship with the tribal religious leaders. I would be afraid that if Mike ever caught pot hunters in action he might kill them. He feels that passionately about this work."

"I understand. Let's continue with your narrative. The filming and photography has ended. Then what happened?"

"It was nearing sunset and Mike told Jack that we were going to shut the dig down for the night. He told him to cover over the "hot" area, the place where the current pots are located, and we would continue tomorrow. Then we drove down the creek maybe a mile or so to a find they had made at the junction with a little side canyon."

"Sorry to interrupt, but who drove down the creek?"

"Mike, Jill, and I. We each drove our own ATV."

"Thanks. Go ahead."

"They had earlier found the ruins of a very unusual Apache site. It appears to be more permanent than most of our old camps. For example, there are some low rock walls, and I saw quite a bit of evidence of pottery and stone artifacts. They made one test dig and found a pointed-bottom pinched clay pot, which is an Apache indicator. So they assigned me to survey the area more thoroughly, and I noticed what might be more dwelling sites up the side canyon. I told them I wanted to look at that for a few minutes. Mike told me to not take long; he wanted me down the trail before it got too dark. They loaded their ATVs in the truck and left for their place in Superior. I went up the little canyon and marked a couple of interesting places. Then I realized I needed to get back to my ATV.

"I heard a truck go up the road and thought the Fulton's were going back for something. I wanted to get on that trail before it got any darker, so I was on my ATV and headed up about five or ten minutes after the truck went by. As I neared the crest of the little hill coming up out of the creek by the dig, I noticed a lot of light and sped up to see what was going on. As I topped over the ridge, I saw a silver pickup and Jack down in the hole digging. The guy holding the light shined it on me, blinding me. I figured I had run off the road and hit a tree branch, which knocked me off the bike, but the doctor said I was shot."

Consternation showing, Lester continued, "That's funny because I never heard a shot or saw a flash of a gun being fired, just felt a hard blow to my head. I don't know how long I was out, but when I woke up it was really dark, only the stars for light. I could feel myself bleeding and was in a puddle of blood, so I rolled up my shirt and tied it tight over the wound. I was cold and shivering. I don't think I was thinking too clearly, because I was kind of mad at Jack for not coming to help me, and I decided to go find him. When I stood up, I passed out. I woke up after the sun was coming over the hill, so I crawled to a sunny place to get warm. I slept on and off until Mike and Jill showed up. The paramedics came and took me to the hospital. That's pretty much it."

Al said, "Tell me everything you can remember about Jack when you first saw the dig after coming over the hill."

"Jack was down in the hole on his knees. I could barely see his face above the edge of the dig. He looked up at me kind of startled. That's all I can tell you about him."

"Could he have been the person who shot you?"

"No, he was in the hole. He would've had to shoot me with his face. Even if he had a gun, he couldn't have shot me without standing up."

"And he didn't stand up?"

"No."

"Concentrate on the other guy. What can you remember about him?"

"I didn't see much. He was behind the light, so all the light was on Jack. When I came down the side of the ridge my ATV headlights hit him for a split second. I didn't see anything unusual about him. He had dark hair. He was either a white guy or a Mexican. I think he had on a blue long-sleeve shirt with white shiny buttons."

"What about his pants?"

"Couldn't see 'em. He was on the other side of the truck. I saw him from his chest up, and it was just a flash."

"So he was standing near the back of the truck, on the opposite side from you?"

"Yes, so I could only see him above the bed."

"You say the truck was silver. What kind of truck?"

"It was a full-sized—one of those ugly ones like the Chevy that makes into an SUV . . . or that Ridgeline rice-burner truck. It has kind of a sloping side on the bed and a lot of black plastic. I can't figure why anyone would want one of those things. Dumb kid maybe. I really can't tell you anymore about it than that."

"A kid? Did that man look young?"

"No. I was just talking about who might have one of those trucks. I don't know why, but I think the guy was older . . . maybe forty or fifty."

"When the ATV lights flashed across the unknown man, you said you saw shiny buttons, is that right?"

"Yes. Kind of like cat eyes shining in the dark."

"How many buttons did you see?"

Lester thought for a minute before replying, "I saw two on his right sleeve and two on his chest."

"One last question . . . was Jack left or right-handed?"

"He was left-handed."

"Thanks, Lester. I'll have this transcribed and let you review it. You can make any corrections, and then I'll need you to sign it."

"No problem."

"Do you know if anyone contacted your family?"

"Yes, Mike got hold of Mom, and they're going up to Peridot to bring her down tomorrow. I talked to her on the phone a while ago, and she seems okay. I told her I was doing fine, but she wants to come stay with me for a couple of days to be sure. Mike said I can't come back to work until the doctor gives me a clearance, so I'll be home a day or two at least."

"Sounds like a good idea to me. Call me if you need anything or if you think of anything else I should know."

~

As Al Victor drove back to San Carlos, he thought through the signs, evidence, and statements from the people at the scene. As far as he could determine, every piece of evidence fit well with the statements given.

When he reached Globe, he pulled into Cobre Valley Motors near a used Chevrolet Avalanche. He stepped over to the back and noted how many of his shirt buttons were above the edge of the bed; four of his buttons would be visible had he been standing behind the truck when Lester's light flashed across him. His buttons were four inches apart, so he was eight inches taller than the suspect; the suspect would be about five-foot-eight inches tall. He got back in his car and drove off before the hurrying salesman could reach him.

Al called Deputy Tomkins and told him the new information about the suspect and said he would e-mail him the taped interview. Al asked to be kept informed about the progress of the case, as his boss would want him to stay involved since a tribal member was a victim. The deputy promised that he would alert Al to everything that happened in the case.

Al then called his close friend, Graham County Sergeant Brendan Allred.

"Hey, Bren, are you still on the Arizona Antiquities Strike Force?"

"Yeah, we have a phone conference every Monday, but there's not too much going on right now. The only current activity is a small-scale investigation in the Kingman area."

"Well, lucky you. I have one for you that not only involves theft of artifacts but a murder."

"In Graham County?"

"No, it's in Pinal County between Miami and Superior. I don't think Pinal has a member on the strike force."

"That's right. So how did you get involved in a Pinal County case?"

"I was asked to help with some tracking, and since one of the victims was a tribal member, Chief Walker authorized my involvement."

"An Apache killed?"

"Fortunately no, but he was shot in the head and left for dead. It looks like he is going to be all right. He is an ASU archeology student working a dig in the headwaters of Queen Creek. The fatality was also a student working on the project but a different dig."

Bren said, "That's sounds like a rough case. I'll help any way I can."

"Hey Bren, I'm coming up on Peridot and need to go report to the boss, so I was wondering if we could meet at your office so I can give you the details."

"Let's meet at the office about 4:30."

Chapter 3

After the Friday night shootings, the man Jack called Middleman didn't go to his rented place in Superior, but instead turned East on Highway 60. He drove through Miami and Globe to Highway 70. There he stopped briefly at a service station and called Edward Hale, Indian Trader to the World, and told Ed that he was on his way to process some great new buys through the lab. Then he continued to Safford, turning south on Highway 191 for about 15 miles where he took a dirt road for four miles to a secluded ranch.

This was no ordinary ranch. It was a real working ranch, but also a rich man's toy equipped with the best of everything. He drove to a six car garage and using a remote in his truck he opened the leftmost door, drove in, and closed the door. He used an electronic keypad to enter a fully-equipped antiquities laboratory. He carried the four plastic storage cases inside and carefully unpacked each valuable relic.

Placing them one at a time in a large sink with a soft neoprene lining, he gently sprayed them off inside and out until all the centuries of dirt had been removed. The owl had some hard, dry leather stuck solidly to the face, so he filled a sink with hot water and immersed the artifact, leaving it to soak.

Turning his attention to the other pots, he carefully blotted them with thick, soft terry towels and placed them on the cushioned countertop while he inspected them. The white had taken a bit of red staining from the soil and the red and black painted areas were dulled by calcium and mineral buildup, but a gentle acid wash would brighten that right up.

He had two large effigy pots, a small storage olla, and a sixteen-inch shallow bowl four inches deep and fully painted on each side with an intricate sun, rain, wind, and lightning pattern. The olla was similarly painted, including about two inches of the inside lip. The effigies, made of fine white clay, were an owl and a ceremonially-clad woman, both beautifully painted with red and black.

He placed the ceramics into a weak acid bath. The acid reacting with the thin coating of calcium at first created small bubbles, and as it did, the colors became clearer and brighter. He started peeling back the edges of rawhide from the face of the owl. To his joy, it came off easily, and he was startled to see two beautiful turquoise eyes staring at him.

The owl was the most unique piece he had ever seen; it had large pale blue eyes consisting of matching inset turquoise disks. He had never heard of Salado pottery artifacts having stone inlays. He smiled as he anticipated the bidding war this beautiful piece would set off.

He drained the sink and refilled it with water, letting the pieces soak for a few minutes. Then he used a gentle spray to carefully rinse each item and patted them dry with soft, clean towels. The treasures were now bright and beautiful. It was hard to believe they had lain in the ground for over 800 years.

Each piece was then moved to the photography area where he captured close-ups from each angle. He also took X-ray photos from the top, one side, and the front of each object to show any cracks or repairs that might exist.

The next step was affixing a radio frequency ID chip smaller than a grain of rice inside the three jar-like objects. The shallow bowl did not have a place to hide the chip, so he selected an area of black paint on the bottom and affixed the chip covered in matching black putty so it looked like a minor imperfection in the pottery.

He scanned each relic in turn with an RFID reader into a computerized artifact registry and cataloged them with a proper archeological description, a mnemonic name, a general visual description, and provenance (the area of discovery, the contextual description of the find, and what artifacts were with it). In this case, he cataloged them as purchased from a private collection. The items were listed as found in 1949 on private property in a Salado ruin at Queen Creek headwaters, NW Pinal Mountains, two feet down along the eastern wall, carbon dated circa 1250. Examined and cataloged by Dr. Emile Haury, University of Arizona.

Middleman attached the digital photos and X-rays to each item. He saved his work and selected *Preview Catalog Presentation*. The new items appeared in all their glory, with all the information from the catalog in a slick eye-catching format. He then selected *Add Minimum Bid* and entered $25,000 dollars for all but the owl, which he listed at $150,000. He set the final bid date for one week away and clicked *Publish*.

The catalog was now in the hands of a group of eighty-seven museums and very wealthy collectors from around the world. In the first five minutes, the bid for the owl had reached $200,000. He wondered where it would go over the next week.

Middleman clicked on a U of A icon near the top of the screen, and clicked *Load Selected Files*. A counterfeit three-by-five Anthropology Department catalog card for each item was displayed in faded manual typewriter font with the blue ink signature of Emile W. Haury. He slipped on thin cotton gloves and placed four blank antique cards in the printer and printed a period card for each newly-cataloged item. The final product was a card that was indistinguishable from the real cards on file in the archive. He placed them in a small manila envelope and tucked them and the gloves in his jacket pocket.

He called the same cell phone number he had called from Globe. Edward Hale answered, "I see the bids are rolling."

"Yes. It is all yours from this point. They are in the collections vault and everything is ready for delivery next week."

"Okay. I'm tempted to bid on the owl myself. It is spectacular."

"Go ahead. It would sure make delivery easy if you win. Just don't forget my forty percent."

"Be sure to activate all the perimeters before you leave."

"I always do."

~

Al Victor drove to the Sheriff's substation in Central, Arizona, arriving at 4:30. Brendan Allred came to the door of the office. At six-foot-one inches and seventy pounds lighter than Al, Bren had the slender but tough look of a working cowboy, and his blonde hair, blue eyes, and fair skin created an interesting contrast when the two good friends were together.

Bren said, "Here you are, right on time."

"Just like always."

"True. You *are* always prompt. What happened to 'Indian Standard Time' with you?"

"The army."

Bren laughed. "Pull up a chair and tell me about your artifact case."

Al went through the details of what had taken place at the Queen Creek headwaters and explained what he concluded from his observations. He said that Pinal County Deputy Dan Tompkins would be sending his report to Bren along with the witness statements and scene photos.

"Give me your impression of the people involved. I've actually met Mike Fulton. He donates his expertise to the Antiquities Strike Force when needed."

"Well, starting with him. I think what you see is what you get. He's a very real person. He loves his work and knows what he is doing. His employees really like him. He seems to be a very honest and caring guy. Jill, his wife and business partner, is a female version of him—just about everything I said about him applies to her. She is very well organized and seems to be the one with the business expertise. Have you met her?"

"No, just Mike. I've never seen her."

"Well, you've really missed something. She's about the best-looking female I have ever seen. On top of that, she has a sparkling personality, a quick sense of humor, is caring and compassionate, and just oozes competency and self-discipline."

Bren chuckled, "She sounds downright scary."

"Next is Dan Tomkins, a good cop, very capable, and easy to work with. He's been on the job only about three years, so he's still learning. I know him pretty well since I did some wilderness tracking for Pinal last year, and he was partnered with me.

"The murder victim Jack Hager was well-liked by his employers and coworkers. Nobody can understand how he would be involved in artifact theft, and all of them are certain he would have nothing to do with violence. The esteem they hold for him is hard to reconcile to any criminal involvement."

Bren asked, "Are they just being loyal, or are they trying to cover for him?"

"I think they are being completely open with us. It's possible he may have been forced by the gunman to participate in the looting.

There's much investigating to be done before we can say much more about him.

"Lester Kenton, the attempted murder, is also well-thought-of by the Fulton's and his fellow workers. He is a dig supervisor and has six students working for him. I know him very well. He was one of my Police Explorer Scouts when he was a kid. Raised by his widowed mother, he's smart, hardworking, respectful, and a heck of a nice guy. He's a very good student, gets good grades, and the Fulton's have already promised him a junior partnership when he graduates next may."

"He's not a suspect?"

"No," Al replied, then continued. "The last one that had any direct connection to the scene is another student supervisor named Greg. I either didn't hear his last name or wasn't told. I talked with him at the camp by the Silver King Mine, and he came across as a good person. He's pretty shook up about his coworkers being attacked."

"So that's everybody that was involved, then?"

"Except for the unknown suspect. Pretty much what we know comes from the brief glimpse Lester got of him, and the conclusions I reached from my observations of the tracks and the height relative to the truck."

Bren thought for a minute, then said, "So if I remember what you told me. He is about five-eight, 170-190 pounds, has dark but not black hair, and Lester's opinion is that he was something over 40 years of age. He drives a silver truck similar to an Avalanche, has expertise with a gun, and may be coldly brutal. He had on a blue shirt with shiny white buttons."

"Yes. One other thing, Lester is certain he had never seen him before."

"The strike force conference call is Monday morning, so I'll urge that we get actively involved in this investigation. I'm sure they will all agree."

"That's good. Do me a favor and get me involved with your investigation. Lester is important to me, and I would like to help get this guy. Being on the strike force will keep me close to the murder case as well."

"I'll request that Chief Walker assign you to the degree needed for the duration of the investigation. How's that?"

"That should do it. Tell me this, why would anybody kill two people over some old pottery?"

"Like so many crimes, the driver is greed. These artifacts bring in a big payoff. Just a simple unpainted red clay pot can easily draw a thousand dollars. A really nice effigy or fetish pot can bring ten thousand dollars. If it is something really unique or rare and of very good workmanship, it can be worth hundreds of thousands."

"So if a dealer in stolen artifacts can sell a hundred good pots in a year he can make a good living."

"Depending on how good the pots are, selling a hundred could give him a multimillion dollar income, but that would have to be a dealer with strong contacts in the world black market. Most of the people we deal with are pot hunters who sell locally for a small percentage of the world value."

"With somebody drawing that kind of income, it should be fairly easy to spot them."

"The problem is that there is also a robust legal trade in artifacts. The only things that are always nationally illegal to deal are human remains and funerary objects. In most states other items found on private property, or grandfathered in private collections, belong to the land or collection owner so can be legally sold. If they are on land owned by the federal government or by the State of Arizona, archeological items belong to the respective governments, and they could sell them but usually don't. So there is a big legal market from private owners that can be used to hide illegal sales."

"So to get someone you must have to catch them in the act."

"That's what usually happens when an arrest it made, but the belief is that we are catching only the pot diggers, not the dealers."

"I had no idea it was such a big deal. Why doesn't the government just take ownership of all unexcavated artifacts within the nation no matter whose property they are on?"

"I would be opposed to that. I think that when you own property you own everything on the property. I have some mixed feelings about the lost scientific information and the cultural insensitivity, but I think these are outweighed by property rights. I do agree with the remains and funerary rules applying to private property."

"This is interesting stuff. I think I'll enjoy working on this case."

Deputy Dan Tompkins called Al to give him an update on the medical examiners findings. Al asked permission to set his phone on speaker so Bren could participate in the conversation.

"I just thought I would let you know what has happened with the ME and the crime lab. The crime lab hasn't supplied a final report yet, but they say that it looks like the conclusions Al reached are right on.

"Something we didn't know was that there were two cell phones in Jack's pockets. One was his personal phone, which he used for almost everything, including work calls. The other was an inexpensive Tracfone. The lab got the call records and the Tracfone was activated four months ago. There have been several calls in and out, all to and from the same number. It turns out that number is also a Tracfone, activated at the same date as Jack's, with all calls either to or from Jack's Tracfone. It looks like Jack made all his Tracfone calls from Superior or the metro Phoenix area. The second Tracfone shows the user was in Superior, Globe, Safford, or the Tucson area when calls were made or received. This makes me think that Jack was willingly involved with the pottery dealer."

Al asked, "Is there any way to use the GPS history to pinpoint locations?"

"I'm not sure about that. The lab said that during a call that can be done, in the same way that 911 can use GPS or tower triangulation to locate a cell call, but there probably isn't a card to hold the historic call coordinates. They are going to check on that. One thing they did try to do is call the number of the second Tracfone so they could get a pinpoint location, but the phone has apparently been completely disabled."

"You mean it's turned off?"

"No. They say that even if it is turned off the emergency locator will work. It has probably been destroyed."

Bren said, "Sounds like our relic thief is tech savvy. At least we know the area of the state that he normally operates in. When you said the Tucson area, was the location actually listed as Tucson or one of the suburbs?"

"A couple of them were listed as Tucson proper, but the others were Oro Valley." Dan continued, "The most important thing is that, as Al suggested, the medical examiner looked for and found blunt force trauma underlying the entry point of the bullet. It matches the butt of the weapon, so we do have murder, not suicide."

Bren asked, "Dan will you be able to continue working with us now that it's confirmed as homicide, or will the Sheriff move a detective onto the case?"

"Kind of both, Bren. I'm certified as a homicide investigator and the sheriff plans to promote me as soon as the budget will allow. So he is leaving me on the case, but the Chief Homicide Detective will be closely overseeing me."

"That's great. It's a really good opportunity for you."

Al said, "It really is! Congratulations. You'll do well."

"Thanks, guys."

Bren said, "Dan, if Jack was communicating with our murder suspect for four months it probably means he was selling artifacts for most of that period. If so, there has to be a big change in Jack's income during that time. You will want to look closely at his finances—his debts to find motive for the theft and income to confirm he was involved in the trade."

"I will do that."

"The debt will probably be easy. I'll bet he has a lot of student debt for one thing. The income is likely to be more difficult. The illicit artifact trade at the source is almost always in cash. A lot of times you can spot an uptick in the paying down of debt without any visible change in income. That indicates an infusion of cash. Also check for a safe deposit box. The traders often recommend that diggers save their cash that way and slowly meter it out as a way to hide the extra income."

"That's good to know, Bren. Thanks again. I'll keep you both in the loop."

After they were disconnected, Al said, "Well, Bren, that was interesting. Looks like we have a pretty clever bad guy out there. But it's good to know he made some mistakes."

"Yes. He seems to have worked out a good system and manages to not leave much of a trail when he has time to plan, but when he has to improvise, he isn't so clever. I would like to go look at the scene tomorrow before the work restarts. Would you be able to go with me? We could go in the afternoon after church, and the cost will be covered by strike force funds. I want to look at the excavation where Jack was killed, so we won't be there more than an hour. Do you think one of the Fulton's could meet us at the dig? If not we can go anyway, but I want to look at the pot impressions where Jack was working. They could be a help."

"No problem for me going. We'll go to Mass tonight, so I could go whenever you want. I'll call Mike and see if they could be there."

"Thank you. We finish our meetings at eleven-thirty, so let's go after lunch. Will it work if I pick you up at two o'clock?"

"Yes, that sounds like a plan."

~

Middleman checked the time as he arrived in Tucson. It was nearly one o'clock AM, so the campus police would have made their inspection of the Arizona State Museum and would be on the other side of the campus. He drove to the museum. As expected at this time of night on a weekend, he had the building to himself. He didn't go to his office, but went to Assistant Archive Curator Sally Gaona's office, put on his thin cotton gloves, and removed her access card from her center drawer.

Using her card to enter the vault where the original 1930-1963 artifact registry is kept. He put the very genuine-looking fraudulent registry cards in the correct files. He returned Sally's access card to her desk, put his gloves back in his pocket, picked up his briefcase, turned off the light, and headed home.

The stolen artifacts were now legitimately registered as private property, by one of America's most famous, albeit long-deceased, archeologists, no less than the namesake of the Emile W. Haury Anthropology Building at the University. Any museum or collector in the world would not hesitate to bid on the pieces if they were interested. Middleman had increased his value by two million dollars in just a few years by this pottery-laundering scheme, and as he contemplated what this last haul would bring in, he wondered if he should get out of the business before the unlikely event he slipped up and got caught. It was not that he needed any more wealth, he was already a multimillionaire by inheritance, but he was pleased that his cleverness was well rewarded.

~

Bren, Monica, five-month-old Layton, and almost-five-year-old Lizzie attended their three hours of meetings on Sunday morning, leaving the church at eleven-thirty and walking the three blocks to their house. On the way, Lizzie explained her primary lesson: "When we pray, we should only pray for good things. If we pray for things that will hurt us or someone else, Heavenly Father won't give them to us. He always wants what is best, but sometimes even good things aren't the best thing for us, so he will give us what we need instead. That's kind of like Mommy. Sometimes I want candy and soda, but she says I've had enough and that I have to eat something that is good for me. What are we having for dinner? I hope it's good and good for me."

Monica asked, "How does roast with carrots, potatoes, and gravy sound?'

"Mm mm . . . good, I'm hungry!"

After dinner they all cleared the table and cleaned up the kitchen, then Bren changed into his uniform. As he came into the living room, Monica was reading the newspaper, Layton playing on a blanket at her feet, and Lizzie was coloring. Lizzie looked up and said, "Oh no, do you have to go to work?"

"Yes, but for just a few hours. You will still be up when I get home, so you can show me your picture and we'll have a snack, read, and say our prayers."

"Good, my picture will be very pretty, so I want you to see it."

Bren sat on the edge of the couch and tickled Layton, hugged and kissed his two girls, and headed for his car. After he left, Lizzy asked Monica, "Can we say a prayer to keep Daddy safe?"

"We already did that this morning, remember?"

"I want to do it again. Can I say it?"

"Yes. Come over beside me, and let's bow our heads."

"Dear Heavenly Father, thank thee for all our blessings, especially for our family and for our baby. Please keep Daddy safe from the bad guys, and help him to choose the right. Bless that he will stay between the lines and not be hurt by the crazy drivers. In the name of Jesus Christ, Amen."

"Amen. That was very nice, Lizzy. Thank you. You better get to work on your picture, so it will be ready for Daddy." As Lizzy resumed her careful coloring in her normal happy-but-intense way, Monica thought about their efforts to shield her from the dangers of Bren's job.

They tried to strike a balance by having her understand the dangers without causing her to feel insecure. They reinforced the security by telling her about the various positive things: helping stranded motorists, helping with fires and emergencies, and encouraging people to drive safely.

Monica lived with a barely-suppressed fear of Bren losing his life or being grievously injured. In all his years in law enforcement, he had only been injured once when he was one of three Mesa officers shot when a drug bust got out of control. One of the officers was critically wounded, but Bren and the other officer had only minor wounds. Each time she remembered the policeman coming to her door and rushing her to the hospital with no clue of how badly Bren was wounded, she relived the waves of nausea and panic. She didn't want Lizzy or Layton, or any of her future children, to ever experience that.

~

As Bren pulled up in front of the Victor house, Bonny came to the door with Al. As he kissed her, the two kids ran to the car and chattered at Bren, who laughed and kidded them. Al hugged each of the kids and sent them back to their mother. They all waved as they headed to the highway. They turned west toward Globe and continued west on US 60. Just west of Miami, they crossed Bloody Tanks Wash. Bren asked, "So was the Battle of Bloody Tanks an actual event or a tall tale?"

"Without question it was real, because there are families at San Carlos who are descended from the survivors and recite the story. I think the main story, as written by white men who participated in it, is pretty accurate. Part of the problem is that history has intermingled two different fights—the Pinole Treaty affair was at a place in the Superstition Mountains called *Tu Tog* (water fish, possibly fish creek) by Apaches; the Bloody Tanks fight was mostly Pinal and Aravaipa bands, and it happened at this place.

"The *N'dee* (Apache) and *O'odham* (Pima and Papago) were mortal enemies and the *Beligana* (Americans) were allied with the O'odham, so that made them mortal enemies as well. The Apaches and their enemy both planned treachery against the other at peace talks. Both sides had secreted weapons in their clothing or blankets, and both planned to signal when to attack the other. One of the white men noticed the Apache weapons and sounded the alarm. The Apaches were the ones surprised, with a very bad outcome for them, since the Americans and their allies were better armed. So yes, it was real."

"Was it unusual for Aravaipa and Pinal Apaches to band together?"

"No, most Apaches would join with other bands for warfare or sometimes to harvest and prepare food or to perform ceremonies. Most of the Pinal Apaches lived on the northern slopes of the main Pinal Range in the warm months and along Pinal Creek, Russell Gulch, the West Branch Pinal Creek (now Bloody Tanks Wash), or Ruin and Granite Basins in the winter.

"The Aravaipa lived along Aravaipa Creek in the winter and summered in the Santa Teresa, Hayes, and southwestern Pinal Mountains. Eskimenzen, best known chief of the Aravaipa's, summered at Mason's Valley, known popularly as Top of the World now. So the two bands lived in close proximity to each other."

"So what group was living on upper Queen Creek where your friend Lester found an ancient Apache camp?"

"Who knows? If it was inhabited in the last hundred and fifty years, they most likely were Pinal or Aravaipa. If older than that, the clans and tribes were perhaps differently defined than they are now. The first Apaches in this area are thought to have come from the north through the Rockies and west from the plains, perhaps as early as the mid-1300's. So if the site was theirs, they are as much a mystery as the Hohokam or Salado."

As they started into Devil's Canyon, Al Said, "Devil's Canyon actually was named by the Apache. The tall monoliths that make up the canyon were seen by the ancients as resembling *ga'an bikoh*. The ga'an are mountain spirits and bikoh means dancer. The ga'an are called crown dancers or devil dancers in English; ergo, Devil's Canyon. The Apache name for Queen Creek Canyon with it's even taller monoliths is *ga'an dizen*, meaning ga'an standing. And yes, the Battle of Apache Leap did happen, no matter what revisionist historians say. It is part of the oral history of the San Carlos Apache."

"I've always loved this drive between Miami and Superior because of the amazing scenery. Knowing this history makes it even more interesting. Here's our turnoff. So I just keep left at the fork and keep going?"

"Yes. Mike said he would meet us at the dig about 3:30, so he might already be there."

As they approached the area of the work, Al pointed out the area where Lester was surveying the possible Apache site before the murder, then said, "When you get to the top of this little rise, stop there and I'll orient you on the crime scene."

Bren stopped as directed, and Al pointed out each location and described how the crimes happened and what the scene investigations revealed.

"Wow, that's some shot!" Bren exclaimed. "I understood from what you told me yesterday it was a difficult shot, but it's even tougher than I thought. Lester was apparently moving pretty fast. The guy must be really good with a pistol."

"Yes. That's something that everyone working this case should remember. If this guy starts shooting at you, you are in trouble."

"Take a look in your mirror. There's a truck approaching."

"That's Mike. Go ahead and pull up to the dig, and park on the left side of the road."

Bren pulled to a stop as directed, and Mike parked behind him. Following their greetings, Bren said, "Mike, I would like to do a little forensics on the placement of the artifacts that were in the hole. If the loose dirt is removed, we should be able to see the base impressions from which the pots were taken. That may tell us how many were stolen and give us an idea of their size and shape."

"You're right. We can at least know how many were removed. After I clean out the hole, we can discuss what we see. We took some photos and video of Jack digging out the first pot, and we can actually see parts of the ones adjacent to it. If you have time when we finish here, come down to Superior and we can look at them together. I'll give you copies as well."

In less than thirty minutes they had photographed the cleaned-out dig showing the impressions made by the pot taken out by Mike and the stolen pots. The one Jack was uncovering at the time of his death was clearly visible, and Mike guessed there remained at least one more in the undisturbed portion of the corner. Mike said, "Let me finish taking this olla out, so it doesn't get stolen. Would you hand me some bubble wrap and a storage tub out of the back of my truck?"

Mike gently wrapped the olla and handed it Bren. They stowed the pot and belted it on the back seat of the truck, and Bren took some photos of the impressions. They left for Superior with Mike leading the way. At Mike's place Bren was introduced to Jill. They watched the video, capturing still shots when it showed the pots in situ. Bren noticed that Jill quietly shed tears as the video focused on Jack.

They agreed that the pot Jack and Mike removed and the one removed today, plus four additional impressions meant that a total of six had been removed, four of them stolen. All of the artifacts they had photographed in their partially uncovered state were polychromes, and at least one of the stolen pots was an animal effigy with pointed ears. Another might have been an effigy, because the base appeared to be two oval-shaped feet. The other two were round-bottomed, most likely pots, vases, or ollas. At least they had an idea of what they were looking for.

As promised, Mike gave them each a digital copy of the video, the screen captures, and the still photos. Bren thanked the Fultons for their time and assistance and the officers left for home.

~

Deputy Manny Sanchez spent the Sunday dayshift covering his area and the Stockton/Bonita area because of a shortage of deputies. This remote district of Graham County covered Manny's area in the northern Sulpher Springs Valley, eastern Aravaipa, and the eastern boundary with the San Carlos Reservation south of US 70. The Stockton/Bonita area covered the eastern part of the county between Cochise County and the Swift Trail. Deputy Patricia Haley would be the night shift deputy working both areas, so Manny drove over to the Bonita store to meet her and review what transpired on his shift.

Manny wasn't comfortable with Deputy Haley, though he wasn't exactly sure why. He'd had very little interaction with her during his three years on the force. His first impression of her was that she was cute and fit and had a professional air about her, but it didn't take him too long to realize that she was always in professional mode. There didn't seem to be any other dimension to her.

Manny chuckled at the only negative comment Bren had ever made about her. When Bren told Manny that he would handoff to Deputy Haley at shift change, Manny commented, "She's kind of hard to talk to, isn't she?"

Bren chuckled, "Not as long as you strictly stick to business. Believe me, you don't want to say anything about politics, society, or religion to her, or you will end up wanting to shoot her."

"So you recommend no friendly chatter?"

"Exactly. Strictly business—of course, it's up to you how you handle it."

As Manny caught site of the store, he saw Deputy Haley leaning against the front of her squad car, looking fully in charge with close-cropped hair and a business-like look on her face. He parked next to her in the opposite direction, picked up her copy of his shift notes, and walked to her, offering his hand. She had a strong, almost challenging handshake. He said, "How are you doing Deputy Haley?"

"I'm doing great. Ready to take on all the minor perps that fate might send my way."

"Well, if your watch is as boring as mine was, you will be ready for it to end. I had two traffic stops, a bust of minors for drinking, a missing bicycle, and an assist of a stranded motorist. There's nothing really pending tonight. So any questions or anything I can do for you?"

"No." Haley held up the notes. "This should do it."

"Okay, I'll head for Safford to take in a movie. I should be back at Klondyke by midnight if you need anything."

"Shouldn't be needed. I've got it covered."

"Don't hesitate if you need backup."

"I won't."

As he drove off, Manny muttered to himself. "Well, I made it through that unscathed. It was almost pleasant." What little he knew about Deputy Haley was that she was raised by her mother, a radical women's studies professor at U of A. Her dad was a Tucson cop who couldn't put up with his wife so left when Pat was six years old.

He married a secretary in the Tucson PD and moved back east where they're raising four kids of their own. The gossip was that he faithfully paid child support and turned a $10,000 education fund over to her when she turned eighteen, but that was the only contact she had with her dad. She didn't know her half siblings, three brothers and a sister.

Deputy Haley's mother considered her choice to go into law enforcement a slap in the face. Pat had grown up hearing what chauvinist pigs men were, especially cops.

Manny thought, "It was pretty gutsy of her to go into law enforcement. No wonder she seems so messed up. Well, I have much happier things to think about—a date with Jenny, the living antithesis of Deputy Haley."

Chapter 4

Edward Hale had started out as a young man working at his dad's trading posts on five Indian reservations in Arizona and New Mexico. Ed was the third generation of traders. His half Navajo grandfather Edward Hale started their first trading post. Ed's business no longer resembled the old barter-or-buy system of his grandfather and father.

Edward still maintained the reservation trading posts, where he bought and sold Indian jewelry, crafts, and art, as well as general merchandise. He even continued to trade with the Indians by barter when they wished to do so. But he had moved to the top tier of Indian art dealers and craftsman jewelers with high-end stores in Scottsdale, Sedona, Tucson, San Francisco, Santa Fe, New York, Vienna, and Tokyo. He had, in fact, become a billionaire and sat on museum and foundation boards.

His big break had come before his dad passed away. He met and developed a romantic relationship with Marie Artiste, an ambitious young archeologist, who was working on projects in Chaco Canyon. She proposed a business arrangement in which she would broker artifacts from private property owners who would allow her to dig their ruins for a cut of the sales, and she knew private collectors from whom she could buy low and sell high.

Marie's problem was that the Park Service frowned on that type of extracurricular activity by employees; however, they would allow her to do private consulting as long as it didn't interfere with work. So Ed could pay her twenty-five percent of the proceeds and her consulting fees to validate and classify the artifacts.

Marie provided some samples and certified them as coming from private owners, so Ed began offering a few legitimate high-quality artifacts for sale to tourists. As his reputation for quality legal artifacts spread, demand grew and prices increased. When his dad died, he aggressively entered the artifact market, opening his first Indian fine crafts and artifacts store in Scottsdale.

All went well for about ten years, when the collector Roland Fernandez, from whom many of Marie's items came, died. Ed scrambled to buy the collection from the heirs, and they were happy to sell the entire collection for a half-million dollars—a lot of money in the 1998.

In that same time period, Ed asked Marie to marry him, but she said she did not want to marry—that she loved him but did not want a family and wanted to keep their relationship as it was. This was more than a disappointment for Ed, because he wanted to have children and realized his age would soon preclude the likelihood of that happening.

He tried to end the romantic relationship with Marie, while keeping their business relationship, but she went berserk, throwing furniture and threatening to turn him in for selling stolen artifacts.

"When did I sell anything that was stolen?" Edward asked Marie.

"At least half the stuff you bought for resale came illegally from my Chaco digs, and Roland certified them as being his for a price."

"That had nothing to do with me. If I had known you were doing that, I would not have sold them."

"Well, if you leave me, I'll go to the police and say the whole scheme was yours and you tricked me into cooperating. It won't matter if you are arrested or not. The scandal would ruin you."

"All right Marie, but no more stealing artifacts. That business should have never happened, and it is over with. I'll pay you a finder's fee for each of the current collection items sold, but don't bring me any more artifacts. I figure I'll make at least four million from the Fernandez collection. At your twenty-five percent, that will pay you one million dollars." Edward ended up making over seven million dollars from the collection, so Marie's share was close to two million dollars.

The relationship with Marie straggled along, because Ed felt he had no choice. He had to admit that he usually enjoyed being with her, but he was grateful they were separated by distance and didn't see her very often.

About two years ago a man came to his office and introduced himself with a card reading *Dr. Robert Middleman, Anthropology, Middleman Consultancy LLC* and a Vail, Arizona post office address. The man was an obvious academic in his appearance and conversation. Ed knew immediately Middleman was a professor who had a private consultancy on the side.

Dr. Middleman showed him the official University inventory, which included the contents of Ed's recently-purchased Fernandez collection. Ed had never heard of such an inventory and had difficulty trying to control his rising panic. Middleman showed him a list of several stolen artifacts from Ed's own advertising catalog.

"You see, sir, I have figured out that, without your knowledge, Miss Artiste has been forging certifications with the cooperation of the collector. If you persist in doing business this way, some cleaver law officer will decide to validate the contents of that private collection, which is listed in the archives of the University. When that happens, your kingdom will collapse.

"If you will allow me to be your partner in the legitimate artifact business, I can both clean up the problems with Miss Artiste's past dealings and greatly enhance your business. I have direct access to hundreds of private collectors. We will both make more money than you can imagine. Not only do I know the collectors who will sell, but I know the ones who will buy. I can sell to renowned museums and galleries as well as to very wealthy private collectors. I'll also assure that every item I procure for sale is legally certified. What I'm proposing is to vastly improve your direct sale online auction both by better technology and by my vast number of contacts."

Ed interrupted, "I can see real benefit in such an arrangement for my business; but since you already have the contacts, why do you need me? How does the arrangement benefit you?"

"In two ways, Mr. Hale. You already have a world-wide reputation for legal sales, and my employer has no objection to my private consulting, but would be very unhappy if I were to conduct direct sales of artifacts.

"For forty percent of future online auction sales that I bring you, I'll become your broker between those willing to supply certified artifacts and my legitimate market. It will be completely separate from your gallery and trading post sales, which you will continue to own and profit from.

"I will also settle with Miss Artiste, and you will be free of her, I believe I can be as persuasive with her as I am with you. But the best part of the deal is that I have contacts worldwide with big money collectors and museums, and can guarantee that you will greatly increase your sales prices and volume."

Ed, being a cautious man, listened but didn't bite until the man demonstrated that he could do what he said. Within two years of making the agreement, the online auction was making more money than his other businesses. Ed was pouring a lot of his new profits into his stores and galleries, expanding his modern Indian jewelry, craft and artifact sales. He was persuaded by Middleman to build a state-of-the-art archeological lab near Safford. Under Marie's scheme, he had averaged $6,000 per artifact. He was now drawing nearly $20,000. So even with Middleman getting forty percent, he had doubled his profit.

As it turned out, his trouble with Marie ended when she died in a freak accident as boulders fell from the kiva she was working in before Middleman was able to make his pitch to her.

Ed was surprised that he felt as bad as he did at Maries passing. He would have been very happy if she had married him, and he had loved her for years. He was relieved that he was out of the situation, but not that she died. She was clingy and emotionally needy, but she was also very pretty, a good conversationalist, intelligent, and witty. They had enjoyed a rich and rewarding relationship and active social life for a long time.

Her next of kin was her sister, but she was unreachable in the depths of the rain forest. Colleagues identified Ed as her closest friend, and he ended up handling funeral arrangements and burial in Grants. Ed and half a dozen park employees attended the brief services at the mortuary.

Unknown to Ed, Middleman was the cause of that accident. He had gone to the remote dig where Marie, who always preferred to work alone, was excavating. Middleman offered her two million dollars to sever all ties with Ed.

She rejected the idea by hurling a sifting screen in his direction, barely missing him. He smashed her head with a large boulder and then went above and tipped a half dozen more down on top of her. He took time to make sure there was no trace of his being there. When she did not return to the park housing that night, her unfortunate accident was discovered.

From that time on, Middleman's carefully-selected group of suppliers, mostly archeologists or excavators, would steal some of the better artifacts and be paid very well by Middleman.

The business had performed flawlessly. Middleman laundered the artifacts before posting them by surreptitiously adding them to the original private collections inventories at the museum archives.

His exposure to the latest trends in archeology, including computer applications, had allowed him to build Hale a most enviable electronic clientele who gobbled up their laundered artifacts as fast as he could supply them. And as with Marie, Ed Hale was unaware of Middleman's illegal scheme.

The money from the artifacts was unimportant to Middleman. He was rich enough already, but the feeling of satisfaction he got in duping the pompous academics who, in his mind, stabbed him in the back was an even greater reward. The fact that he used the legitimate work of one of their mentors, the esteemed Dr. Emil Haury, to make fools of them pleased him immensely.

~

Deputy Sanchez parked his SUV in the parking lot of the Sheriff's station and called his fiancée, Jenny Mondragon, and told her he was at the office and would need about ten minutes to drop off his report. She said she would be waiting in the parking lot when he came out.

Manny walked in and greeted Jessica in dispatch, who was listening to a call on her headphone. She rolled her eyes and gave a "crazy" sign, as he sauntered past and dropped the report in the shift notes inbox. On his way out, Manny rolled his eyes and blew a raspberry, making it hard for Jessica to keep from laughing.

Jenny was waiting in her parked car when Manny came out of the building. He slid in beside her while pulling her close and kissing her. "Hey good lookin'. Whatcha gotta cookin'?"

"What's for dinner? Whatever you want."

"Nope, you have to pick this time."

"They have posole tonight at Tony's Kitchen. That sounds pretty good to me."

"Tony's it is. Take us there milady."

They ordered large bowls of posole and had some garlic cibata on the side. As they were eating, Manny said, "You know this was a ritual stew of the Aztecs. We make it with hominy and pork now, but the Aztec used the giant local corn and the flesh of temple sacrificial victims."

"Get out of here—that's gross! Are you trying to spoil my appetite?"

"No, just the facts, ma'am. After the conquest, the priests insisted that it be made with pork instead of people."

"Things like that make me glad I'm not of Mexican heritage. At least the Basques didn't eat people."

Manny nodded. "That's true. In fact the Basques are thought to be descended in prehistory from Indian Hindus, so at one time they were probably vegetarian. Of course that was thousands of years ago. Basques now are really into mutton and beef."

"You are a never-ending storehouse of little-known trivia."

"Are you making fun of me?"

"No, I enjoy learning from you. You're an interesting guy on so many levels. You're always learning. What's that new online course you're taking from ASU?"

"Classic Pueblo Cultures of Central Arizona. It's an overview and comparison of Hohokam, Salado, and Mogollon archeology."

"But it has nothing to do with your work."

"Actually, almost everything has to do with my work. The more you know the better policeman you are. Then there's the fact that I'm just interested in learning about new things."

"Well, I'm glad you are."

Manny, finishing up his bread asked, "So do you want dessert?"

"No, I can't handle another bite."

They drove to Roper Lake and walked the trail as they talked, something they did frequently at the lake or one of dozens of trails in the area. Sometimes they were fairly aggressive hikes up Bonita Creek, Ash Creek, or Mt. Graham.

"Okay, now let's get down to business." Manny continued, "You are all moved home, and you graduate next Saturday. In two months, we will have completed the marriage preparation classes. We have arrived at the moment when we have to make some big decisions. We need to set the date and decide where we will live."

"Where we will live?"

"I live in a thirty-by-eight-foot trailer house at Klondyke. There is no next door. Neighbors are far between. So either you move out there with me, or we will find a little more populated place, and I'll commute out to my assigned area."

"I don't mind Klondyke as long as you are there, and I don't think your trailer is bad. A woman's touch can make it pretty nice. Living there would mean we get to spend more time together. If you commute, that will be extra time apart every day."

"All that's true, but you will spend four or five hours, morning and afternoon, stuck out there by yourself. We *will* get to have lunch together, but it'll get pretty lonely and could be boring."

"I'll have my books, computer, radio and television, and I can take some distance learning courses. I heard somewhere the more you know the better. Besides, there are some neighbors out there and there must be some level of social life. I might put in a garden. And I love to take walks in the desert. I'll be just fine."

They stopped watching fish jump in the lantern light from a distant camp. Manny moved to face Jenny and said, "Okay then, one last thing before setting the date . . . your safety. You are a small and beautiful woman, and I worry for your safety being that remote and all alone. So I'd like you to get certified for concealed carry and to keep your firearm on your person at all times. We will also attend the hand-to-hand self-defense training the department offers to spouses. And I'm going to put some security measures on the trailer."

"You think all that is necessary?"

"I sincerely hope not, but it's not optional. If we live there, I have to be sure of your security. If you call the sheriff's office for help, it could take up to an hour for me to get to you . . . and I'm the closest officer."

"Okay, I'll do it."

"Now our moms are going to be all over us to set a date. Let's preempt them and get it done. How much time do we need to get everything planned and take the vows?"

"To get everything done and send out invitations with time for people to attend, we need at least two months. That would put it toward the end of July. I've never wanted to get married when it is really hot, so why don't we set it sometime in September? Let's get married on a Friday, so we have the weekend to start our honeymoon."

Manny took out his phone and pulled up his calendar. "How about Friday, the twentieth?"

"Good! Yahoo, we are really getting married!"

"So do we just casually tell our parents tonight? Or are we supposed to do some kind of folderol to announce it? I'm not sure how that works, so anything you want to do is fine with me."

"Let's tell our parents tonight. I'll ask mom if she wants to do anything more than send out invitations. Some people have an announcement party, but since we've been engaged for two years, that doesn't seem necessary."

~

Deputy Tomkins contacted the Motor Vehicle Division and asked for a list of Chevrolet Avalanche trucks registered in Pima County, with year, color, and owner information. They sent him a spreadsheet with the results of the search. He knew there would be quite a few, and there were. The list had 1,105 vehicles listed. If he were to include similar trucks by GM, Cadillac, Nissan, and Honda, the number might double. He decided that the list would not do him much good unless they uncovered more information that would thin down the search.

He requested a search warrant for Jack's apartment, car, computers, electronic devices, and any storage area or lockers he might have, and a second search warrant for his bank accounts, safe deposit boxes, and general financial information, including detailed printouts of all transactions.

When the warrants were issued, Dan called Chief Homicide Detective Paul Espinoza and they arranged to drive to Jack's apartment together. Dan stopped by the property room and checked out Jack's key ring, so they could enter and search his property and car.

On arrival at Jack's apartment, the officers went to the office and presented a copy of the search warrant. They took evidence boxes, bags, and tags with them into the apartment.

Detective Espinoza asked, "What do you want to look for first?"

Dan looked around. "Let's check his financial information: savings and checking accounts, tax records, pay stubs, loans, debts, safe deposit box, electronic data, and e-mail. Then let's look for any cash, which might indicate he has been selling artifacts. After that, anything that might indicate he knew how to handle a gun, any relationships that might expose him to artifact dealers, and information as to who his circle of friends were."

Nodding agreement, the detective said, "Okay, let's not bother starting the computer and electronic devices. We can take them as evidence and examine them at the office. Why don't you start looking for check books, statements, bills, passwords, and that kind of stuff and box them as you go. I'll search for hiding places for guns, money, drugs, and illegal items."

It took an hour to do a thorough search of the apartment. They found everything they expected to find and nothing unexpected; there was no gun or anything to indicate Jack had any interest in firearms, no stashed cash, and no artifacts of any kind.

They walked to the garage and opened it. Jack's personal car was a 2008 blue Ford Focus four door, in which they found nothing of interest. Metal shelves had been placed along one side and the front of the garage on which Jack had some camping and climbing gear, dozens of college textbooks, a few tools, some cleaning supplies and a few boxes of clothes.

Nothing on the shelves could help the case. Other than Jack's financial information, the one tiny bit of evidence they found was back in the sheriff's office as they examined the packages of items taken in bulk from the apartment. Near the top of a stack of business cards was Dr. Robert Middleman's card. It was checked for fingerprints. It had Jack's prints and had two partial prints, one on each side of a corner. Not enough to even run against the data base.

Detective Espinoza said, "Let me see his keys." As he looked at each key, he identified it. "This is the car key, the garage key, the apartment key . . . this little brass key is probably to the mail box at this complex, and this odd silver key might be to a safe deposit box. Let's go see what's in his mailbox."

The mailboxes had the same numbering as the apartments. They opened Jack's and found a couple of bills, a note from Emily Hager, a National Geographic magazine, and a bunch of bulk advertising mailers. The detective said, "Put it all in an evidence box. We will inspect it at the office."

"Even the ads and coupons?"

"Yes, everything. The ads might tell us something about his tastes and habits. Add them to the receipt, and we'll take everything down. Leave a copy of the receipt on the table and note that a copy of the warrant is with the apartment manager. Did you get the name and address of his bank?"

"Yes. It's the Desert Schools Credit Union at 1245 E. Broadway."

"Let's get this stuff locked in the trunk and head over there. We might as well complete that search while we're in Tempe."

At the credit union, Detective Espinosa and Deputy Tomkins showed their identification to the attendant at the reception desk and asked to speak with the branch manager. The attendant, name-tagged Louis, buzzed Mr. Weston and told him police officers needed to speak with him. He was told to show them in."

Detective Espinoza introduced himself and Deputy Tomkins, with each of them again showing their badges. Espinoza explained, "One of your members, Jack Hager, has been killed under suspicious circumstances, and we are investigating his death." He handed the search warrant to Mr. Weston, adding, "We need the information requested on the search warrant immediately, and we need to inspect the contents of his safe deposit box and possibly impound them."

"I have never dealt with a search warrant. I need to make a call to our legal department first, just to make sure that I follow proper procedures. It shouldn't take long."

Mr. Weston spoke with an attorney who had him read the specifics of the search warrant to him. The attorney asked if he checked the officers' credentials, and after getting confirmation, he told Mr. Weston to give them everything they had on Mr. Hager, help with anything that they needed, provide the requested access to the box, witness the contents of the box, and write a detailed record of everything and send it and the search warrant to him.

Mr. Martin called his assistant and told her to bring the account information requested as quickly as possible. Then he invited the officers into the safe box privacy room and asked if they had the owner key for the box.

Dan said, "Is this it?"

"Yes, I believe so. Just insert it here, and turn it to the left." After Dan did as instructed, Watson inserted the bank key and removed the box placing it in a privacy station, saying, "Would you like me to stay and witness the contents with you?"

The detective said "Yes, please" as he opened the box.

Dan exclaimed, "Bingo!" at the site of a loose pile of currency.

Mr. Weston said, "I'll have a cashier come in and count the money and she and I'll certify the amount."

The detective asked that the money only be handled using gloves in order to preserve any finger prints, and produced a small pack of gloves from his coat pocket. The box contained nothing but cash, which totaled nineteen-thousand, five-hundred dollars.

~

Middleman became interested in quick-draw competition his freshman year at U of A. He and some friends discovered the timed quick-draw booths at the Old Tucson Movie Studio and started competing against each other. Middleman was a natural and soon was outdrawing all his friends. He attracted the attention of the gunfight actors group and ended up working as an entertainer, Rot-gut Rupert, for five of his six years at the university.

Later, still in character as Rot-gut Rupert, he entered the live ammo sport of Cowboy Action Shooting, and was twice the trick shooting national champ. When in character, he went unshaven for a couple of days and attached a huge, bushy mustache, matching eyebrows, and a heavy pompadour wig, all in jet black. It changed his look from a refined and educated gentlemen to a drunken old west gunslinger.

As he aged, he lost some of his speed and was noticeably shaky, which took a bit of the edge off his accuracy; however, he still did very well in the various Arizona competitions, often placing in the top tier of shooters.

The only competition he did not engage in was the horse-mounted shooting; he didn't like horses and was sure they didn't like him. Through the years, he had competed in all three gun types and had done well, but his true love was single-action pistol. One of his favorite tricks was shooting skeet with his pistol from a quick draw. He was still the best in the state in that skill, taking first in pistol and high enough in rifle and shotgun to take overall first in state in the most recent competition, which meant he had another trophy.

It was a plaque-mounted chrome-plated colt revolver with pearl handles; set in the base was a photo of him shooting. He had long ago put all his minor trophies in boxes in the garage and only displayed his national trophies in his living room, but this one was too pretty to not display. He had a bookcase in his office at work that had a space on the top shelf that would be just right, so he took it to work and stuck it on the shelf. Thereafter, each time he looked at it he smiled.

The only other thing in his life that had given him as much satisfaction as his sport was his career choice. He had been a brilliant student and had excelled as an archeologist and researcher, writing scholarly papers and articles. He was even a student instructor. But it all soured for him when he presented his doctoral thesis, and it was rejected. He reacted by turning against his mentor and trying his best to discredit his work and character.

When he was bypassed as an associate instructor in favor of lesser peers, he finally hacked into the doctoral candidate files and found that he had been blackballed by the university. They recognized his talent and intelligence but found that he lacked the ethics and character required. His mentor had entered the opinion that he was a sociopath and could be harmful to the university, and possibly dangerous.

The senior researcher position at the state museum opened, so he applied and was awarded that position. His former close associates at the university were relieved to have him relegated to near obscurity. He did a very good job, but he had no passion for what he did. Still, he was promoted to curator of the museum archives. For nearly two decades now his only real passion had been the shooting competitions.

Then he invented the illicit business for Edward Hale and found a new passion. It wasn't the money that provided the joy, though that was a nice perk, but the pleasure of outsmarting the stuffed shirts who had ruined his career. It was also satisfying to be able to do his work under the good name of Mr. Edward Hale, simply because he was the best in his business.

He came to realize that his former mentor was correct; by all logic he was a sociopath. He concluded that the difference between a non-sociopath and himself was that he was far more intelligent, could do whatever was needed for success, and did not need their approval.

~

As Bren had predicted, the Antiquities Task Force agreed to support the investigation of the Queen Creek thefts. They also authorized Bren to cover the expenses of part-time officers from Pinal and Graham Counties, the San Carlos Police, and others on an "as needed" basis. He contacted the two sheriffs and received permission to use Deputies Dan Tomkins and Manny Sanchez, and he already had an agreement with San Carlos Police Chief Walker to use Sergeant Al Victor.

Bren arranged for a meeting in Globe to orient these new team members on both this case and the administrative procedures of the task force. They met in a private room at Guayo's Restaurant near Globe. Bren introduced Manny and Dan, the only attendees who had not met.

After they placed their lunch orders, Bren updated the group on the task force decision and the approvals of their bosses. He then explained the administration rules, basically time keeping, expense reimbursement, and requests for extraordinary expenses.

Lunch meetings were old hat for Bren and Al, having worked on these types of investigations many times through the years, but it was exciting stuff for the two younger deputies who sensed a change in status from junior level to being considered seasoned officers. The food arrived and Bren said, "Enjoy your dinner, and we will get down to business when we've finished eating. Since I'll be paying for this meal, you won't need to report it on your expenses."

After the enthusiastic consumption of their various combination plates, Bren explained, "The Task Force is investigating theft of artifacts, and in relation to our case, Pinal County is investigating a murder and an attempted murder. The sheriff wanted me to emphasize that if there is a priority question between the two investigations, murder gets the nod. Since Deputy Tomkins is the lead investigator in the murder, in a sense we are all supporting that investigation as well, so I doubt we will have any such conflicts."

He then asked, "Dan, would you run through what we know about the case to date? Then we will discuss it as a group."

Dan started with his call to the scene and told the history of the investigation up to the present. It was the first time Manny had any details and the first Bren and Al had heard about the results of the search warrants.

Al asked, "Jack's left-handedness, Jack having a lack of gun-handling expertise, and the prior blunt force wound, do you feel that suicide is ruled out?"

"Yes. There's no question in my mind Jack was murdered."

Manny commented, "You know, we are all well-trained and well-practiced in firearms, but I doubt that any one of us would have been able to execute that headshot on Lester." There were unanimous nods of agreement. "I don't know how it could help us, because there are so many shooting enthusiasts in the state, but have you heard of action shooting clubs?"

Dan said, "You mean the urban battlefield ranges where targets pop up in a maze? There are several of those in the state."

"That's not what I was thinking, but it is a valid place where a person can hone their quick shot skills. What I'm talking about is a form of quick-draw shooting with live ammo. They are usually old west affairs. These guys can toss a coin in the air, then draw and put a bullet through it. That is the kind of skill I think it would take to shoot Lester off a fast-moving ATV."

Bren said, "You say there are several of these clubs?"

"Yes, I have no idea how many, but there are probably hundreds of enthusiasts in the state that are involved in the sport."

"Well, I agree," said Bren. "The shooter either had an incredibly lucky shot or was very skillful. Having a pool of people that can routinely shoot like that will give us a place to look. Manny, you research it for us—both the quick-draw clubs and the action shooting ranges."

Bren asked, "Do we have any more questions for Dan or discussion on the state of the case?" There were none, so Bren continued, "I would like to orient you on the world of artifact theft. There is an informal society of people who are involved in the illicit trade of Indian artifacts. At the bottom of the barrel is the common pot digger. These people generally come as one of two types. The first is lowest level petty thief. A lot of times this is the typical local guy who loots ruins, graves, or other archeological sites for the sole purpose of selling pots and other artifacts locally to make a few bucks. In some ways this guy is the worst of the lot because he typically destroys more artifacts than he recovers, and he does so with no regard for the site at all.

"They locate where to dig by shoving steel rods into the ground, "feeling" for pottery. When he breaks through a pot, chances are there are others at that spot that he recklessly digs up. They sometimes will take a backhoe and completely destroy the site to recover some of the pots. He will sell them to local collectors or tourists for what he can get . . . typically from ten to two-hundred dollars.

"The second level is the personal collector. These people are not as destructive as the pot digger, because they are actually interested in the culture and in preserving the artifacts intact . . . and even sometimes in capturing the archeological context. So the site continues to exist for future investigation, and the artifact itself has more meaning and value. Some of these people are actually very good amateur archeologists. Often they understand the law and dig only on private property with permission, so they aren't doing anything illegal.

"So just because somebody digs up a pot doesn't mean they are breaking the law. However, some private collectors do not hesitate to dig on public land, which *is* against the law. In some ways, they are harder to catch, because they keep their finds secret and just add them to their current collection. They don't look for a buyer. They are pretty much only vulnerable to the law prior to putting the artifact on their shelf.

"The next level is the artifact gatherer. This person has knowledge and training in archeology and knows how to price and sell on the international black market. He most usually does not dig the item himself, but carefully trains others to do so and pays them well for the artifacts they supply him. He is relatively safe from the law, because at this level the black market is very careful and very secretive. The money involved at this level is in the hundreds to thousands of dollars per item.

"The highest level is the rogue archeologist. This guy is actively involved in the science of archeology and may work for the government or a respected foundation or museum as a contractor, professor, scientist, curator, or some similar position of trust. He has established himself as a supplier to the high-dollar black market, only taking rare artifacts of high quality. Because they are the only ones who know of the existence of the artifact and move so few of them, the chance of being caught is small. They can make thousands or hundreds of thousands of dollars per relic."

Bren paused a moment, then continued. "So those the types of bad guys we will be looking for. Unfortunately, those we usually catch are the lowly pot diggers. In addition, there are legitimate art dealers who buy from private collectors, estates, and such. On occasion this results in them selling an illicit artifact without even being aware of it. There are handlers that ship and deliver to buyers around the world. The problem being that at this upper level it's nearly impossible to spot criminal activity. So now you know what we are dealing with.

"Follow all the rules of procedure and evidence, and if you feel something isn't right, listen to your intuition. One element to this case that the task force doesn't normally deal with is the violence. We have a skilled killer, so be on your toes."

Chapter 5

Deputy Patricia Haley grew up with very few friends. Her mother was concerned that those children whose parents subscribed to traditional home structure and religion would counter the progressive feminism she was hoping to instill in her daughter. Consequently, Pat had known only two or three kids whose mothers were feminist enough that she was allowed to spend time with them.

These children were precocious, like Pat, and were better at conversing with adults than other children. They didn't play with dolls or do other girly things, so their activities were much the same whether they were with the other feminist children or their mothers. Pat never had a close friend, much less a best friend, until she went to work for the Sheriff.

When she went through her on-the-job training, as designed by Sheriff Bobby Bitters, she spent three months working in dispatch. During that period, she was amused by the irreverent and outlandish wise cracks and humor displayed by one of the senior dispatchers, Jessica Martineau. The fact that Jessica accepted her without judgment and listened to her thoughts and ideas without either arguing or pandering made it easy for Pat to open up and talk about her true feelings—something she had never experienced before.

In many ways the two women were very different. Jessica was religious, Pat was agnostic. Pat was a political liberal, Jessica was a conservative. Jessica was happily married, Pat thought marriage was an institution for subjugating women. Jessica enjoyed her heterosexual relationship. Pat was asexual and, in fact, did not know if she wanted anything to do with sex of any kind. But on a level beyond thought and opinion, the two were able to enjoy the intelligence and spirit of the other. As weird as it seemed to both, they had become best friends.

Pat called on Tuesday, Jessica's day off and arranged for them to have lunch, saying she needed some advice. They met at La Casita in Thatcher at eleven o'clock, ordered, and exchanged pleasantries. Then

Pat said, "I think I'm being discriminated against at work because I'm a woman."

"Really? Tell me about it."

"They recently started using me and Deputy Sanchez as fill-in supervisors. Well, to start with, I have two years more experience than Sanchez, so it seems unfair that they didn't think about giving me the temporary promotion until they wanted to promote Manny. I think they just promoted me because they wanted to promote him. Now the latest thing is that Bren Allred just appointed Sanchez to the Antiquities Task Force. By all rights, I'm the senior, and they should be appointing me instead. I'm thinking I might file an EEOC complaint."

"Are you sure? I know you all really well; you, Manny, Bren, and Sheriff Bobby. I've never seen anything but fairness and honesty from them. If you feel like you are being discriminated against I recommend you discuss it with Bren, and if you don't get a satisfactory outcome, then discuss it with the sheriff. Just blindsiding them with a legal complaint wouldn't be fair to them. They should at least get a chance to discuss it with you."

"Yes, I guess that makes sense. Do you think my complaint has any justification? I'm asking because I trust your judgment."

"There might be a question of why they waited so long to let you fill in as supervisor. For one thing that involves a temporary increase in pay. But serving on a task force is not based on seniority. It is at will, and the request for a specific resource from the force is usually granted. It also doesn't involve an increase in pay. You know when you were in the Solomon/Bryce district, you were junior deputy there. So you were unlikely to have ever gotten the fill-in call because of that. How long have you been in Stockton/Bonita?"

"About four months."

"Are you senior in your district now?"

"No, Lopez and Smithson are both senior to me, but Lopez has refused to serve as a supervisor. So if Smithson isn't available, then I'm next."

"And you have been filling in for the last few weeks, right?"

"Yes."

"On the other hand, Manny is second in seniority in Aravaipa/Ft. Thomas district, and he only fills in when Woods isn't available."

"That makes sense. I hadn't thought about it in relation to district seniority."

"Since you feel kind of threatened by the situation, I'd still discuss it with Bren. If nothing else, it will make him more aware of any potential for prejudice. It will reinforce your interest in promotion and serving on special assignments, and it will let him know that you are willing to come to him with problems. None of that can be bad."

Pat smiled. "Wow. I'm glad I have you to talk to. It would have been bad to file suit with no supportable facts. I can't see that helping my career."

"Want a suggestion? If you think you have a problem like this, try looking at it from the other guy's perspective. Assume there is a good reason and that they are not trying to hurt you."

"That's a good idea."

"Do you remember when you asked me if your feminist views were hurting your relationships with other deputies?"

"Yeah, I laughed when you said, 'No, it's your man-hating that's hurting the relationships.'"

Jessica laughed. "Really, a lot of the guys are afraid of you. They walk around you on egg shells believing you are going to accuse them of chauvinism. They aren't afraid of your feminist views, they are afraid of offending or creating enmity. Relax a little bit, and look at things from their perspective."

"I don't think I hate anybody. But I guess I'm pretty intense."

"Hey, you are a good person and a good cop. You're smart, hardworking, honest, passionate, and professional. Everybody respects that. You go get the bad guys . . . not your coworkers Keep it safe, kid. I need my friends."

"Okay, Doctor Jessica. I'll probably need a few follow up sessions. You've given me a lot to think about. I *will* talk with Allred."

~

Dan called Deputy Espinoza and said he wanted to run a couple of ideas by him.

"Okay, Dan. Fire away."

"As you know, we don't have much of a lead on who our pot thief murderer is. I wonder if it would be worth my time to talk with the Fultons and their employees to find out if there is anyone that they feel is either a potential artifact thief or might be recruiting people to provide him with artifacts. Right now we don't even know where to start looking. Maybe somebody has had questions asked of them that made them uncomfortable or have dealt with somebody that they felt was kind of smarmy.

"Or maybe Fulton has fired somebody that might warrant looking at. It is just a shot in the dark, but maybe we could stumble into something. Also, I would like to run background and financial check on employees and former employees to see who might be vulnerable to an unethical offer."

"As you said, Dan, we don't have anything to work with now, so go ahead and follow that as far as it will take you. Let me know if anything interesting turns up."

Dan drove from his apartment in south Superior to the Fultons' rented home a short distance away. Noting that their truck was there, he stopped and rang the doorbell.

Jill answered the door. "Hi, Deputy, I hope you don't have more bad news for us!"

"No, in fact I have some kind of good news . . . and a favor to ask of you and Mike."

"Come on in and have a seat. Mike's back in the office working on some reports. I'll go get him."

The Fulton's returned shortly and sat on the couch across from Dan.

"I thought you would like to know that we are now sure of two things. We know that Jack could not have been the person who shot Lester, and we know that Jack did not commit suicide. He was murdered. I would like you to keep that to yourselves for now, because for a short time the murderer will continue to think he is in the clear."

Mike said, "Good. We never believed it was Jack. I'm glad he's been cleared."

Dan continued, "We also found out that Jack was selling artifacts, probably to the man who killed him. He appears to have started about four months ago, during which time he sold about $20,000 worth."

Jill said with a catch in her voice, "Why did he do that?"

"I guess we can't be sure why, but he had student loan and credit card debt and his mom had recently been diagnosed with cancer and has no insurance. That need for money might have made the offer to sell on the black market enticing."

Jill again wept as she murmured, "Poor Jack . . ."

"I will interview each of your employees to see if any of them have been contacted by a black marketer or if they have suspicions that somebody they have dealt with might be dirty or trying to recruit. I would like to have a list of all those that have worked for you since the first of the year, with their contact information."

"If it will help get the scum who did this, we'll be happy to cooperate. Before you leave, I can go print out the roster for you."

"That's great. Instead of printing it, could you just copy the document to this flash drive?" Dan handed the drive to Mike. Then Dan asked, "What I would like to ask you to do is think about everybody you deal with in your business and think if they have shown an undue interest in the monetary value of artifacts. Also consider each of these people and identify if you have ever had the thought or impression that you doubt their integrity. And finally, list anyone you have ever fired or rejected as an applicant because of integrity or theft issues."

Mike said, "Dan, I don't feel very comfortable doing that. It is like accusing them when I have no evidence."

"That's not what you would be doing. We are simply trying to find a starting place to look for the perpetrator. We will build a pool of people from these nebulous feelings and experiences, then conduct background checks and only investigate those who have some convincing evidence. You would be surprised how often a first impression that someone is lying or covering something up proves to be true. This is the only way we have to find viable suspects or material witnesses that can lead us to our killer."

"Well, let Jill and I think about this. We'll write down potential problems and get back to you. As far as those we have fired or not hired for ethical reasons, there are very few of those, but I'll put them on the drive for you. Give us a couple of days to work on listing people whose integrity we question."

"That sounds good, Mike. I appreciate it."

"I just wish Jack had come to us. Maybe we could have helped somehow."

Jill said, "Jack requested an insurance change form about a month ago, and I provided it to him. The completed form goes straight to the insurance company, but I did get an increase in both his life and medical insurance deductibles a couple of weeks ago. I wonder if he added his mom to his insurance."

~

Manny and Jenny called the church secretary and reserved the evening of September 20th for their wedding and reception. They visited her parents and then his to announce their date. All were thrilled and plans were made to start shopping for dresses and invitations.

Manny took Jenny back home, and they sat on the porch swing for a while, talking dreamily of their future life together. Before Manny left, Jenny agreed to accompany him to the range the next week to start her weapons training. Manny was home before midnight.

He was too keyed up to sleep, so he logged in and began searching live action shooting clubs and ranges in the state. He quickly found over thirty action shooting clubs and sixty-three gun ranges scattered all over the state.

He decided that since the murderer had communicated by Tracfone most frequently from Tucson, which was most likely where the suspect would participate in shooting competitions. This narrowed the list to five cowboy action clubs and two ranges that provided cowboy action shooting. It appeared that the standard competition was single action pistol, rifle, and shotgun. They also had horse-mounted competitions.

The action shooting clubs all listed long rosters of events. The clubs required that members select and register an old west alias and dress in old west style, so the member lists contained names such as Ann E. Ookly, Bad Jim, Deadly Dan, Earp's Nemesis, and such. Most of the clubs seemed to have monthly meets. The national championship was held annually in Phoenix, and they reported having 1,000 competitors from forty-two states and five foreign countries.

In addition to the Cowboy Action Clubs, there were three tactical ranges in the Tucson area that provided training and practice in quick response shooting at pop-up targets. Manny sent this information in an e-mail to Bren. Then he went to bed.

~

Jill Fulton walked into the office in their rented Superior house and said, "Mike, let's talk about the slimy characters we've encountered. Maybe something will fall into place, and they can arrest the creep that shot our boys."

"Okay. The only ones I thought of were the ones we let go or that I didn't hire because I don't feel good about them, and I've already given that list to Dan."

"What about Marie Artiste?"

"It couldn't be her. She was killed some time ago. Besides, there was no substance to that . . . except that her bringing up how much money could be made on the black market was unprofessional."

"So did I, but I also felt she was feeling us out to see if we might take the bait. I think we should mention it. Maybe if they look into her background it will point them to somebody else."

"Maybe so; that might be what Dan meant when he said to go with our instinct. It's kind of casting a big net and seeing what you catch."

"What else do they have to go on? Lester is the only one that saw anything, and it wasn't much. I really think that for those two boys we should give it our best effort. On that big Chaco project, I always felt that Mark Derwood was kind of off in the ethics department. I think his ego was more important than his science."

"That's true. Then there's the whole Benson-Colley Engineering bunch. I was afraid that we and every contractor working for them would end up being arrested for violations. I've never seen anything as sloppy and careless as the surveys they did. They took shortcuts on everything. I'm still convinced that they paved over the funerary sites we had marked for recovery and repatriation, so they could make their schedule bonus. They paid and released us, and the next week the road bed was laid. People who would do that are not above doing anything for money."

"So we've got six or seven names that we can give to Dan and as we continue to think about it we might come up with more. I'll go ahead and e-mail this list as a spreadsheet with our reasoning and whatever we have in the way of contact information."

"I hope it helps catch the murderer. It would also be nice if we could weed out some of the bad apples in our field. There is little enough known about these cultures without thieves stealing and destroying it."

~

Dan Tomkins called Bren Allred and told him that he had interviewed the Fulton's and all their current employees and asked if they had colleagues or others in the archeological work that they felt had a problem with ethics.

"I ended up with nine names and have done background and financial checks on them. There are some that I would like to track down and interview, and there is a pre-construction survey company we may want to investigate. In addition to that, there's an archeologist who worked for the National Park Service whose finances are very suspect. I think we need to investigate that situation."

"You said *worked*. Did he get fired?"

"No, *she* died in a freak accident on a remote dig several months ago. But I think we might be able to find some illicit connections by investigating her."

"What kind of accident was it?"

"She did excavation and analysis of kivas and other religious sites and generally insisted on doing the work by herself. She was about nine feet down when there was a rock fall with several large boulders dropping down on her. One crushed her head, probably killing her instantly. The FBI and OSHA investigated and concluded it was an accident. They cited the park service for not providing trench walls on a deep dig."

"What are the financial inconsistencies you discovered?"

"She had a good salary, $65,000 last year. She had a very nice home, two new cars, and zero debt. The home was valued at just under $400,000. She bought a new car every two years, and at the time of her death she owned a Jeep Rubicon with every bell and whistle, winch, front and back protection racks and custom bumpers—that's at least $45,000. Her other car was an Audi R8. That's around $100,000. She also traveled a lot, and in style. Yet she had no debt. So in ten years of averaging $60K, she paid off well over half a million in debt while living a 'rich and famous' lifestyle."

"Well, that's too much smoke not to have some fire. Go ahead with your research. Start by getting the full file on the accident. Work any of the other possible leads you've identified as well. Where did the death occur?"

"It was in Chaco Canyon."

"That complicates it a little bit. That's in New Mexico on federal property. Once you've gotten everything you can via computer and phone, let's get together and plan the next step. We may need to go to Chaco."

~

Bren's cell phone rang and caller ID showed Deputy Haley's number. "Hello, Deputy. This is Sergeant Allred."

"Hi, Sergeant. I have something that I want to discuss with you. It isn't critical, but it's personally important to me. I was wondering if we could get together sometime soon."

"Sure," Bren said. He opened his calendar. "I have a couple of things in the early afternoon, but I could meet you in Safford at three o'clock. We can use an office or interview room to talk, if that will work for you." Bren tried to get on personnel-type things as soon as possible to reduce the anxiety level of the officer and because usually this type of meeting was really to deal with a grievance. It was best to deal with problems quickly.

At the appointed time, they were able to use a small interview room. Bren got a bottle of water and asked Pat if she wanted a beverage. She poured a cup of coffee and carried it into the room. As they settled in, Bren said, "I can see that you seem a bit tense. To put your mind at ease, I can promise you I will listen carefully to what you say, will consider it fairly, and be straight up with any questions or answers I might have."

"I appreciate that. It's all I want."

"Okay, you have the floor."

"I have two different, but related, issues. First, I've felt that I've not gotten the same consideration for promotion as the male deputies, and second, I feel I've been bypassed by a less senior deputy on a task force assignment."

"I'll need you to lay out your reasoning on the two issues in detail, but first let me review the department policies on both promotion and areas of assignment. In general, we operate on assignments *at the will of the Sheriff*, which means we have more flexibility than some people realize. Assignments are made to best cover the current need, so they may sometimes be based on a particular skill or simply availability and staffing considerations.

"For promotion, we are governed by personnel laws that require proven competency, significant experience, and consideration of performance criteria. In promoting, all other things being equal, we generally fall back on the senior qualified officer. If it is an actual rank and pay promotion, we consider all personnel department-wide. If it is a temporary or fill-in promotion, we consider it within the district you are assigned. So understanding that framework will make it easier to analyze your issues. Unless you need more clarification on any of this, let's get into the details of your issues."

Pat nodded and began, "Deputy Sanchez and I started working fill-in at the same time, but I have two years seniority over him. I hadn't realized that fill-in was strictly in the district, and I've not been the senior in either district that I've worked in. Sanchez has second seniority in his district, so I understand that inequality better. But on the other hand, why wasn't I assigned earlier into a district where I would be able exercise my seniority sooner?"

"The answer is that seniority is not considered in making area assignments. We try to put people where we feel they will best fill a need. In your case, when you were green, we wanted you with very experienced officers, and we knew you had worked in a municipal department—the University Police in Tucson—so we have used you in two of our more populated districts. Deputy Sanchez was even greener, so he was put directly under me. His prior experience, unlike yours, was part-time for a two-man college police department. He grew up in a rural area, so the Aravaipa district with no concentrated population seemed a good fit for him."

"That makes sense. So honestly, did my being a woman have anything to do with me not making fill-in sooner than Sanchez?"

"It was strictly the make-up of your assigned districts."

"On the matter of the task force assignment, I have the same issue. I have seniority and experience on Sanchez, yet have never been given a task force assignment. I don't consider it fair that he got one before I did."

"On that issue, task force assignments are 100 percent *at will*, and seniority is not a consideration. It is not a promotion and does not involve increased pay. It is strictly an assignment just like an area assignment. Also his assignment is an as-needed assignment, meaning he is not on the task force full-time and will likely spend most of his time on his regular duties. If there was a mistake in making that assignment, it falls on only one person—me. I personally requested Deputy Sanchez on the task force, because I could see we needed someone who is a whiz at data analysis, statistics, and computer research. Manny has a particular talent for that."

"I'm fairly strong in the computer aspects, but statistics and data analysis is not an area of expertise for me. I think you have settled the issues for me."

"Are you sure, because I don't want to minimize your concerns?"

"I'm sure. I appreciate you being up front with me."

~

Newspaper and electronic media had been given very little information on the ongoing investigation of a shooting and possible suicide in rural Arizona, in hopes that the perpetrator would become over-confident and perhaps careless enough to make a mistake that would help resolve the case.

However, Emily Hager felt that the police were casting aspersions on her son by implying he had shot his friend Lester and then killed himself. She contacted Lyla Tran, a television reporter who, through use of hyperbole and sensationalism, conducted a somewhat yellow brand of investigative reporting.

Tran pieced together enough facts and innuendo to break a story of police cover-up of crime on state-highway projects involving murder and theft of ancient Indian artifacts. The story was picked up and spread around the world, ending any hope of keeping the perpetrator misinformed.

Edward Hale was mortified when he saw the report. It was the first he had heard of the murder, but it was the location that startled him. The murders took place on a dig on the headwaters of Queen Creek, and it was believed that rare effigy artifacts were taken. He had just sold an extremely rare effigy pot for $800,000 that was listed as coming from the headwaters of Queen Creek. Middleman had assured him he was buying only from legitimate, certified private collectors.

He was furious at Middleman and couldn't imagine a scenario in which murder would be justified. As far as he knew, the pots were coming from private collections. He had an excellent lawyer, and he decided that he better run his concerns by him and see if he might be able to distance himself from yet another insane partner.

Peter Villa was, in fact, a top-tier lawyer who had practiced criminal law for fourteen years before moving into more lucrative business law. He specialized in enterprise expansion, intellectual property, and executive liability. He and Ed had been friends since college when the two had been in the same fraternity. He had helped Ed expand his business from a million dollars a year to fifty million per year.

Ed called first thing in the morning. "Pete, I'm afraid I made a compact with the Devil, and he's about to call in the payment. I need your help."

"Don't a say any more about it. When can you come to my office?"

"I can be there in ten minutes."

"All right, I'm working on a brief, but I can have my associates keep the work going. Come on down."

Ed was standing in Pete's office seven and a half minutes later. He explained the situation to Pete in detail. "I was told all the artifacts were certified legal. I honestly did not think we were operating a theft ring, and I never thought violence would be involved. I don't know that Middleman killed that student, but the description of the items missing and the location seem like too much to be coincidence."

"As your attorney, I'm advising to not mention your suspicions, because you have absolutely no fact or evidence to support the hypothesis. I'll look into the whole thing, and if we have anything of substance, we will step up with it. This started with Marie acting as a buyer for you. So I'll ask again, did you know she was stealing articles from her dig and selling them through you?"

"No. She told me that she had legitimate private sources. But I'm not concerned about Marie. She died before this other idea was initiated."

"That's fine, but the fact remains that if what she threatened you with is true, then that could put you in a bad place with the law. You should have come to me when she first went nutsy on you. Why did you feel you needed to move so heavily into artifact sales? Your business was doing well, and we were ramping it up."

"It was the difference on return. We could buy objects from collectors, which is perfectly legal, for a few hundred or few thousand dollars and sell them for tens of thousands or more on the legitimate market. These aren't black market sales, but sales to museums, galleries, and wealthy private collectors. I sold them through a limited-subscriber online catalog completely separate from my gallery sales. So the *why* wasn't simple greed. It was being able to create something new, have it take off so successfully, and place my goods in the finest museums. It was a pretty heady feeling."

"So what are you looking for from me?"

"I want you to insulate me from the excesses of Middleman and to minimize my personal risk, liability, and culpability. And if worse comes to worst, I want you to represent me in court."

"Okay, I can do that. Your part is to not stir the pot. Don't talk with your silent partner or anyone else about this. In regard to the most recent sale, how is the partner paid?"

"He has a contract for 40 percent of the net. He invoices the catalog company, and it is paid as brokering services with a company check."

"We don't want to cause him to become alarmed or think you are reneging on your contract, so handle it normally. Don't do anything more or less than you have normally done in the course of business."

"Okay."

"Do you have your catalog business set up as an LLC or corporation?"

"No. My on-line catalog and auction is *Edward Hale, Indian Trader to the World OnLine*, so it is under the same umbrella as my gallery stores and trading posts. But I maintain exclusive books for the online sector."

"I'll want to see your books and your operation for the catalog business. Do you remember the executive liability insurance we've been paying for you? If we handle this right, it will pay any financial liabilities that might come out of this. I want you to go to the corporation commission today and modify your file to list me as general counsel and give me an appropriate executive salary and bonus package. That way I can speak for the company in legal matters."

"Thanks, Pete."

"When can you let me see your catalog business and books?"

"Do you want to see my physical facilities, online sites, and business records?"

"Yes, the whole operation."

"I'll make time whenever you can do it."

"The sooner the better. How much time will it take?"

"We'll have about six hours travel time and probably no more than that to review everything."

"Okay, let's do it tomorrow. I'll pick you up at 6:00 AM."

Chapter 6

Bren arranged a call for the strike force team consisting of Assistant Attorney General Barry Dirocco, the five district representatives, and guest Detective Paul Espinoza, all calling in from their respective offices and Sergeant Bren Allred, Sergeant Al Victor, Deputy Dan Tomkins, and Deputy Manny Sanchez calling in from Bren's office in Central. The agenda included an update on the Queen Creek thefts and a request for permission to have the team travel to New Mexico.

Dirocco welcomed the three new members and the guest and told the new members that he had received and approved their application to serve on the task force. He had them stand and take the oath of office, then said, "Sergeant Allred will now present the task force badge and ID wallets to you."

Bren called them forward one at a time, gave them their wallet, and shook their hand to the applause of the other members.

"Now Sergeant Allred, go ahead and report on our progress with the Queen Creek theft."

Bren explained the results of Deputy Tomkins research into the suspect vehicle, interviews, and background checks. He then gave a detailed review of the findings on Marie Artiste and said investigating her was probably the best opportunity to develop leads to illicit activities. Dan had gotten a copy of the Marie Artiste accident from OSHA, and Bren mentioned that he had sent copies to all the team members. He talked about Deputy Sanchez's data on cowboy action gun clubs and shooting ranges in the Tucson area.

Bren asked permission for a team to go to New Mexico and search for leads, which was granted. Then he asked for a contact in the New Mexico Attorney General's office who could work with them in that state. Dirocco said he would arrange that when the call was finished.

At the end of the conference call, since they were at Bren's office in Central, the four officers decided to have lunch at La Casita. They ordered and Bren turned to Manny, "Okay, Manny, you seem so happy you can't contain yourself. What's going on?"

"We set the date . . . getting married on September 20. We're going to neaten things up at my trailer, and we'll make our first home in Klondyke."

"Aha! It's about time. Congratulations!"

Al said, "That's great news! You better get some vacation scheduled. You don't want the night watch on your honeymoon."

"That's a good idea, Al. Okay, Bren are you going to let me start my vacation on a Friday?"

"We'll make sure it works out for you. I bet a couple of moms were pretty excited to hear that news."

"Yes, they were. I think the wedding plans are practically done already."

Bren's cell phone rang. "This is Bren Allred."

"Sergeant Allred, this is Assistant Attorney General Fred Rose in Albuquerque. I just had a conversation with Attorney Dirocco, and he sent me your background information on Marie Artiste. I wholeheartedly support your looking into the possibility of corruption on her part. I have already sent you all the files on her death. I also checked on her estate, and settlement is still pending, so all her belongings are still in her home. Let me know when you want to come to our fair state, and I'll have a search warrant for her home and property."

"That's good news. I would like to bring a couple of members of my task force with me. We want to visit the death scene in Chaco Canyon, talk with her boss and associates, and go through her belongings and records. We will pursue any useful leads related to our case. Beyond that, if we uncover other New Mexico leads, we would like to give them to you. I assume you or your people would like to participate in these activities with us, so when would you like us to come?"

"I'm very interested. Artifact theft is one of my areas of responsibility. I'm sure you want to do this soon, so you let me know when, and I'll rearrange any conflicts. I suggest that you stay in Grants. Miss Artiste's home is just north of town on the foothills of Mt. Taylor, plus there are several good hotels there. It is a long drive to Chaco, but we could handle both searches in two days."

"If it will work for you, we'll drive to Grants Wednesday afternoon, spend Thursday executing the search, and drive to Chaco to inspect the death scene and talk with the Park Service people on Friday. Then we'll travel home that afternoon."

"Good. I'll make sure the Chaco people make themselves available to you on Friday. I'll join you in Grants on Wednesday. Let's plan to have dinner at about 6:30. I recommend the Holiday Inn Express. That's where I normally stay."

"I appreciate all your help. We will see you at the hotel on Wednesday."

Bren hung up and said, "Al, I would like you to travel with me to Grants. Would that be a problem for you?"

"No, I'm approved to help as needed."

"Dan, can you travel with us? I want three of us there executing the search."

"I may not be able to go. The Sheriff has me scheduled to participate in a raid on a cattle theft operation."

"I'll give him a call and let you know." Bren continued, "Manny if Dan can't go, I'll need you to come with us."

~

Deputy Andy Lopez recognized that he was in a strange position in the department. He was a designated field training deputy, which made him sort of supervisory over deputies who had not yet completed the full course of task training. He was happy to be a trainer, but he turned down being a fill-in supervisor, because he simply didn't want to be the boss.

Deputy Pat Haley was the fill-in supervisor over him but he was assigned to finish the five out of forty task training points left for Deputy Haley. She had passed all the required training, but these five items were things that she has never had an opportunity to actually perform. Today he had an order of protection to serve in Artesia, so he called Pat on her cell phone.

"Hey, Pat, Andy Lopez here. I need you to help serve an order of protection in Artesia today. When could you do that?"

"I'm on 191 right now heading north. Where should I meet you?"

"Let's meet on the pullout by Artesia Road. We'll walk through the procedure first. It shows that you observed a serving earlier, but this will be the first time you've executed a protection order, right?"

"Yes, that's affirmative."

"Okay, see you in a few minutes."

Pat arrived at the pullout and Deputy Lopez had her tell him what she thought was the best way to serve an order of protection. She had the process right. He then emphasized that this was often unpleasant and could easily become dangerous because of the emotions involved, so it was important to maintain professional detachment.

Deputy Lopez had printed a satellite image of the place they would be serving, and they discussed the safety issues and where they could take cover if needed. Then he said, "Now, I'm not saying this in a chauvinist way, but since we are serving an order of protection for Mr. Bowens ex-wife, your being a woman could make you more of a target of his resentment. As usual, we will maintain a little distance from each other so we can approach him from different sides if it turns violent."

"Got it. I'm ready when you are."

"Let's go in my car. When we are finished, we'll come back here, and I'll go through the review and sign you off."

Pat performed execution of the order without incident. Mr. Bowen accepted it and acknowledged by signature that he understood and would comply with the order. He had no questions. The primary emotion involved seemed to be a resigned sadness.

When they were back at the highway pullout, Sanchez told Pat she had performed perfectly. There was nothing he would have done differently. He signed her off as task-trained for order of protection. She thanked him and asked, "Deputy, do you feel uncomfortable working with me? A friend told me that men were uncomfortable around me because I'm a man-hater."

Andy laughed, "You are asking the wrong guy. I don't think you are a man-hater. That would be your mom. She taught you that men only wanted you to serve them, and that your father was a bad as any. She isolated you from him. You grew up without normal friendships, mystified by and afraid of males. You know what she taught you, but you don't know how much of it you believe.

"I know this because my mom was the same way. I grew up thinking I was genetically damned to be something only slightly above an ape. Even my name was weird. It is actually *Andee*. She named me that because it wasn't a macho name. She is still furious with me for becoming a cop, because it is just living out my male authoritarianism."

"Holy Moly! I thought my childhood was confusing. I can't imagine how it would have been if I had been a boy."

"So I'm actually quite comfortable with you. But don't be surprised if I occasionally challenge the sacred tenets of feminism. I've been on my own for fifteen years now, and I've only had one romantic relationship. I abandoned that because I was afraid it would lead to marriage and that would turn us to hating each other. So I have issues, but I have been working through a lot of them. You still have that to look forward to."

"So, short of going to a shrink, how do I identify and *work through* my issues?"

"Good question. I wouldn't trust a shrink, because I think they are the types that gave birth to this whole mess. Actually, believe it or not, the Mormons helped me more than anything else."

"You're a Mormon?"

"No. Probably like you, I was raised without religion. It was no big deal to my mom, but we just didn't even think about religion. When I moved up here from Tucson, I rented an apartment in Thatcher from a Mormon family. They invited me to go to church with them, and I thought, why not? I actually enjoyed it, the people are friendly, and happy, and they are very supportive of each other. I didn't understand a lot of the religious stuff, though it did get me to reading the Bible." Andy shifted a little uncomfortably, and continued, "I guess I went through an epiphany as I read about Jesus, because I found myself believing."

He paused again and said, "But that's not the point. The big breakthrough for me was the time I spent with that family. The family was different from mine. There was a lot of cooperation, fun, and love. The husband and wife respected and treated each other with kindness. And the children had wonderful lives. They had dozens of friends, and they were allowed to be children. They played, teased, and had fun. Oh, they had to study and do chores, the same as I did, but they didn't seem to resent it the way I did. They participated in family decisions and discussed why they do what they do. The whole thing was so different for me."

"As for the religion, it's very intense. I really like the Mormon Church. I think some of their doctrines make more sense than others, but being a Mormon takes such a commitment."

Andy chuckled. "It's more than I can handle. They give more than one-tenth of their income to the church, they make a huge commitment of time . . . heck, their Sunday meetings are three hours long. They also have very strong standards of behavior, and I do like my beer. I simply did not want to make that kind of commitment. But I really enjoyed the fellowship and intellectual stimulation, so I found a non-denominational protestant church where I can be more casual in my religious commitment and still have fellowship with good people.

"Anyway, seeing that their families were polar opposites from how my mom described marriage and family was the real breakthrough for me. It caused me to start questioning all the feminism and liberalism that my mom had indoctrinated me in."

"So they have perfect families?"

"No, not at all. They have disagreements and kids argue and teenagers rebel, but they just handle it better. I guess it's part of that commitment thing."

"That's interesting. So how does your mom handle your 'rebellion'?"

"Well, she's certainly disappointed, but we've reached a balance where she doesn't press me. I think we are in a live-and-let-live equilibrium."

"That's got to be nice."

"It is. Well, we better get back to work, huh boss?"

"*Boss*? That's funny. Speaking of that, why don't you take fill-in when it's offered?"

"Like I just told you, I don't want the commitment or the responsibility for somebody else."

~

When Bren contacted Detective Espinoza to request permission to take Dan to New Mexico for the last few days of the week, Detective Espinoza was hesitant. "I won't refuse to let him go, because we agreed to let the strike force use him when needed, but it is really a bad time for the department right now. If it wouldn't cause you problems, we need to have him here this week. We have several deputies, including two of my investigators, on sick leave, and we are about to move on a commercial cattle theft ring on Thursday."

"Dan is not specifically essential to this activity. I have another resource I can use. We are actually following up on the lead that Dan developed, so I wanted to give him the chance to be part of it. We will be executing a search warrant, so I have other officers that can go."

"Then if it won't hurt your operation, I would rather keep him here."

"Please let him know that we made the request, so he knows we have nothing against him."

"I will do that. I'll tell him you are acting on his lead. Thanks for giving me a pass on this one."

After telling Dan his request for his service and been turned down, Bren called Manny and told him that he would need to make plans to travel to New Mexico with them. He then called Deputy Smithson and asked if he wanted to work his days off on Thursday and Friday as acting sergeant, but he had plans he couldn't change so declined. That left Lopez, who had asked to be taken off the substitute list, and Deputy Haley, so he called Deputy Haley.

"This is going to seem weird; since we just discussed this, but I assure you our discussion has nothing to do with it. The Antiquities Task Force is going to be in New Mexico Wednesday through Friday, so Manny Sanchez and I will be away. Carl Smithson would usually be acting sergeant in my place, but he is on leave and is not interested in changing his plans. Lopez has taken himself off the substitution list, so that leaves you as next in line to be acting sergeant in my absence. It pays a little more per day and would require you to work overtime on Friday, because that's your scheduled day off. Do you want to accept this assignment?"

"Yes, but I have no training at all on the sergeant's administrative duties, so I'll have to get some fast task training."

"Thank you. I appreciate your willingness to do this. How long will it take to get your shift assigned tonight?"

"No more than an hour."

"When you finish, drive over to my office in Central, and I'll walk you through the things you will need to do and provide you with a copy of the command procedures manual in case something unusual comes up. You should also be able to call my cell phone most of the time if you need to talk to me."

They met in Central at five o'clock. Bren had made a daily checklist and gave it to her. They talked through the administrative forms and procedures that Pat would need to know, and Bren showed her how the manual was organized and how to quickly find procedures for a specific circumstance. She understood everything quickly and said, "I feel comfortable with doing this now. Thanks for all the help."

"Good. You're a fast study. Here is your duty roster for each shift. As you can see, we are pretty thin—each area will only have one deputy on duty. Make sure that each area knows who is in the neighboring areas and are prepared to provide backup for each other when needed. Also, in a critical situation, ask for assistance from other agencies if appropriate. If you or your people log more than your eight hours per day, you will have to justify the overtime. The eight hours on your day off is already approved. If you want to split time between shifts, that's okay as long as you don't exceed eight hours per day."

They walked outside, and as Bren was locking the door, Monica and Lizzie walked by pushing Layton in the stroller. Bren called them over and said, "This is Deputy Patricia Haley. She's going to be taking my place while I'm in New Mexico. This is my wife, Monica, and Lizzie and Layton. Lizzie is five and Layton is almost six months old."

Monica said, "Nice to meet you," and offered her hand. Pat shook Monica's hand, and eased her grip when Monica winced. "Oh, I'm sorry. I'm used to shaking hands with these macho guys. I'm happy to meet you, Monica."

Lizzie stuck her hand out, and Pat gently shook it. Lizzie said, "You will like dinner tonight. It's meat and noodles. After supper you can read to me."

Monica laughed and said, "Lizzie, Patricia is only taking Daddy's place at work, not at home." Turning to Pat, Monica said, "But we do have plenty of food for supper and would love to have you join us."

"Oh, I don't want to intrude, but thank you very much."

Bren said, "No, it's a good idea. It's almost time for your break. Call it in and join us." Then he chuckled, "Don't make me have to give you an order."

Lizzie walked over and took Pat's hand and said, "I'll show you the way. We live right down here in this brown house."

The meal was good, and Pat was thoroughly charmed by Lizzie. When dinner was over, Pat thanked the Allreds, hugged Lizzie bye, and reported back on duty. As she was driving away, she thought that she had a taste of the family life that Andy mentioned . . . and nothing about it seemed oppressive to her.

~

On Wednesday, Al and Bonny Victor had a late breakfast after the kids left for school, and then she drove him to the Allreds' home. Bren was putting his luggage in the back of his sheriff department SUV, so Al got his bag and stowed it with Bren's. Monica was sitting on the porch rocking Layton, and Lizzie was standing near Bren, holding his jacket. Bren accepted the jacket, placed it in the truck, and picked Lizzie up. "Thank you, Sweetie." Bren motioned to the chairs on the porch. "Let's wait in the shade until Manny gets here."

Bonny was already sitting next to Monica, holding and tickling Layton, who was giggling at the new attention. Bonny asked, "So how are you going to Grants?"

Bren said, "It's convoluted any route you choose, but the shortest time is through Mule Creek and Luna to Springerville, then Highway 60 to Quemado and north through the Malpais to Grants. It will probably take six or seven hours. At least it is a beautiful drive . . . lots of amazing scenery."

"What time should I pick my man up on Friday?"

"I guess we will have to call after we leave Chaco Canyon, because I'm not sure how long the crime scene visit and interviews will take. We'll also have an hour or two more travel time back to Grants. If we get off by mid-morning, we should be home by six."

Al said, "Don't worry. We'll be sure to keep you current with the travel. I'll send a text as we pass through different towns coming home. The miracle of electronics . . . sure beats smoke signals, doesn't it?"

Manny drove up, parked in front of the house, and locked his car. He came over and said, "Am I late?"

Al said, "Nope. Ten minutes early."

"My rifle is in the cargo box. Should we drop it by the SO on our way out?"

"No, go get it, and we'll lock it in my gun safe until we get back. Hopefully we won't need our weapons on this trip, but if we need a rifle, we will have mine."

Manny handed the AR15 to Bren, stowed his bag with the others, and shut the cargo door on the SUV.

Bren asked, "Did you remember to bring that Seagate hard drive?"

"Yes. It's well-protected and packed in my bag."

Lizzie came over to him and said, "Manny, will you be sure my Daddy stays safe?"

"Of course I will, Lizzie, and so will Al."

She reached up and Manny bent over and hugged her. "Thank you. I will pray for all of you to be safe."

"And we will all be praying that all of you will be safe while we are away."

"That's nice," Lizzie said. Then she turned to Al and hugged him.

Bren kissed the kids bye, the wives received their hugs and kisses, and the Antiquities Strike Force began their journey. Six and a half hours later, they were in their rooms at the Holiday Inn Express, where they reported their safe arrival to their ladies and went to the lobby to meet Attorney Fred Rose for dinner.

As they exited the elevator, a thirty year old man of medium height and build dressed in khaki's and a light blue polo shirt waved and walked them. "You must be Deputy Allred. I'm Fred Rose," he said and extended his hand.

Bren shook his hand and said, "Yes, I am. This is Sergeant Al Victor of the San Carlos Tribal Police and Deputy Manny Sanchez of Graham County. Both are members of our Antiquities Strike Force."

"I'm pleased to meet you, gentlemen. I have an investigator with New Mexico State Police with me, but he had to make a few phone calls. Let's sit down until he arrives. Do any of you have a favorite place to eat in Grants?"

Bren said, "The only place I've ever eaten here is Blake's. I like their green chili burgers."

Al said, "I've never stopped in Grants. When we're travelling through, we usually stop in Gallup."

Manny said, "The same for me. We are usually in a hurry so have never stopped here."

"That being the case, I suggest that we eat at La Ventana Steakhouse. They have good steaks, excellent prime rib, and a pretty robust menu. If you like Mexican food, they have a good selection. I especially like their green chili stew."

Bren said, "We'll take your recommendation. Meat sounds good to me."

They were joined by a five-foot-seven barrel-chested Hispanic man of about 45-years-old. He wore a plaid western shirt and Levis, slung with a fully-equipped gun belt and state trooper badge. Fred Rose introduced Investigator Jesus "Chuey" Reveles, and they left immediately for the restaurant.

The food was good as was the conversation in which the lawmen got to know each other. After two and a half hours, they returned to the hotel and agreed to meet in the hotel breakfast room at seven.

~

Acting Sergeant Pat Haley worked up her daily time sheets and field notes and stopped by the sheriff's office to deposit them in their respective boxes. Her friend Jessica was on duty at dispatch, so she stopped by on her way out. Jessica put aside the novel she was reading and asked, "Hey, what's up?"

"I just had to drop off papers. Looks like things aren't exactly popping for you tonight."

"Yeah, it's been unusually slow. That's good I guess, but it makes for a long shift. I see from the duty roster that you are the acting sergeant. You must have been pretty convincing in your talk with Bren."

"I let him have it with both barrels." Pat laughed. "Not really, but it was a very good discussion. He told me pretty much what you did. It just turned out that two days later he is out of town, Smithson is on leave, and of course, Andy is on the permanent refusal list. That put me next in line."

Jessica picked up on "Andy" because Pat always referred to her fellow officers by their last name. "Yeah, what's with Deputy Lopez? He has never once accepted the shift lead."

"He says he doesn't want the responsibility."

"That's pretty unusual. Most deputies want the extra pay and see experience as a fill-in as a step toward promotion."

"Well, his life has been pretty complicated, and it has taken him a long time to come to terms with some life issues. I'm guessing that he feels he has enough to work out just dealing with his own problems."

"That's interesting, because a couple of the deputies had sort of an argument the other day about whether he is gay or not."

"That's crazy. Actually, Andy's problem is that he was raised by a woman that is just like my mom. Can you imagine what kind of self-doubt that would put in a boy growing up? It was bad enough for me as a girl, but a poor little boy, man! He had a longtime girlfriend but ended it because he was afraid his marriage would end up like his parents'."

Jessica said, "Now that could impact self-image and gender doubt. Of course it wouldn't matter if he were gay, because he is a really competent deputy. He has to be to qualify as a department trainer. I've always really liked him."

"Well, the next time it comes up, you can set them straight."

"No, they think it's him that needs setting straight."

Pat laughed, "You can make a joke out of anything. But seriously, I have a lot of respect for him, because he really is a good officer and has come a long way on his own from when he got away from his mom."

"So when did you find all this out?

"Just this week. He task trained me on order of protection, and somehow we ending up comparing our upbringing. They are amazingly parallel. I found myself talking with him the same way I talk with you. That hasn't happened with any male since I was six. It's very liberating to me."

"That's wonderful! We can't have too many good friends."

~

The five officers of the Antiquities Strike Force met at breakfast as planned. The New Mexico lawmen led the way up Lobo Canyon Drive to a paved private drive ending at the house. Marie Artiste's very attractive home was set in beautiful oak pinion pine hills. The lawmen parked in front of the garage and stepped out to admire the panoramic view from Mt. Taylor to the north to the Malpais and Mesa Negra to the south.

As they gathered near Fred's car, Bren said, "Man, this is some place!"

Fred agreed. "It has three and a half acres and abuts the forest. The bedroom suite has a bathroom, a huge closet, vanity, and its own sitting room the size of most living rooms. The house has a large Sub-Zero kitchen, wine cellar, separate pantry, living room, office, antiquities lab, and a three-car garage . . . oh, and two other bathrooms, and a large patio with pool and spa. It's only twenty-six hundred square feet, but that's pretty good sized for a single-bedroom house. Then it's got this million-dollar view. Government archeologists apparently make a large salary."

Bren commented, "Yeah, that's the conclusion that Dan Tomkins reached too. All this, two luxury cars, zero debt, on a $65,000 salary? There's no way to make that add up."

"The judge found it convincing enough that he issued the search warrants we requested. Well, gentlemen, shall be begin?"

They entered the house using the house key taken from Artiste's personal items in the evidence room.

As soon as they entered, Al said, "Uh, oh. I smell rotting flesh. We better check for a body."

Bren flipped a light switch, but nothing happened. "I bet they shut off the power and walked away, leaving the food in the refrigerator to spoil. Wasn't there any next of kin? Surely they would have come to secure the place."

Fred said, "The report says she only had one living relative—a sister who is a doctor in a remote clinic in Brazil. Attempts were made to notify her, and the local polycía said they would get the message to her, but there has never been any response at all."

Bren said, "We probably don't want to open the refrigerator. It will make the stench worse. Let's open up all the windows, so it can air out some."

Fred nodded, "Let's confirm where the smell originates, just to be sure there isn't a body in here somewhere . . . but I agree, don't open the refrigerator or freezer."

Manny had already begun opening windows and doors. When he opened the sliding patio doors, he noticed a shed with a diesel exhaust pipe sticking out the top and went over to examine it. As he came back in, he said, "There is an auxiliary power generator hooked to a relay switch out here. When they shut off the power, it automatically kicked on and ran until it emptied the fuel tank, which has a two-hundred-gallon capacity. It probably lasted for a few days. If we do need lights or cooling, all we have to do is add some fuel and start it."

Bren said, "The odor is from the walk-in refrigerator, so we know that's the source. Just opening the windows has made a huge difference. It ventilates well."

"No wonder it's working so well," Manny said, "This place is designed with natural air flow cooling. I noticed what looked like several chimneys on the roof. They're actually solar chimneys. The sun heats the chimney, which moves the warm air up and draws cool air from below. See the long narrow vents along the base boards? When they are opened, they pull cool air off the landscaping near the ground. So it pulls cooler outside air in and warmer ceiling air out. It costs quite a bit to put this stuff in a place, another sign that Marie had more money than she should." Manny then moved through the house opening the lower vents.

Fred asked Bren, "Is that kid an engineer or something? He sure seems to know about a lot of things."

Bren chuckled, "He is mostly self-taught, and he never ceases to amaze me. It often comes in handy when we are working on a case. He's kind of our version of MacGyver."

"I can see why you like him with you. Now that we can breathe in here again, let's get everybody together and make sure we are on the same page with the search warrant. Then we can each start searching a different room. We need to search everywhere, but let's start where we are more likely to find things of interest to artifacts theft or that raise questions about her death."

When all five officers were once again together, Fred talked about the judge's order for the search, what type of things they should be looking for, and the methods for documenting evidence impounded during the search.

After explaining these in some detail, he summarized, "The search is to be non-destructive to property, and each room should be left in nearly the same state as it was found. Take before and after photos. Take photos of items impounded in situ, if possible. We want to be thorough; look at the undersides, backs, and potential hiding places in furniture and home features such as shelves, drawers, cabinets, crawlspaces, etc. Document what you impound, exactly where it was found, and what other items were with it.

"Bring all keys found to the kitchen island. We need financial records, PINs, passwords, usernames, cash, artifacts, or anything that might be illegal or could reference illegal activities. Look for information on people she knew or did business with. Look for notes, journals, diaries, letters, or cards that might be useful for the case or to identify others to investigate or question.

"Chuey and Manny, you guys start with the garage, cars, outside areas, sheds, and patio, and then do the kitchen, pantry, and wine cellar. The car keys are on this ring. The Jeep won't be in the garage; it's in the impound lot. Bren and I will start in the office and the living room. Al, you start in the bedroom suite.

"We'll save the computers for last. I think we will fire up the power so we can copy the hard drives to Manny's back-up drive before we move them. If you find a gas can, set it aside to use later." They were well into the search before eight o'clock.

About eleven o'clock, Fred said, "Let's have Chuey go pick up some lunch. The nearest fast food is on First Street. There is a Blake's and, a little further down, a Sonic. Since Bren likes the green chili burger, I suggest Blake's."

They all placed their orders and Fred asked, "Did you find a gas can?"

Chuey replied, "Yes, there's a five-gallon can in the garage."

"Good. Take it with you and pick up diesel before you get the food." Fred handed a paper to Chuey. "On your way past the State Police Office, pick up these five respirators."

They ate in the shade of the patio, and then Fred said, "I've looked at your evidence logs, and we're finding a lot of interesting stuff. We found some sticky notes in the main desk with what are probably usernames and passwords. We're keeping them together on that desk in case you need them, Manny. We also have a key Al found in the dresser, which looks like a security box or safe key, so keep an eye out for a hidden safe.

"There are a few artifacts scattered around the house, mostly as displays, and five in the lab that look like they've been cleaned up. Chuey and Manny got pictures of those. We will want to ask about each of them when we are at Chaco Canyon.

"I called the county supervisor and told him about the rotten food. He has agreed to send a trash truck up at five-thirty to haul it away, so we want to have everything else done by then. Let's get back to it."

They were finished by 4:30 with all the evidence bagged or boxed, the hard drives copied, the computers logged and boxed, and everything loaded in the SUV. Using the odor filter respirators they cleaned out the refrigerator and had the trash bin in place when the garbage truck arrived.

Chuey said that the partially-filled, algae and mosquito-infested water in the pool and spa was a hazard, so they opened the pump valves to drain and pumped out the water. The building was secured, and the generator was shut down. To keep people away, they marked the house and yard as a crime scene with do not enter warnings.

The evidence was taken to the State Patrol Office in Grants where it was temporarily stored and secured. They agreed to just pick up food, so they called an order to El Cafecito and ate in their rooms.

Manny organized the photos he took of the artifacts in Marie's home so they would be ready to show the NPS people in the morning. Then he hooked the hard drive to his laptop and began going through the files.

In the *Pictures* file was a folder called *Eddie*. It was filled with photos of Marie and a man over a long period of time. They were camping, horseback riding, lying on the beach, swimming in pools, and on ships. Some of the pictures were in Hawaii, Machu Pichu, and Paris. There were occasional pictures with additional people, but often the shots looked like they used the camera timer to get them both in the shot. Eddie looked somewhat familiar to Manny, but he couldn't figure out why. Miss Artiste was quite pretty and had a flair for the dramatic in her fashion.

Manny found Marie's Wells Fargo online banking icon and tried the various user ID and passwords they had gathered. *LaBelleMarie* and *Ed602* worked. He found several accounts. They included a savings account of $145,000, a checking account with $50,000, $1,200,000 in CDs, a safe deposit box, but no loans. Twice a month the US Government deposited $2,112 into her checking account, of which $1,500 was automatically moved to the savings account. All but about $200 dollars went to utilities, and $200 was taken out in cash.

Most months she had a check from EHIT for consulting services ranging from two-thousand dollars to fifteen-thousand, but six months ago a one-million dollar deposit was made, and three-hundred thousand was sent to the IRS. Some of the EHIT money was also transferred to savings and some withdrawn in cash. One regular monthly expense of $2000 was automatically transferred to Amazônia Indianos Clínicas, OSCIP, Manaus, Brazil. Finally, at eleven o'clock, Manny shut off his computer and went to bed.

Chapter 7

Deputy Dan Tomkins researched Benson-Colley Engineering online and found they were a civil engineering general contractor, specializing in preconstruction environmental and cultural surveys. Steven Benson and Oscar Colley were the majority stock holders, with Benson as CEO and Colley as COO.

He found several news stories of Benson-Colley winning contracts for preconstruction surveys, and some as the general contractor. They were the third largest preconstruction company in Arizona by income, yet they were listed as having only five full-time employees. They typically hired subcontractors for the actual work.

Benson-Colley had a violation of the Endangered Species Act filed by the EPA for failure to identify the existence of an endangered Arizona Hedgehog Cactus population at a contracted construction site, resulting in the destruction of an unknown number (at least three) of the species. They were fined $60,000. The contract was for the location of a state highway yard, and the bonus for completing the survey on time and budget was $300,000.

If they knew of the species but covered them up (in this case literally) to meet the deadline, they still had a net gain of $240,000. It would not be a stretch to do the same type of cover-up of native burials to avoid the costs of exhuming and repatriating to earn the schedule bonus. The Fulton's may have been right about the ethics at Benson-Colley.

On the Benson-Colley Web page, Dan found a picture gallery in which most of the people were identified. He made a list of names and located them online, gathering what information he could. He ran background checks and looked into their finances. Nothing of interest turned up until he went onto Elton Godwin's Facebook page. There he found that Elton, who was described in the Benson-Colley photos as a part-time field technician, had toys in the form of a three-year-old Trail Blazer, a Rhino quad, and a toy hauler trailer.

According to Mike Fulton, a field technician is basically a site laborer with training in excavating a dig. They are generally paid by the hour, usually in the ten-to-twelve dollar range. Dan decided that was an expensive lifestyle for a guy who didn't seem to earn enough to rent a decent apartment.

Studying Mr. Godwin's poorly-written posts, mostly pictures of his quad, it soon became apparent the he worked sporadically, yet spent a lot of time playing . . . not really elaborate, but excessive for a part-time income.

Dan wanted to talk with Detective Espinoza about going after Benson-Colley and getting a search warrant for Elton Godwin's property and finances, but decided against it. Since this would most likely have nothing to do with the murder, Espinoza would probably not be amenable to following those leads. Instead, he called Sergeant Allred and explained what he had found.

Bren told him that he would talk with Attorney Dirocco about it. Most likely the person who had persuaded Jack Hager to supply artifacts was doing the same thing on other digs. Bren told Dan he had done a good job on finding those leads, and he would keep him updated on what was happening.

Bren called Barry Dirocco and updated him on the search of Marie Artiste's property and on the investigative leads that Dan developed.

Barry said, "There has been suspicion about Benson-Colley for a long time, but other than the protected species judgment we won against them, we've come up blank. I'm inclined to go after Mr. Godwin with a search warrant. If we can get anything of substance on him, maybe he will testify against his bosses. I'll have it on the agenda for discussion at Monday's conference call."

~

Manny showered and was ready to go to breakfast, but it was still half an hour before the others would be down. He decided to call Jenny.

She answered, "Well, I'm surprised to hear from you so early."

"You're out running, aren't you?"

"Not exactly. I'm out, but I'm walking to get loosened up."

"I bought a surprise for you and was supposed to pick it up today because the shop is closed tomorrow. Would you mind stopping by Gila

Outdoor and getting your new handgun? It's all paid for and has all the accessories you need. Tomorrow we can go out to the range, and I'll teach you how to use it."

"Of Course! Will they let me pick it up if you're the one who bought it?"

"I'll call today and tell them you'll be picking it up."

"What kind is it?"

"It's the Ruger .380 LCP that you liked, except it has been customized a little for you. It will include three clips, a loader, a cleaning kit, some ammunition, and three different holsters to fit different clothes."

"Now I'm curious to see those customizations. I'll go as soon as I get back home. I was going to call you with some news . . . I decided on my wedding dress!"

"Which one, the one with the big bow or the one with the pearls?"

"The pearls."

"Good! One more step taken."

~

The law officers met for breakfast as planned and decided to ride in the same vehicle so they could discuss the case. The Graham County car was a full-sized SUV, so they decided to travel in it. Investigator Reveles drove, since he was most familiar with the route. Al's size gave him the *shotgun* seat, and Bren, Manny, and Attorney Rose rode in the back. As they drove, Manny explained the research he'd done and suggested they follow up on Marie's consulting services, which appeared to be a very lucrative sideline for her.

Manny told the others about the many pictures of her romantic interest named Eddie. He also mentioned that Eddie seemed vaguely familiar to him, but he had been unable to come up with anything. Manny told the others that he had made a slide presentation of all the artifacts that were in the house, plus those that were in Marie's snapshots. He suggested they have the NPS people at Chaco review them and give them any information they could.

Fred Rose agreed with Manny's conclusions and said, "Today we are set up to interview Marie's three closest associates, individually–her boss Jacob L. Goetle, assistant Gib Yazzie, and fellow archeologist

Elwood Heatherly. We are set up for 45 minutes each, but I doubt that we'll require that much time. Afterwards, we can meet with all of them together, plus any others they deem appropriate to review the archeological photos.

"We are scheduled to be taken first to the scene of her death as soon as we arrive at the Park. Then we will go to the headquarters for the interviews. Knowing what we do about Al's tracking skills, Chuey and I would prefer that Al take the lead on the scene visit."

Al said, "I don't mind doing that, but this scene is so old, I doubt that we will find very much in the way of evidence or tracking sign. Just in case, it might be a good idea for me to do a perimeter search for any sign of people coming into the dig from an unexpected point. I'll talk with our guide at a point where we can overview the scene at a distance, and then I'll do a wide walk around before we actually approach the ruin itself. Will that be okay?"

"Yes. You are in charge of the scene visit, so we'll wait for instructions from you before we do anything."

Because he was familiar with the route, Investigator Chuey drove. They travelled east on I-40, then north on NM 371 through Crown Point to the turn off on NM 57, and about 25 miles on that rough dirt road to the Chaco entrance road. It took them two and a half hours to make the trip.

As they drove into the park, Chuey asked Al to set the radio to the NPS frequency and ask for Gib Yazzie, the park guide who was to meet them and lead them to the death scene. Yazzie replied that he would meet them at the visitor center so they could have a chance to stretch a bit, get a drink, and *drain their lizard*, which drew a chuckle form the cops.

Gilbert "Gib" Yazzie was a tall, slender Navajo in his late twenties who looked like the marathon runner he was. He wore a National Park Service uniform and hiking boots. He introduced himself to them as Marie Artiste's archeological assistant.

As soon as they had completed their bathroom visits and received cold water bottles, Gib told them he was glad they had an SUV. They were going on a primitive trace for about ten miles. He led the way in an NPS F150 4x4.

Al rode in the truck with Gib, and they conversed in Navajo-Apache. The two languages are dialects of the same language, similar to British and American English, so they understood each other.

Al asked Gib to describe Marie. He said she was very good at the work and extremely picky. She watched what he did closely, but he didn't mind because he learned a lot from her. She wasn't always easy to work with and could be moody and bossy. She and Elwood had equal pay grades, had a competitive relationship, and disagreed often, to the point of rather loud arguments. The boss never let those two work together; and only rarely let Sharon Camacho, the third staff archeologist, work with Marie. He pretty much had her always work by herself.

The route was open country with good visibility, so Chuey allowed Gib to pull away from him for about a quarter mile to allow the dust to disperse ahead of them. After about nine miles, Gib pulled over on the summit of a little rise and waited for them to catch up. He unrolled a topo map onto his tailgate and, using it as a reference, oriented them on the small pueblo that contained Marie Artiste's death kiva, visible about a half mile away.

Bren asked, "Is there any chance of original tracks being there? Wouldn't they be obliterated by visitors?

"No," Gib said, "This ruin is not open for visitors; only park employees. It's not shown on any of the public maps and the dirt trace to it is unlabeled. Tracks last a long time up here; that's why we encourage visitors to stay on authorized paths."

Al asked, "So where did the responders and investigators park?"

"We can drive almost to the pueblo on this trace. They parked in that flat just to the left of the north wall. It's only about a hundred feet from the kiva."

Al nodded and asked, "So most of their tracks will be contained between the kiva and the parking lot?"

"Yes. Later I brought the OSHA investigator and the county sheriff detective to review the scene, and they walked around the outside of the kiva, paying special attention to where the boulders came loose. It was kind of interesting. The detective went first and very slowly looked for any sign of someone being up there, but it's mostly hard, smooth sandstone on that side . . . no sign of anyone ever being up there," Gib said, pointing with his lips toward the upper area of the pueblo.

"If I wanted to surprise someone working in the kiva, where would I park to keep them from hearing my vehicle?"

Gib studied the landscape for a while before responding, "The canyon picks up sound when you get close to the narrow, so I would park where the road crosses the little sand wash. It would be easy to walk up it to within a few feet of the kiva and go to the top side of it."

Al said to the group, "I'll get my camera. Gib can drop me off at the wash and go on up to the parking area. After I've looked the scene over, I'll let you know to come on up. I'll get a couple of shots from here for overall reference. It'll probably take twenty minutes to walk the perimeter."

At the wash, Al noticed that there were indentations indicating someone or something had been walking in the sand, but the wind and maybe a little rain had rendered them indecipherable. Rather than walking in the narrow wash, he stayed on the sloping side, looking for entry points in or out of the wash. Near the head of the wash, he found faint boot prints with a fairly clear outline of the heel coming both into and out of the wash. He noticed a single small, dried juniper branch lying some distance from the nearest tree.

The tracks disappeared about twenty feet from the spot where the clean sandstone began. The only possible explanation was that the tracks were deliberately wiped out. After documenting his findings with photos, Al carried the broken branch to the tree and found where it had been broken from the tree. He also found that the area between the flat stone and the tracks had a concentration of small stones to the side of the area that had been swept with the branch.

He looked for scuff marks on the sandstone, but found none. He then examined the disturbed spot where the stones had dislodged and fallen on Marie. There was nothing he could conclude from that, but he did note that the soil imprint left by the lowest stones that fell seemed to be squarely set on the stones below them. It might have been possible that the lower, more firmly-set stones were dislodged when the stones above fell, but it didn't seem likely to him. He examined the kiva itself, but it had been so disturbed by the body recovery and subsequent examination that little of value could be found there. He photographed the scene as he found it and called the others up.

Al explained what he had found and presented his conclusions. Someone had walked to the kiva and back some weeks or months ago. On their way out, they had gone to the trouble of cleaning their tracks for some distance with a juniper branch. He felt the stones falling by natural means seemed unlikely, but had no evidence of manual manipulation. Perhaps an earthquake could have made them fall; they could check with the Geologic Survey for seismic activity on the day of Miss Artiste's death. So there was reason to suspect foul play but not much conclusive evidence.

Gib said, "This region is considered aseismic. There has never been an earthquake recorded here."

Al asked, "Could we get the original scene photos from the accident?"

"Of course," Attorney Rose said. "I'll request them from OSHA. Thanks for the great analysis, Al. I think your conclusions are spot on. Let's head back to the visitor center to meet with the Park personnel."

~

Jenny Mondragon felt a little silly that she was so excited to get the pistol Manny had ordered for her. Her dad had taught her to shoot a rifle at an early age, so she was not afraid of guns, but she had never used a handgun and was a little nervous about learning to handle it. It was exciting to her that Manny had bought her something that he considered essential for her safety. She had never thought of a gun as an object of affection!

She cut her run short, showered, and took time to get her looks perfect. She decided she wanted to look professional, so she selected light grey dress slacks, a silver, silk short-sleeved blouse, and her shiny gray two-inch heels.

When she walked into the store, the clerk, a balding man in his late forties with "Gunny" on his name tag, looked up from the cabinet he was dusting.

"Morning! How can I help you?"

"I'm here to pick up an order for Manny Sanchez."

"Well, it's really for Jenny. Would that be you?"

"Yes."

"Manny said I would know you because you would be the prettiest woman that ever came through our doors. I think he's right, but I still need to see your driver's license for the federal background check."

Jenny extracted her license from her purse.

Gunny said, "Jenny Mondragon. He told me how to pronounce your name and warned me not to make any dragon lady jokes."

Jenny laughed, "Thank you; he was trying to save you from my wrath."

As he was talking, he laid her merchandise on the counter for her inspection. "I know how it feels. My name is Dagfinn Dustin Gunderson. I got teased about it all my life. Then, in the army, the sergeant said, 'You better watch it. We'll have no dusty guns around here.' So everyone started calling me Dusty Gun. Fortunately, my dad was a gun nut, and I was very proficient at gun handling and marksmanship and ended up being a gunnery sergeant. I like Gunny Gunderson better'n Dusty Gun."

"Name teasing gets old fast, that's for sure. Wow, all this is mine?"

"Yes, and the best for last." Gunny laid a raspberry pink Ruger LCP .380 pistol on the counter.

"Oh! It's beautiful! I didn't know they made guns like that."

Gunny said, "Normally, I would walk you through all the features involved with each of these items, but Manny specifically told me to leave everything in the bubble packages, and he would work through it with you. He's pretty excited about this."

"That's perfect. I can hardly wait for him to get home."

"While I bag it up, sign right here, and you are free to go. If you ever have any questions or concerns, feel free to call or come in."

~

After introductions of the national park personnel by Ranger Yazzie, Attorney Rose explained why they were reopening the investigation of Marie Artiste's death and that they needed to get to know as much as possible about Miss Artiste and her work. They decided to reverse the order of the meetings and review of artifacts found in her home, so began the general meeting by having Manny present his slide show of the artifacts.

The mood of the meeting changed from one of confusion about what was going on to consternation mixed with outrage as the beautiful artifacts were shown in close-up shots of the design details from three sides. After about the third slide, Dr. Goetle could stand no more.

"This is outrageous! None of these artifacts have been cataloged in our system. Have you seen these Elwood?"

"No, I have not," the archeologist answered.

"What about you, Mark? Didn't she normally bring them to you for cataloging and cleaning?"

"She didn't work in the lab herself. It was always me," Mark Bisti replied. "She would drop off the pots with her field notes, and I would clean and catalog them. The artifacts you're showing didn't go to the lab. Even during a dig, she would use me to carry the gear, help lay out the grid, do rough excavation, and be a gofer. But when we got to the artifact layer, she worked by herself . . . didn't trust that to nobody. She would have me screen the dirt pile for small items at the end of each day."

Manny asked, "Is it unusual for your people to work a dig by themselves, Dr. Goetle?"

"Yes. Each dig normally has a crew. Depending on the scope, it could be up to a dozen or more people. As you probably noted this morning, the dig Marie was working was in a very small kiva. It wouldn't be practical to have more than two people working in it. Marie was a perfectionist and was difficult to work with, but her science and knowledge was excellent. She preferred to work small remote digs, because she didn't have to deal with people issues."

Bren said, "Mark, you said she used you for lab work and to run errands. How frequently was Marie alone at a dig for extended periods?"

"A lot. Sometimes she would give me enough lab work that I would be here for two or three days in a row. She would bring things in on her way to the apartment or before she drove home."

"What apartment is that?"

"She had a small apartment at the park employee housing. If she didn't have business in town, she would stay here at night instead of driving to Grants."

Fred Rose said, "Dr. Goetle, would there be any of her personal belongings in the apartment?"

"No. Her personal property was boxed and taken by the state police. Someone else has been in the apartment for a month or so."

Bren said, "Mark, getting back to Marie's habit of working alone, what happened typically at the end of a day?"

"Well, it wasn't always the same. Sometimes she would tell me to head back, so I wouldn't go into overtime, but she would work as long as there was light. Other times when she had to go into Grants, she would leave at two or so and tell me to finish up by quitting time. We always had our own vehicles, so our schedule could be different."

Dr. Goetle interrupted. "The professional staff is paid a salary so get no overtime. The technicians and helpers are wage, and we are very careful about overtime. Most of our staff works an average of ten to twelve hours a day, but we don't track their time on the job. Other than organized activities and meetings, they pretty much set their own schedules. It's not unusual for the archeologists to work a dig until dark, long after the crew has gone, or for them to work late into the night on documenting or analyzing finds. They have a lot of autonomy."

Al asked, "So if Miss Artiste decided to remove something from the kiva, it would have been easy to do so without anyone else being aware. Could she have packed an artifact in her personal gear and then transferred it from the park vehicle without suspicion?"

Looking somewhat offended at the suggestion, Dr. Goetle thought about it a moment. "Yes, I suppose so. It would be a terrible breach of trust, because we are dedicated to protecting the antiquities and preserving the science integral to them. It is the same as a law officer who conspires to break the law for gain. Just talking about the possibility feels like casting aspersions at the profession."

Manny suggested that they get on with examining the photos and confirm whether the remaining relics were also apparently stolen. By the end of the slideshow, all were confirmed as unknown and uncatalogued.

The officers then paired up and interviewed each of the park staff, completing that task in a little over an hour. Nothing revealing or seemingly helpful came from the interview, except for a picture of the personality and work habits of the late Miss Artiste.

The officers had their sack lunches in the shade of a ramada near the visitor center. By twelve thirty they were on the road returning to Grants. As they drove, they rehashed everything they had discovered in the investigation. It was agreed by all that Marie Artiste had been involved in a lucrative artifact scheme, that she had most likely been murdered, that the murder was most likely related to the theft ring, and that resolving the murder would require first identifying the others in the theft ring.

Fred said, "Obviously, we are most interested in solving the murder and bringing the murderer to justice. Since the theft of artifacts from Chaco Canyon, and likely their sale, happened in New Mexico, we will take over the investigation of those crimes committed here. You have a similar murder and theft in Arizona, and you will be investigating that. I think we should conduct these as separate crimes and the coordination should be informational only. We don't want to prematurely give anyone the impression this is interstate crime, or we will have way more help than we need or want."

Bren asked, "Have you discussed this with Attorney Dirocco?"

"Yes, and he agrees. We want to keep any possible connection as late as possible in the investigations . . . much less complicated that way."

"Less complicated is always good."

~

Ed Hale was waiting on one of the portico seats of his circular drive when his newly-appointed general counsel Peter Villa arrived in his white S65 AMG Mercedes. Ed put his briefcase on the back seat and eased into the passenger seat. Adjusting the seat to fit him, he said, "I thought you might bring your Roadster since we're going through the mountains."

"I decided to go for comfort, since we will spend most of the day driving. We are heading for Safford, right?"

"Actually, it's a ways south of Safford. The lab is on my ranch."

Pete took the shortest route to the 202 East. He would stay on that until it connecting with US 60, then to US 70 in Globe and on in to Safford. "So we will take 666 South to your ranch?"

"Yes, except it's not 666 anymore, it's now 191. They changed the number in 1992 to be compatible with other north-south routes, and because ADOT said the 666 route signs were the most frequently stolen in the state."

"I didn't know that. It will be interesting to see your lab. Why did you feel it necessary to build a state-of-the-art archeological lab? You never needed one before."

"Middleman said it would be more economical than having to pay to have the artifacts cleaned, photographed, and x-rayed. He pointed out that I hadn't had to deal with that, because Marie took care of it before delivering artifacts to me. He also suggested it would be more secure, since only we would have physical contact with them."

Ed continued, "As it turns out, the cost was recovered within a month, and having our own facilities has enhanced our reputation and marketing. It has the advantage of allowing us to get the items documented, cataloged, and on the market within hours of receiving the item."

"So it's probably an easily-justified business decision."

"Absolutely. We saved a little on the building by incorporating the lab as a wing of the residence."

"How did you handle the cost of the lab?"

"The construction of the lab and the equipment purchased were through the business. I paid for the ranch and residence with my personal funds."

"So for tax purposes, there is no mingling of the costs?"

"No. Even the utilities for the lab, including phone and computer connections, are separate and billed to the company. Those for the residence and outbuildings are billed to me."

"Good. If there's anything that you think could be perceived as less-than-ethical, you need to let me know. If this ends up as an IRS or FBI investigation, we want to disclose anything amiss or dubious upfront and accurately. In fact, once we understand where we are with everything, which hopefully will be late today, we should take any concerns we have to the authorities ourselves. Preemptive full disclosure is the best defense."

As they entered Queen Creek Canyon, they took a break from conversation and admired the dramatic pillars and cliffs, as well as the challenge of the curves as they flew up the highway fifteen miles over the speed limit. The Mercedes performed beautifully on the mountain curves, easily outpacing other cars. Pete was meticulously obedient to staying within the law in everything but speed limits. He owned and loved fast cars. This sedan had a V12 turbo engine with amazing acceleration and excellent road-holding characteristics. As they topped out at Oak Flats, they were caught in slow traffic.

Pete asked, "Didn't the murder at the dig happen around here?"

"Yes. The place is described as the headwaters of Queen Creek, so it would be a little ways northwest of us now. I've never been in that area."

"Why would anyone kill for pottery?"

"Why would they kill for any reason but defense?" Ed asked. "I suppose it was for money. Ultimately, greed is the cause of a lot of evil."

"True. If these artifacts are worth thousands, people kill for less than that all the time. Do you think this guy Middleman is the killer?"

Ed pondered that before answering, "I can't imagine that. The guy is an academic. He comes across like a professor. I suspect that Middleman may have been scammed by a artifact dealer he trusted, not knowing he was lying about the source. The murderer could be that illicit dealer."

"I hope you're right. If Middleman is a brazen murderer, you could be in danger because you could identify him. That's another reason to keep your business and communication with him as normal as possible. Don't do or say anything to him that would make him think you are a legal threat to him. Take his calls, be happy about sales; behave exactly as you have in the past. Do you owe him anything now?"

"No. He invoices me for his services on sale, so I'll be getting an invoice for our latest transactions probably today or tomorrow. I normally pay them as soon as I open the e-mail."

"Do the same with this one. We want him to feel safe and happy."

As they ascended out of Devils Canyon and reached the passing lane, Pete managed to pass all the cars that had been held back by the laboring semis and had a clear path all the way to Miami. Once out of Globe and past the Apache Gold Casino, he once again opened up the Mercedes, and Ed nodded off to sleep. They reached US 191 in Safford, and Ed directed him to the ranch.

They toured the house and the lab, and Pete asked questions about the purpose of the equipment and made sure all the assets were properly accounted for. Though he wasn't an expert on the system, Ed demonstrated the online catalog and showed the ads for the recently-sold items. Pete was duly impressed with the quality and ease of working with the system. They had a drink at the ranch house bar and started the trip back to Scottsdale, stopping only to buy fuel and grab a quick lunch. They were back in Scottsdale by two o'clock, going directly to Ed's office where Pete met with the accountants and reviewed their books and practices.

When he finished, Pete stopped by Ed's office and told him that everything looked really good. He would spend part of the next day putting together a strategy for the next move. Ed felt some easing of his anxiety, but knew he would still be facing some difficulties, both personal and professional.

~

The members of the task force said their goodbyes in the parking lot of the New Mexico State Police building in Grants and began the long drive home. The trip was fast and uneventful except for an incident about halfway home as they were approaching Reserve.

Bren had driven to Springerville, where Al relieved Bren of the driving. Near the town of Luna, the road sloped down to a small creek crossing with a cornfield on the other side. They had just reached the bridge when a nice-sized wild turkey walked out of the cornfield unto the shoulder of the road. Al said, "Uh-oh, a turkey," as he slowed from 65 mph. He moved into the empty on-coming lane to put some distance between the car and the bird. It looked as if the evasive effort had worked, until the turkey took flight, flying straight into the top center of the windshield.

A jagged hole the size of a quarter was punched through the windshield, and the insides of the turkey, mixed with granules of safety glass, sprayed through the hole hitting Al in the face. Instantly, he was coated from mid-chest to the top of his head with pieces of internal organs, blood, feathers, glass granules, turkey excrement, and mostly what looked like creamed corn.

Blinded by the slime, Al jerked off his sunglasses and handed them to Bren, who cleaned them with napkins and handed them back to Al. He put them on to keep any of the stuff that was still dripping into the truck from getting in his eyes, as he continued driving into town.

They were shocked to silence. Bren hadn't gotten any of the spray at all, Manny's left sleeve was somewhat soiled, and the spray had stenciled a perfect outline of Al's head and shoulders on the back window. The windshield was spider-webbed for about a foot around the hole. Al grabbed some of the napkins and wiped the stuff from around his mouth and nose.

Finally, Bren asked, "Are you hurt, Al?"

"Only my dignity and all I can smell is turkey crap." At that moment most of what remained of the turkey flipped from the windshield, and a sliver of liver slithered through the hole, down the mirror, onto the steering wheel, into the steering column, then out again onto Al's shoe. A little flap of turkey breast covered with down slapped into the hole, making a nice plug. That broke the tension, and they all burst out in laughter.

Al looked grievously injured, covered with flecks of skin, flesh, blood, and creamed corn. He appeared to have had his skin peeled off. His upper torso was blood-spattered and filthy. They pulled into a service station mini-mart, and Al took his overnight bag into the bathroom to clean up and change clothes. Bren and Manny cleaned up the car.

The girl at the counter almost fainted when Al came through the door. "Oh my heavens, what happened to you? I better call the paramedics!"

"No, I'm not hurt. We just hit a turkey on our windshield, and everything in him ended up on me. Is it okay if I clean up in your bathroom?"

"Yes. Delbert, take him an extra roll of towels."

A local deputy came by and talked to Bren and Manny. When Al came out, the Deputy told Al that he should ticket him for hunting out of season, but guessed he wouldn't out of professional courtesy.

In forty minutes or so, they had gotten themselves and the car cleaned up, and they were back on the road. Al said he'd had enough driving for the day; it was Manny's turn to drive. They drove through a light rain and Manny complained, "Dang! The rain's hitting me in the face. We should have left the turkey flap in it."

Al said, "We can call you Chief Rain-in-the-Face."

"I guess that's better than Chief Poop-in-the-Face," Manny laughed.

"I'll never be able to eat creamed corn again."

They arrived home without further incident. But the story of the turkey pureed through the windshield continues in the lore of three families, as well as being filed under *weird stories* in the local police agencies.

Chapter 8

Deputy Dan Tompkins was disappointed that Detective Espinoza didn't let him make the trip to New Mexico with the Antiquities Task Force, but he understood the reasoning. He found the raid on the cattle theft ring both interesting and exciting, so that made up for missing the trip.

It was a big operation, stealing cattle off ranges from all over the state and hauling them to a sham ranch in the Ninety-six Hills between Florence and Barkerville, where they would drop the cattle long enough to change brands and other markings. They preferred to grab unbranded calves, but had registered six brands that were designed to alter other brands by applying over them. They operated their own stockyard and slaughterhouse near Casa Grande, where they bought legitimate cattle and mixed the stolen cattle with them, effectively "laundering" them.

They called their ranch Hell South Ranch. It consisted of a trailer house, a barn, a well and tank, portable aluminum holding and working corrals, and a twenty-acre pasture smack in the middle of a fenced section of land with no nearby roads or neighbors. The pasture was only used to allow reworked brands to heal. Hell South was located in a basin behind a hill referred to on maps as 3130 Hill from the topo map altitude.

Hell South actually owned the 160 acres containing the ranch, along with the lease on the entire fenced section it was centered in. There were only two gates on the section—one on the south side and one on the west side. Both were kept locked, as was the only gate into the ranch. No cattle ran in the section surrounding the ranch. The ranch was positioned in a C-shaped basin on the east side of 3130 Hill, so nothing could be seen of the operation from any direction, and they were several miles from any other ranches or ranch roads.

They didn't have a single horse on the property. For getting around on the ranch, they used quad ATVs. There was natural feed in the pasture, but they occasionally fed the pastured cattle. The pasture connected directly to a working pen, and that was where the cattle were fed and where the water troughs were located. To move them, all they had to do was put out feed, and all the cattle would come. Closing the gate behind the last one had them all rounded up.

The pens and squeeze gates for branding were easily worked on foot. The foreman and one cowhand lived at the ranch. The others were called in when needed, which was mostly in the middle of the night when a new load came in, or when they shipped a load to the slaughter house.

They had been operating for about six years with no suspicion from anybody. The downfall began when they were rude to a visiting rancher from about ten miles away. There was no way to open the gate to drive in, but there was a talk box, so he buzzed it.

A man's voice said, "Whatcha want?"

"This is Marv Plunkett. I run the Starvation Ranch over by Barkerville. I just wanted to pay a neighborly visit."

"Well, the boss ain't here right now, an' he don't want nobody comin' around. That's why he keeps the gates locked. Y'see he's got a lot a persnal difugalties. He's shell shocked from the war, and a mean ex-wife wants to make his life a livin' hell."

"And who am I talking to?"

"I'm Gem Hamling. I jest work for Mr. Ike Coppin."

"Well, Jim, would you tell him I called? I'm in the phone directory. Marv Plunkett. I'm a veteran myself. I'd sure help him any way I could."

"Mighty nice of you, Marv. I'll tell im, but it won't do no good. I been here since he moved in, and I don't think in the whole five or six year he said more'n twenty words that wasn't tellin' me what to do. He ain't intersted in socializin' or sympasizin'. He just wants left alone."

"Clear enough, Jim. I won't be back, but if you or he ever need something or just want to visit, I'd be happy to see you. Best of luck to you."

"Mighty nice. Thank ya." click.

Marv left them alone, but over time he began to notice that, for a place with absolutely no visible cattle on the range, they regularly shipped cattle. In fact, they shipped cattle when nobody else was doing it.

Then late one night as Marv returned from visiting his brother in Phoenix, he passed a big truckload of cattle heading to Hell South Ranch. These were not feeder cattle, they were mature shipper cattle. Something didn't seem right. The next time the Pinal County Range Deputy Jake Jacobson stopped by, Marv mentioned his strange neighbor.

The deputy agreed that it was suspicious and began paying attention. He finally crept to the top of 3130 and tunneled through the branches of a large juniper tree until he could use it as a blind to observe the operation. At the time, ranch hands were busy rebranding cattle.

The sheriff assigned Paul Espinoza to work with Jake to identify how the operation worked and to build a court case. They set up surveillance on the main gate by placing a fake air quality monitoring station on public land opposite the gate. It was contained in a white trailer surrounded by an eight-foot chain link fence.

The unit was signed with the Arizona Department of Environmental Quality seal and the words *Portable Air Quality Monitor*. It had obvious weather instruments on it, but disguised among them were high resolution video cameras and an infrared video camera, which were monitored via satellite and controlled from the Sheriff's office.

By the use of the monitor, they were able to record the cattle being moved in and out of the ranch. When a shipment came in at night, a deputy would take his place in the juniper blind on 3010 Hill before daylight. He would video the activities and capture photos of each of the individuals involved. In about a month, they had accurately figured out the operation and obtained enough evidence to file charges.

The deputies had noted that both gates were equipped with alarms and video cameras. All those on the ranch were armed with sidearms, and their ATVs and trucks carried rifles.

To avoid the alarms, they cut the fence a safe distance from the gates and drove cross-county. They surreptitiously put snipers on each of the points overlooking the ranch, positioned deputies in the washes that could be used as escape routes, and had a deputy in position at the house and Dan at the barn. At the designated time a SWAT team sped into the ranch yard, and a helicopter hovered overhead.

The speakers announced, "You are surrounded. All escape routes are blocked. Snipers have you targeted. Put your hands on your head, and move to the center of the yard."

Coppin obeyed and shouted, "We don't have a chance! Do what they say."

One cowhand was working away from the rest of the group and he decided he might be able to hide in the barn, so made a dash for it, pulling up short when Dan stepped in front of him pointing an M&P-15 rifle at his chest. The suspect raised his hands above his head.

Dan ordered, "Use two fingers to lift your sidearm out of the holster, and toss it on the hay to your right."

The suspect did as instructed. Dan told him to interlock his fingers on top of his head and walk slowly to the others. The deputy followed about eight feet behind. One of the SWAT members covered the suspect and told Dan to cuff him, which he did.

All the suspects were frisked again before they were loaded into a prisoner transfer van, and the SWAT team accompanied them to the jail in Florence. A similar raid was simultaneously executed on the slaughterhouse, but no weapons were wielded by the suspects. Many of the workers had no clue that anything illegal had been taking place. The ring leaders were arrested.

Dan helped to conduct the search of the property for evidence and was released to resume his regular duties.

~

Manny Sanchez, though tired from the travel, had a difficult time getting to sleep on Friday night. He had asked his parents if he could spend the night at their house, since he was going to spend Saturday with Jenny. His parents were pleased with that idea. They asked him if he and Jenny would have dinner with them, which they did. The meal consisted of thin-sliced fried pork chops, green beans, mashed potatoes and gravy, and mom's yeast dinner rolls. A real home-cooked meal was great after having eaten restaurant and fast food for three days.

After dinner, the couple went for a drive out to the darkness near Roper Lake to watch what was predicted to be a pink moon due to red dust being lofted high into the atmosphere by heavy winds in northern Mexico. They cuddled as they sat on the hood of Manny's old Stratus and talked about the things that had transpired during their separation. It was a spectacular moonrise and delivered as pink a moon as anyone could imagine. Finally, Manny began to yawn, and Jenny insisted they go home so he could be rested for tomorrow.

Jenny's parents were watching the TV news, so he visited with them briefly, kissed Jenny goodnight, drove to his parents' home, and went straight to bed. Now he had lain there for an hour without going to sleep. He was a little aggravated at himself that he was so excited about his shooting-range date with Jenny tomorrow that he couldn't sleep—like a kid on Christmas Eve. He got up and poured a glass of milk and sat in the porch swing enjoying the cool air and moonlight. After half an hour he was able to get back in bed and sleep.

Manny picked Jenny up at nine, and they headed out to the range. He went through all the safety rules and had her handle her pistol empty for a while, putting the clip in and out, cocking, aiming, and pulling the trigger on an empty chamber. He explained all her accessories and had her load her clips first manually, then using her quick loader.

When it came time to fire for the first time, Jenny said, "I don't know what to expect. I want you to fire it a few times, so I can be prepared for the noise."

"Okay. It won't be as noisy as the other guns you've been hearing today. It is not as powerful as those guns, but it is a lot louder than a twenty-two."

He fired a couple of shots then said, "There are a couple of things I'm surprised by. The trigger has a pretty long pull on it. You have to pull it back a long way before it fires. And there is a little more recoil than I expected. It's not bad, but you will want to grip it firmly with both hands. Use the two-handed grip you've been practicing, and put the front sight in line with the back and right at the center target. Then pull the trigger all the way back, smoothly without jerking. Be careful to keep it pointed straight ahead between each shot. Re-aim and fire till the clip is empty. When you're through shooting, lay it down on the pad while we talk."

And so it went for two hours. Jenny was a natural, and by the end of the session, she was hitting the silhouette target every time and spot targets in the silhouette most of the time. She handled the pistol correctly, was aware of the muzzle each time, and was able to quickly change and reload clips. Finally, he showed her how to use the laser to aim and shoot. Once she got used to keeping it steady, she became amazingly accurate.

"Wow, Jenny you are doing great. I didn't expect you to develop this level of skill so quickly. Our time is almost up, and I see Deputy Haley is waiting for a lane, so pack all your gear up. Check your weapon first. You have done much better than I did on my first range session."

"Thank you. I have a wonderful instructor."

"We have a few weeks before the wedding, so by then you will be an expert. I'll train you on all our police weapons as well. By the time you are Mrs. Sanchez, you will be more proficient than me. Let's go have lunch."

"Sounds great. I have to be back home by one thirty. The fitting for my wedding dress is this afternoon."

"I like the sound of that. More progress!"

Pat gathered her gear and moved toward the lane. Manny introduced Jenny to her as his fiance. Pat laughed, "So this is your idea of a romantic date, Manny? You need to watch some chick flicks."

"You know people are always telling me I'm not sensitive enough. Maybe a few romantic movies would help."

"That's okay with me," Jenny said, "As long as you watch them with me and don't make fun of the sappy parts. But being on the range with my guy is pretty romantic too. Noisy, but romantic."

As they were leaving, Deputy Andy Lopez came in, waving at them as they passed. The lane next to Pat opened and Andy took it.

~

On the weekly Antiquities Task Force conference call, Attorney Dirocco discussed all the week's previous activities. He finished by mentioning that New Mexico had officially opened an investigation into the murder of Marie Artiste. Attorney Rose thanked the team for bringing it to his attention.

Attorney Dirocco also said he was preparing a request for a search warrant on Elton Godwin's home, property, banking and finances, and asked, "In which county would you like it issued? He lives in Maricopa County, but would it be easier for you to pick up if it were issued from Graham or Pinal County?"

Bren answered, "Dan will be serving it, so issue it from Pinal County. I'll assist him in conducting the search."

"Okay, I'll request it for first thing in the morning. Will that work for you Dan?"

"Yes, we can usually pick them up at the courthouse within an hour of the request. Bren, do you want to do this tomorrow afternoon?"

"That will be fine. I'll call you after this call ends, and we'll work out the details."

"I'll notify Maricopa of our search, because Godwin lives in a county island in Tempe."

The next morning, Bren traveled to meet Dan for lunch at Ted's Hot Dogs in Tempe. When Dan talked with MCSO, they said they would provide a deputy to assist, so Deputy Miguel Lopez was also invited to the lunch meeting. Dan introduced him to Bren. Deputy Lopez requested they call him Mike.

They looked at the satellite photo of the small house Godwin rented off Curry just north of the Salt River—a small, white, lap-side cottage with a front and back door, set on the back half of the lot. A concrete block wall enclosd the backyard. There was a vehicle gate through the block wall at the end of the single-car driveway and a small access gate to the alley. The only thing in the back yard was his trailer with an ATV on it. There were no outbuildings.

Dan said, "I doubt he will resist or run. If he did run, there is no place to hide, so we would catch him pretty quickly. I guess we will just do a search, and unless we find some unexpected damning evidence, we probably won't arrest him at this time."

"I agree. Of course you know that we get surprised with violence in pretty innocuous situations, so stay alert for trouble."

Mike said, "Just in case something goes south, I'll park in the alley and wait at the back gate. Once you're inside, call me in and I'll help with the search." The other two officers nodded agreement.

The search went without a hitch. Elton Godwin asked what they were searching for and was shocked to hear they were looking for evidence in a murder.

"That's crazy. I haven't hurt anyone, ever."

"Then you don't have anything to worry about. We can't find evidence of anything you didn't do," Bren replied.

Bren turned to the others. "Deputies, check out this room first. There's not much in here, so check under, behind, and in everything, then move to the other rooms. I'll check his personal stuff and join you."

Bren asked Elton, "Do you have any contraband or anything illegal you would like to tell us about before we find it ourselves?"

"I don't know what that is."

"Drugs?"

"No, I don't do drugs."

"Do you have any weapons on you or in the house?"

"I have this folding Leatherman knife on my belt. Not really a weapon. And there are two rifles in my bedroom closet and a 9 mm handgun in the top dresser drawer."

"As part of the search, take everything out of your pockets and the knife and put them on the table."

"My comb and wallet too?"

"Yes. I'll look through your wallet and everything else. They are through searching in here, so you can continue watching the game while we do the other rooms if you want, or you can follow us . . . just don't get in our way."

"Nah, I'll stay in here."

Bren checked through the wallet. There were the normal things you'd expect to find in a wallet, and thirty-six dollars. He had a debit and credit card both from Arizona Security Bank. Bren wrote down the account numbers.

"You have quite a few keys here. Two appear to be house keys, and you have a car key or two. What are these for?"

"The house keys are for front and back doors, the GM key is to my Trail Blazer, and the smaller one is to my ATV. The padlock keys are to the storage shed and tool box at work."

Bren held up a safe deposit key and asked, "What is this little cabinet key for?"

"I have a safe deposit box."

"The search warrant allows us to also search your bank and financial accounts and records, and your safe deposit box. What are we going to find at the bank?"

"I've got almost $2,000 in my savings," Elton proudly stated, "and maybe $1,000 in checking."

"What about the box?"

"I keep some cash in it."

"How much?"

"I'm not sure."

"Okay, maybe it will be to your advantage to be honest and up front with us. The murder we are looking into is related to theft of artifacts. We have figured out that you don't make enough money at work to even pay your monthly rent. I bet we will find several thousand dollars in the safe deposit box. That means you are probably stealing and selling artifacts, and that makes you a leading suspect in our murder."

"Look, if I tell you, will you stop talking about murder? I don't know what you are talking about."

"Yes. It looks like the deputies have found everything they were looking for, so let's all just talk about it. Tell us the truth about the money in the safe deposit box."

"I never steal. I actually do a lot of work for Benson-Colley. They don't want to hire an archeologist, so they pay me ten dollars an hour to dig up the pots. Then they have me package up the stuff and leave it in a tool box, and the archeologist picks them up overnight.

"The thing is . . . they don't want the government to know that I'm working full-time, so they pay me $1000 a week in cash, plus regular part-time pay. I could never make that anywhere else.

"I have to be careful about spending it and am supposed to put a little bit of money into the savings account each week. I give some to the food bank and my mom, and the rest goes into the box. I've got about sixteen-thousand in it now. I can't report it and I can't pay taxes on it, and if I do something that gets me caught, Mr. Benson said they will charge me with stealing. I never have stolen. Not one thing."

Dan asked, "So how did you get training doing archeological digs?"

"I wasn't doing very well in high school. I was going to flunk out, so I quit. One of my teachers said he knew Benson could use a hard-working laborer, so they gave me a job helping Mrs. Fulton when we were working on the road by Sunflower. She showed me how to mark the squares and dig the pots without breaking them, and wrap them in bubble wrap. She was very nice. They left after a couple of weeks, but Benson-Colley let me keep digging. Sometimes they have me dig up plants and bury them, or cover up snake holes in the right of way."

Bren said, "Elton, I believe you have told us the truth, so we won't need to arrest you. It is very important that you don't talk to anyone about us coming to see you. Just keep doing what you have been doing. And don't worry, we know you are innocent. We will need your help later, but until then, no talking about anything we talked about with anyone else, okay?"

When the officers were outside, Bren said, "Let's meet down Curry at Papago Park. We need to talk about this."

In the park, they sat at a ramada table and discussed what they learned. Bren asked, "Did you guys hear enough of that conversation to know that Elton is a true innocent?"

Mike said, "Yes, he's being used by those jerks."

Nodding agreement, Dan added, "He has the developmental capacity of about a ten-year-old. They think they have set him up to take the fall if anything comes out about artifact theft. They pay him a thousand a week to do their dirty work, and they probably make ten times that from the pottery sales . . . and they've been doing it for two years."

Smiling, Bren commented, "I think Elton will be the key to getting these guys not only on artifact violations, but also conspiracy, tax evasion, and multiple protected species violations. It sounds like they have him get rid of problem plants and owl burrows before the inspectors get to them. I just want to make sure the kid doesn't get hurt by any of this."

Bren turned to Mike. "Normally this would be the end of your involvement, since we've successfully served the warrant, but in this case we might want you to be a witness to Elton's cooperation and honesty."

"I'll be happy to do that."

"Thanks, fellas," Bren said, shaking hands with them. "Dan, I'll call you tomorrow, and we can start working on the next step."

~

Wednesday was a normal day for the Graham County deputies and Al Victor, as they handled their routine patrols. Each of them spent much of their solitary time thinking through the evidence they had uncovered in the archeology thefts and murders.

Bren called Dan about midmorning and told him to go execute the order for Elton Godwin's banking records. Instead of seizing the money in the safe deposit box, Bren told Dan to have the manager count it and sign a validation of the amount and to keep it strictly confidential. Then return Elton's key, so he could maintain his normal activities.

Al had a report of vandalism at Black Point Cemetery. Someone had thrown red paint on the Veteran's Memorial. He took photos of it and called the local veteran's leader, who said he would clean it up. Al said he would meet him there at five o'clock to help. Al found footprints and beer cans with liquid residue. He photographed the footprints and took the beer cans as evidence, thinking they would likely provide finger prints. Looking more closely, he decided it looked more like the paint can might have been dropped. He followed drops of paint to a trash barrel where the paint can was deposited.

Manny patrolled his area without incident. He also spoke briefly with Richard, the defacto leader of Beautiful Land Commune, and provided directions to an older couple wanting to photograph Aravaipa ghost buildings.

The officers met at the Pima Taylor Freeze for lunch. A school bus from Globe stopped there to let the kids get lunches. Several students were still waiting for their orders, so the cops decided to wait outside until the place cleared out. They quickly compared notes about what they had been doing, and Bren updated them on the search warrants.

Alf Hesse pulled in beside them and came over and greeted them. After the pleasantries he said, "It looks like we'll be able to get in and order in about five more minutes. I just backed into a kid's car over at the mini-mart . . . made a little dent, so we looked at it, and I said it wasn't worth making an insurance claim. He said he could probably pop it out himself. I gave him $100 and told him if it cost more to fix, I would pay it. He seemed happy with that, so we didn't call the sheriff. Hope I did right."

Bren said, "It's always a good idea to get a policeman there, if only to verify that you owned up, but its sounds like you negotiated a satisfactory agreement."

"Negotiation has been a mainstay of my business success. Two tactics work: making them feel like they are winning, or scaring the living hell out of them."

Manny burst out laughing, "I have learned in my business classes that win-win is the first choice, and presenting a scenario of possible loss is the second choice, but I never heard it put so succinctly."

"Believe it or not, a man from right here in the Gila Valley—in a place called Franklin, which doesn't seem to be a town at all now—demonstrated negotiation in a way I will never forget. I was a brand new Boy Scout. My word, that was over seventy years ago."

The cops knew they were in for a story when Alf seated himself on the hood of his car.

Alf said, "My dad was a geological consultant, and we lived in Vancouver, British Columbia. He took a two-year assignment in Los Angeles helping develop some oil fields, so we moved down. I just completed the equivalent of Cub Scouts in Canada and became involved in the Boy Scouts when we moved to the States.

"Our troop did a lot of great activities, in spite of the fact we were in the Depression. In our area the only active troop was at the Mormon Church. It was the only show in town, so it became my troop even though we were Episcopalian. Most of the scout leaders worked for California Edison, including George Campbell, who went to Cali to find work. And the president of Cal Ed was a big fan of Scouting, so we got lots of support in funding and equipment, and even personnel from the company for activities.

"California Edison and some other big corporate donors had poured a lot of money in developing a scout camp up in the mountains by Arrowhead Lake, and they paid for all the kids in the troop, about thirty kids, to go to camp for two weeks. The company provided a man-truck for George to drive us to camp. It was a GM diesel truck with rows of benches installed in the back and canvas top and sides that rolled up for good weather. All our gear was in a trailer hooked to the truck.

"We went most of the way on graveled highway, but near the lake, it turned into a single-lane road cut into the steep canyon side for ten miles or so. Every so often there would be a wide spot gouged out so a car could pull in to let one going the opposite direction pass. It was terrifying.

"Some of us younger boys were so scared that we started crying. I was sitting by my best friend Richard. All the other kids called him Dickey but he preferred Richard, so that's what I called him. He was the only one of the younger boys who wasn't frightened.

"George heard us crying, so he parked and came back and talked to us. He was funny and colorful, but he had a lot of credibility with the boys, because he could do just about anything and was always good to us.

"He said, 'Now you boys don't have anything to be afraid of. I helped build the camp and this road, and it's made right and safe when you have a good driver. I have driven bigger trucks than this on really bad roads in the mines and never had an accident. Think about it. Have I ever done anything that would get you hurt? Nope. You're my friends, and I'm going to take care of you . . . so just calm down and don't worry. I'm going to roll the side down so you don't have to look down in the canyon. Now I'll drive, and you guys keep me awake by singing scout songs. We'll be in camp in about an hour.'"

Alf interrupted his story and motioned, "It looks like we can go order now. I'll continue my tale inside after we order, if that's all right with you fellows." They placed and picked up their orders and went to a table, ready for Alf to finish his tale.

"As George promised, all went well to the loud serenading of the scouts (we certainly didn't want the driver falling asleep) until about the last mile. We came around a corner and George stopped and started blowing his horn. We all stood up to see over the cab. There was a beautiful new green-and-black REO Speed Wagon flatbed coming toward us. George hopped out and started signaling to the guy to turn into the pullout, but the guy just kept coming. George gets back in and starts down toward the guy, honking his horn all the way, but the guy passed the pullout and kept coming. They met bumper to bumper . . . well not really. The bumper of the GM was even with the headlights of the Speed Wagon. They shut off the engines and set their brakes.

"George got out of the truck and offered his hand. 'I'm George Campbell, and what's your name?'"

"I'm Henry O'Hare, and I'm not about to try to back up on this road."

"Henry, let's be logical about this. It would be nearly impossible for me to back up on this curve. I've got thirty Boy Scouts in the truck, which is close to two feet wider than yours and needs every bit of the road, and I'm pulling a trailer to boot. You only have to back up a few hundred yards on straight road to the pullout, and I can get by you with no problem."

"Henry was resolute. 'I'm not backing up.'

"George took his cap off and scratched his head. 'I'm a professional driver. How about I drive your truck down to the pullout and then get my truck and drive on past you?'

"Nope, you gotta back up.'

"George puts his hat back on, takes a step closer to Henry, and looks him straight in the eye. 'Mister, I've offered some reasonable solutions. The only thing you offer is your way and that can't be.'

"Don't try getting tough with me fella. I'll throw you in the canyon."

"At that, my pal Richard holds his scout hatchet up in the air, and says, 'Hank O'Hair, pick on George and lose your hair!' All the other scouts took out their hatchets and started chanting, 'Hank of Hair, Hank of Hair, Hank of Hair!'

"George said, 'Sit down boys and put your hatchets away. If Mr. O'Hare gets violent, then have at 'im.' Turning back to Henry, he said, 'There are two other things that might work. One I don't like, but could use if I have to. This GM will easily push that little Speed Wagon off the road, but I don't want to do that because this is a Cal Ed truck, and they wouldn't want me getting all the green and black paint on the bumper. That leaves one other possibility. First I'll back the GM up a little ways to show you how hard it is with this big truck. Then I'll come back and we can discuss the third option.'

"George backed our truck up about a hundred feet. Then he got something out from under the seat and said loudly, 'All you boys get out of the truck and go back around the corner until you can't see the truck anymore.'

"Even after we could no longer see the confrontation, we could hear every word because of the canyon walls. George walked back towards the REO, fiddling with the stuff in his hand. Henry says, 'What have you got there?'

"Oh, not much—just dynamite! I figure if I toss it under your truck, neither one of us will have to back it up." He struck a lighter in one hand and held the dynamite in the other. "I'm giving you ten seconds to start backing down the road. Park as close to the bank as you can. Ten, nine, eight . . ."

"Old Hank of Hair started the REO and did a fine job of backing it up. George pulled the fuse and cap out, lit the fuse, and tossed it over the side. It made a good pop! He told us to load up and tell Mr. O'Hare thanks when we drove past. George carefully piloted the GM by as we shouted, 'Thanks Mr. Hank of Hair. At the last second, George wobbled the truck so the trailer dug a deep scratch in the REO's beautiful green rear fender. The rest of the trip was anticlimactic."

"Great negotiation! He appealed to reason and fairness, asked for and offered alternate solutions, firmly stated the strength of his position without threatening, and finally offered a solution O'Hair couldn't refuse."

Manny said, "Holy cow! Dynamite on a scout trip? They'd drum him out nowadays."

"Yes, and more's the shame for that. Boys are being raised to be helpless cowards now, as if it's immoral to solve your own problems. They get expelled from school for defending themselves or drawing a picture of a weapon. Pure idiocy.

"I stayed in touch with my friend Richard for many years . . . finally gave up on him when he started associating with Tim Leary and shacking up with kids young enough to be his daughter in some California commune back in the seventies. He's probably dead from effect of drugs now. Such a waste. He was a great, smart, fun kid too."

Chapter 9

Bren called Deputy Tomkins to discuss the situation with Elton Godwin and Benson-Colley. Bren asked Dan, "How do you think we should handle Elton?"

"I don't know. The guy is an innocent dupe. He thinks he's doing honorable work. I sure don't want to complicate his life or put him in danger."

"Eventually he will make a great witness. I will strongly recommend to Dirocco that no charges at all be filed against Elton." After a brief pause, Bren continued, "I do have an idea of how we can use him to gather evidence, though. Did you notice in all the worksite pictures Elton had his iPod?"

"No, I didn't, but I saw he had it in his ear when we went to his house."

"My guess is he's never without it. It would be a simple thing to switch his iPod for one with a high-capacity digital recorder in it. We could capture all the conversations Elton has. I talked with the guy in our local electronics store, and he can rig one up for me that would automatically turn on when anyone talks. It wouldn't interfere with any of the iPod functions, so even Elton wouldn't know. If nothing else, we can get instructions given to Elton by his bosses, and we might get more than that. I'm pretty sure Dirocco would get us a tap warrant. "

"That's a good idea," Dan replied. "Since Elton wouldn't know he was tapped, he would behave perfectly normally, and that would be much safer for him. He is transparent. I don't think he could successfully lie. Of course, we would have to copy his music from his machine to the tapped one before we substitute it. Do you know what model it is?"

"Yes," Bren chuckled. "I was a little amused because Elton had left the foil sticker with *iPod Slate Classic* on the front. We need to be sure the substitute has the sticker as well. Once we have the warrant, I'll get the bugged one made, and we can decide how to make the substitution."

Bren called Attorney Dirocco and told him about the idea. He said he would get a warrant for a wiretap.

~

The way Manny Sanchez's mind worked sometimes surprised him. When there was a missing bit of information on a case, he would find himself mulling it over as he went about his other duties. Eventually he would decide there was nothing more he could do about it, so he would put it away somewhere in his head and leave it alone. Then hours or days later, it would pop back into his consciousness with a solution he could try.

Such was the case with Eddie, Marie Artiste's mystery boyfriend. The action his mind recommended was something so obvious, that he couldn't believe he hadn't thought of it before. He had been patrolling on the old Cedar Springs road. He pulled into a shady alcove, parked, and turned on his computer.

He searched the key words 'Marie Artiste Eddie Edward Pottery'. Among the hits was an old article about the gala opening of Edward Hale Indian Trader's new gallery in Albuquerque. The picture showed Edward Hale with a group of six celebrants toasting the new opening. One of those celebrants was Marie Artiste.

Manny used the clip function and saved the article, then e-mailed it to Bren. Bren in turn forwarded the e-mail to Barry Dirocco, with the message "Bingo!"

~

At the exact moment Manny pressed send, Pete Villa, general counsel of Edward Hale Indian Trader, picked up Ed at his home. They had requested an appointment with Assistant Attorney General Barry Dirocco to explain a possible legal matter they had great concern about. Villa believed their company may have inadvertently been involved in a criminal scheme. Ed and Pete drove down Washington Street to the state government buildings, parked near Twelfth Avenue, and walked to the AG's office.

Barry finished reading the article Deputy Sanchez found about the Albuquerque grand opening just before his assistant announced the arrival of the article's subject. He walked around to meet his visitors and shook their hands. "Nice to see you, Pete, and it's nice to meet you, Mr.

Hale. I've visited your excellent galleries. I'm sorry I don't have more time for you today, but I have an important deposition in about forty minutes."

Ed said, "Thank you for seeing us on short notice. It means more to me than you could imagine."

"Let's sit at the table, and you can jump right into the meat of the subject. We will try to determine what, if any, follow-up actions are needed by the time you leave."

Pete said, "A very high-level summary of the situation is that an archeologist of good reputation offered our company the opportunity to purchase valuable Indian artifacts for resale on the world market. These artifacts were all certified as from private property or private collectors. It proved to be a very profitable venture. We have been involved with this for several years.

"We recently learned that the archeologist took artifacts from government property and possibly worked with one or more private collectors to fraudulently certify them. This came to our attention when another archeologist provided evidence that a number of our sales had, in fact, been falsely certified. Almost simultaneously, the first archeologist died in a workplace accident.

"The second archeologist then told us he could offer premium artifacts from private collections registered in the Arizona State Museum registry, which provides absolute assurance that they are legal. For forty percent of the sale, he would contact the collection holders, receive artifacts, and verify they are in the private registry files prior to providing them to our company. This proved to be even more profitable and has attracted top museums, universities, and other institutions, as well as wealthy private collectors.

"We had every reason to believe that this new arrangement was fully legitimate, until recent events caused Mr. Hale to have apprehensions. There was a murder at a dig near Superior, Arizona, and in the same week, our supplier provided us with some excellent articles that came from the same area. He provided photo copies of the registration in a private collection, but now Mr. Hale is concerned that the supplier may have, in fact, stolen them from the Superior dig . . . and possibly committed murder in the process.

"We are willing to cooperate in any way to clear this up, but we do not wish to approach the supplier, as it seems he may have murdered two archeologists. I have advised Ed to interact normally with the supplier to avoid raising suspicion."

Barry said, "I definitely want to pursue this as part of our ongoing investigation into the Superior murder and a possible link to artifact theft. I'll need an in-depth interview with Mr. Hale that includes names, dates, and details. I'll ask you to set up an appointment with my legal assistant Ronnie when you leave. Will three hours be long enough?"

Pete replied, "I think so. Actually, I have prepared a report for you with what I think is all the pertinent information, including accounting entries, duplicated documents, and photos." Pete took the report out of his briefcase and laid it on the desk. "I think this might shorten the length of time needed for the interview."

"I'll ask Ronnie to schedule a two-hour time slot with you. Ed, it would be advisable to have Pete attend with you. I would like to do this in the next day or two." If we have no other option, I'll stay late to get this done soon."

After Pete and Ed left, Barry called Bren Allred. "I'm impressed that your man identified Eddie. I read the article just before he came to my door with his attorney."

Barry then described the meeting with Ed and Pete. "Whenever the appointment can be made, I would like you there, along with any members of your team you could include. I'll ask my assistant to call you as soon as we have an appointment."

"Do you think he was really involved in the theft scheme and is trying to shift blame?"

"I'm favorably impressed with Mr. Hale and am inclined to listen with an open mind. I know Pete Villa rather well and respect him. They seem to want to do the right thing."

Bren asked, "Could we have a copy of the Hale report as soon as possible?"

"I'll have it copied and sent by courier in the morning."

"Why not have her make digital copies and e-mail them to us?"

"Good idea. I will."

~

Deputies Haley and Lopez finished up their monthly range regimen and walked out to the parking lot at the same time. Neither of them looked like they were ready to say goodnight.

Andy said, "Hey, I'm going to go grab a sandwich at Tony's. Want to join me?"

"Sure. I'm kind of hungry. I'll meet you there."

Andy ordered a Tony's special and Pat got the Italian. They sat away from the busy counter area and talked about their performance on the range until the sandwiches came. The conversation quickly turned personal. Andy said, "I've wondered about your dad. I understand that he really wasn't in your life from the time you were about six. Do you have any kind of relationship with him?"

"I loved my daddy. He used to play with me and make me laugh, and he would read to me. It really hurt me when he just disappeared from my life. Mom said I was better off because he really didn't love us. I found out later from mom's friend Erma that every year he sent me a gift or a card, but Mom threw them away. He also paid child support all my life and had an education fund, which was transferred to me when I turned eighteen. He never forgot about me, but I didn't know it. Since my mom worked for the University, my education was practically free, but the money from dad let me move out and choose the courses I wanted to take."

"So that's . . . what now . . . eighteen years since you last saw him? And you haven't made an effort to reestablish contact? He must have cared about you a lot to make the effort he did. He gave you the ability to declare your independence. Isn't that how you were able to go into justice studies?"

"Yeah. I guess I haven't thought about it exactly that way. I think I would complicate his family life and confuse his other children. They probably don't even know they have an older sister."

"I bet they do. His wife knows about you for sure if she supported sending money from their budget to you every month. My guess is he told them about you and all of them would welcome you."

Deputy Haley smiled. "Don't you think they would be put off by my macho persona?"

Andy laughed. "Their dad is a cop, too, you know. You and he probably have a lot more in common than you realize. I think your becoming a cop was not only a swipe at your mom's domination, but a bow to your dad. If I had a father like that, I would walk across the continent to reconnect with him. You are half him—not all your mom."

Andy paused for a moment. "I know nothing about my dad. He contributed nothing to me but the seed that planted me. My mother refused to tell me anything about him. I don't know if he ever knew I existed, or if he cared. Your dad was nice to you, and he sacrificed to support you. I would love to have that. Please don't waste any more time. Get hold of your dad."

Pat notice tears welling up in Andy's eyes, and without thinking, she took his hand. They sat for a long moment holding hands and looking misty-eyed at each other. Then Andy burst out laughing, saying, "Can you imagine if our fellow officers could see us now, sitting moon-eyed and holding hands? They think I'm gay and you're lesbian."

The tension broke, and Pat laughed at the image Andy had conjured. "Sounds like a story from a really loony chick flick." They continued to hold hands.

Andy walked Pat to her car and said, "I really like being with you. I've never known anyone I feel more comfortable with."

"I guess that makes sense. We're two odd ducks that understand each other. Thank you for what you said. I would like to meet my dad again, but I'm very afraid."

"You came out of a woman's world and have mastered a man's game. You're stronger than you think. Why don't you give your daughter side a chance? I'll help you any way I can."

~

Sergeant Allred called Deputy Dan Tomkins and told him they would be getting an order to set up Elton's iPod as a wire in the morning. He instructed Dan on a plan to set up an appointment for the next afternoon. In a short time Dan called back and said they had an appointment at eleven thirty.

When they arrived, Elton was showing a little anxiety. So Bren put his mind at ease by telling him they were sure he had not done anything wrong, but they forgot to write down some of the things on the search warrant. He told Elton to put all his things from his pockets on the table, including the iPod.

Then he said, "Elton have you had lunch yet?"

"No, I was going to make a sandwich in a little bit."

"We haven't eaten yet either. Is there a place nearby we could pick up lunch and bring it here for all of us to eat?"

"I really like Deli Trio Sandwiches from Jack in the Box. There's one down the street. But it costs quite a bit . . ."

"That sounds good. Do you want one of those too, Deputy?"

"Sure."

"Well, you work on this while Elton and I go pick them up. Elton can show me where to go. Would you like to ride in my police car?"

"I sure would."

After they left Dan downloaded everything from Elton's iPod then loaded it on the wired substitute. He compared the two, and except for Elton's being a little dirty they looked identical. He tried the new one out making sure it worked correctly. He slipped Elton's device into a cargo pocket and zipped it.

Since he had time, he walked across the room and spoke a test sentence. Then, using a pin-plug device he inserted into and out the back side of the bugged iPod charging receptacle, where it connected with the tap storage device. The memory was downloaded to a small digital recorder. He played the recorder and heard his sentence clearly. He put up his pin connector and recorder, and placed Elton's new iPod back with his other property.

Bren and Elton returned with the food. Dan said, "Okay, I think I got everything right this time. You can have all your stuff back. I saw that your iPod was a little dusty, so I cleaned it up for you."

"Wow. It looks really nice. Thank you."

Bren said, "Let's eat."

After the officers were in the car, Dan said, "I'm impressed that the tap is a completely independent device within the iPod with no visible, audible, or functional difference from an untapped one. I know how they make the connection with the tap by passing the pin all the way through the body of the power connection to the chip. But the charger has one pole on the side of the pin, and the other pole on the end, so why does the charger still connect and charge?"

"The tech said the tip is spring-loaded to stay in position, but it is hinged so that when the pin is pushed in too far, it swings up, sliding back in place when it's extracted. The pin is non-conductive, except for the female sockets in the end that mate with the memory, so it doesn't short the battery. Now let's just hope it captures some good information for us."

~

Deputy Sanchez was making his routine patrol driving past the entry to Beautiful Land Experimental Commune on his way to check the area near the Turkey Creek cliff dwelling, when he thought of the story that Alf Hesse told at Taylor Freeze. After checking out the area further up the canyon, he drove into the Beautiful Land parking lot.

The commune was a farm staffed by volunteers and supported by donors. They studied environmentally-sound farm techniques, permaculture, and native and regional crops. Three to ten volunteers lived for weeks or months at a time at Beautiful Land and several dozen volunteers, mostly from Tucson area colleges, worked there on weekends or during special projects.

While they had a board of directors to handle routine business matters, they operated on a democratic vote of the members without appointing a leader. However, Richard, the longest-tenured member, lived full-time at the commune and, whether the members realized it or not, had become the de facto leader.

Richard had no last name. Back in the seventies, as a young assistant professor at UC Berkeley, he befriended Dr. Timothy Leary, who ended up so bending Richard's mind that he gave up academia and became a hippy living in a Bay Area commune. During this period, he had his name legally changed to just "Richard." For many years he's been drug and alcohol free and takes his work very seriously.

During Manny's first month on the job, he became friends with Richard when Beautiful Land suffered some vandalism. Richard was working in a field of heritage Indian corn when he saw Manny drive up, so he took a break and walked over to visit.

"Hello, Richard . . . looks like your corn is getting up there."

"Yes, that's about as tall as it will get. It's a pygmy variety of multicolored corn that yields small ears, but they are hearty and produce a very nutritious grain. In a couple of weeks I'll give you a bag to try."

"I look forward to that. Is everything all right with the place?"

"No problems at all. It does get a little lonely this time of year, but I've got some boy scouts coming in Thursday night for a couple of days."

"Well, that should enliven things a bit."

Richard laughed. "I'm sure it will, especially around the fire pit at night. I really enjoy scouts coming. It brings back memories of my own time in scouts—some of the few things I can remember prior to my ill-spent young adulthood."

"I didn't know you were a scout," Manny said.

"Oh, yes. I was a patrol leader and went to Camp Arrowhead several years. None of them could beat the first year for adventure," Richard said. He then told the same story about traveling to camp that Alf had told. "I wish I could remember that man's name. He wasn't one of the leaders, but he was on the Scout Committee and helped us a lot. He was a smart guy and really funny."

"Well, Richard, I better get back on the road. I might be bringing a ride-along citizen with me when I'm up here tomorrow or Wednesday. He's kind of interested in subsistence farming. Would it be all right if I drop him off for an hour or so for a little tour?"

"Sure. Part of our mission is educating the public."

"Great. Do I need to let you when it will be?"

"Maybe just let me know which afternoon. It can be any weekday. The boys won't arrive until late afternoon Friday."

As Manny drove away, he was pretty excited with the idea reuniting old friends. He called Bren and said he was going to invite Alf on a ride-along, if that was all right. Bren told him, "Yes, but be sure he has the rules and signs a waiver. Let me know when you pick him up and bring him back, and get a copy of the waiver to me."

Bren added, "I was about to call you. We have an interview with Edward Hale at the AG's office at two on Friday afternoon. I'd like you to go with me."

"I'll plan on it."

~

Manny called Alf Hesse's cell phone.

"This is Alf."

"Hello, Mr. Hesse. This is Deputy Manny Sanchez. We occasionally do citizen ride-alongs as a public relations type of thing, and I need to do one in the next couple of days. I would enjoy having you ride with me on a routine patrol one afternoon. Would you be willing to do that?"

"Sure," Alf answered. "Tomorrow works for me."

The next day Manny met Alf for lunch at Taylor Freeze where they took care of the paperwork. Alf asked lots of questions about the work done by the Sheriff's office. After they got into the car, Manny called Bren and told him he had picked up Mr. Hesse for the ride-along and that they would be patrolling Aravaipa and Turkey Creeks and chatting with a few citizens along the way. He then radioed dispatch and reported back from lunch, and said he had Mr. Alfred Hesse riding patrol with him as a guest.

Sheriff Bitters came on saying, "Mr. Hesse, this is Sheriff Bobby Bitters. Welcome. I'm pleased to have you riding with one of our excellent officers. Enjoy your time with Deputy Sanchez, and remember to carefully follow his instructions in any crisis or emergency. He will keep you safe."

Manny handed the microphone to Alf, who said, "Thank you, sir. I'm already enjoying the experience."

As they drove, Manny described the car and its equipment and the sort of things he did on his rural patrols. He explained the procedures he used to protect himself on his solitary patrols and that, other than drunkenness or domestic disputes, most of the situations he dealt with were routine and not dangerous.

He stopped by Gil Howell's ranch to check on them and introduced Gil and Donna to Alf. They stopped by the Begay Foundation where Mrs. Kennedy explained their mission of preventing fetal alcohol syndrome and helping mothers who have FAS children.

Manny also pointed out the local ranches and points of interest and explained their history. He showed Alf the location of the old military camp, Camp Goodwin, and the site of the Wham Robbery in

Cottonwood Canyon. He also explained that this road was originally built as the military road between Fort Grant and Fort Thomas.

Manny and Alf saw Jim Martin and Cliff Nolan talking by the Nolan Ranch turn-off and visited briefly with them. As they drove, Manny explained that he knew every person that lived in his area and often picked up helpful information by simply visiting with them. He said it was one of the most pleasant things about his work.

Alf heard about the history of Klondyke, Aravaipa, and the Powers Brothers as they drove and was impressed with the beauty of the canyon as they reached the riparian forest and the narrowing of the valley. As Manny traveled west in Aravaipa Valley, he radioed as usual that he would be out of both cell and radio range for about an hour.

Alf asked, "So when you are down in this area, you are truly alone? There's no help available if something goes wrong?"

"Yes. If I'm going far enough up the canyon, the road tops out, and I get service again. Beautiful Land has a radio tower up on the ridge with a wire to the main house, so if needed, I can radio from there. But here in the chasm I have only myself."

Alf was pleased with Turkey Creek, a tributary canyon, and the tall trees in the narrow defile, and as they parked at Beautiful Land, Manny explained the commune's purpose.

Alf commented, "What beautiful little fields, gardens, and orchards."

Manny said, "In just a few years they've done some amazing work here. It's all watered by springs on the property."

As they walked down the main path to the houses, Richard came toward them. He had changed out of his traditional shirtless bibbed coveralls to jeans and a plaid shirt, and he was wearing a pair of mocs instead of his usual work boots.

Manny introduced them as simply Alf and Richard. Manny explained that Alf was doing some similar things on a smaller scale over by Eden. Manny said he couldn't stay, but he would pick up Alf after about an hour or so after checking up the canyon a ways. As he drove off, he wondered if the two would catch on that they were boyhood friends. He could see them in the mirror talking as they walked toward the gardens.

Because there was no radio reception or cell service in the depths of the canyon, Manny checked his cell phone voice mail when he topped out on the ridge. He checked in with dispatch, and they had nothing for him. Manny said he would be returning through the canyon for the next half hour so would be out of range again.

He could hear voices echoing off the little side canyon at Beautiful Land, so he walked to the rim of the canyon and saw the two old men gesturing at the spring boxes and water delivery systems that Beautiful Land had constructed. The last time Manny had taken this view, he had cast a shadow into the canyon, but the sun was too far west now, so he remained undetected. He was pleased to see the two men absorbed in affable discussion.

He drove back to the parking lot, but could see no sign of his friends. He walked down to the little complex, but they were still nowhere to be found. He had actually been gone for almost an hour and a half, so he went to the large call bell near the fire-ring amphitheater and gave three yanks, sending out clangs than could be heard for half a mile.

The men came from the Turkey Creek branch of the property, where they had been looking at the vineyard. Manny was sitting on a comfortable bench when they arrived.

Alf said, "Sorry, deputy. The time got away from me. This has been really interesting. I've told Richard I'd like to become an associate member and help out some with what they are doing."

"I just got here, but I thought I'd let you know I was here. If you need to finish a discussion, go ahead."

Alf replied, "Ha! We'd probably never finish. This has been most interesting, but I don't want to make you late. We better get back on the road."

Manny said, "Richard, it looks like you hit it off pretty well with my friend Alf."

"That's true. He is a very knowledgeable fellow and good company. I feel like we've known each other for years."

"Same for me. It's been a wonderful time."

Manny said, "Richard and I were talking the other day about a man he once knew, but he couldn't remember his name. Alf, I think the name was similar to the fellow who drove the truck you told us about at Taylor Freeze. What was his name?"

Alf said, "His name was George Campbell . . ."

Richard shouted, "That's it! How did . . .? Alf?"

Alf laughed. "Richard! Hank of Hair! I thought you were dead!"

Richard grabbed Alf in a bear hug and said, "I should be dead, or at least brain dead . . . but thankfully I'm alive to see you again, my old friend."

Richard turned to Manny. "Could you go on without Alf? We'll have dinner, and I'll take him home. We have a lot of catching up to do."

"Of course, but I need one more signature. Alf has to sign that he was treated well, kept safe, and has no grievance related to his ride-along experience."

They all walked to the parking lot. Alf signed the form, and when Manny drove out, the two men were busily engaged in conversation. When he was back in radio range, Manny radioed that the ride-along was completed.

~

Because of his inflated ego, Middleman was more concerned about anyone thinking his shooting was off than the prospect that he may get caught. Middleman felt comfortable with the way he left the scene at the dig—that was until the news broke that there was a survivor, and that Jack's death was a murder, not a suicide. Middleman's mistake was overconfidence in his shot, that he didn't check the first victim. That left a witness. It was a good shot; it had to be the helmet that caused the bullet to deflect and lose energy.

Middleman was so upset with the situation that he had neglected to bill Edward Hale for his consulting services. Now he was concerned that the uncharacteristic oversight might cause Hale to begin to worry and possibly even link it to the murder, which was a hot story in the local news. He went to his desk and prepared and sent the invoice. He apologized in the cover e-mail that he was behind in billing because of a bad summer cold.

Each evening he searched internet news for information on the murder, but it appeared that the police actually had very little evidence.

In fact, a story in the Casa Grande Dispatch quoted Pinal County Investigator Espinoza: *This is a very difficult case with little evidence and few leads*. Middleman was also fortified by his conviction that cops in rural counties were incompetent, and therefore unlikely to get very far with the investigation.

He heard his e-mail ding and, as always upon the receipt of the invoice, Hale had electronically paid. Hale also responded to Middleman's apology:

Sorry to hear you've been sick. Hope this means you are feeling better. I made your payment. Don't worry about a late billing. It let your money earn me a little more cash. Lol.

The cheery note relieved him of any concern as to Hale.

~

Elton Godwin drove to the construction site on the Ft. McDowell Reservation, listening to his iPod. This job was a little one; some kind of a water plant and erosion control. Mr. Colley said it was a good job because there were a lot of rain water control measures to put in. Elton wasn't exactly sure what that was, but he got to do a lot of work digging between ditches the trenchers had made and filling in behind concrete aprons. There was also some work on a ruin, but Mr. Colley said they would only work on that when they didn't have something else to do.

Elton went to the tool trailer to put on his hard hat, glasses, and vest. The trailer was his responsibility. He kept the tools in the right place and swept it out each day. Workers would sign out tools in the morning, then check them back in after their shift. They never put the tools up, though. They left them for Elton to put away. He wouldn't have to worry about it today, because he and the bosses were the only ones working.

Elton had just got out his shovel and pick and grabbed a bottle of water, when Mr. Colley called to him to come to the engineering trailer first. Elton leaned his tools on the steps to the trailer and did as told.

"Hi, Elton," Colley said. "We may need you to do something else. Let's wait until Steve gets off the phone to find out. Fix yourself a cocoa while you wait."

Elton didn't like coffee, but they had hot water and packets of cocoa, and he really liked hot chocolate. He mixed it up, then added one ice cube to cool it down some. He could hear Mr. Steven Benson talking on the phone but paid no attention to what he was saying.

Benson hung up and said to Colley, "Middleman will make a pick-up tonight, so have Elton get three or four good items out of the corner dig."

Colley looked at Elton and asked, "Okay, do you know what we want you to do?"

"Yes sir, Mr. Colley. You want me to take three or four whole, painted pots from the corner room, wrap them, and put them in the yellow toolbox . . . and cover up the ugly and broken ones."

"Very good. And make sure you lock the yellow toolbox. When you finish that, I saw one of those little round cactuses over by the big mesquite. Put that in a hole too."

"Okay. I will bury it in a hole and put a big rock where it used to be like you told me. Then should I go back to the ditch I'm working on?"

"Yes. Thanks, Elton. You can get to work now."

Chapter 10

Deputy Dan Tomkins had to deliver an order of protection in Tempe in the early evening; it went without a problem. Since he was so close, he drove by Elton Godwin's place, but his car was gone, so he decided see if he could visit the Fultons for a few minutes. They lived in the 2000 block of East Pebble Beach and the EcoAnthro Office was attached. As he parked on the street, he saw their office light on, so went to the business entrance.

He tapped on the door and opened it slightly. "Is it okay if I come in?"

Jill looked up, smiled, and said, "Yes, come on in!"

Mike was on the phone and Jill was doing something on her computer.

Dan said, "I wanted to ask you about a Benson-Colley employee. I talked with Elton Godwin, and I wondered what you could tell me about him."

"A redeeming quality of Benson-Colley is that they seem to treat Elton very well. If they didn't, I would have hired him away from them when we left. He is a really good worker and learns well. They had him work with us as an excavator, and within the first week, he was doing as well handling artifacts as any of our techs. He is just a sweet young man . . . doesn't have a mean bone in his body."

Dan asked, "I have thought about using him as an informant, but I'm afraid he wouldn't be able to do that."

Jill thought a few seconds before anwering. "That would never work with Elton. He is far too honest. He would not be able to lie to save his life. He's the most transparent person I've ever known. I don't think he could keep a secret—with the exception of doing something nice to surprise somebody. On the other hand, anything he knows about Benson-Colley he would unhesitatingly tell you. You would never need to interrogate Elton, just chat with him. He's an open book."

Mike had hung up the phone and had heard Jill's statement. "Jill's absolutely right. Elton is totally without guile. I assume you picked up on his mental limitations, but he is also a clear thinker and learns fast by example. He has a strong sense of right and wrong. Not that he wouldn't break a law, but if he knew something was illegal, he would never do it. He simply would not do anything he knew to be wrong . . . not for me or anyone else."

"Looks like I reached the same conclusion you two did. I just wanted to confirm it with someone that knew him better than me." Dan paused and changed subjects. "We're making some progress on Jack's murder but may have been thwarted some by Mrs. Hager getting the murder in the news. I know she only wanted the stigma of suicide removed, but it took away an advantage we had over the murderer. That's probably my fault. I should have explained to her what we were doing."

Mike added, "Maybe so. I'm sure she wouldn't have done it if she thought it would hurt the investigation. His death was awfully tough on her. She is struggling hard against her cancer, but she's now having a tough time focusing on the fight. Having people think Jack killed and committed suicide was more than she could bear."

"That's really rough. I wish we could make some faster progress on the case to give her some peace of mind. I feel bad for her."

"There is one good thing," Jill said. "Mrs. Kenton has decided to stay with Lester a while. During the day when Lester is at school or work, she spends the time with Mrs. Hager. She helps her with her medication and household chores and takes her for treatments. They have become very close. And Lester is happy to have mom living with him. He goes over when needed to Hager's in the evening and takes care of the yard and other such things. I think it's helping her much more than just physically."

Dan said, "That's great. She has enough to handle with her grief, medical condition, and financial worries without having to deal with chores."

Mike said, "Ed Hale called me and wants to help with Emily's medical expenses. We've talked with our insurance company. Jack had his mom covered on both his medical and life insurance, but even combined, they are not sufficient to meet her expenses. I'm working with her case worker to get all providers to charge only the bare minimum above what the medical insurance will pay, and with Ed, we will quietly cover the necessary charges beyond that.

"Most of the doctors and other providers are not charging for their time, so it's making a difference. We helped her apply for medical disability from SSI. Hopefully, we can make Mrs. Hager understand that Jack loved her, so he covered her and would want her to live. Of course the life insurance will not pay until the cause of death is official."

"That's mighty nice of you. Let her know that we have some good leads we're working on, and I believe we will get the guy. Maybe it will help her to hang in there."

~

Bren, Al, and Manny met for their traditional lunch meeting at the Taylor Freeze. Nothing unusual was pending on their beats, so Bren updated them on the activities of the Antiquities Task Force and the murder investigation. They agreed to meet in Pima in the morning and ride together to the meeting with Attorney Dirocco. Bren would arrange to pick up Dan on the way through. The food was ready so they picked it up and were eating when Alf Hesse and Richard walked in together.

Richard was in the lead as they approached. "Gentlemen, Alf said you would be here, so we wanted to come in and thank you for reuniting us. It is just amazing that after fifty-five years with no contact, living in different countries and states, and taking very different paths in life, we have ended up living so close together in the wilds of Arizona, doing much the same thing."

Bren and Al looked at each other in confusion. Manny just grinned.

Alf immediately caught on that it had been Manny's doing. "You rascal, Manny! You set the whole thing up! You knew what you were doing from the beginning, didn't you?"

"Yes, I confess."

Bren said, "Okay, how about including us in it now."

"You remember when we were here last time, Alf told us the scout story about Arrowhead Lake?"

The senior officers both nodded, and Manny continued. "Well, the next day I paid Richard a visit as I was patrolling, and he told me that exact story. In the earlier story, Alf had said his pal was called Dickey, but preferred Richard. I still thought it unlikely they were the same children. But I guided my discussion with Richard to scouts, and he told the same story. I arranged the ride-along for Alf and dropped him off for about an hour while Richard gave him a tour of Beautiful Land. They hit it off immediately, but never recognized each other. I brought up the story, and it suddenly dawned on them."

Richard said, "Alf has become an associate member of Beautiful Land, and he's shown me his springs and garden and his wonderful reference library. It's amazing that a formerly drug-addled hippy and a business mogul have retained very common interests."

"Richard and I were so excited that we didn't properly thank you before you left, Manny. So we are here to say thank you. Also, I completely neglected to tell you that I thoroughly enjoyed making the patrol with you. It was very interesting, and I didn't realize even a portion of what you fellows do. So to all of you, thank you for the duty tour; thank you for getting us together; and thank you for the great service you give."

The older men shook hands with them and departed.

Bren said, "Nice community-relations work, Manny. You made those two fine characters very happy."

~

Dan Tomkins called Bren. "Lester Kenton has been released to return to work. The doctors said they first worried about possible bleeding on the brain due to concussion, but everything has cleared up. Lester is good as ever."

"Well, that's great news," said Bren. "I wonder where they are going to have him working."

"Mike didn't say. I imagine he would go back to what he was doing."

"Yes, that worries me some." Bren paused as he thought, then continued. "Because of the news, the killer knows his first victim survived. He may decide to eliminate the witness."

"I hadn't thought about that. I have paid very close attention to the news and done regular internet searches to see how much information is getting out. All the focus has been on Jack. I don't think the news outlets even know Lester's name. Another good thing is that Lester's main job is not at the Salado dig at all. It's about twenty road miles from it, so the bad guy probably doesn't even know where Lester would be."

"True. There's a three-mile trail between the two sites, but it's too narrow for a vehicle. I'm not comfortable with the situation, though, so let me conference Mike Fulton into this conversation."

Mike answered his cell phone, and Bren added him to the call.

"Mike, I hear Lester is doing a lot better. I bet his mom is relieved."

"She sure is," Mike agreed, "but you know she has stayed with him constantly since the time of the incident. The close call really scared her. An interesting thing is the two of them visit Mrs. Hager every day. The two ladies have become very close, and I think it is a real help to Mrs. Hager."

"That's good to hear. Dan told me she seemed to be losing her will to fight the cancer. Someone who understands the horror of what she's been through the way Mrs. Kenton does may be exactly what the poor lady needs. We understand Lester will be going back to work. Do you know when?"

"He's starting tomorrow," Mike replied. "I'm having him replace Jack and promoting Greg to lead on the lower work."

"I'm a little concerned about that." Bren then explained the situation that he and Dan had discussed.

Mike thought for a moment before saying, "I sure don't want to put him in danger. I know he will be disappointed because this is a promotion and because he has a connection to that secondary Apache site. If I could provide an armed guard to secure access to the site, could we proceed with our plans?"

Dan said, "Mike's idea might work, Bren. There's an agency in Florence that has a contract with the sheriff to use uniformed off-duty deputies and reserve officers to provide security. They would have a patrol car as well. If they set up a checkpoint on the northwest edge of the Oak Flat plateau where the road drops into upper Queen Creek, they could control all vehicle access. That vantage point would also provide a view of any vehicle activity on the north side of US 60, as well as any pedestrian approaches."

"Mike, can you afford that?" Bren asked. "You are already incurring some big additional expenses."

"Fortunately, it is a federal project so we have a generous contract and a generous incentive to complete it on time. Being able to continue the work in the most efficient manner makes the most business sense for us and assures that our employees are able to keep working, even with the additional cost. However, if you still think it's too risky, we won't do it. I would shut the job down and take the loss rather than have another of our people hurt. My question for Dan is, can the security company provide enough off-duty deputies to cover ten hours, six days a week?"

"No problem, Mike," Dan explained, "Pinal is the third largest SO in the state we have 700 people, plus reserves, so there's not a supply a problem for the security company. They may have twenty different deputies cycling through on their days off."

Bren endorsed the idea, "It sounds like a rational approach. Dan, tell your sheriff what we are doing and why, and ask him to issue instructions to the officers hired that it is critical to be vigilant. Let's make sure they log every vehicle and movement on the road with descriptions, license plate numbers, and—for each new person entering—a driver's license. Provide them the description of the suspect vehicle, and have them call for backup if a vehicle like that turns off Highway 60."

~

Bren picked up Al and Manny in Pima for the trip to Phoenix, leaving their vehicles parked in the church parking lot. They picked Dan up at the Superstition Springs Mall. They had all read the report prepared by Ed Hale's lawyer, Pete Villa, and they spent most of the trip discussing it. Each of them had made notes of questions and weak points in the narrative. These would be used to clarify or expand on the information in the report.

The receptionist at the attorney general's office told them they would be in conference room six. She gave them a building diagram, circling their room and the nearest restroom with a marker.

They were the first to arrive. The took advantage of the restroom, then selected a drink and pastry from the snacks laid out on the credenza. The round conference table would seat twelve, so they sat in twos across from each other. The subjects would sit across from Attorney Dirocco and his team.

They stood as Barry Dirocco and two women entered the room. Barry shook their hands and introduced them to his assistant, Ronell Blair, and clerk, Carolina Matta.

Carolina had a large odd-looking tablet computer. Barry explained it was both the control panel for the room and a data entry terminal that connected to Carolina's computer.

Ed Hale, Pete Villa, and an unknown woman entered to introductions and handshakes. The unknown woman was introduced as Pete Villa's assistant, Ann Eiffel. Pete paused and warned, "If you want to get along with Ann, do not ever point out that her name is an apt description. She doesn't like that."

Ann smiled. "It does get old after thirty-five years. I need to get married."

Manny joked, "Just don't marry a guy named Teak."

Ann laughed at that. "At least not 'til I'm very old!"

Barry said, "We are still about five minutes early if anyone needs to avail themselves of the facilities. We also have some refreshments and beverages if you would like."

All three took a beverage, but only Ann took a pastry, and they took their seats.

Barry continued, "Thanks to all for showing up so promptly. Let's get started. First, Carolina will turn on the room recorder. If at any time during the meeting you want to go off record, make the request. She will announce each time it is turned off and each time it is turned on during the meeting. We will be happy to provide a digital copy to Mr. Hale at the end of the meeting."

Pete said, "We are fine with the electronic transcription. So start it when you wish."

Barry nodded to Carolina, who touched her screen and said, "We are recording."

Pete said, "Could we have a test of the recording quality?"

"I'm Barry Dirocco. Would you each, in a normal conversational voice, say your name as we go around the table from right to left." Each person did as requested, and Barry again turned to Carolina. "Stop the recording, and play the test back to the room speakers."

Carolina touched the screen, and said, "Recording off. Starting playback." She touched the screen again, and the roll call was repeated from the speakers.

Pete said, "That's excellent. Let's get started."

Carolina said, "We are recording."

Barry began, "We have all read the report, so we don't need to go through it again. My team members have some questions or clarifications, and we will have them discuss those. First let me bullet-point a summary of the situation.

"Mr. Hale met Miss Artiste at the Albuquerque Gallery opening and they became romantically involved.

"After some time, Miss Artiste suggested a scheme of purchasing legal artifacts from private property or collectors, for resale by Mr. Hale, for which she received compensation.

"When Mr. Hale tried to end the romantic relationship, Miss Artiste informed him that she had stolen or purchased, and he had sold, illegal relics. She blackmailed him into continuing both the business and personal relationship, threatening to go to authorities and blame Mr. Hale for the whole thing. She promised to not provide any more stolen objects.

"From that point it appears that all the items delivered by Miss Artiste were legal.

"Later, Mr. Hale was told by a Dr. Middleman that Miss Artiste had dealt in some illegal artifacts and said he could resolve the legal situation while replacing Miss Artiste in a similar agreement.

"Miss Artiste died in a workplace accident before any action had taken place on the new agreement, but the new agreement worked even better than the one with Artiste.

"Mr. Hale became concerned when he heard of the theft and murder near Queen Creek and Middleman showed up with extremely valuable artifacts from that location in the same timeframe, though they were certified as private decades ago.

"Mr. Hale contacted the company General Counsel, Mr. Villa, who acted on Mr. Hale's direction to review and report on the situation. That report was subsequently delivered to me. Is that a reasonable summation?"

Ed said, "It is."

Barry said, "We appreciate you bringing it to our attention. Sergeant Allred will direct the review from this point on."

"Thank you. My team members have been told to interject or ask questions at any point in these discussions. I would like to get clarification on two things first.

"A business card like the one Dr. Middleman gave you was found in possession of another person related to the case. Only the phone numbers were different. I suspect that he probably only actively works with a few people at a time, perhaps two or three, and communicates with each on a separate throw-away cell phone.

"We have asked Mr. Hale to continue to deal as usual with Middleman and not to do anything that would make him suspicious." Bren turned to Ed. "That means you should let us know immediately if his phone discontinues working or if he changes his phone number."

"I will do that."

"Good, it's very important. Can you tell us about your communication methods and habits with him?"

"He calls infrequently, and when he does, it is very short, usually to say he has made an acquisition or that he has completed cataloging and putting a piece on the digital market. Occasionally, he will make a congratulatory call when we've made a big sale. The calls are rarely more than one or two exchanges between us, so less than a minute long.

"We also communicate via e-mail when he sends an invoice for payment. My habit is to pay it electronically immediately upon receipt. We sometimes exchange pleasantries in those e-mails. That is pretty much the total communication. I have a copy of our most recent exchange for you. This followed the sale of a beautiful owl effigy to a museum in Vienna for nearly a million dollars."

That hit the room with a jolt. Dirocco exclaimed, "A single item brought one million dollars! I knew we were talking big money here, but that's astounding! Who would pay that kind of money for a ceramic?"

Ed said, "It was the most unique ancient Southwestern piece I've seen—wonderful craftsmanship and color—but what was most unusual was its gemstone-quality turquoise disks as eyes. As to who would pay, there were still four bidders at seven hundred thousand: three museums and a private Asian collector. The winning bid was actually $800,000."

Attorney Dirocco tried to shake off the surprise of the last disclosure. "Sergeant, if you can pick up your line of thought, please continue."

"Let's move away from the Queen Creek case back to Chaco Canyon. The next thing I'd like to explore is why Mr. Hale believed Miss Artiste when she said the artifacts were legal."

Ed thought for a moment. "I knew her well by then, both on a personal and professional basis, and she knew clearly how I feel regarding looting of antiquities. She had a spotless reputation as an ethical, thorough, and knowledgeable archeologist. I also trusted her with my affection, so I had no reason at all to distrust her, nor any expectation that she would go against my principles related to artifacts. Perhaps her deception is the most painful thing to me."

Al said, "Miss Artiste revealed her deception when you decided to end the romantic relationship. What made you decide to end it?"

"Marie was in many ways a delightful person. She was very good looking, refined, smart, witty and fun, and we shared a lot of interests. I had asked her to marry me, but she made it clear she was not interested in marriage. As time went by, she became more demanding and mercurial, and not even willing to discuss marriage and family, even though she now knew it was important to me.

"I decided my opportunity to have a family was slipping away in a dead-end relationship and that the relationship was costing me too much emotionally. It was tough, because every time we were together we had some great chemistry and good companionship, but I could see that's all it was ever going to be."

"A follow up on that," Al added. "Were you angry when she told you what she had done and that she would ruin you if you left her?"

"I should have been, I suppose, but I just felt shocked, then incredibly sad. Then she became more animated and wild I was frightened. I actually thought she was going to kill me. I wrapped my arms around her and restrained her that way for fifteen minutes, and she finally started crying. When I eased up, she threw her arms around me. We stood like that for a while, and I suggested we open a bottle of wine. From then on everything was the same as it had been—nothing was ever said about the argument. The next morning she promised me that she would never sell an illegal relic again."

Dan said, "On the day Marie died, you were in your store from nine to ten a.m. Then, according to Mr. Villa, you signed the deposit slip that night at nine thirty. What happened during the intervening eleven hours?"

"I don't know. I might be able to find out by looking back at my calendar."

Mr. Villa spoke. "I didn't specifically mention this in the report, but if you look at the documents I added to the end, you will find a receipt from a barber shop just before eleven a.m., one for Burger Rehab at one thirty, and a liquor store at about five—all in Scottsdale. The store log and time sheets signed by Mr. Hale show he was in the store from shortly after five until close. Miss Artiste's death happened sometime in the afternoon. Even with the fastest jet to Farmington, there is not a time period that would have allowed Mr. Hale to travel to Chaco and back and be in store by closing."

Mr. Hale said, "I didn't know you checked on me. I never thought I was suspected in Marie's death."

Villa said, "I wanted no surprises."

Manny spoke, "You met with Dr. Middleman. Give us a detailed description of him."

"He was about medium height and weight with heavy black hair, eyebrows, and mustache. His eyes were rather small and dark, and he wore rimless, slightly-blue-tinted glasses. His hair seemed somehow uncharacteristic of the rest of him. It was rather long and combed back on the top and sides, with kind of a pompadour . . . the same thing with his eyebrows. They were thick and untrimmed. His mustache was black and thick, shaped like Sam Elliot's.

"Other than that, he was clean-shaven and well-groomed. He wore a nice, medium-gray suit with a light-blue shirt and a navy-and-white tie, black wingtip laced shoes. His hands were smooth and well-manicured for an archeologist; no dirt under nails, no chips, no callouses.

"His air was definitely academic—confident, very well spoken, precise, and knowledgeable of archeology. I'm sure he is a professor, but one that does no fieldwork."

"That's good," Manny said. "Let's talk more about his basic description. What was his complexion?"

"He was white . . . didn't appear to be mixed race or Hispanic, but he had a little darker complexion." Ed gestured towards Manny and Dan. "Somewhere between that of you two deputies—maybe kind of a light southern Italian tone, as opposed to the Tyrolean complexion of Mr. Dirocco."

"So maybe about the same as your skin tone?"

Ed laughed, "Yes, I guess so; but I'm a quarter Diné, so I might be a little more coppery than he."

Al noticed that Dan looked a bit confused. "Diné is Navajo." Pointing at Ed with his lips, Al said, "Bilagáana bizaadísh dinits'a'?"

Ed laughed. "He asked me if I speak English, so I guess I better do that."

Everyone chuckled.

Ed said, "Sorry, back to the description. You were about to ask something else, Deputy Sanchez."

"Can you be more definitive on the height and weight?"

"Could you and Deputy Tomkins stand up?"

Ed and the deputies stood, and Ed compared their height. "He was an inch taller than Manny, but not as trim . . . and not close to as robust and muscular as Dan . . . probably about midway between them."

Bren said, "You mentioned that Middleman had shown you an inventory of the collection you were buying from and identified several items on your webpage that were not part of the collection. Where did he get the inventory?"

"He said it was in the archives . . . I assume the University archives. He said that archeologists made a real effort during the forties and fifties to catalog private collections, so they could be included in studies . . . and to protect private collectors from prosecution after the antiquities laws were enacted. He used that registry to validate the artifacts we sold."

Al asked, "How many of these private collections are there?"

"Nobody knows. Most of them are not documented, but probably tens of thousands. Ranchers and early settlers were impressed with the beauty of the artifacts and began collecting them in the 1800s, and people have been collecting ever since. Some collections are small with a dozen or so items and others are vast.

"I bought the entire Fernandez collection that Marie was claiming as her source for artifacts from the estate after Fernandez died, and it took a full-sized moving van to deliver it to Arizona. I can't contain it in my storage. I rented warehouse space."

"So you are saying there are tens of thousands of legal artifacts out there?"

"Easily, Sergeant Victor. I'll bet there are people on your reservation who have prehistoric artifacts in their homes."

"I do know families that have pots, axes, and beads from pueblos like Kinishba, Besh-ba-Gowah, and Tonto. I suppose there are quite a few who do, even though Apaches wouldn't have them if they were associated with a burial."

"Yes, Navajos generally won't touch artifacts because of *chindi*, the bad part of the spirit that stays behind when a person dies."

"Apache belief in this matter is not as defined or strong as Navajo chindi, but we have a similar belief for items related to death of friends or family."

Bren remarked, "So this discussion demonstrates our problem. Thousands of private artifacts exist all over the Southwest, and that complicates our ability to identify stolen ones. It's a problem our Antiquities Task Force is very familiar with. I believe that covers the concerns the investigators had. Do any of you have anything else?"

The officers indicated they did not.

Ed Hale spoke up. "Mr. Dirocco, there is one other item of business that I would like to discuss, if I could."

Barry said, "Go ahead."

"Because of the information that Dr. Middleman gave me, I know of several specific stolen artifacts that I sold through my company. I intend to discretely contact the buyers and inform them that that my supplier fraudulently certified artifacts stolen from a national park and our company unknowingly sold one or more to them.

"I'll offer to refund the purchase and pay the shipping so they can be returned to the park. I'll offer them an additional 20 percent discount from their winning bid on the next item they buy from us. If the state or federal government wishes to fine us, we will not contest it. I would like to have Mr. Dirocco assist me in communicating with the correct people in New Mexico."

Barry replied, "The New Mexico Attorney General's Office has been privy to our investigation from the beginning, and I'll relay your plans to him. I'll also ask him and you to delay any such action until we complete the Arizona investigation of the Queen Creek thefts and the associated murder being investigated by Pinal County. It is best that we don't cause any interest outside of those directly involved in the investigations."

Pete looked at his client, and said, "I recommend that you fully comply with Attorney Dirocco's request and that, as we move forward with restitution, you allow me as your general counsel to completely handle it on our end."

Ed nodded. "I'll help with anything this task force needs, but since I've agreed to Mr. Villa's advice, please arrange for my cooperation through him."

Pete added, "I'll begin to research the stolen pieces, but we will not act on any of it until you give us the go-ahead."

Barry said, "I think that's most prudent, and an agreeable arrangement for both our Office and the Task Force. Thank you all for your participation. That concludes our meeting."

Carolina said, "Recording off."

Chapter 11

Middleman received a text from Benson-Colley that they had some product ready to be picked up. He left work early and stopped by his house in Oro Valley where he put on the wig and facial hair of his Rotgut Rupert costume. He brushed the hair back and combed the mustache and eyebrows, so he looked less wild, and put on his tinted wire-rimmed glasses. He didn't look like Rupert, but he certainly didn't look like himself. He was now Dr. Middleman.

This customer was working a Hohokam dig on the Ft. McDowell Apache-Yavapai Reservation. For whatever reason, over the last decade Hohokam pottery had become less popular with collectors than Salado. They probably would only get twenty thousand or so from this, but it was still worth the trip.

By the time Middleman reached the site it was dark and everybody was out of the construction yard. He walked to the big yellow toolbox, extracted three pots and a soapstone tablet of some kind. He secured them in a plastic storage tub and strapped it into the back seat of his truck. He drove to Superior and spent the night in his apartment. The next morning he touched up his disguise and reapplied the wig, then headed for the Safford lab.

He cleaned and cataloged the three items of pottery. The pots were nice, intact pieces but nothing unusual. He set the bidding at five thousand for the best item and three thousand on the other two. In the text, he made more of them than he felt and hopefully they would get some bidding going.

Then he set about forging a registry history for them. He certified them as coming from a private collection first recorded by Gladwin in the 1930's as belonging to a collector in Globe.

The soapstone "tablet" he had seen through the bubble wrap at the construction yard, proved to be a very nice piece. It was carved of green-black soapstone paint palette. Dimensions were nine by six inches. It had raised flat serrated edges and a bear head handle on each end. He cleaned and photographed the palette, and entered it in the catalogue, saving it as a draft; he decided to do more research before putting it on the market. He had seen something similar out of Snaketown. The piece would probably be attractive to museums, so he wanted to set the opening bid properly.

Middleman texted Hale. *Posted three new acquisitions from a Gladwin recorded Globe collection. Good, but not unusual. Expect moderate return. A very nice stone piece from same; evaluating before setting price.*

Hale texted, *Thx!*

Middleman printed off his fake Gladwin-signed cards, careful to handle them with gloves, and delivered them to the Museum. He had included the Gladwin certification for the as-yet unpriced stone piece, and filed all of them.

Using a computer in the museum reading room he did some market research and saw a similar piece with a prominent crack across it sold for $8,000.

He typed in the address for his Safford lab server and logged in. He completed the catalog entry on the stone tray by setting the starting bid at $12,000. He logged off, erased the browser's history, and sent a short text informing Hale that the bidding was open.

~

Manny Sanchez was nearing completion of his ASU Pueblo Cultures distance learning course and was writing his final paper on the differentiation of Salado from Hohokam pottery. His instructor suggested doing research at the Arizona State Museum in Tucson. The instructor told him to be sure to take his student ID card with him.

The Arizona State Museum, Tucson, is located on the campus of the University of Arizona. It was originally the artifact repository of the University Anthropology Department. In 1893 the Arizona Legislature established the state museum with a separate administration from the University. The museum includes the Arizona Historical Museum in Tempe. The archeological collection at Tucson is the largest repository of southwestern native artifacts in the world. The museum also includes over 70,000 volumes in its non-circulating library, and houses archeological labs.

When Manny arrived at the museum the receptionist pointed to the elevator and told him to go to the second floor and see Assistant Archive Curator, Sally Gaona. The second floor lobby was little more than a bare alcove with a wall directory pointing to restrooms on the right and Archives and Library on the left.

Past some small glass-walled meeting rooms and the library entrance he came to an open office area with two desks each occupied by a young woman. Doing a fast scan, Manny decided the most professional looking of the two must be the Assistant Curator. Approaching her he said, "I'm looking for Ms. Gaona…"

The other woman said, "That would be me."

Sally Gaona, an attractive woman in her late twenties, looked to Manny more like a hostess in a second rate club than an academic. He explained why he was there.

"You should be able to find everything you need here," Sally said. "Let me give you a tour of the facilities and tell you how you can be most efficient. What will you be researching?"

"Methods of distinguishing Salado pottery from late Hohokam pottery. I'd like to identify the scientific means as well as site-based, stylistic, and any other methods."

"There are some comparative exhibits in the main museum that may be helpful, and we have a great deal on that in our manuscript and research paper library. The index is available to you online. We have a reading room in the book and manuscript stacks where you can examine our material and take notes and photographs. Or for a fee we can make photo copies. In the Museum labs we also have graduate students actually working on classifying sherds by composition, design, and context, and you could observe and discuss with them."

Sally inserted Manny's ASU ID card in a device on her desk, typed a bit on her computer, and out came a laminated student researcher ID badge. She removed his ASU card and handed back to him. She then attached the new museum card to a lanyard, and told Manny to wear it at all times in the museum. His new ID badge had a color copy of the ASU photo ID on the back side, and the front had the ASM Seal, Manny's name, and an eight digit number. It also had an RFID patch in one corner.

Sally turned to the woman in the next desk and told her to cover for her until she was back. Manny noted the desk name placard, *Olga Jordan, Admin. Assistant*.

At Sallies command, Olga smiled and agreed, but she seemed irritated; Manny noticed that as soon as Sally turned away Olga rolled her eyes and shook her head.

Actually Olga was rightfully irritated; they weren't supposed to take students in the secure room. She thought, *Sally is really vamping this guy. She gets most of her dates that way.* Olga was pleased at Sally's irritation when Manny nodded and smiled at Olga. Manny on the other hand, besides wondering what was bothering Olga was oblivious to the tension between them.

Sally took an electronic key card from her center desk drawer and said, "Let me show you our document archives first. This will probably be the only time you are in this room. I'll fetch the things you want from here and bring them to you in the reading room."

She explained that the *secure room* was a sealed environment, kept dust free at a constant temperature and humidity. Even the lights were special to protect the old paper. They went into a long room about forty-feet wide filled with book stacks, map tables, filing cabinets, and various shelving and cupboards all clearly numbered and labeled. She walked him through and pointed out the general areas where different types of documents were kept.

About the center of the room she passed a large group of old wooden library index card files with a sign that read *Private Artifact Collection Registry*. Manny stopped. "What is this?"

"Starting back in the twenties or thirties the Southwest Archeological Center in Globe started examining and indexing artifacts in private collections. Over the next several decades they created that card file with a description of the artifact and a coded registration number, along with as much other information as they had on it, and of course, the owner and location of the collection. As you can see, there are thousands of items recorded. The neat thing is each card is signed by the archeologist that created it, so we have many signatures of people like the Gladwins, Emil Haury, or Ned Danson and others that are considered the founders of modern archeology."

"I've heard about this. I wondered if it was real or just an old archeologist's tale."

Sally smiled at his sudden interest. "It is real. Would you like to take a look?" She took gloves from the top of the cabinet and handed them to Manny. "We strictly practice safe research, so put these on."

Manny pointed to a bound tablet on top of the cabinet. "What's this?"

"That is an index that lets us locate artifacts listed by some general type descriptors. It would help so much if these could be digitized and indexed on a computer." Sally sidled up to Manny. "We will have to get close so I can show you how this works." She randomly opened a card drawer. "Can you read the tabs okay?"

"Yes." Manny's first thought, *I wish Jenny could have come with me.* Then he realized that having Sally remain friendly would give him a better chance to investigate this file that was integral to the artifact murders. Instead of rejecting her, he decided to not react.

The cards were darkened with age, but were in very good shape. As he thumbed through the file he could see a few were written by hand, but most were typewritten on old typewriters with occasional irregular letters.

"Take one of those blank green tab cards in the front and place it in the middle of some of the registry cards, then pick up the card immediately behind it. That way when you put the card back, it will be in the right place." She pressed against him and pointed out the information on the card he was holding. "There's Dr. Haury's signature!"

"That's so cool; who has access to these files?"

"Only Mr. Morra and I have keys . . . he's the archive curator . . . but we allow professors to use these files. There's a workspace behind the cabinets, and we remove the file drawer so they can use it there, but we have to let them in."

"How often do they do that?"

"Rarely. It's only happened two or three times in the four years I've worked here. One of the professors has talked about using students to digitize the cards so they can be more easily used, but apparently he's never been able to get a grant for that."

"This has been a real treat. Thank you." Manny put the card where it belonged, moved the green index card back to the front, and closed the drawer.

"It's my pleasure. If there's anything at all you want, just ask." Sally replaced the key card in her desk and showed him the rest of the floor, a quick walk through of the Museum on the first floor and Labs in the basement. They returned to the second floor and she oriented him on the library, and he settled into a work station where he worked for two hours collecting information for his term paper.

As Manny was leaving, he waved at Sally, who was talking to a middle-aged, balding man in a tan sports coat. Manny thought, "That's probably Mr. Morra. He looks just like a museum curator," though he wasn't sure he had ever seen one before.

~

Deputy Tompkins dropped by Elton Godwin's house and asked if he could talk for a little bit. He brought two sodas from Jack in the Box, and they sat at the table to drink them. Elton emptied the contents of his pockets onto the table.

Tompkins pointed at the iPod. "What were you listening to?"

"It's *Rocket Man,* by Elton John."

"That's a good song."

"Yeah, I like Elton John. He has good music. My mom says I'm named after him."

"Lucky for you she didn't like Snoop Dogg."

Elton laughed, "Especially since I don't like him. I'd hate to have that name."

"Can I listen to Rocket Man?"

Elton picked up his iPod and loaded the song, then handed it to Dan. "I'm glad you like it too."

Dan put in the earbud and began to keep time with his head, to Elton's delight. Dan held the player under the table while he downloaded the bug chip. The green LED on the downloader started blinking, indicating the download was complete. As the song started to fade, Dan sang with it, "I think it's gonna be a long, long time." Then he switched it off and gave it back to Elton.

"So Elton, how's work going?"

"Pretty good. I'm working out by the big fountain. I get to see it just about every time it shoots up."

"What are you doing out there?"

"Mostly cleaning up water control measures. Mr. Colley says this is a good job because there's a lot of water control measures. I mostly clean out the ditches the big trencher-machine makes, and then after the concrete sets I fill in around the aprons."

"Do you like that?"

"It's okay . . . kind of boring but pretty easy work. I did get to recover some relics the other day. Mr. Benson was on the phone and told Mr. Colley to tell me to just take three out of the corner room, and then cover up the hole again. We aren't doing a dig, just taking a few things out when they need them. I found three Indian pots, and a little flat stone tray. It had handles that looked like bear heads."

"What do you mean you aren't doing a dig?"

"When you do a dig you have to make a grid and keep track of things. We don't need to do that on this job. When the owner says to dig something up, we go find something. Maybe it's because the Indians are the owner on this job?"

"Maybe. I don't know why either. So did you put them in the yellow toolbox?"

"Yes, but I wrapped them real well in bubble wrap first."

"You're very conscientious."

"I know what that means. It means I always try to do a good job. Mrs. Fulton said that about me, and my mom told me what it means."

"It's a good thing when people say that about you. Well, I better get back to work. My break is over. When I'm up this way again, I might stop and visit."

"I'm glad you're my friend."

"And I'm proud to have a friend like you."

~

Pat didn't have to look up her Daddy's phone number, she had written it in the front of her address book. She never called it, but she knew the number by heart. Her dad sent roses to her at the school when she graduated from University High School, and on the attached card he wrote, "So proud of your accomplishments. Find your own calling.

Don't let anybody dictate to you. Call Mr. Santillanes at Compass Bank about your education account. If you ever want to, I would like to talk with you. Love, Dad." He included the banker's number, along with his own phone number and address.

She hid the card from mom and wrote the phone number with no name on her address book. She told mom the roses came anonymously from a secret admirer. She put the roses in a vase and kept it on her desk in her room. When they began to droop, she hung them upside down and let them dry. They had made the move with her to Safford, and were still on her desk. They were the first and only flowers she had ever received.

That was six years ago. She had the phone in her hand, but she couldn't dial the number. Instead she called Andy Lopez.

He was surprised to hear her.

Pat blurted out, "I want to call my Dad. Can you come and be with me?"

When Pat opened the door, Andy was startled at her appearance. She was pale and shaky. He put his arm around her and led her to the desk chair. He read the open card from her dad, where she had left it by the phone.

"Don't you see that he's begging you to call him? He wants you in his life." He grabbed a chair from the dining table and sat beside her. "Call now. It will only get harder the longer you wait."

She took a deep breath and dialed, hoping her father would answer, then hoping he wouldn't. It rang the third time, and she was about to hang up, when a female voice answered.

Sounding like a scared ten year old, Pat asked, "Is this Lois?"

"Yes, it is."

"Mrs. Haley, this is Patricia, your husband's daughter. Could I speak to him?"

"Oh, he will be so happy to hear from you! So am I, Patricia. He's still at work, but you can reach him there. He's been waiting a long time for this call."

Lois gave Patricia the number and said, "We would all love to meet you. I'm just so excited. Call him right away, and maybe you and I can talk another time."

Pat jotted down the number. "Okay, thank you."

She smiled through tears as she told Andy, "She was happy I called. Daddy's still at work. I can call him there."

She recognized his voice when he said, "This is Lieutenant Haley."

"Daddy, this is Patricia."

"My Pattie! Oh my darling girl. How I've missed you!"

Pat could hear his voice breaking as he talked. They both sat for a period with sniffles the only sound on the connection. When she regained some composure, she couldn't believe what came out of her mouth. It wasn't what she meant to say.

"Daddy, why did you leave me? Why did you have to go away?"

"I tried to get shared custody of you. My lawyer was working on it, but the judge was a radical feminist, and she struck down every motion or filing he made. The judge finally said that if I moved, she would grant me right to communicate with you and to contribute to your care. I sent you cards and notes but never heard back. I was sure they were never making it to you, but I kept trying. Losing you from my life was the worst thing that ever happened to me. I'm so sorry."

"I found out that you always paid child support and sent me birthday gifts, but Mom never gave them to me. I thought you didn't love me anymore. I was too young to understand."

"Sweetheart, I still don't understand. It shouldn't have been like that."

"I wanted to call you ever since I received your flowers, but I was afraid to call. My friend Andy kept encouraging me to call you, and now I'm so glad I did."

"Tell Andy thank you for me. This is one of the greatest days of my life. Tell me more about Andy."

"He is a fellow deputy, and we have become very close friends." The conversation lasted over an hour and ended with a promise to call each week. They agreed that he would call her on Skype next Sunday at six p.m., so she could "meet" her brothers and sister.

~

The church was reserved, invitations had been sent, the dress was altered, and the tux was rented. Manny had also secretly bought thirteen American Eagle Gold coins in a decorative silver box for $5,000 to use for the arras. But there were lots of details to be figured out while there was time to accomplish them, so Mrs. Mondragon had invited Manny and his parents to dinner and an evening of planning at their house.

Dinner consisted of traditional Basque-American fare. Appetizers were served in the living room: pintxos of soft ewe cheese filled with ground veal on rosemary sheepherder's bread with thin-sliced sweet peppers.

The dining table was set family style with cool foods on cold platters and hot foods on hot, covered platters or bowls. They each had a small bowl of a spicy garlic soup; a fresh tossed salad with grated Basque cheese; hot, soft rosemary bread with olive oil; thin-sliced, marinated, and seared rib eyes; and roasted mixed vegetables. They served a hearty red wine and for dessert had cold cherry soup with a scoop of vanilla ice cream. The dinner was a hit, and they all assisted with clearing and wiping the table, where they sat to begin the discussion of wedding plans.

Jenny opened the conversation. "Manny and I have decided we don't want to have sponsors, since both of us have saved enough to pay for our wedding."

Mr. Mondragon objected. "We have saved since the day you were born for both your college and your wedding, and we plan to use it for its appointed purpose!"

Mr. Sanchez agreed. "You kids have your lives in front of you, and you should use your savings to assure the wellbeing of your family. We are willing to pay the expenses as well. You need to continue to build on your savings so when you are ready to buy a real home, you have a good down payment. Plus you need to always have $15,000 or more built up as an emergency fund."

Manny said, "We are all willing to pay for the wedding, so we don't have to worry about that. I suggest we put the cost discussion off until we settle some of the other details."

Mrs. Sanchez spoke quietly. "We will be sensitive to your wishes because it is your wedding and the start of your new family; but likewise, you need to be sensitive to the desires of your families and understand that we want what is best for you. And it is not just us. For example, my cousin Emilio has already spoken that he would like to sponsor some part of the wedding, hopefully as a padrino. Are you planning to have an all-American wedding, or will you use padrinos and madrinas?"

Jenny replied, "We'll have kind of a traditional American wedding in English, because everyone attending speaks English and many don't speak Spanish. But we want to include some of the Mexican traditions like the lazo, arras, cushion, and offering bouquet. Father Brady says we can insert them where we feel they are appropriate. We will have some honorary padrinos and madrinas, but we won't ask them to sponsor the cost. We would be honored to have Emilio be padrino de arras."

Mrs. Mondragon said, "Between the three families, we certainly don't *need* any sponsors, but if it would hurt Senor Campos's feelings perhaps he should be allowed to provide the coins."

Manny spoke up, "I think Emilio will understand that I want to give Jenny gold that I bought for her. I would be honored to have Emilio handle and present them in the ceremony."

Mrs. Sanchez said, "I think that would be perfectly fine."

Jenny said, "Speaking of Emilio, I would love to have Mariana come and sing for our wedding. I suggested it to Manny, and he agrees, but we aren't sure how she would travel. Also, she has a fiancé now, so we would need to invite him to come with her. How do you think Emilio would feel about bringing them with him?"

Mrs. Sanchez smiled, "I'm sure he would be very happy to do that."

Jenny asked, "Would it be improper to have our parents be our Padrinos de Lazo? Manny and I would like that if it is acceptable. Also we each have a grandmother. I know that with Grandmother Rowe it might not be possible, but do you think they could do the cushion and bouquet? We know it's not traditional, but Father Brady said he had no problem with it."

Mrs. Mondragon looked at Mrs. Sanchez, who nodded yes. "I see nothing wrong with that. Momma is pretty cognizant most of the time, and we could have Elena assist her with her part. And we would love to help wrap the bonds of love around you two."

Manny said, "I've decided to have Tommy be my best man."

Jenny added, "And I want Elena to be my maid of honor. We have always been close, and I can't think of anyone that would be more appropriate."

The discussion continued in this manner, point by point through the remaining details. After almost three hours, Mr. Mondragon said, "So the only remaining issue is that you must use the money in your wedding account before you spend any of yours. What you don't use will be cashed out and given to you, because it belongs to you."

Mr. Sanchez added, "And if you need more than is in your account, we will pay the excess. I'll provide enough cash to cover your honeymoon and help you get your home ready for a civilized lady to live in, so that it doesn't come out of your wedding account. You two pool your savings accounts and start saving for your soon-to-be children."

~

Ed Hale asked Pete Villa to stop by his office to discuss some concerns Ed had about their online marketplace. As Pete entered the office, Ed turned his monitor to face Pete and moved to the front of his desk, sitting beside Pete. He had the Salado owl with the turquoise eyes displayed on the screen.

"Thanks for coming, Pete. This effigy owl is one of the finest Salado pieces I've seen, and was the most expensive I've sold. It will be a real embarrassment to have to recall it from the museum. My reputation, and my personal self-esteem will be damaged, and rightfully so, but we need to have a strategy to minimize the impact on the business.

"I'll assume, though it may not be true, that everything Dr. Middleman sourced is stolen. The same is not true for the artifacts provided by Marie, because a number of them probably did come from the legitimate Fernandez collection, but it may be impossible to prove which is which."

"It may not be as bad as you think," Ed commented. "The Fernandez inventory provided by the heirs included several dated versions that they found stored in different places. Since Roland Fernandez included his date of ownership on each item and each of the lists are also dated, we can probably identify many of the legitimate ones by comparing the older dated copies to the more recent ones.

Postdated items are most likely stolen. Of course, those for which we find no such documentation will still be in question."

"This is very important, Pete. If there's any question at all as to the source, we have to treat it as stolen property."

"I think it would be helpful if I could get a temp person familiar with archeology to research these lists. Is it all right if I contact Barry at the AG's office and ask if they can recommend anyone?"

"That would be fine, but you might be better off just asking Sergeant Allred. He is more familiar with people in the field than Barry would be."

"I'll do that."

Ed continued, "The other concern I have is that Middleman is continuing business as usual, which means we will be continuing to sell stolen items to my customers. I'm not at all comfortable with that, but if I don't do it, it will tip him off that something is wrong. He just posted three items, and will soon post a fourth.

"We will be able to contact the buyers and make amends, but it makes the problem grow larger with each sale. Could we set up a couple of new customers as a front and buy them ourselves, so we can protect against any more damage to our reputation than we already have?"

"That's a good idea. In fact, I bet the AG would love to help us with that. I'll get on it as soon as the meeting is over. And I'll check with Allred for a contact for our research and get somebody started as soon as possible."

~

Manny Sanchez called Bren, who answered his cell phone.

"Hey, Bren, do you have a couple of minutes to talk?"

"Sure, let me get in a better place to stop." Bren pulled further from the shoulder of US 70 just outside of Ft. Thomas. "Okay, go ahead."

"I started working on my term paper for my anthro class by doing some research at the Arizona State Museum on the U of A campus. They have the register of private artifact collections there that was mentioned in our meeting with the AG. Do you remember that?"

"Yes, that's the one Middleman used to expose Marie Artiste's theft and convince Hale to partner with him."

"Right. Well, I was there as a new student and was given a tour of the environment-controlled room in which those records are kept. They are in an old card file, like the Dewey Decimal files they used to use in the library before computers. They are grouped by collection with a card for each artifact.

"It occurs to me that one way fraud could be committed is to match stolen artifacts with a similar one in a collection, then sell the stolen one as from the collection. For example, a five-inch polychrome Hohokam pot with black-and-white internal paint could be used to represent many similar pots."

"That is interesting. But if it is being used that way, since it is available to researchers like you, anybody could do it."

"That's the catch. Access is restricted to a couple of museum personnel and professors in the university's Anthropology Department. They keep a record of who accesses it, and in the last two of years, it's only been accessed two or three times."

"Whoa! If it is being used in the scam, that narrows down suspects to maybe six people. Likely maintenance and security would also have access. Did you get access because you are law enforcement? I hope not, because we don't want anybody there to think we are on to them."

"No, boss. I was there strictly as a student researcher. Nobody knows I'm a deputy. I think I was given special treatment because the attendant thinks I'm hot. She was overly friendly. I didn't discourage her, because I thought it might be helpful in future investigation."

"Ah, the sacrifices one makes for law and order. So besides making friends with some lonely librarian, did you get any research done on your paper?"

"I doubt that she's lonely. I think she's *very* friendly to pretty much any male. Yes. I have a very good start on it. The tour only took about twenty minutes. Adjacent to the secure room they have a pretty nice little library that they call a reading room. I was able to find everything I was looking for on those open stacks, so I didn't need any special files."

"Did you happen to see a man who matches Middleman's description?"

"No. There were a few students too young to be our suspect, two young female employees, and their boss, the curator—a guy named

Morra. He looks like I would expect a curator to look: fiftyish, balding, bookish, fastidious, and stuffy. He was otherwise pretty average. No heavy head of hair or bushy facial hair. He wore slacks, a golf shirt, and a sports coat."

"Do you plan to make another research trip?"

"That might be a good idea. I want to get a few photos for my paper, and perhaps I can talk with the girls about their work to pick up some more helpful tidbits. I don't want to alarm Middleman should it be he is creeping around in the archives. The only problem I have is there are a lot of little chores preparing for the wedding, so I might not get back until after the big event."

"Go tomorrow as undercover work, and it won't take up any of your limited personal time. Don't let anybody have a hint about your occupation. You better have a plausible cover just in case. Say you work as a night watchman for Allred Farms in Thatcher. I'll send you the number. If anyone is curious have them call. Monica answers that phone and will vouch for you. Take your personal car and turn in an expense report."

"Thanks, Bren. That will help me, and maybe we can find something to move the case along."

Bren hung up the phone, but before he could pull back on the road, he got a call from Pete Villa, who asked about someone with an archeology background who might help him sort through the Fernandez collection paper work. Bren said, "Let me check on that, and I'll get back to you."

"I appreciate that. It's kind of urgent, so the sooner the better."

Bren called the Fultons' office and explained what he was looking for.

Jill said they had to suspend work on the US 60 realignment for a three-day scheduled break while the state evaluates them. All their students are idle now. Lester Kenton would probably like the work.

Pete immediately put Lester to work on the lists.

~

Deputy Dan Tomkins had found the original bid notice for the Ft. McDowell project that Benson-Colley had Elton Godwin working on. It was being built with federal grant money provided by the Economic

Recovery Act and was considered a sustainability improvement. It would include a water storage tank, a small treatment plant, a large concrete apron, a solar panel array with supporting circuitry and batteries, and a number of drainage channels, containment ponds, erosion dams, and pipelines. The nearly one-acre apron and water tank would be by far the largest structures. Dan thought, "Another generous distribution of taxpayer money for something nobody asked for in the first place."

He decided to drive up to Fort McDowell after work and have a look at the site. It was near the existing community water tanks a few hundred yards from the eastern limit of the town of Fountain Hills. As expected, the small construction yard was unattended and locked.

In addition to Elton's large yellow industrial toolbox, the yard contained two trailers—one a typical twenty-by-twelve-foot construction office and the other a thirty-foot semitrailer with steps attached to the back, no doubt the tool trailer that Elton attended. The back of the yard was a laydown storage area with forms, steel, aluminum, pipes, scaffolding, and other construction materials. There was a backhoe/loader, a small dozer, a blade, a tracked trencher, and a GMC dump truck.

Dan drove past the yard to the large earthwork that would be the concrete apron, and on the southern edge of the construction zone he spotted the remnants of the Hohokam pueblo that Benson-Colley was looting. There were places where the stone-clay walls were a foot high, but they were mostly visible as a grid of buried stones.

If they were doing this as a legal dig, the non-funerary artifacts would belong to the Ft. McDowell tribe, but the human remains and accompanying funerary would be repatriated to the neighboring Salt River Pima-Maricopa people for reburial, since the Hohokam were their ancestors. Dan could see where the ruins had been probed with a rod to find pottery, as well the disturbed area where Elton had been removing artifacts and carefully depositing them in the yellow tool bin.

Dan had been considering the possibility of installing surveillance, but it would be rather difficult to do anything without being noticed at this location. He thought it might be possible to put fake ADQ monitor at the cul-de-sac on the north of Sunset Drive in Fountain Hills. With zoom lenses they could closely monitor the ruin, gate, and yellow box. He would suggest that to Bren.

As he walked back to his car, Dan thought it must be seven o'clock because the fountain in the middle of the Fountain Hills pond began gushing skyward. It shot its column of water 560 feet into the air each hour for fifteen minutes—a sight that Elton mentioned enjoying.

Chapter 12

Deputy Manny Sanchez left his trailer at seven thirty a.m. and drove the back roads, half of which were dirt, to Willcox where he took I-10 to Speedway and the Arizona State Museum in Tucson. He considered taking the longer route through Safford, because of it being mostly paved, but the direct route was thirty miles and about twenty minutes shorter.

Manny arrived at the parking garage at nine forty-five, so entered the museum and proceeded upstairs a few minutes after the ten o'clock opening. He felt his main purpose was to talk with the museum personnel to better understand the functioning of the organization and figure out how Middleman might fit in. His obvious "in" with Sally was a key to getting insider information.

When he reached Olga's desk, it appeared she was the only person on the second floor. Manny gave her a friendly smile and said, "Good morning, Olga. Is Sally busy today?"

Olga seemed pleased that he had remembered her name. "She doesn't start until after closing today. We have a group of researchers with an evening appointment. Mr. Morra has taken a personal day so won't be in at all. I'm the only show in town this morning. But I should be able to help you with anything you need. I'm glad you came actually, because the only thing I have to do right now is answer the phone, and we don't get that many phone calls."

"Well, good. It will give me a chance to become acquainted with you. The only problem is, Sally let me look at the private collections card file in the secure room when I was here last and I was going to ask if I could spend about fifteen minutes looking at it to examine differences in how different people cataloged and when the last entry was made. I would also like to look at the cross index book for the files. With both Sally and Morra gone, I guess that's out of the question."

"No, not really. When Sally is gone, I'm delegated her responsibility, and her key card is always kept in her desk," she said as she picked up Sally's card. "I can take you in there; however, I can't stay away from the phone for more than about five minutes, so you may have to let yourself out."

"So this is the only key?"

"No. I think there are three. The curator has one; the museum director has one; and this one stays in the office." Olga took him to the files, and Manny took gloves from the box on the cabinet and put them on.

Olga said, "Now that you are gloved up, do you know how to use the green index card to keep the files in order?"

"Yes. Sally said to find the card I want to look at, insert the green card in front of it, remove the card and examine it, then put it back in the same place and remove the green card."

"She missed it a little bit. The preferred method is to place the green card in front and remove the card you want to review, like you said, but when you put it back, put it in front of the green card. That makes the next card in order available behind the green card if you want to look at multiple cards, and it keeps them all in the right order."

Manny nodded agreement, "That makes sense. Is there anything I need to know about the index tablet?"

"The tabs are each one a searchable reference. So *Location* has the alphabetical locales of where each artifact was found; *Collection*, the private collection it's in, etcetera. For example, if you go to location and pick Adamsville, you will see a list of alpha numeric IDs. Each of these represents a drawer and Dewey-type number in the card file. So each of the twelve tabs represents a different type of cross reference with an ID for each item cataloged."

"Wow. To think of all the manual work that went into this. We are really lucky to have computers for this now. This is great."

"You were asking about the last entry date. On the tab marked *Date*, are all the entry dates, with the ID of each item entered on that date. Turn to the last page, and the date at the bottom of the list will be the last entered date."

Manny did so. "February 3, 1964." He jotted down the ID of the item entered and asked, "So if I go to drawer R and pull the card with this number, I'll see who did it?"

"Yes. If you want to take one drawer at a time to the work station back there, you will be more comfortable and have a desk for writing notes. I'll be up front if you need me. Just press 'O' on the phone. It rings to my phone."

"Thanks, I won't take long. Ten to fifteen minutes at most."

As soon as Olga left, Manny started taking pictures of the files, the door, the work station, and the index book. He pulled the card IDed as the last card entered which he thought should be the last card in the file, but it was not. He took a photo of the typed card. The card read, *four inch dia., two-inch deep Salado Polychrome from the Ellsworth Collection in Globe* and was signed by Gordon Vivian.

He then looked at the cards behind it. There were three and, as they should have been, were entered on that same date. Two were signed by Vivian, and the third was signed by Dr. Emil Haury. Chances were that Dr. Haury's registration was the last item entered in the collection.

Manny took photos of these three cards as well. He took a blank 3x5 card from his pocket and laid it over a fan of the old cards, which clearly showed discoloration of age compared to the new card. He took a photo of this as well. Something nagged at his subconscious, but he couldn't form a thought from the uneasiness.

He then opened several of the drawers and compared the new card to the old ones in the files. While the old cards were not exactly uniform in color, they were all obviously much older than his card. That was consistent with the range of years from the twenties to the sixties. He carefully returned everything back to its proper order and left the room.

Olga was walking into Mr. Morra's office with a stack of newly-opened mail, so Manny walked in behind her. "I'm finished with the files."

Olga asked, "Did you find the answers you were looking for?"

"I think so, but I need to get my ideas organized. That may take a while. The other thing I wanted to do today is see if I could get some photos of comparable pottery from both the Hohokam and the Salado. Any ideas about that?"

"You should be able to do that on the computer. Enter your pot specs plus the word Salado, and then the same specs substituting Hohokam. Then pick the two that best serve your purpose. Here is a citation card, to give credit to the museum if you use our photos." Olga paused, pointed at the wall, and then said, "Also take a look at the poster."

The poster, titled *A New Religion? Meaning in Ceramic Decoration*, featured a comparison of a Hohokam and Salado pot. Manny asked, "Is it okay if I take a photo of that?" Olga nodded, and he snapped the shot from across the desk.

It only took another thirty minutes for him to find half a dozen photos that would work for his paper. He thanked Olga and said goodbye.

~

Ed Hale thought about the conversation he had with Mike Fulton. They had discussed the feasibility of anonymously donating through Mike's company whatever additional funds the victims of the shootings might need, including Emily Hager, Mrs. Kenton, and Lester. Mike was happy to comply and thought it would be a big help with Mrs. Hager's medical expenses.

Ed wished there were something that could be done in the way of emotional support. The poor lady was having it hard, and losing her son had almost done her in. Ed walked over to the office that Lester was working in and asked how he and his mom were doing, then asked about Emily. Lester said, "She was ready to give up, but she and mom have become good friends. She seems to be perking up some."

"Is there anything I could do to help her spirits?"

"Maybe. Having friends is good for her."

"I noticed your mom dropped you off today."

"She needed to do some shopping. They are about out of things to eat at Mrs. Hager's."

"Can Mrs. Hager get out at all?"

"Yeah. She likes Mexican food, so a couple of times a week we go with her to Taco Bell. It's nearby."

"Call your Mom and tell her I'm taking you home tonight, and that I'll take you all for Mexican food at a very good place. It's casual, so they won't have to dress up."

Ed and Lester picked up the ladies at five o'clock. They were pretty excited to be going out and had freshened up, done their hair, and put on makeup.

Lester introduced them, "My boss, Mr. Hale."

"Please, just call me Ed."

"I'm Emily."

"My friends call me Nettie," Mrs. Kenton said.

"Nettie and Emily, we are going to Casa Reynoso in Tempe. It's not far."

Emily exclaimed, "Oh, that's great food! One of the girls in the neonatal nursery used to bring it to us."

Proudly Nettie said, "That's a family from Globe. We eat at La Casita all the time . . . same family."

They drove the short distance from Emily's home near Evergreen and Broadway to the restaurant, ordered and ate. The conversation was interesting and lively and Ed was gratified to see Emily joking and laughing. He found out that as a neonatal nurse she had gone to work with a registry where she had no insurance about two months before she was diagnosed, leaving her uninsured.

She teared up with a smile. "Mike Fulton, Jack's boss, told me that Jack had me on his insurance, so I have coverage I didn't know about. That's a big help. It was so thoughtful of Jack to do that. Mike also told me that his company and some other people in the business will cover additional expenses. I'm just overwhelmed by the kindness."

Nettie said, "You have done so much good for people. It's just coming back to you."

They decided to have dessert. Ed and Emily had flan, and Lester and Nettie had fried ice cream. After dinner they drove home, and they visited for over an hour.

Displayed on a credenza in the living room Ed saw a beautifully-woven tray basket with the weave portraying ga'an dancers. He was attracted by its fine craftsmanship and beauty and could tell by the lack of patination on the willow weave that it was a new creation.

He said, "That is a wonderful basket tray. Is it okay if I examine it?"

Emily nodded yes.

He picked it up and looked at the tightness of the weave and the use of red-dyed yucca, which added accents to the white of the willow and black of the devil's claw. He looked for an artist's mark, but there was none. Finally, he said, "This is marvelous work. Emily, where did you get it?"

"It was a gift from a special friend," she said, laying a hand on Nettie's arm. "Nettie made it."

"Do you make many of them, Nettie?"

"No. I make seven or eight baskets a year, maybe two or three trays."

"Where do you sell them?"

"Oh, I've never sold my baskets. I give them as gifts for special occasions, like marriages, sunrise dances, or graduations. I don't have money to buy gifts, so I give baskets."

"Nettie, if I sold a tray like this, I would get enough for you to buy a new house. This is like a Van Gogh or Rembrandt. It is high art. Emily, be careful who you let see this. It is valuable enough someone could hurt you for it."

"Maybe I better keep it in my bedroom where I can see it, but not everyone who comes in can. I really like it, and agree that it is wonderful."

Lester talked a little about ancient basketry from his archeological studies. He had told his mom that her work was really good, but she didn't think it was anything special. From there they ended up discussing Indian crafts in general and what made some pieces better than others.

The conversation somehow evolved to childhood experiences of living on rez. They laughed and joked as they compared Lester's Apache reservation experiences with Ed's Navajo ones. Ed delighted Nettie by speaking to her in Navajo for a few minutes. Finally Ed decided he should not tire Emily, and said his goodbyes.

As he left, Ed realized he was free of tension that he had been unaware of even having. Ed genuinely liked all of them. He admired Emily. She was quick-witted and kind in conversation, very cultured and intelligent, and he thought incredibly brave. He was surprised that she was very young looking and attractive, even though she had lost too much weight due to her illness.

~

Pat Haley waited eagerly on Sunday for her scheduled video call from her dad and his family. At six the call came up, and the family appeared on Pat's screen. Pat was surprised at how different her dad looked since she last saw him. Instead of the dark-haired, slender thirty-year-old preserved in her memory, he was a fit fifty but much more muscular. His dark hair was well salted with gray, almost white, on the sides.

Lois was pretty, poised, and had a great smile. She had light-brown hair streaked with gray. Pat wondered if the gray was natural or if she had it added as highlights. Pat remembered that her mom said she was five years younger than daddy.

Daddy said, "It is hard for me to see you so all grown up. But your bright eyes and smile are still exactly the same . . . delightful."

Each of the kids introduced themselves, from oldest to youngest.

Larry would be eighteen in November, a senior at Blacksburg High where he played fullback in football, guard in basketball, and third base in baseball. He would be attending Virginia Tech next year.

Paul was fifteen, a guard in varsity football, yearbook photographer, and played cello in orchestra. He just got his learner's driving permit.

Kenneth was eleven, won the city spelling bee and played shortstop in little league. He earned his Arrow of Light in Cub Scouts and was going into Boy Scouts in two weeks.

Carol was eight, in third grade, played piano and was learning to play the flute. She also played Tee League baseball and was taking dance and riding lessons. She was really excited to have a sister! Too many boys in her family.

They talked for an hour and a half about their jobs, their families, and their communities. Mr. Haley said he had never been to Safford, so they would have to schedule an Arizona vacation sometime. Pat said that would be fun . . . it's a pretty place with a lot of interesting things to explore. She laughed and described Graham County as being rural except for Safford and Thatcher which are connected, saying jokingly that three of the suburbs were Eden, Gripe, and Lizard Bump.

Before they finished, Mr. Haley said, "Pattie, we want you to come soon and spend a week with us so we can become reacquainted and you can get to know your family. I'll buy your tickets, and we have a nice guest room for you to stay in. How soon can you come?"

"I could schedule some vacation in October. September is pretty well taken up by other deputies' vacations, and I have a friend's wedding then too."

"Okay, let me know as soon as you can, and I'll get the ticket booked so we can get good rates. I'll take the week off too. The week of Columbus Day would be good because school will be out that day . . . give us more time together with the brothers and sister."

Pat was elate; she felt that the family had fully accepted her. She was excited to think about the upcoming visit. She felt pure joy for half an hour, before a twinge of anxiety began to creep in. When she was with them for so long, would she be a disappointment?

~

Ten months ago Manny decided to buy the trailer in Klondyke when the owner decided to sell his property and move to Sierra Vista. A veteran, he felt he and his wife needed to be close to a military base since they needed more medical care. He found a buyer for his twenty acre home about two miles from his rental, but the realtor said it may be months or years before the trailer property would sell.

He told Manny he would be willing to let him continue renting until the property sold, or if he wanted to buy the property he would let him have the whole package for eight thousand cash. He said, "No telling how long it will take to sell and I'd really rather just be done with everything here when we move."

"Give me a day or two to think about it."

"Sure, take as much time as you need. I won't be evicting you, so no hurry."

The deal included the land, the trailer, a well, tank and water treatment system, a barn and a corral. Manny checked with a rural realtor who told him the place would eventually sell for between twenty and thirty thousand. If it weren't forty miles from a town and only two acres it would be worth a lot more; people who live this far from town usually want some pasture land and a more substantial house.

Manny took the deal figuring that he could always get his money back from selling it, and if he transferred he could move the trailer if he wants. It has been a pretty good deal for him. Once he and Jenny set a date, Manny started fixing and upgrading his trailer. Even though it was old, it was in good shape and everything worked. Now it was time to make sure she would be safe. People in Klondyke had to be able to protect themselves.

He ordered steel-clad solid oak security doors with reinforced mounting, hinges, locks, and hardware. At the same time he ordered reflective film installed on all the windows—primarily for security, but also to help cool the trailer.

He installed aluminum slats in the sliding windows He also installed video cameras with a view of the front and back yards. Not only would Jenny be able to see both yards on her computer and phone, but so would he, no matter where he was.

On the plain wall between the living room and the kitchen, he installed a horizontal gun rack and placed Jenny's new Remington 870 Express compact shotgun loaded with 2-3/4 shot.

He knew all this might seem extreme, but Jenny was worth it. Finally, he cleaned out the barn so her car could be garaged out of sight. He parked the department car behind the house when home, and his Stratus was always at the sheriff's office.

He brought Jenny over to see the improvements. She was impressed, and somewhat touched that he was making such an effort to protect her, though she felt it was unnecessary.

She smiled and punched his arm. "I didn't know the conspiracy theory neurotic side of you, Manny?"

"No theory; the fact is that you have no help here when I'm an hour out. If some crazy is set on harming you we have to be prepared. In a sense a place this remote is exactly like the old west."

"Well, you may be way over protective, but I love my neurotic survivalist!" She threw her arms around his neck and he kissed her.

~

At the Monday Antiquities Task Force phone conference, Attorney Dirocco reported on the work being done by his office. He explained the plans to assist Ed Hale and Pete Villa in setting up dummy customers so Ed Hale can purchase stolen items from his own company rather than duping an innocent buyer. It's costly for Ed since he has to pay the fee to Middleman; but it does protect his customers.

Bren mentioned that Lester Kenton had been hired by Hale to help analyze the sales that had been made from items supplied by Miss Artiste and Dr. Middleman to determine which of them were illegal. When the time is right for our investigation, Ed can refund the customer and return the stolen property to the rightful owner.

Once the general discussion was concluded, Barry Dirocco asked if anybody had anything else to report.

Dan told of his conversations with Elton Godwin and the information recorded on the iPod bug. He pointed out that they had recorded some solid evidence in the conversation, including instructions to remove artifacts and dig up and bury a little round cactus.

Dan said, "I drove out after work and looked at the Benson-Colley construction yard where Elton is working. It is fairly well secured and lighted, and there is a watch-clock key station mounted on the gatepost. It would be difficult to surveil either electronically or by stakeout. However, our department has access to a remote surveillance station disguised as an ADEQ Air Monitor. We could park it off the north cul-de-sac of East Sunscape Drive in Fountain Hills and have a clear shot of the gate, the yard, and the drop box. It would not arouse suspicion, and we could capture Middleman picking up the stolen property."

Barry said, "Let's do it! I'll contact your sheriff."

~

Manny reviewed the photos he had taken of the private collections files and realized he had failed to notice something important. He had checked for new white cards that would indicate recently added files, but found none. But in looking at his photos he realized that several file drawers contained a supply of unused cards stored in front of the first tab. They had been placed there for convenience of those entering new files. They, like the files themselves, had browned with age.

If those cards were used in creating a fake entry, they would not look any different than the others in the file. He really had not thought about the possibility of creating fake files. He was guessing that Middleman was simply reviewing the files, finding an entry that closely matched the stolen item, and attributing that ID to the stolen item. Manny had almost eliminated this scenario because there had been so little access to the files—only three visits in two years would not work.

But he could now see the fallacy of that thinking, from what he observed on the last visit to the museum—Sally's access key in an unlocked drawer of her desk. Anybody who knew about the key could surreptitiously use it to enter the secure file room.

That meant his original scenario could be possible, as was the second scenario—simply adding a new file card for a stolen artifact. The second method would work because it is unlikely that anybody would ever even see the fake card.

Of course if a fake card were created, even on one of the original spare cards, it would have to be done with an old typewriter and would require a forged signature. Otherwise it would be an obvious counterfeit to even an untrained eye. Plus, a fake card would not be on the cross-reference table, but that would not matter since it would be like a counterfeit needle in a stack of needles.

After pondering for some time, he hit on a possible solution. Ed Hale said that Middleman provided verification on the online catalog to assure the bidders that the item was legal. Manny thought, *If we get the private collection ID number from the catalog, or any of the cross references, we could pull that specific card and possibly determine if it is real or fake.*

By the time he reached these conclusions, it was too late to call Bren about it, so he sent him an e-mail laying out his thoughts. Having disposed of his work on the case, he worked for an hour or so on his term paper and, for the first time, included comparison photos in it. He added a sentence mentioning recent work on the possible religious meanings to the differences between Hohokam and Salado designs. The photo of the poster had a reference to a paper, which he noted on his endnotes.

As he was scrutinizing his shot of the poster, something in the background of the office caught his eye. It looked like a Colt .45

Peacemaker on the top of Morra's bookshelf. He zoomed in as much as he could but could only see that it was mounted on some kind of plaque. It had a logo or photo and engraving on it, but it was out of focus and indistinguishable. He made a mental note to get a look at it the next time he went to the museum.

~

Driving a plain white pickup truck with a magnetic ADEQ seal on each door, Dan Tomkins and Frank Landon, the asset manager for Pinal County Sheriff's office, pulled the fake air monitor to Fountain Hills. The device was solid state and powered by solar-panel-charged batteries, and the signals were transmitted via satellite to the 24-hour clerk's console in the sheriff's office. In addition to the two video cameras, it had a long-distance directional ear that could transmit conversations from up to a mile away. They set up, leveled, and tested the device and installed portable chain-link fencing and no trespassing signs around it.

Tomkins and Landon then talked to the nearby residents and left printed notices that the monitor would gather data for ten days to three weeks in order to establish a baseline air quality record. They asked the neighbors to keep children away and call the number on the notice if anyone tried to damage or steal the monitor. The notice listed a phone number that routed through the sheriff's office. It would ring on the clerk's desk phone marked *Air Quality*, so they could respond appropriately. The setup and notification took less than an hour.

~

Bren Allred called Manny Sanchez about the e-mail Manny sent pertaining to the private collections file.

"Manny, that was good work on the artifact files in Tucson. I called Ed Hale's attorney, and he gave me the private collections reference number on a piece that they believe was taken from the dig at the murder scene. I know you are taking off for most of this week to get ready for the wedding, but would you mind making a quick trip back to the museum to check out that specific file this morning? I'll pay it as overtime so it makes up for infringing on your vacation."

"Yes, I can do that. If I leave now I can be back in time to have lunch with Jenny."

Bren asked, "So if the card is authentic, what do you expect to see? And how will a fake card be different?"

"A few of the cards are handwritten, but almost all are typed with the small type called Pica. I expect an authentic card to first look like the other cards in degree of discoloration and fading of the printed lines on the card. The typing is not great on the cards because they were actually typed by the scientist making the entry, not a professional typist. The text is not square on the cards, and it looks like no effort was made to align with the printed lines. Contrast between characters will vary; capitals will likely not be fully aligned. If it's printed by a more modern device, it will be neat, with even contrast, and capitals will always align with the lower case."

"Good. It sounds like we should be able to spot any new additions. If we don't then we will have to assume Middleman, or possibly an accomplice, simply matched a stolen artifact to a registration card. Take a good close-up of both sides of the card, and email them to me with your evaluation. I'll not bother you about work for the next two weeks. I'll see you Friday at the wedding."

Manny was tempted to take his patrol SUV with him, since he could make much better time in it, but decided it wasn't worth risking being seen in a police vehicle by Middleman . . . or his accomplice.

Manny realized he had not thought about the possibility of an accomplice until Bren mentioned it. Manny was just assuming that Middleman worked in the museum or university and was using the files himself. He wondered about Sally and Olga as possible accomplices, but rejected that idea. They both had been willing to let him not only see the files, but handle them . . . and do so without their oversight. If they were doing something illegal, they would probably be careful as to whom they gave access.

Manny drove as fast as he could safely drive on the secondary roads to Willcox, knowing that his fellow officers there would not bother him. Once on the freeway, he set his speed control at 84 mph, nine miles over the speed limit. Hopefully the Highway Patrol would pay him no mind. He arrived unmolested.

Olga appeared to be the only one in the office, though Morra could be behind the closed door to his office.

"Hi Olga, I'm back! Looks like you have the place to yourself again, unless your boss is in his office."

"Hola, Manny! You got it right. Morra has a meeting at the museum in Tempe today, so most likely Sally won't come in until after lunch. She isn't here much unless she has no choice."

"I won't bother you much. I just had one reference I wanted to check in the private collections file, and I'd like to take another look at Morra's poster. The reference information on the bottom was too fine for my camera to get."

"We won't have any problem with the first request. I'll let you in, and you can take your time." She got the key card out of Sally's desk and headed toward the secure room. "But Morra's office is locked, and I don't have a key. However, there is an identical poster in the main hall downstairs. It's on the south wall on the far left as you head toward the door. There's a little cluster of chairs there. It's just behind them."

Manny thanked Olga and slipped on white gloves as she returned to her desk. He opened the file drawer and withdrew the reference card in question. The card certainly looked legitimate. It was dated 4/7/48 and signed by Emile Haury. The Pica type was slightly crooked, about half the upper case letters were not properly aligned, and the contrast varied widely between letters. He took a close-up photo of each side of the card as requested and reinserted it into the file. He checked the cards before and after the card in question. They were all entered on the same date and signed by Haury, and all three were consistent in appearance.

Manny visited with Olga for a few minutes. In the course of the conversation, having picked up on Olga's pique at Sally, he said, "It seems like you are frequently left alone here, and that Sally gets a better deal."

"I didn't know it was that obvious. Sally and I started out as administrative assistants. Morra said that he hired us because we looked like someone he would like to work with. He made it clear that we could get promotions and other privileges if we were accommodating and cooperative. Sally was willing to pay the price, so she is now an assistant curator. I made it clear I work strictly according to my job description and the law pertaining to employees."

"Wow. So is he rewarding her for sexual favors?"

"Well, I haven't seen them in the act, but once or twice a week they have a date. She comes and goes as she pleases and does anything she wants to do with never an objection from Morra. If I take off half an hour early, my pay gets docked. She probably isn't actually here thirty hours a week and gets her full pay. I do all the office work, handle all the phone calls, fill most of the archival requests, and I write grant requests, purchase requests, and budget proposals. She does little guided tours with VIPs and gives special tours of the file room to good-looking guys who happen in. I was surprised when you came out so soon. Sometimes it lasts and hour. You didn't notice she rubs against you like a cat in heat? It doesn't take a genius."

"Now that you mention it, she did hang awfully close. I just figured she had to be that close to see the files I was looking at. But why do you keep working here?"

"Because I actually like this place. I enjoy working with the students and professors and the sense of mission and history here. I refuse to be driven from a job I like by someone like him. One of these days someone is going to catch on and it will hit the fan, but I'll still be here when they clean the stuff out."

"You know that is sexual harassment, right?"

"Yes. But it would be my word against the two of them, and I'm the bottom of this totem pole. Also, I have to say that once I told him no, he has left me alone. I guess I can thank Sally for that."

"Well, I hope everything clears up for you soon."

Manny was on the road by 10:45 and made even better time on the return trip. He put together the report for Bren, attached the photos, and pressed *Send*.

Chapter 13

Pat Haley called Jessica Martineau and offered to buy lunch if she could spend a couple of hours with her. They met at Denny's.

Jessica said, "What's up?"

Pat answered, "I just needed to talk with Dr. Jessica. My life is becoming overwhelming and confusing, but in a good way."

"That sounds wonderful. Fill me in."

"You know Andy and I have become friends. We happened to be at the range at the same time, so when we finished we had lunch together at Tony's. We talked for a long time, and it was wonderful. We shared real feelings and encouraged each other. It was kind of like you and me."

"Uh oh. Should I be jealous?"

Pat laughed. "Not yet. This was the first time I've shared my feelings with a guy since my daddy left. Andy encouraged me to call my father, pointing out that he had continued to support me and had given money for college that allowed me to do what I wanted instead of what Mom wanted. He said if he had a dad like that, nothing could stop him from going to him.

"He teared up as he was talking about it, and without thinking, I took his hand. We held hands for the rest of the conversation and as we walked to our cars. I've never done that before. The last thing he said was to call my dad. When I told him I was afraid to do it, he said he would be with me when I called if it would help."

"That's really neat, Pat."

"I thought about it for days and finally decided to do it, but I couldn't make myself dial the number. Instead I called Andy. He came over and made me call. Daddy was still at work, but his wife was really happy to hear from me and gave me his work number. Daddy cried when he heard me, and we talked for a long time. Then last Sunday I met the family over Skype—three brothers and little sister. They are wonderful. I'm going to their house for a week in October. Now do you see why I'm overwhelmed?"

Jessica smiled. "What? You get your first boyfriend, talk with your dad for the first time in decades, and are introduced to siblings you've never meet? Why would that be overwhelming? That's a lot the get a mind around. But it *is* really wonderful!"

"I'm frightened about several things. Adjusting to my family is a big one. My little sister, Marie, is thrilled to have a big sister; she has three older brothers and is really looking forward to spending time with me. She is eight, plays T-ball, Piano and flute, and is taking dance. I don't have a clue what to talk to her about or how to play like a little girl. I only have about a month to learn, how do I do that?"

Jessica smiled reassuringly and said, "That's a lot of time to bone up on little girl stuff. Mainly just listen to what she says and ask questions about what you don't understand; it's not as different from talking to adults as you think. If she wants to play dolls, you just play the part of one person talking with another and take your cues from her. Kid's aren't usually limited by any topic of conversation."

Pat asked, "So just talk like we are talking?"

"Kind of, except talk about what she wants to talk about; she probably will never run out of something to say."

Jessica continued, "As for learning about early childhood, there are some simple things you can do. Ask Bren if you can visit with Lizzie a few times, or volunteer to babysit a couple of evenings while they do something. Try watching shows for little kids on TV, maybe even pick up a few children's books for eight year olds and read them. Kids love Dr. Seuss stuff."

Pat visibly relaxed. "That makes me feel better, and you are right that I do have time to find out more about the tastes of children. The two more urgent things are the wedding next week; and what am I going to do about Andy?

"I have never been to a wedding. I've been invited to Manny's and want to go, but I have no idea what I would do there."

Jessica said, "Well, I'm going. You can sit by us. I'm not too sure what to expect myself. I've heard Catholic weddings are long and complex. You can come with us and we will be confused together."

"That's nice of you. I would like that. The second thing is I want Andy to go with me but don't know how he would feel about it or how I would ask him."

"Just tell him you're going and would like him to come with you. If he really doesn't want to, he will tell you so . . . but I think he'll jump at the opportunity."

Pat hesitated a bit. "I don't have a dress and don't know what to wear to a wedding or a church . . . or anything else for that matter. I don't know how to use makeup. Could you help me?"

"Now that will be fun! I don't go to work until four this afternoon. Let's go shopping when we get through eating."

They finished up and headed to the dress shops where they bought a burgundy voile fitted midi with cap sleeves and a flared bottom. Jessica accessorized her with black three-inch heeled shoes, a crystal quartz arrowhead necklace and bracelet, and a little jeweled handbag. The outfit looked really good on Pat, much to her amazement.

Jessica stood back and admired her work. "You look hot!"

Jessica suggested that Pat set up an appointment at a salon to get their hair and makeup done on the day of the wedding. Jessica also offered to help her select makeup and teach her how to use it. They agreed to that plan.

Pat asked, "What should I do about my hair? It's time I would usually get a haircut, so it's a little longer than usual, but my #4 buzz-cut doesn't match the feminine look."

"Don't worry about it. It's long enough to part, and there are a lot of very short cuts, that look great. The stylist will make you look girly."

Finally Pat was persuaded to call Andy and ask him to go to the wedding with her. He immediately agreed and said he would get a haircut and new tie. She told him to get a burgundy one so they would match.

Jessica laughed when Pat told her about Andy's response. "That's about the sum total of a guy's preparation for a big event! Women spend hours getting everything just right, and the guys comb their hair and put on fresh clothes."

"Well, I can certainly identify with that. But I have to say, this girly stuff has been a lot of fun. Thanks, Jess."

Middleman called the Benson-Colley office on his burner phone and said he was ready for a few more items, and asked if they would be able supply a couple that night. He received an affirmative answer and the conversation ended.

Mr. Benson called Elton to the office and told him to put a polychrome jug and one of the medium-sized bowls in the toolbox before he went home. He did as instructed.

The fortunate thing for law enforcement was that both the ADQ monitor and the iPod bug picked up parts of those conversations and had them recorded. Unfortunately, the sheriff's clerk had been told to monitor activity at the construction yard after it had closed for the day, so no one at the sheriff's office was aware that a theft would be completed that night.

The computer on the sheriff's end of the system ran live video and audio feed continuously. Though nobody was actively monitoring it during the daylight hours, all the feeds were digitally saved. From 6:30 p.m. to 6:30 a.m., the system was programmed to sound an alert any time motion was detected on the screen. The infrared video would come on as soon as it was sufficiently dark, and if it detected motion and the regular video didn't, it would also sound an alert. An alert from either source would call the clerk's attention to the monitor. If a vehicle was at the yard, the clerk was to call Deputy Tomkins's cell phone.

Deputy Tomkins lived in Superior, over an hour away from Ft. McDowell, so he had made arrangements with Maricopa County to respond for him.

Middleman arrived at the Benson-Colley yard at 8:05 p.m. The alarm on the monitor started beeping at the sheriff's office, but it took the clerk a while to figure out what was going on. Once he silenced the alarm and looked at the monitor, he could see that a pickup truck was parked parallel with the gate, and the gate was open. He dialed the number taped on the console, but the cell switched immediately to voicemail. He left a message to call him as soon as possible.

The clerk zoomed the camera in on the truck and could see that it was a Chevy Avalanche. It was light colored, but he couldn't really get the color because the lot lights made the truck look yellow. The driver walked to the toolbox and returned with an armload of packages. As he approached the truck, the clerk zoomed in and got a fairly good image of a shaggy-looking cowboy with a huge mustache. He captured that shot as a still photo.

The subject locked the gate, put the packages in the backseat, and backed around the side of the fence and went out toward the north. The clerk was hoping he could capture the license plate when the car got past the city water tanks and turned east, but there was too much brush, and the Avalanche disappeared from sight. He called deputy Tomkins again.

Dan was just stepping out of the shower when he heard his phone ring. He grabbed the towel, dried his hands, and answered his phone. The clerk explained what happened.

Dan called the Maricopa sheriff's office, asked them to put out a *be on the lookout* on a late model Chevrolet Avalanche pickup with silver paint. "The driver is armed and dangerous. The vehicle is probably on Highway 87 in the vicinity of Ft. McDowell, Fountain Hills, and the Salt River Reservation."

The sheriff had two patrol cars in the area and both checked Highway 87—one to the Verde River and the other to Country Club and the 202—but the suspect was not found.

Since the guy operated from this area and Safford, Dan decided there was a good chance he would head to Superior. Dan asked the clerk for the time that the suspect was first seen on the monitor and figured the truck could be to Superior in as soon as half an hour. Dan waited for him at the west side of town. He alerted the deputy on duty in Superior and told him to listen for a backup call explaining what it was about. Dan waited, watching traffic for two hours, before finally giving up.

Middleman, without knowing he was being watched had, by sheer luck, eluded the police. Instead of heading to the freeway system, he went east on Highway 87 to meet with a potential accomplice who was working a small dig near Rye Creek. By the time Dan called the MCSO, Middleman was already west of the Verde River.

Middleman decided the guy was too unstable to deal with; counting it as a wasted trip he decided to go all the way to Safford. He traveled to Globe then on to the lab outside of Safford. He arrived near midnight, where he cataloged his new items and spent the night. He left the next morning in time to get to work by ten.

~

Pat picked Jessica up for the appointment at the salon. Pat's apprehension increased once they were there, as she looked at the strange goings-on with the six other women in the place.

When Jessica made the appointment, she explained the situation in detail to her hairdresser, Sylvia, so she had time to form some ideas as to how she could make Pat's "cop cut" look feminine.

As Sylvia studied Pat's hair, she made conversation hoping to ease the obvious tension Pat was feeling. Sylvia was amazed at how blemish-free and healthy Pat's skin was.

As she brushed Pat's hair this way and that, she said, "You have really nice skin. What do you use on it?"

"Not much," Pat answered. "I wash it morning and night with Ivory soap and warm water, and before I go out in the morning I use Bert's Bees to keep it from drying. I'm outside a lot."

"Burt's Bees. I've seen that," Sylvia said. "What's the lotion called?"

"They call it 'Day Lotion.' It has SPF sun protection plus moisturizers. I also use their beeswax lip balm, so my lips never crack anymore."

"Jessica says you work at the Sheriff's office with her, but she spends all day inside."

"I'm a patrol deputy, so I'm either in my car or outside for pretty much the full shift. I wear a cap or hat all the time too."

"Wow!" Sylvia said. "So are you out writing tickets and arresting bad guys all day?"

"Yeah, just like all the other deputies. I'm the only female deputy on the force right now."

Jessica returned from getting her hair washed and heard the last part of the conversation. "Pat is one of our best officers, and she is a fill-in supervisor. You remember the big drug fight out at Aravaipa last year?"

"Yes."

"Pat responded on that call. Fortunately, the druggies had knocked each other off, so none of the officers had to use their weapons, but Pat was put in charge of guarding several million dollars' worth of cocaine. She's the real deal."

Sylvia smiled at Pat. "That's just so cool!"

Sylvia said, "Okay, Pat. "Here's what I think will work well with your hair. I'm going to make a high part with some of the longer hair layering over the shorter, and most of the long hair will be kind of layered and sloping forward and down on the right side. You'll have some light bangs on the right side of your forehead, and I'll make some little curls along the sides of your face. I've got a picture here that is similar to what I recommend. What do you think?"

Pat thought it wasn't bad, but instead of answering, she asked Jessica, "What do you think?"

"It looks kind of like a pixie cut; I think it will be really cute."

Sylvia added, "And you will be able to maintain this style for several months as your hair grows out. Then we can keep it or change it to any way you like. A hat won't mess it up, and it won't take much to whip it into shape in the morning."

"Yes. Let's take the plunge."

Sylvia made a snip here and there and used texturing shears to thin a few places. She styled the ends to flip in little swirls that framed Pat's face and finished with a light spray of hairspray. Then she spun the chair to face the mirror and held a hand mirror to show the back, saying, "Ta da!"

Pat turned her head from side to side. "Oh, that looks really nice! Thanks."

"Now for the cosmetics." Sylvia said, "You don't need foundation . . . your skin is perfect . . . just a little blush, some brow shaping, a nice lipstick, and some emphasis on your pretty eyes."

The touch of makeup was light, but had a powerful effect.

Jessica exclaimed, "Holy moly! You are gorgeous!"

They went to Jessica's house, where Jessica helped Pat get dressed and bejeweled. She worked with her on walking in her high heels and told her, "Now you have to work on walking like a lady. You're not thinking about taking down a bad guy, but of relaxing with friends.

"Keep your back straight, shoulders back and neck aligned with spine, but try to stay relaxed. Let your shoulder swing slightly, and let your hips gently sway. When you step, start in you solar plexus, take shorter steps . . . not too fast . . . but gently flowing, as one leg moves forward, the other bending back. And smile!"

Pat said, "You know I feel quite awkward. I'm afraid I'm going to look a fool."

"You're doing great! Just practice walking in these shoes between now and when we meet at the church. Be positive, happy. When your date picks you up, it's time to forget about you and think of what you like about him and the people you are with. Your self-doubt will go away."

Jessica's husband Rob came home from work but did not recognize Pat.

"This is my friend Patricia," Jessica said.

"Nice to meet you, Patricia."

Pat cracked up. "You really don't recognize me, do you?"

Jessica said, "This is Deputy Haley, in her civvies."

"Man! I thought you were cute, but had no idea you were this pretty. You should do this more often."

"All right, Bucko, curb your enthusiasm." Jessica laughed. "We've only got an hour and a half, so go take a cold shower and get your suit on."

Pat headed home, where she spent most of the time prior to Andy's arrival walking around her apartment in heels. She even went outside to practice going up and down stairs. She was surprised at the reaction she got from the men she passed. She usually drew little notice, but not today. It was strange and a bit disconcerting, but kind of fun too.

Pat opened the door for Andy. He stammered a bit. "You are beautiful. I'm afraid I'm completely outclassed here."

"So you don't think I look silly?"

"Geez. No. You are terrific.

"I really like your tie—a good match to my dress, wouldn't you say?"

~

For Manny Sanchez, the last few days before his wedding were almost a blur. With Tommy and Elena home for the wedding, he tried to visit and catch up on their lives as much as possible. The same was true for Mariana and her fiance Antonio, and their host Emilio. It was difficult to find adequate time to visit. Between family dinners and events, necessary last minute tasks and details, the rehearsal and rehearsal dinner, and the afternoon Mass, Manny found himself running from one place to another. He barely arrived at the church on time.

Manny and Jenny and the wedding party greeted guests as they arrived. The organist played a prelude medley of their favorite traditional hymns and classical music.

Manny was pleased by the number of fellow officers who came, Sheriff Bitters, Bren, Al Victor, his highway patrolman and game warden friends, and it looked like all the off-duty deputies. Most of the officers were in suits, but a few wore their dress uniforms. The back four rows of the sanctuary soon filled with the officers and non-Catholic attendees.

Manny, like everybody else, was completely stunned by Deputy Haley's appearance. He told her, "You are a great officer, but I had no idea you were such a Babe! Andy, I appreciate you and Pat. It's great to have you both here on our special day."

At the appropriate time, Father Brady gave the signal and the organist played "Jesu, Joy of Man's Desiring." The processional began, led by the ministers and Father Brady. Following in turn were the wedding attendants, the padrinos and madrinas, Tommy (the best man), and Manny with his parents.

Once all were settled in their places, the familiar tune of the "Wedding March" began. Jenny started down the aisle, accompanied by her father and mother. Elena, her maid of honor, controlled the train of Jenny's dress.

It seemed to Manny that Jenny floated down the aisle. *Angels would not look more graceful, but would feel homely beside her,* he thought. He felt his heart pounding, and a hint of tears challenged his manly poise.

Manny had paid close attention in the rehearsal and had gone over his part in great detail, but he felt slightly panicky as though he no longer knew what he was supposed to do. Fortunately for him, Father Brady smiled and tapped the book in his hand with his index finger. Manny relaxed a bit as he remembered that the book was held flat and had "cue cards" that could be seen by the bride and groom.

As Jenny reached the front pew, the two grandmothers met her—one with a white satin kneeling pillow, and one with a bouquet.

Mariana Villalobos sang "Ave Maria," as the grandmothers and Elena escorted the Bride to the niche with a statue of Mary.

One grandmother placed the kneeling pillow, the other took Jenny's bridal bouquet and handed her the offering bouquet. Jenny placed the offering bouquet before the statue and said a short prayer. The grandmothers returned the bridal bouquet to Jenny, accompanied her back to her parents, placed the pillow in front of her chair, and took their seats.

The parents hugged and kissed the bride and groom and took their seats. Jenny and Manny joined hands and sat in the two chairs that were set before the altar, and the priest gave his greeting. Mariana sang "The Song of Ruth," and the parents placed the *Lazo* or lasso, a long double Rosary hung as a sideways figure eight over their necks, symbolically binding them as one.

When the hymn ended, the priest explained that the Lazo represented the love of God and His honoring the couple's covenant before Him to be faithful to each other and to God. The shape of the symbol for infinity was a reminder that the grace of God and the sacrifice of Christ assure eternal life for believers. The priest then recited the Penitential and Gloria, in which Mariana sang, and he offered the invocation.

Mrs. Mondragon read *Ruth* 1:16-17, the text on which the "The Song of Ruth" was based. With Mariana singing lead, the choir sang "On Eagles Wings." Mrs. Sanchez read *Corinthians* 13:1-7.

The choir joined Mariana in singing "Alleluia," and Father Brady read *Matthew* 5:1-12 and gave a brief personal homily relating the example of the couple to the blessings of living a Christian life.

He asked the Padrino de Arras to come forward. Emilio Campos carried a small silver box and handed it to Manny, who passed the open box of coins to Father Brady, who blessed them and handed them back.

Manny placed the thirteen gold coins in Jenny's cupped hands and pledged them to her as a token that all he owned now belonged to her. She pledged to give all that was hers to him and to protect their treasures and care for them as a stewardship to their God. Emilio held the open silver box for her to place the coins and took them to guard until the ceremony was over.

Father Brady asked Manny and Jenny if they each were there of their free will, and they declared their consent to each other. They joined hands and recited in unison the wedding vow, and the priest blessed their marriage. Tommy presented the rings to the priest, who blessed them and presented them to the couple. They placed the rings on each other, in turn dedicating them as a sign of faithful love.

The priest told them they could now kiss for the first time as husband and wife and called for the register to be brought forward. The church register and the marriage license were signed by the couple and their witnesses. Father Brady announced they were the parish's newest family and were recognized as married by God, the church, and the law of the land. The benediction was offered, and the organ played the recessional as the bride and groom exited arm in arm, with Elena again managing the train. They were followed by the wedding party and guests into the church hall for the reception.

Once in the hall, Jenny detached her train and replaced her high heels with comfortable flats. A plentiful assortment of finger foods and refreshments were immediately available, and the dance band started before the guests began to filter in.

The wedding party formed into a receiving line, and the traditional events of the reception moved quickly. The formal pictures were taken as soon as they entered the hall. The professional photographers continued to get both candid and posed shots throughout the evening.

The reception line was finished in about fifteen minutes, and the new couple spent most of their time visiting each table and doing the traditional bouquet and garter toss, cake cutting, and first dance.

The dancing and partying would go on long after the honored couple had departed to start their honeymoon. They thanked the members of their wedding party, hugging and kissing most of them.

They danced a slow dance, then before the music ended, they briskly left the hall followed by their families, who cheered them on their way.

Manny said, "This is already the best day of my life, and we still haven't enjoyed all the wonders yet!"

Their last view as they drove away was of their two sweet abuelas standing arm in arm. With tears in their eyes and smiles on their faces, they waved goodbye.

~

Middleman was happy to have the catalog updated with the new items. As soon as the final bid was in, he would bill Hale for his services. He put the pots on the market early because he knew that he would not be able to do anything with the artifact business this week.

He had two guest lectures at the university and would be conducting a series of sessions at the American Archeological Society Symposium. His series was titled *Working with Dusty Data: Making the Most of Past, Present, and Future Science.*

It pleased him to make prestigious presentations to the body of stuffed shirts who earlier pooh-poohed his research, blocked his doctorate, and denied him a professorship. Now they bought his books, and even lectured their classes out of them. They would scoff at his $65,000 salary, but he earned millions from selling stolen artifacts to these same ninnies.

Middleman often wished he could tell them what he was doing, so they would know they had been fools. That was the one thing that would comfort him if he should ever be caught. Of course the likelihood of that eventuality was slight. His system left no evidence. The secrecy was essential to the success of his scheme, and having to keep his triumph secret was the most unpleasant part.

He had no confidant in his life. He had never trusted anyone enough to share thoughts or feelings with them. The best he could tell, he didn't have normal feelings. People talked about love, but that term made no sense to him. There were a few people he enjoyed talking with because of their intelligence, but he had no actual friends.

Even Sally, who was pretty and provided physical comfort, was not a friend or love interest. It was simply a quid pro quo. She provided some companionship and pleasure, and he paid the most salary the museum allowed and let her do whatever she wished related to work. They would go on a date and spend a few hours together once or twice a week, and she occasionally accompanied him to an event. It was the most human contact he could ever want or need.

The one actual regret he had was killing Jack Hager. Jack had produced the best product of any of those he dealt with. Losing him was like losing a tree that constantly bore good fruit. It also ended for the foreseeable future any chance of finding a source in Mike's company.

Mike Fulton was one of those people that Middleman actually enjoyed talking with—intelligent and witty, and very knowledgeable in the science—but Middleman also considered Mike unnecessarily burdened with concern for people and ethics. For that reason, Mike would never reach his full capabilities. However, at this moment, there were no intelligent conversationalists available. So in lieu of intelligent conversation, he spend the evening exerting his power over Sally.

~

Pat Haley and Andy Lopez enjoyed the Sanchez wedding and reception. They had planned to have a late dinner following the reception, but the little Basque sandwiches, rolled taquitos, spicy sausages, and veggie spears were so good and so plentiful that they replaced the meal. By the time they had cake, polvorones, nuts, candies, and the frozen punch laced with sangria, they didn't need any more food.

They enjoyed the mix of music from the band, and Andy encouraged Pat to dance, but she was hesitant because she had never danced before.

"You've never danced?"

"Well, when I was little Daddy used to dance with me, but it was really just holding me or letting me stand on his feet while he danced. And as a teenager I used to watch the dancing on TV and try to imitate it, but I never really learned to dance."

"That's one thing mom let me do," Andy said. "Along with piano lessons, I took dance. We did a lot of folk dancing and some ballroom stuff, and even a little bit of tumbling and acrobatics. No pressure, but you don't have to really know how. I'll just kind of lead you through it."

"I'm sorry, Andy. I'd be really embarrassed."

"No problem. I'm happy to just be here with you."

Several men, including some of the deputies, asked if she would like to dance, but she declined. After being there a while, and having a few cups of punch, her inhibitions lessened. When *La Marcha Zacatecas* struck up and the wedding party started a grand march, Andy said, "Okay, we have to do this." So they did.

After they completed the last pass under arching arms, the band leader said, "Switch to *la corrido*: the runner," and the band sped up the tempo. Everyone interlocked their arms in a line across the dance floor and, in a trot to the beat the swung forward and backward the length of the floor, sometimes rotating, sometimes weaving. As the tempo increased incrementally, couples began to drop out. Andy and Pat were among the eight couples who lasted to the end, and Pat was having the time of her life.

The music was a mix of classic and popular dance songs and Mariachi standards, and all was very well done. When *Unchained Melody* began Pat said, "Oh, I love this song! Daddy used to dance with me to it."

Andy stood, lifted Pat from the chair by her elbows, and began a slow dance that led through the tables to the crowded dance floor. They ended up as close to cheek to cheek as they could manage with their nearly one foot difference in height. By the time they left the reception, Pat could no longer say she didn't know how to dance, or that she had never had a boyfriend.

They drove to a point that overlooked the valley with the town lights below and the Milky Way above. They visited for about two hours, sitting on the tailgate of Andy's pickup. Andy took her hand. "You are very special to me. I've liked you from the first, including your tough cuteness. I'm amazed at what a classic beauty you are when you decide to show it. I'll never be able to think of you as just one of the deputies again. Something has changed for me tonight." He touched her face, and leaned over and kissed her lips.

Another first for Pat. She was glad it was dark. She felt her face turning red, but she was very happy.

~

Deputy Dan Tomkins went to Detective Espinoza's office at the Pinal County Sheriff's Office. He had asked for a meeting to talk about the upper dig murder. Dan liked and trusted Paul Espinoza and knew he could say what he meant and he would get a straight answer.

They shook hands as Dan entered. Paul opened a little refrigerator, got out two Pepsis and handed one to Dan. "It's kind of rough luck missing getting your pot thief the other night."

"It's more than that. It's about as frustrating as it gets," Dan groused. "But the truth is we already had all the intelligence needed to nail him. We had our murderer in our hands and let him get away."

Paul said, "We don't really even know who our murderer is, only an alias and a vague description . . . and what intelligence are you talking about? The clerk made the first attempt to contact you within five minutes of the suspect showing up. We can't monitor the kid's iPod real time. It gives great evidence, but only after the fact."

"Yes, but we missed a daytime phone call between Middleman and Benson-Colley in which he ordered another theft for that night. If we had a clerk on the monitor during business hours, we could have known about the pick-up six hours ahead of time. It would have been really easy to trap him."

Paul asked, "You're sure that order was made by phone?"

"Yes, we have the recording of the B-C side of the conversation." Dan laid a little recorder on the table. "I got that day's sound recording from the clerk and listened to it last night. This is what I found."

Dan Pushed the play button, which started with the sound of a phone ringing.

"Benson-Colley, this is Oscar."

There was a pause as the caller talked.

Oscar said, "Yes, we have several ready to package anytime you are ready. We'll put two nice ones in tonight."

There was another pause as the caller spoke, then, "Okay, thanks," followed by the beep of a cell phone hanging up.

Oscar then said, "Steve, that was Middleman, he wants two tonight. He specified *nice*, so let's give him the polychrome basin and four-inch pot with the in-and-out painting."

Steve clicked something and spoke. "Elton, come to the office."

Elton answered, "Be right there."

After forty seconds, Elton said, "Hi, Mr. Benson."

"Elton, package up that pretty four-inch pot with painting on the inside and out, and the big shallow pot with the painting inside, and leave them in the box. But wait until the electricians leave before you do it. We don't want anybody to know when we have artifacts, or they might steal them."

"Okay. I'll keep working on the trench until they're gone."

"Good, thanks."

Dan turned off the recorder. "So if we had been monitoring, we could have waited in the brush until he made the pick-up, then nailed him. We would have the head of our theft ring and, no doubt in my mind, the murderer."

"Dan, you are right, but we can't do it. We have to cut hours already. We would have to keep somebody on the monitor for eight or ten hours every day without any assurance as to how long we would have to wait to get another opportunity like this. We do have a few trained temp clerks that work part time as needed, but the Sheriff doesn't have money in the budget to pay them. Is there any chance the antiquities team would pay? It could be a month before anything happens, so we are talking about maybe five-thousand dollars."

"I don't know if they can do that or not."

Paul nodded and said, "It's worth a try. Give the same pitch to Bren Allred you did to me, and explain our budget problem. Use one of the spare workstations here to get hold of him."

Dan found an empty desk and tried Bren's office on the off chance he would be there. He was, and Dan made his proposal, played the tape, and explained the Pinal budget problems.

Bren was encouraging and said he would call Barry Dirocco. "I see you are at the office. If you wait there, I'll call you back as soon as I talk with him."

"Good. It'll let me work on my reports while I wait."

Bren called Barry's cell phone. The attorney would almost always take his call when he saw Bren's caller ID, but his receptionist would rarely connect him when he called the office phone.

"Hello, Sergeant Allred. How can I help you?"

Bren recited the proposal.

Barry thought a minute before responding. "We don't have an unlimited budget either, but this is a really good opportunity. Let me talk to the AG to see if I might tap into some RICO funds."

"That's a good idea, but I have another possibility. I bet Ed Hale would be happy to provide the task force with a five-thousand dollar grant. He would probably appreciate the chance to be part of the solution to the mess he's in."

"Whoa, you're right. That will be a lot faster than my red tape. Let's add Pete Villa to this call."

Pete came on, listened to the proposal, and said, "Our company will be pleased to support you with a grant. In fact, I'll provide a ten-thousand dollar grant to help in any way you chose to use it for the Antiquities Task Force. I'll have a check printed and messenger it to your office today. Do you have some administrative requirements I need to comply with?"

"Yes. I'll send you an e-mail. We occasionally get grants from various museums or archaeological organizations, so we do have forms and a process. As far as the check goes, make it out to Arizona Attorney General Antiquities Task Force, and send it right away. We will have Pinal get some people on the monitor today if possible."

Bren relayed the news to Dan; Dan and Paul told the Sheriff, who had HR arrange for the temps to get started first thing the next day. Dan felt a lot better driving back to Superior than he did on his trip to Florence.

Chapter 14

On Saturday morning following the wedding, Pat Haley called Jessica and asked, "What do I do with my hair and make-up? It's a total mess and so is my pillow."

"Umm, you're supposed to remove your make-up every night before you go to bed. For one thing, you really don't want to get it in your eyes. For another, it's not good for your skin.

"Just brush your hair in the general direction of the cut and it will pretty much fall into place. Rob is working today, so give me a few minutes to put myself together, and I'll be right over. Wash off your makeup, and we'll shop for cosmetics."

Jessica picked up a freshly scrubbed Pat, and they bought the few cosmetics and hair styling things Pat would need. Then they went back to Pat's apartment.

Jessica explained that for everyday use, you don't need to put on all the eye shadow and such. For Pat, mascara, lipstick, and a touch of blush was all she would need. Jessica talked Pat through applying the makeup.

Pat was pleased with what she had done. Then she brought up the other problem that was bothering her. "This is great for my free time, but I don't want to look all that feminine when I'm working."

"On workdays just do exactly what you have always done: wash up, put on your beeswax, slap on your hat, and you are back to no-nonsense Patrolman Pat. When you get home, you can soften the look a bit in time to impress Andy."

"I can do that. Thanks for helping me, Jess."

"You two were darling together last night, and I was impressed with your dancing. It looked like you had a great time."

"I did. I think it was the best time of my entire life. I appreciate you and Rob sharing a table with us. It was a wonderful evening."

~

The newlyweds had fled the wedding in Manny's 1998 white Dodge Stratus, which was wildly decorated; they had anticipate that, so they drove to the Mondragon's house changed their clothes and took Jenny's 2010 Civic, which they had pre-packed.

They had reservations in the Hilton Hotel at US 60 and Alma School in Mesa, and arrived there a few minutes before ten, thinking they would eat in the hotel restaurant. However, the restaurant had been reserved for a high school formal, so they decided to go across the parking lot to the Red Lobster. But it had closed at ten so they ended up eating at a Village Inn down the street on Southern.

It didn't matter that all their plans didn't happen as expected because they were so happy nothing seemed bad. It turned out that the manager was so impressed they were having their wedding dinner in his restaurant, he covered the meal. Everybody applauded and congratulated them as they left. Manny appreciated the good service of the wait staff and the generosity of the manager so he left a very generous tip.

On the drive from Mesa to Oak Creek, Jenny asked about the murder and artifact theft. Manny explained what was going on and told her that the only real clues they had to the murderer were that the suspect drove a silver Chevy Avalanche and was average sized with a lot of dark facial hair.

"He is also a deadly shot with a gun and very dangerous."

"What's an Avalanche?"

"It's a pickup truck . . . kind of a combination of SUV and truck. Or it could be a Honda that looks the same. It has some ugly, sloping plastic work between the bed and the cab."

He also told her that the suspect would most likely be caught the next time he went to Ft. McDowell to pick up artifacts. Then he said, "No more talk about work. We have much better things to think about."

They spent a lot of their honeymoon driving and hiking. After the wedding night at the Hilton, they drove the next day to Sedona. There they spent two days in a wonderful little cabin on Oak Creek. They hiked to Vultec Arch, Bell Rock, and Cathedral rock at Sedona, and waded in the chilly water of the creek.

They spent four days at the Grand Canyon. Manny had booked their stay with the El Tovar at the Grand Canyon, which included one night in a cabin at the Phantom Ranch. The most strenuous hike of the honeymoon was to Phantom Ranch in the bottom of the chasm where they spent the night and then hiked out the next day. They spent their remaining time there using the Canyon shuttle to visit viewpoints and taking it pretty easy. Even as experienced hikers the trek in an out of the Canyon left them sore.

The last two days they stayed at a Hampton Inn in Flagstaff. There they celebrated with some of Jenny's college friends, and while in Flagstaff they hiked through Walnut Canyon National Monument.

For the first time since the marriage, one of Manny's flashes of clarity about a case popped into his mind. As they were returning to their car at Walnut Canyon, Manny suddenly realized what he had missed when looking at the Private Collections file. When he checked the owl pot's card for typing irregularities and differences in tone of the letters, it looked as it should, but he should have checked for letter impressions on the cards.

Typewriters worked by metal letters smacking inked ribbon against the paper. This left an ink letter but also a detectable impression in the paper. If it were a computer forgery, there would be no impressions. The same applied for the signature; if an ink pen was used, there would be no impression. But by the 1960s, people were probably using ball points, which would leave impressions.

He told Jenny what he was thinking. "When we get back to the car, if there's cell service, I'll text Bren about it and tell him I need to go back to the museum again on Monday."

She laughed, saying, "I was wondering how long you could go without falling into police mode. I'm amazed it took six days!"

"Well, I have been preoccupied with other things."

Giving him her most fetching smile, she said, "So what was your favorite part of our honeymoon, Mr. Dudley Doright?"

Deliberately seeming to think about it, he finally said, "I don't know because it's not over. Right now I'd have to say it was all the exploring." She jabbed him in the shoulder.

"I'm talking about exploring you."

"Pretty quick on your feet."

"Yeah, I have a good sense of survival. Besides, you knew it was a stupid question when you asked it."

There was a good signal at the car, so Manny sent his text to Bren.

Bren texted back, "Stop it. You are on your honeymoon."

"Just took a short break. Need to know about Monday."

"Okay, make the visit, but don't think any more until Monday."

Jenny was amused by the exchange.

They headed back the next morning and, instead of taking the interstate, they traveled through Payson and Globe, arriving home at four.

Manny had spent hours detailing the trailer, but they were surprised when they entered. Their mothers had been there. They had replaced all his throw rugs and put in new bedding, linens, and towels. The kitchen cabinets, refrigerator, and freezer were stocked with their favorite things, and their wedding gifts were put away or stacked neatly in a corner of the living room. There were roses by the bedside table and flowers on the dining table and coffee table.

Later when asked, Jenny would say the very best part of their honeymoon was moving into their own little place together. It was the most wonderful feeling.

~

As directed by the AG's office, Pete Villa set up the two dummy buyers on the Hale vendor file. When artifacts were purchased by them, the shipping address would automatically print as soon as Middleman selected the *ship to* icon on the Marketplace.

Shortly after Ed Hale received the notice that the most recent Benson-Colley pots where on the market, he notified Pete who made a bid five hundred dollars higher than minimum on the big pot and bid the minimum on the smaller pot. They monitored the bids. Only one competitor placed a bid, for the smaller pot, one hundred dollars higher than Pete's offer. So he the raised it two hundred higher, which ended the bidding.

The two fake the companies were *Antiquities Preservation Society* and *Collegiate Studies Sourcing*. Each was set up with nice-looking web pages and a phone number to their own phone at the AG's office, as well as a physical address. The shipping address was actually a mail-forwarding center, with the boxes labeled *Suite 1, Suite 2*, etc.

Their web pages said *Antiquities Preservation* provided finding services for member institutions and collectors. Collegiate Sourcing procured lab samples and study items for a wide range of scientific purposes for American colleges and universities.

Normally when the products sold Middleman packaged them with the required documentation and sent them out the day of the sale. With these orders, it took a few days before he actually sent the product; he simply had too much to do.

~

The Pinal County Sheriff's office trained six temps to man the monitor on the Benson-Colley yard from six a.m. to seven p.m, or until the yard closed. They were trained to log the time and a brief description of each event, arrival, departure, phone call, and when possible, the name of the people involved. They were required to immediately notify the sheriff's clerk of any mention of Middleman, pots, pottery, artifacts, or ruins. They were also to alert the sheriff's clerk of the arrival of a Silver Chevrolet Avalanche.

Because of the monotony of their assignment, the temps were limited to one six-hour shift per day. The sheriff's clerk would relieve them for fifteen minutes after three hours, and for a five-minute bathroom break as needed.

Dan Tomkins dropped by the office near the end of the first day's shift and looked through the logs. Nothing pertinent to the investigation had happened, but Dan realized that the logs were valuable because they are effectively an index of the video and audio recordings. The recordings were date and time stamped, so he could pick an event from the log and jump immediately to it on the recordings.

~

During the Antiquities Strike Force conference call, the business was mostly repeating small items of new information so that the team members were all aware of what was happening. There had not been a great deal of progress in the last week, but the outlook was good with the work that Dan was doing on Benson-Colley and Manny's investigation at the museum.

Al Victor said, "I have an update that has nothing to do with the investigation but something I think you will all be glad to hear. I had a conversation with Lester Kenton yesterday, and he is doing well.

"We spoke about Mrs. Hager's medical situation. Her treatment seems to be taking effect, and she is improving. Lester also said the cancer center will bill her insurance for the full amount, and for her not to pay anything to anyone billing her. They said that the center and most of the providers have agreed to write off her share of the costs. Once it is all settled out, she may be billed by a few providers or services, but she's not to pay those either. Her son's employer and an anonymous donor have agreed to pay those. Lester and Mrs. Kenton have really been taking good care of her, and she has a real desire to make it."

"That's great," Attorney Dirocco said. "In our line of work it's good to hear about the good things people do out there. When you spend most of your time in the dark side of society, it's easy to think mankind is a festering pool of greed and hatefulness. This is the kind of perspective we need to add to our normal cynicism."

~

Dan Tomkins was patrolling in the area of Queen Valley, when a call came through from Bren Allred. Dan pulled to the side and picked up the phone.

Bren said, "Dan your monitor on Benson-Colley and bug on Elton is producing great information. Of course the best thing we could get from it will be arresting Middleman, but we don't know when that payoff will come. Keep up the vigilance, and we will jump on Middleman the next time he appears.

"For now I want you to concentrate on building a strong case against B-C. Put together a case history with precise dates and times and significant statements and actions. Merge the same information from the iPod record into the monitor records. Where we have video footage, capture some good stills to include in the case file. That way when the arrest of Middleman happens we can move at the same time on B-C."

"Will do."

"Be sure to also reference specific violations to the law each time they occur. Include the protected species violations as well. We want to hand a ready-for-court file to Barry as soon as the case breaks. Also build the same type of file on anything that relates to the Pinal Murder case. That way we can move much faster and not step on each other."

"I'll start working on it today," Dan said. I'm covering a shift for a sick patrol deputy until four, but I'll start detailing the file as soon as I'm off. I'll include my interviews with Elton and the notes I've already made on the earlier monitor tapes."

~

Mr. and Mrs. Manny Sanchez enjoyed their first weekend in their own home. They rested and relaxed on Saturday, sleeping in until ten. Jenny fried up some of her custom huevos rancheros, which consisted of chopped green chili in scrambled eggs. She served warm toast, and orange juice fresh squeezed from the bottle. Manny never enjoyed a meal more.

They spent almost an hour inspecting their place as Manny explained how to reset the electrical breakers, open the barn doors and the various gates, start and stop the well pump, and check the water-treatment system. He explained that for the most part, the well and treatment systems were automatic and needed no attention. They walked about a mile up the wash that ran past the back of the property, flushing out quail, doves, rabbits, and jackrabbits.

Jenny asked, "How come jackrabbits have such long ears and cottontails don't?"

"It's because natural selection allowed the jacks with longer ears to survive better than those with short ears. You know the jackrabbit isn't a rabbit, don't you?"

"Then why is it called 'rabbit'?"

"Just the name its momma gave it maybe," Manny joked as Jenny poked his shoulder. "I suppose it was a case of mistaken identity. Jackrabbits are actually hares. Cottontails are rabbits."

"But still, aren't hares just a different kind of rabbit?"

"Seriously, no. The hare is a different species: Lepus. There are some big differences. Hares are born ready to go. It takes them about an hour to be able to live independently. Rabbits are born hairless, blind, and immobile and are not capable of being weaned for weeks. Hares have large, strong back legs and are bigger than rabbits. Rabbits live in colonies, and most rabbits burrow in the ground. Hares are loners and make nests on the ground. Rabbits depend on running down a hole or hiding for survival. Hares are very fast and run from danger. Hares eat bark, twigs, mesquite beans, and cactus. Rabbits like tender vegetables, grass, and shoots."

"Well, now I know."

They took a drive to Turkey Creek, and Manny took her to see the cliff dwellings there. He stopped at Beautiful Land and introduced his bride to Richard and Alf, who was visiting. Jenny was introduced to two more neighbors on the way home. The rest of the day was spent talking, napping, and eating one of the mother's prepared dinners in their refrigerator.

On Sunday they drove in to ten o'clock mass at St. Rose and had lunch with Jenny's parents. After a couple hours visiting, they drove to the Sanchez home where they visited and had dinner. They left at seven thirty. Manny thought about getting the Stratus to drive to Tucson in the morning, but Jenny thought they should just go home together, and he could drive the civic. It would be much better for traveling, and they could go pick up his department car Monday night.

"You know if I do that, you will be stuck out here all day,"

"But you'll be home by two or three, right?"

"True."

"I can use the rest after all the exercise I've had lately. I'll do some reading and just loaf."

Manny and Jenny were up at six thirty. Jenny made some bacon, eggs, and toast while Manny showered and dressed. They ate, kissed good-bye, and Manny headed out to his car. Jenny called out to him, "Be careful! And call me when you get there and when you leave to come home."

"I will. I love you."

"I love you too."

They had been together, mostly alone, for the last twelve days, and they were both somewhat surprised to be feeling some separation anxiety. Jenny immediately started cleaning the kitchen, a task that took her less than thirty minutes. She thought "Now what am I going to do?" She decided to figure out where to put their remaining wedding presents, but that only made her miss Manny more. She sat on the couch, then smiled through dewy eyes when she thought "our couch."

Mom's intuition must have been working because the phone rang, and it was her mother asking if she would like some company since Manny had to go to work. They visited for about an hour, and when the call ended, she thought, "I have my big girl pants on now."

~

Manny tried hard to get himself into professional mode, but thoughts and tantalizing flashes of memory from the last few days kept interfering. He did manage to think through and prioritize the things he wanted to accomplish.

When he parked in the second floor of the parking garage, he called and told Jenny he was heading into the museum and would be there an hour or two. They exchanged routine, but meaningful, pleasantries and he was off.

As he approached the entry way, he thought of one more question to ask Sally or Olga. He hoped it was Olga. On entering the office, he was happy to see Olga was alone again. She explained, "Both Mr. Morra and Sally are in a meeting at the university today."

Manny asked with a smile, "I was wondering if an archive curator drives a Town Car or a Ferrari?"

Olga laughed, "Not even close! Morra drives a pickup truck."

"One of those big black Escalades?"

"Nope, just a truck. It's silver or gray. Nothing fancy."

He saw that Morra's office was open, so he asked, "May I have a look at that trophy in the boss's office?"

"Sure, take a look. When you get through looking, what do you need?"

"I thought of one more thing I would like to check in the Private Collections. Is that okay?"

"No problem. I'll let you in, and you can let yourself out. For once I have work to do. Morra has me working on a presentation for him."

"This will just take a minute." Manny stepped into the office and took a close-up photo that clearly showed the photo and the inscription on the plaque: *Rot-Gut Rupert—First Place Overall competition—Arizona Live Action Cowboy Shooting*.

A chill ran up Manny's spine. He examined the photo on the plaque; it was not much of a leap of logic to conclude Middleman was a cleaned up version of Rot-gut Rupert. He took a close-up photo of the trophy. He was reasonably sure he had identified their suspect.

As he came out of the office, Olga picked up Sally's key and opened the door, saying, "Remember the gloves, keep everything in order, and turn out the lights when you leave."

"Will do. Thanks!"

Manny had gotten four other reference numbers in addition to the one for the owl. He pulled the card for the owl first. There were no key depressions on the card, but those on either side had depressions on the text side and slight raised points on the back side. The same was true for the other four cards; they were all fakes. He removed and threw away the gloves, and turned out the light as he left.

He stopped by Olga's desk and thanked her. She said, "I notice on your ID file that when you first were granted entry to the archive room, Sally failed to note the nature of your business."

"Research on incorporating old sources into modern studies," Manny said and then thought, "Where did that come from?"

Olga typed his answer into her computer and smiled. "Morra would love that. He did a two day seminar on it last week."

"It's a concept I had for a future paper, but it sounds like it may already be over researched. So that information is on my museum ID card?"

"Yes. Everybody who has a card is tracked in the system, and every time a card is used to open a door, it records that. We enter the items you pull to review and the copies you make. It's easy to review what is being used, when, and by whom. For example, I always prop the door from the elevator lobby on this floor open, but if it were closed, you could open it with your card." She laughed again, "Of course in your case, that's the only door on the whole campus your card would open."

"So if you want to know who has been visiting the secure room, you could see that?"

"Yes, for all the good it will do since Sally's card is almost always used."

"I guess if the card were used after hours, you could probably see that?"

"Yes. It shows the door, the date and time, and the individual card information."

"Be careful, Olga. Big Brother is watching . . ."

"That's for sure!"

"Well, I've got to grab a quick bite and get home. I'll see you soon, I'm sure. Thanks for all your help."

The elevator was already on its way up when Manny reached it, so he stepped back to let the occupants exit. The door opened and Sally and Morra stepped out just as Manny place his hand against the door to hold it open. Sally said, "Oh, Manny. Are you leaving? I had hoped we could visit next time you came."

"Yes, I need to be back to Safford this afternoon and need to grab a bite, so have to be on my way."

Morra gave Sally what Manny thought must be his Rot-gut Rupert deadly stare.

Sally said, "Mr. Morra is the archive curator and my manager. This is Manny Sanchez, a student who has been researching here for a few weeks."

"Are you a doctorate student?" Morra asked.

"No, I'm actually a distance-learning undergraduate. I've been doing a paper on comparison of Salado and Hohokam culture. I really appreciate the help your department has been to me. Sally and Olga have been wonderful."

"I'm sure they have. Sally usually gives way more than required of her," he said rather snarkily.

"They were both very helpful. I'm really pleased with the paper."

"Well, I hope your instructor is as pleased."

"Thank you, so do I!" The door started buzzing, so Manny stepped inside. "It was nice meeting you, sir. Maybe next time, Sally."

~

Sally, sensing that Morra was miffed, decided to avoid his wrath. "Excuse me, I need to go to the bathroom."

Morra asked Olga, "What was that Sanchez student doing today?"

"He was only here a short time. Last time he was here, he was looking up Salado Hohokam comparison. Your office was open, and I let him take a photo of that poster. When he came back, he had noticed your gun trophy and wondered if he could look at it, so he did. Then I let him into the Private Collections file."

Morra spluttered, "You what? Why did you let an undergrad into the secure vault?"

"Because his ID is set up for full research rights."

"Who on earth did that?"

"Sally."

"I suppose each time he was researching she was locked in the vault with him for an hour. He looks like someone she would want to help a lot . . . ignorant tramp."

"Sir! I will file a complaint about that slur!"

"Not you. It's Sally. I'm not mad at you. Print the full ID and visitation information on Sanchez right now."

Olga quickly complied and handed the report to Morra.

"When Sally gets through with her convenient bathroom break, tell her to come to my office," Morra half-yelled as he slammed his office door.

Olga thought, "This is out of control. He might kill her." She put her cell phone on video and propped it up to record what was happening through the office windows.

Morra punched in Manny's ASU student ID number, and it confirmed he was enrolled in a distance learning ANTH 321 class. That calmed him a bit. Then he remembered that Manny was interested in the shooting trophy. He called Olga's phone. "Did Sanchez ask any questions about me at all?"

"Not really. He joked that a curator must drive a Town Car, and I said, not really- a pickup truck. That's the only conversation we've had about you."

Sally came in, and Olga said, "Morra has gone nuts and said to send you into his office as soon as you get here."

Sally didn't seem overly perturbed as she let herself into Morra's office, leaving the door slightly ajar. Olga could hear what was being said because there was no effort to speak quietly.

"What were you thinking breaking every rule we have on access to the secure vault? You know it is only for professors, doctoral students, and university-validated specialists. You and maybe I could be fired for that."

"I don't know what you're so excited about. I've taken fifty underclassmen on a 'special' tour of the secure room. Just the same as I've taken you on the exact same tour several times. If you report me for my special tours, I'll report yours as well."

"This is different. During those playtimes you were there the whole time. They didn't access our files. Sanchez has full research rights, the same as a professor. I don't care if you are a whore . . . in fact that's the only reason you work here, but your job description does not have 'stupid' in it."

She lunged toward him across the desk, "You can't talk to me like that!"

He jumped to his feet and slapped her hard enough that she fell back in the chair, her mouth bleeding slightly. "I can do anything I want with you and don't you forget it."

"I didn't give him that access," she whimpered.

"Look at the security screen," he said turning the screen to face her. "Not only does it require your password, but it takes your picture when you create or modify a card. The date, time, your login ID and your picture convict you of creating it."

"I didn't know I did that. I must have hit the wrong checkbox. Besides, he was only in there one time, and I was in there with him the whole time. He didn't touch the files," she lied.

"No, he happened to come back three times, and his access ID told Olga to let him in the room. He has spent a considerable time doing who knows what to the files. We will be lucky if this does not cost us both our jobs."

"I'm sorry. It was just a mistake."

"It sure was. Leave. Go home. I can't stand any more of you today."

"But we have a date tonight."

"It's cancelled. I would just as soon put a slug in your head as touch you. Now get out of her before I lose my temper again."

Sally stormed out without saying a word.

Morra got back on his computer and did a search of Manny Sanchez, Safford, Arizona. Up popped several news stories about Deputy Manual "Manny" Sanchez being involved in detective work. Then it all fell into place for him. *The cop probably got a description of my truck from the survivor at Queen Creek. He now knows I'm a crack shot. He knows I'm an archeologist. He was overly interested in the private collections files. The young punk detective thinks he's about to solve another case.*

Quickly Morra searched property transactions for Manual Sanchez in Graham County and learned that he owned a rural property in a place called Klondyke. He typed the museum address and the street address in Klondyke as the destination and got a map and a satellite image of the route, which he printed out. He unlocked his bottom desk drawer and took out his 1911 Colt. As he stuck it in his jacket pocket, Olga came to his door with the print jobs he requested. He grabbed them and said, "Thanks. I'll be out the rest of the day and may be late tomorrow. I don't think Sally will be here in the morning, so take care of things." Then he practically ran out of the office.

~

Olga had caught a glimpse of Morra putting what might have been a gun in his pocket. He was mad at Sally and had made a threatening statement, but people said things like that all the time when they're upset. She thought and stewed about it and decided that since Morra had threatened Sally, she should warn her.

Sally answered.

"Sally, this is Olga. Morra just took a gun out of his desk and left the office running. You may need to go someplace he can't find you. I heard when he told you that he would just as soon shoot you."

"I'm on the freeway going home. I'll go to my sister's place. He doesn't know about her. Thank you for warning me, Olga. I won't come to the office until we know what's going on."

Morra had left his browser open. Olga could see the map on the screen. She pressed the back icon until it came up with the home address of Manuel Sanchez. On the next screen were the news stories identifying Sanchez as a deputy. She backed through the other screens until she got to one that was an invoice for someone named Middleman for an owl effigy. She remembered the card that Manny looked at.

Was Morra mixed up in some kind of crime? Was Manny investigating him? Morra had taken a print out of the map to Manny's house. She was beginning to panic. If she was wrong, she could cause a lot of trouble over nothing. But if he was going after Manny time was running out. Better to look a fool than let a murder happen. She went back to Manny's ID card file and found a phone number for him. She quickly dialed the number.

Manny was surprised to see the museum on the caller ID.

Olga said, "Manny, I think Morra has gone completely crazy. He got very upset about you visiting the Private Collections and going into his office. He hit Sally and threatened to shoot her. He ordered her to go home. He I think he took a gun out of his desk and left the office running. He printed a computer map to your house in Klondyke. I think he's planning to assassinate you."

"What time did he actually leave the office?"

"At exactly 12:55."

"Does it take him long to get to his car?"

"No. His parking space is right next to the building. He would be on the road before one o'clock."

"Thank you, Olga. Have you warned Sally?"

"Yes. Let me know when things are all right."

"I've got to break speed laws, so later."

Manny called dispatch and Jessica answered. He asked her to get any officers in the Stockman to Pima area to head to his house.

Manny added, "Call Cochise and tell them I'm speeding through north Willcox in a Honda civic, and to not delay me. Then tell Bren that Morra is Middleman, and he's heading for my house and Jenny is there. He's in a late-model silver Chevrolet Avalanche and is armed and extremely dangerous."

~

Manny phoned Jenny and said, "Sweetheart, Middleman is heading to our trailer to assassinate me. I'm about twenty minutes from home, but he is ahead of me. Turn off the lights, make sure everything is locked, and keep your shotgun in your hands. He will think the trailer is empty, so no matter what, do not talk or make noise. I've got the video up and he is not there yet. It's safe to look out the windows. He can't see in through the film. Carefully look out the kitchen window. Do you see anything?"

"Yes, there's a silver pickup stopped in the road by the store. He's just sitting there in the truck."

"Did you do everything I told you?"

"Yes. He's still just sitting there."

"Okay, go sit in the rocking chair and stay there until I come for you. It should be out of everybody's line of fire. Put the video on your tablet, turn off the sound, and you can see what's going on. If bullets begin to hit the house, lie on the floor. If he somehow gets in there, don't say a word . . . just shoot him. Don't hesitate. You will only have a few seconds of surprise to take advantage of."

"Maybe I'll just lie on the floor to begin with and keep my shotgun in my hand. I won't let him get me."

"Okay, but that end of the trailer is the safest. I love you."

"I love you too. Don't let him shoot you, Manny."

"That's my plan. I'll see you when this is over."

Chapter 15

Manny was on fairly rough dirt road in a small car going up to eighty-five miles per hour. He slowed to sixty long enough to call Bren. He told him Jenny was in the north end of the trailer and asked him to tell everyone to avoid firing toward the trailer and not at all toward the north end. Morra had parked his truck with the tailgate backed toward the south end of the trailer.

"I'm going to parallel him to the north," Manny said. "There will only be about thirty yards between us. I'm going to force Morra to have to use the truck body for cover, and I'll use my engine for cover."

Bren said he would advise those responding. Manny hung up, took his handgun and clips from the glove compartment, and covered the remaining distance in five minutes. He had his Glock .45 stuffed in his waist holster and two spare clips in his buttoned shirt pocket. He sped into the driveway and simultaneously hit his brakes, killed the engine, and threw himself across the passenger seat. As he skidded to a halt in a thick cloud of dust, he dived out the passenger door.

Morra could barely make out the shape of the car in the dust, but he accurately put two rounds through the side window where Manny's head would have been and a third in the door post. Manny rested his arms across the hood and fired three rounds where he had seen Morra standing before he was engulfed in the dust. One shot had effect because Morra screamed.

Manny thought, *My only advantage is that Morra has never been a target before.* Manny was careful to stay behind the engine and the wheel. The strategy paid off because Morra tried firing under his truck hoping to hit the legs, but the bullet passed under the car into the desert. Failing that, Morra moved to the back corner of the cab and quickly popped an un-aimed shot in Manny's direction. Manny aimed for that same spot waiting for Morra to try another shot. In the distance they could hear the sound of sirens.

Manny yelled, "Give it up, Morra. It's all over." Morra popped another wild shot toward Manny. Suddenly there was the blast of Jenny's shotgun taking out the kitchen window. Once again Morra screamed. "Don't shoot! I can't fight. Help me!"

Manny dashed across the open ground and made sure Morra's gun was secure. "You won't be doing much of anything with that right hand again."

Jenny was still aiming her shotgun through the window at the downed man.

Manny said to Jenny, "It's all over, sweetheart. Put your gun on the rack and bring me a bunch of my old towels to use as bandages."

Manny tightly rolled a small towel and pressed it into Morra's right arm pit. Morra screamed in pain as the deputy pushed his mangled arm tight against his body.

"You have arterial bleeding. If you want to live to brag about your genius, you better keep the pressure tight. Your left shoulder is a through shot, so I'm stuffing a rag in each of the wounds to slow the bleeding."

Looking at Jenny, Manny said, "Wrap his arm and hand tight to slow that bleeding." Then he called Bren again, "The suspect is down and severely wounded. We have arterial bleeding. Is an ambulance on the way?"

"Yes, he's right behind me. I'll let the others know that they can slow down a little but to come on in to help secure the scene and conduct the investigation."

Jenny and Manny tried to stop as much bleeding as possible. Manny picked up a nearby block of wood and placed it under Morra's feet to send the blood to more critical areas. Morra was no longer screaming. He was unconscious, but he was breathing and had a fairly strong pulse.

Bren and the ambulance arrived, and Bren quickly took a few pictures of the general scene and of Morra as he lay.

The EMT's gathered around Morra with their gear. Manny explained the extent of Morra's injuries and said he had a fairly strong pulse and was breathing. They looked at Morra's injuries and said to

Bren, "He might not make it with a two-hour transport. See if we can get a chopper here in less time."

Al Victor of the San Carlos Police arrived with Deputy Pat Haley just behind him. Some of the neighbors were starting to show up, so Al and Pat set out some cones and strung some crime tape.

A Native Air Helicopter had just delivered an accident patient to Mt. Graham Hospital and could be at Klondyke in less than thirty minutes. It was able to set down thirty yards from the scene. The EMT's provided carbons of their notes and advised the air nurse as to what they had observed and done. They said to tell the doctor that he was shot by a shotgun through a window, so there are fragments of glass as well as No. 1 shot.

Morra was loaded into the helicopter and made it to the hospital alive. He underwent a two-hour surgery just to repair the arteries and veins and remove the pellets and glass. He would need many surgeries to save some of his hand.

A Cochise county deputy and Game Warden Matt Vukovich kept the lookyloos at bay. Klondyke was remote enough that the crowd ended up mostly being residents of the area, and a good number of them were members of the sheriff reserve, so the crowd was made up largely of people who wanted to and could help if needed. Several reservists relieved Al and Pat of traffic and crowd control, so they could help with the investigation.

Bren told Manny and Jenny to go shower and change clothes as quickly as they could, so they could give their statements. "Which means no showering together," he said, "or you two will never get back out here in time!"

It seemed incredibly funny to Jenny. Manny was glad. Jenny was starting to look a little shocky, and the laughter broke the tension.

~

Deputy Pat Haley had recently certified as a crime scene investigator. Bren assigned her to help him mark and sketch the scene, tag, bag, and get photos of the placement of the various bits of evidence.

He asked Al Victor if he would handle the interviews with Manny and Jenny, so it would have the credence of an outside agency. Al agreed.

Manny came out and said, "We are all cleaned up now."

Bren told him, "Good. Al will be coming in to process the scene on the interior, and then he will take an official statement from the two of you. Stay inside with Jenny. We almost have the outside scene work done."

Manny did as instructed. He sat on the couch holding Jenny close. She laid her head on his shoulder and felt safe in his arms. Manny still could not shake the fear he had felt for her for the last hour.

Al told Bren, "Be sure to check the tire tracks on the truck. The suspect truck at Queen Creek had a mud knob missing on the inside of the right rear tire."

Pat said, "He backed in to where he's parked, so it's hard to see the track. If we are through with the truck, I can pull it forward a few feet and we should have a clear track in this dust."

"Good idea," Al said as he went into the trailer.

He told the waiting couple, "I'll get your statement in a couple of minutes. He took a broad shot of the kitchen, dropped a marker by the expended shell, and took a close up. He put a marker on the window sill and took a shot of the blown out window pane, then took a shot of the shotgun in the rack. He bagged some glass fragments and the shell. He removed the remaining ammo from the shotgun and tagged it.

He sat in the rocking chair near the couch the couple was cuddled up on. He asked, "Is it okay if I take your statements now?"

The both nodded yes.

"Okay, I'm not going to separate you. Manny, when I'm interviewing Jenny, don't say anything, don't correct anything, don't agree. It is to be her statement to the best of her recollection. And Jenny, the same for you; say nothing during Manny's interview. If there's any confusion, we can straighten that out later. Both of you be as accurate and complete as you can be."

He started with Jenny and recorded the interview on a small digital recorder. After giving date, time, location, purpose, and his identification, he asked Jenny to give her full name and then to recount the events from the first moment she knew there was a problem.

"I'm Jenny Lynn Mondragon Sanchez. I was at home when I received a call from my husband, Deputy Manny Sanchez. He had learned a suspect called Middleman was on his way to our house to assassinate him.

"He told me to turn out the lights and make sure the house was locked; to get my shotgun and keep it in hand; to pretend that I'm not home; and to make no sound and wait in the north end of the living room. But first he had me look out the kitchen window to see if anyone was there. A silver pickup truck was sitting in the road, apparently looking at the house. He told me to put the security video on my tablet so I could see what was happening outside and to go back to the north end to be out of the line of fire, which I did.

"The truck backed in near the trailer so it was facing the road. The driver got out, carrying a pistol in his hand, and tried the door. Then he walked around back and tried that one. He went back to his truck and stood by the passenger door, still with the gun in his hand.

"I could hear the sound of a car coming down the road very fast, and I could hear it slam on the brakes and skid. Then I saw my Honda with Manny driving skidding into view, but it looked like no one was in it. Then Middleman fired some shots at the car, but the cloud of dust so thick you could no longer see the car. As the dust slowly began to clear, I could see the car door on the passenger side was open and Manny was ducked down by the side of the car.

"Middleman fired some more shots, and I was afraid for Manny because Middleman is an expert shooter. Manny fired three shots, and one hit Middleman in the shoulder. He yelled and fell, but he got up and started firing the gun toward Manny. I crept to the kitchen window and saw him trying to take careful aim at Manny again, so I aimed the gun and shot. The gun disappeared from his hand, and he fell to the ground screaming, but I kept the gun aimed him in case he was faking. Then Manny ran over and moved the dropped gun. He told me to put my gun on the rack and bring towels, so I did. I helped Manny try to stop the bleeding. It was awful."

Then it was Manny's turn for a statement. He started by recounting the undercover work he had done at the museum and what he had found out. He told about the phone call from Olga and his calls to dispatch, Bren, and Jenny. He explained his strategy for creating a dust cloud to give him a chance to get out of the car and of ending up parallel and slightly behind the suspect's truck. He used the engine as a shield. The suspect would be forced to use the body of his truck. The placement of the car would keep all fire away from the house."

He said, "I figure the only reason I wasn't shot driving up was the unexpected high speed and dust, plus I was already lying down before I left the road. Once it turned into a gunfight, I think Morra, Middleman's real name, was rattled. He had never shot at anyone who could defend himself. So for a short time I had the advantage and took my shots. One hit him. I think after that he realized the gravity of the situation and determined to stop firing wild shots. In other words, I was then in trouble. No doubt in my mind, Jenny saved my life."

Al shut off the recorder and said, "Manny, would you download the security video for me?"

Manny loaded the video from both cameras onto a USB drive and handed it to Al. "They are time stamped and are marked front and back. The only thing on the back video will be Morra trying the back door and my cloud of dust floating away."

The officers working outside stowed their evidence and equipment, picked up their markers, cones, tape, and trash. They scooped up the bloodied ground and broken glass and covered the site of the shooting with a layer of gravel from beside the road. They removed the two broken windows and cleaned the broken glass out of Jenny's car.

Bren told Manny, "Call the window guys and get the kitchen window replaced. Also the car had both front windows shot out and bullet hole in the door post. Since you used a personal car for undercover work and the attack was provoked by that work, the sheriff's office will reimburse you for the repairs.

"Also, as you know Manny, you are required by policy to see our trauma counselor before you can resume normal duties. I suggest that both you and Jenny go see Melinda as soon as possible. I'll send the event report to her this afternoon."

Bren asked Al and Pat to meet at his office in an hour so they could put the report together. Before he left, Bren sat in his car and sent a text to Dan. *Middleman just tried to murder Manny. Suspect shot and critical at hospital in Safford. Enough evidence for conviction on Queen Creek Murder.*

Working on our report today, will send it to you when finished. Be alert to B-C reaction when the news is out. Maintain monitored surveillance.

~

Manny told Jenny that he needed to set up an appointment to see the counselor as soon as possible and asked Jenny to see her too.

"Of course I will, but I really think I'm all right."

"Then I'll call and set it up. You may be surprised how this will come back when you are least expecting it. I still have nightmares about shooting the drug hit man and that was well over a year ago." He called Melinda Curtis, a clinical psychologist who, in addition to teaching and counseling for the college, did evaluation and counseling for the local police agencies.

Melinda scheduled them the next day at ten o'clock and agreed that when they came, she would see them together for an initial visit and then visit with them separately. Since they lived so far, she would schedule their future individual appoints in adjacent time slots.

Manny called Olga at the museum to let her know the danger was over. She picked the phone up on the first ring. Manny identified himself and said, "You can let Sally know that Morra is under arrest and in the hospital with gunshot wounds. He tried to murder me but was badly injured in the gunfight. He's under arrest for attempted murder, and other unrelated charges are pending."

Olga asked, "Were you hurt?"

"No. Thanks to your warning, I wasn't surprised. I wounded him, but he was still shooting at me when a third party shot him. That ended the fight. Because of the on-going investigation, I can't tell you anymore. I just want to thank you for what you did. It would have been a very different ending without your warning."

Next he called the dealer in Safford. They asked him to bring the car and leave in their lot overnight and they should be able to get it repaired the next day.

He called the glass company and a young man arrived about two hours later. He replaced it in ten minutes.

They decided to leave right away to take the car to the dealer, then pick up the Stratus at the sheriff's parking lot, go eat and explain to their families what had happened before they hear it on the news. They called their parents and asked them to meet them at La Casita in Thatcher for Mexican food. After they accepted, Dan called the restaurant and reserved a table for six.

Jenny said, "I think you should just give them the short version of what happened without too many details. I might get emotional if I try to tell them. They will be upset, so try to soften it as much as possible."

The Mondragons were waiting in their car. Manny and Jenny got out and hugged them. The Sanchezes drove up and the greetings were repeated.

The waitress took them to their table in the back of the room. "We will try to keep the tables next to you empty if we can to give you privacy. If we get busy, we won't be able to."

As the waitress walked past Mr. Sanchez, he covertly slipped his credit card to her and whispered, "No matter what, don't make separate bills, and once the meal is completed, don't bring the bill. Just ring it up on my card and add a 20 percent tip."

She smiled and nodded, "Sure."

The server brought chips and salsa and drinks, along with a green chili cheese crisp appetizer.

Manny said, "We wanted to tell you about a disturbing thing that happened today before you hear about it on the news. As you can see, we are perfectly okay—thanks in no small part to Jenny."

"There was an attempt on my life this afternoon."

The parents were shocked, and Mrs. Sanchez demanded, "What happened?"

Manny continued, "A suspect in a case I'm working on planned to ambush me at my house when I got home. Fortunately, one of his associates caught on and called to warn me. I called Jenny, and she secured the house and hid inside with her new shotgun in hand. Thank goodness we had the strong doors and reflective windows installed, so he couldn't get in and couldn't see inside."

Manny related an abbreviated version of the event, then taking Jenny's hand said,

"Jenny literally saved my life."

There was stunned silence.

Manny said, "Jenny wanted me to tell you in a way that wouldn't upset you. Looks like I messed that up pretty bad."

Jenny laughed and said, "Well, I guess there was no way to sugarcoat it."

Mr. Mondragon said, "Was the guy from around here?"

"No, he's from Tucson. We were investigating him in connection with a theft and murder at an Indian ruin near Superior. This attack was pretty much a confirmation that he is the murderer."

Mrs. Sanchez said, "And we thought you went way overboard on the security and firearms training. Boy, it was really worth it. Thank dear God you were both protected."

Jenny said, "I want to change the subject. We don't want anybody to forget how wonderful the last two weeks have been. We love all the nice things, food and goodies that you put in our place."

For the rest of the evening, they talked about the wedding, reception, honeymoon, and what they were planning to do with their yard. There was a bit of a stir when they found out Mr. Sanchez had paid the bill, but it was a pleasant stir since all had wanted to pay. Things felt normal by the time they parted to head back home.

~

Sergeants Allred and Victor and Deputy Haley met in the office Bren used for his administrative duties. The office was in a closed store in the community of Central and had the advantage of being a few hundred feet from Bren's home. The owner donated use of the space to the sheriff.

They first looked at the scene sketches, the placement of the two vehicles involved, the skid marks in the gravel, and the shots that could be accounted for by bullet hits versus the shots that were fired. Assuming both pistols were fully loaded and counting the shells, Morra fired six shots from a Colt 1911 .45, Manny fired three rounds from his Glock G21, and Jenny fired one round with the shotgun.

Al said, "Morra's not such a crack shot when the target is shooting back."

Bren agreed, "Yes, thankfully. We can account for all three of Manny's shots: one in Morra's shoulder, one passed through the truck's back window and the right rear window and into the desert to the south, and one penetrated the back wall of the truck and embedded in the frame of the right rear door. Three of Morra's shots made contact with the car, and three went into the desert to the north. Jenny's one shot disabled the suspect."

Pat said with some satisfaction, "Good guys two, bad guy zero."

Bren continued, "Manny had a good strategy and executed it well. The way I see it, the evidence fully supports the interviews. How do you feel?"

Pat nodded agreement.

Al said, "Absolutely."

"Good. Now let's watch the video. First, we'll watch both cameras on split screen and then watch the front one full screen."

The total length of the action from the time Morra arrived until Bren and the ambulance arrived was twenty-two minutes. The video caught all the action, but it was still so clouded by dust that they could barely make out Manny's three shots.

The video, the statements, and the physical evidence were in agreement. They compiled it all into a detailed report and signed it.

Bren asked Al to provide an outside opinion of the justification of the shooting by the officer, the performance of the officer, and whether any departmental discipline or criminal charges were appropriate.

Al provided a signed letter that identified the date, case, and officer involved. It read:

Deputy Sanchez exercised good judgment, skill, and valor in responding to a serious attempt by the suspect to murder the officer, and potentially others. He alerted dispatch and his sergeant, and then with the knowledge that help would not arrive in the needed time, improvised a plan of action that was bold and effective. He made great effort to reduce the chance of injury to the public or to property.

His use of deadly force came only after he was fired upon by the suspect, and his response was per department guidelines and skillfully executed, wounding the suspect in the shoulder in spite of the fact the suspect was taking cover. The suspect continued to brandish the gun, and a citizen seeing the deputy was in danger, fired on the suspect. Deputy Sanchez secured the area after the suspect was down and enlisted the help of the citizen, undoubtedly saving the life of the badly-wounded suspect. All actions by the Deputy were professional and commendable.

Bren said, "Thanks, Al. I appreciate your responding and helping with the investigation; and especially with your analysis of the shooting incident. Now as soon as I get this tied up, we need to compile the new evidence against Morra in the Hager murder and artifact theft. Deputy Haley, I know that you are only directly involved with the tire track identification, but I'd like you to participate with us in this next phase as well, if you don't mind."

"Thanks," she said. "I think it will be very valuable to me."

"You did a great job on your first crime scene investigation, got everything right."

Bren placed the letter in the file along with a list of officers who responded and gave assistance. Later he would recommend to the sheriff that letters of thanks be sent to the assisting agencies and letters of commendation be given to Manny, Jenny, Al, Pat, and Olga Jordan for their actions. He scanned the report and e-mailed it to Sheriff Bitters. Then he turned his attention to the work of the Antiquities Task Force.

"Al, Deputy Haley confirmed the missing mud nob on the right rear tire of Morra's truck."

"Good," Al said. "That puts him at the dig when the murder was committed. We can put the two photos side by side for our Queen Creek report."

Bren said, "I also found an extra .45 shell in the back of Morra's truck. Since we have accounted for all his ejected shells at today's scene, this is likely the shell from the Kenton shooting. I'll have ballistics compare it to the gun from the Hager case as well as the ones from our shooting scene."

Pat asked, "So if it matches our scene, it wouldn't be from the Queen Creek shootings, but if it does not match the gun Morra was using today, it will strengthen the value of a match from Hager, right?"

"Exactly; we know the murder weapon because it was left at the scene, so if the shell is from that gun it's supportive evidence linking Morra to the Queen Creek case. By itself, it could be argued that it got in the truck earlier when Morra was doing some recreational plunking. But even then it still links Morra's truck to the murder weapon.

"Shell marking profiles are not as accurately distinctive as slug profiles. If two guns have exact firing pins, chamber placement, and mechanical marks, they can't be distinguished one from the other. But we are comparing a Colt to a Glock; it will give a distinct Glock characteristic."

Bren moved to the next subject. "This morning Manny was working undercover at the state museum archives in Tucson. He figured out that Morra was printing very convincing registration cards listing stolen items as coming from legitimate private collections years ago. We will now be able to find the forged cards and remove them from the files. Hopefully, we will find the computer program Morra was using to produce them."

Next Bren showed the photos of the trophy plaque and told how Manny discovered it. He pointed to the close-up picture and said, "This greatly resembles a hairy and unkempt version of the descriptions given of "Dr. Middleman." He combed the wig neatly, shaved, and wore a more dignified mustache, but it's the same guy."

Bren then explained what set Morra into his murderous rage that morning. Bren added, "Olga Jordan called and warned Manny or he would probably be dead now; and maybe Jenny as well.

"We need to look into the questionable relationship between Morra and his assistant curator Sally Gaona. Her pay seems unusually high, and she gets special treatment from Morra. It may only be a case of workplace sexual accommodation, which isn't our concern, but it could be she is an accomplice in the artifact fraud.

"Because of the possibility that evidence could be removed, Dirocco ordered security to rekey the card to Morra's office door and the door to the archive vault. They will keep a guard overnight and until we arrive."

Bren finished with assignments. "Al, would you wrap this new stuff up in a report and send it to all members of the Task Force? Also tomorrow we will go to Tucson and interview the clerk and assistant and search Morra's office and home. Will that work for you, Al?"

"Yes." Al replied. "Chief Walker said I'm to make myself available anytime needed. He will be thrilled that we have Lester's attacker."

"I'll write a separate report with these new items as they relate to the Queen Creek murder and send that to Dan Tomkins and our sheriff. I've already gotten hold of Dirocco, and he has requested a search warrant issued from Graham Court first thing tomorrow. Let's meet at the sheriff's office at eight, and we'll pick up the warrant and head for Tucson. Manny will not be able to work until he gets a psych evaluation, so the sheriff gave permission to borrow you, Deputy Haley. Can you come with us to help?"

"Wow. I mean, yes sir. I'll be pleased with that assignment."

"I have requested Deputy Tomkins of Pinal to join us in Tucson, but he hasn't been authorized to do so yet. Hopefully, we can have teams of two for the interviews."

~

Deputy Haley and Deputy Lopez were now seeing each other two or three times a week and exchanging phone calls and text messages frequently. Neither of them had used the word "dating" in describing their relationship, though in reality that's exactly what they were doing. And neither of them would actually call it a relationship, though in reality it was a very meaningful relationship to both of them.

There was definitely romance but not admittedly. When they talked about each other, whether to others or between themselves, they used the term "friends." It was not inaccurate because they had a close friendship in the classic sense. They enjoyed each other's company no matter what the mood, they considered the other a confidant, they enjoyed each other's wit and intelligence, and they understood each other in a way that nobody else ever had.

Physically, they usually held hands when they walked together, embraced often, and even kissed goodnight in private. They were content to keep that part of the relationship at status quo until they felt less awkward about the concept of being together.

Pat stopped by the office to say hello to Jessica, mainly because she wanted to tell her about being invited to the Tucson investigation.

Jessica said, "Well, aren't you looking chipper . . . must be seeing Andy tonight."

"Well, yes I am. We're having dinner tonight."

"That's great. Now you kids behave yourselves."

"We are always prim and proper and very comfortable together. I've also got some good news about work. Bren assigned me to investigate the scene of Manny's gunfight today, and he said I did a good job. But the best part is that he asked for me to sub for Manny on the antiquities team when they execute the search warrant and interview witnesses tomorrow. Manny is off duty until he gets his psych clearance."

"Congratulations! That is so cool," Jessica gushed. "You just barely completed your certification, and you're already doing probably the biggest investigation of the year. Tell me, is it true that cute little Jenny shot the bad guy?"

"Yep. She turned his right hand and arm into hamburger with a twelve-gauge. Manny had wounded him, but Morra was still shooting, so Jenny just shot right through the window glass. The perp never knew it was coming."

"Amazing. I am woman, hear me roar."

Laughing, Pat headed out with, "Gotta go get my girlie on for dinner, but I just wanted to share my good news with you."

"Thanks for telling me. Give Andy a big kiss for me," Jessica said, smiling at the flush creeping up Pat's neck and face.

Chapter 16

Deputy Dan Tomkins called Bren to say he was still waiting for permission to go with the team to Tucson, so he might be a little late. Bren called Amy, the Pinal sheriff's administrative assistant. He explained the request for Dan.

Amy said, "I'm sure the Deputy will be allowed to go. The problem has been that both the sheriff and Detective Espinoza have been beset with meetings with feds in Phoenix concerning our illegal alien situation. I have been trying to reach the sheriff with no luck. I'll try the detective."

"I understand. Tell Deputy Tomkins we expect to be there around eleven o'clock. We have to pick up the court orders before we can leave. He may not be able to reach us in route because there are dead zones along I-10. Tell him just to head to the museum."

The court orders were ready when Bren walked into the clerk's office. They were driving south on US 191 by eight thirty. As they drove, Bren explained his plans for the day.

"We will take care of the tasks at the museum first and search Morra's house after that. When we arrive we will get a quick orientation of the office, then I'll meet with the museum director to explain what we are doing and get a statement from him concerning each of the people in Morra's department. At the same time, Al will meet with the museum HR person to collect the records and discuss them for clarification.

"During this time Pat will get a statement from Sally Gaona of the events of yesterday, starting with when she encountered Manny as she and Morra exited the elevator. When you do that, get a statement from the administrative assistant Olga Jordan of the incident from her perspective. We don't want to interrogate them at this point, just get a witness statement. We will have two officers when we actually interrogate.

"The university police will provide printouts of the access records for the secure room for the last four months and Morra's access records to any part of the Museum during that same period.

"And finally, if we find the need, we will execute a search on Sally Gaona's home as well."

~

The team arrived at the museum at ten past eleven. A young woman in a university police uniform was waiting for them in the lobby, she introduced herself as Officer Sharon Danes and said she was assigned to facilitate Sergeant Allred with whatever the team needed.

Bren introduced the team and said, "We would like to be oriented on the library facility. I understand it is the second floor of this building?"

"Yes." She led them to the elevator and pushed the button.

Pat asked, "Are you a student or full-time officer?"

"I'm a student. I get about twenty hours a week."

The elevator arrived and they stepped in.

Pat said, "I worked for the department all four years I was here. It was a great experience."

Officer Danes asked, "Were you a criminal justice major? That's what I'm in."

"Yes. It's cool you are on the force. It is the perfect lab for the courses. I see you are a certified officer, too; so already on the career track."

They stepped out of the elevator, and Officer Danes explained the layout of the floor, the emergency exits, emergency procedures, and where the fire extinguishers, first aid kits, and defibrillators were located. She explained the access card locks, alarm system, and video cameras in the halls and lobbies. She pointed out the restrooms and drinking fountain and the two small conference rooms that were reserved for them.

At reception she introduced them to Officer Alex Olivas, another student University Policeman. He had provided security for the office and archives since eight that morning and was happy to be relieved of duty.

Olga was the only archive employee in the office. She asked, "Is Manny Sanchez all right? I think it's awful what happened to him. He is such a nice guy."

Bren said, "Yes, he's fine. He would be with us today, but department policy requires an officer involved in a shooting to have a psychological evaluation before they can resume normal duties. So Sally Gaona is not here today?"

"Not here at the moment, but she will be soon. The joke around here is that she runs on Sally time, which is always late. She planned on being here by eleven, and it's eleven-thirty, so she will be here any time now."

Bren said, "Pat will stay here and take Miss Gaona's statement when she arrives, then she will take a statement from you Olga. We will want just a narration of the event as it happened here yesterday. Al and I need to be taken to the director and an HR representative. Pat, you can just visit with Olga a bit until it's Sally time. Maybe it would be helpful to just find out what comprises normal business here."

"When we return to conduct the interrogations and perform the search, we would like to invite you to join us, Officer Danes."

"Thank you. I appreciate that."

Danes led the two sergeants back to the elevator.

Olga said to Deputy Haley, "I'm so sorry about Sally. She can be so frustrating."

"That's not your fault. Don't worry about it. So what normally goes on here?"

"We are a non-circulating library and archive of Arizona and Southwestern archeological and anthropological reference material. People come here to do research for university papers and journal articles, as well as background and historical research. The job of the staff is to take care of the contents and assist the patrons."

"So nothing is ever taken from the premises? All research is actually conducted here?"

"Yes."

"Who are your patrons?"

"The vast majority are students. Probably 90 percent of our service is to students working on papers for a class, thesis, or doctoral dissertation. The next largest group is professors and archeologists doing research for classes, books, or background for fieldwork. The remaining two percent is everyone else."

"So when a student or professor comes in what do you do?"

"Two main things: we assist as a librarian for our open library stacks, and we fetch materials from the archives to be used in the reading room."

"So you help people find books, answer questions, make copies, and make sure the archival material is properly pulled and re-filed. Everybody uses the reading room for this?"

"Yes, typically everybody uses the reading room. However, professors, credentialed professionals, and doctoral candidates are allowed to work in the archive itself—in the secure room or vault—depending on what they are researching."

"So you have a secure room and a vault?"

"No. It's the same place but equally referred to by the staff."

"I see. So that's why Morra was upset? Because Sanchez is just an undergrad?"

"Yes. And that is typical of Sally's work habits. She's a piece of work. She is not a mean person, but she has no concept of propriety or morality. She flirts with everyone, sometimes even the women. She has plenty of dates."

Olga looked toward the lobby. "Here she comes like it's just another day."

They walked to the first conference room and waited for Sally to reach them. Olga introduced Sally to Deputy Haley and returned to her desk.

Conference Room Two contained a small round table, four chairs, a small credenza, and a whiteboard mounted on the wall. The front wall and door were clear glass. Pat stood near a chair with her back to the whiteboard. Sally put her hand on Pat's arm. "Where would you like me to sit?"

"Sit wherever you would like."

Sally slid sideways between the whiteboard and Pat, meaning she pressed and overtly rubbed against her while passing to take the far side chair. Pat felt like punching her.

Pat sat down and waited until Sally was seated. Then in a rather menacing way, she said, "Let's get this straight from the beginning. I don't like girls and I barely like guys. Also I don't mix play with my work. Any questions?"

Sally just had a blank look and said nothing.

"We need a witness statement from you concerning what happened from the time you and Mr. Morra spoke briefly with Manny Sanchez after you got of the elevator. All we need is your chronological narration of what took place between then and your arrival home. I'll be recording this session. Do you have any questions before we start?"

"Am I being accused of a crime?"

"I know of no reason why you would be. Is there something you want to tell me?"

"No, but I don't know why I'm being interrogated."

"You are not being interrogated. If you were, we would have read you your legal rights and told you what crime you are suspected of. You are a witness to what happened immediately before Mr. Morra seems to have gone nuts and attempted to kill Mr. Sanchez. Mr. Morra is the only suspect in that crime.

"We need a clear detailed statement from the only two witnesses as to what might have caused him to react the way he did. We will also get a statement from the other witness, Miss Jordan. So all you have to do is tell what happened in the order it happened as accurately and completely as you can. If I think anything needs clarifying, I'll ask you after you finish you story. I'll make an introductory statement. Then just tell where you had been and what happened once you got off the elevator. Okay?"

She relaxed a bit and said, "Yes."

"I'm starting recording now." Pat placed the digital recorder between them and turned it on. "This is Deputy Patricia Haley. I'm interviewing witness Sally Gaona as to what took place with Mr. Morra in the Arizona State Museum in Tucson yesterday morning. Miss Gaona please describe what you experienced that day."

Sally spoke clearly and the narration flowed smoothly, both signs that she was probably telling the truth. "Mr. Morra and I had been attending a discussion of the museum archives at the university. As we stepped off the elevator, a student, Manny Sanchez, was there and I introduced him to Mr. Morra. We talked only a minute or two, and then Manny got on the elevator. That was the last I saw of Manny."

Sally gave a fairly accurate and complete statement of what had taken place, only omitting a few things that were said about her personal relationship with Morra and about her activities in the secure room with several students.

Sally's statement sounded like what Bren had related, so Pat had no follow-up questions. Pat asked if there was anything else Sally would like to add, but she did not. Pat thanked her for her statement and turned off the recording. She asked Sally if she would send Olga in to give her statement.

Olga came quickly to the room and took a seat. Pat explained the purpose of the interview, made the introductory statement on the tape, and Olga began telling what she saw and heard. It was substantially the same story the Sally had told, without the omissions Sally had made, and with the added information that happened after Sally was gone. Pat had some clarifying questions for Olga.

"You are sure about the part of him accusing her of being immoral, and of her saying he was as well, and about the date that night?

"It was as clear as our conversation is now."

"Were you aware of such activities?"

"To a degree. Mr. Morra had a conversation when he hired me that hinted things could be really good for me, maybe even an assistant curator if we could make a special arrangement. I told him that if he was saying what I thought he was saying, I would file sexual harassment charges. He denied that was his intent and never brought it up again.

"A few months later it was announced that he had hired an assistant, Sally. I confronted him in his office as to why I wasn't promoted. He said Sally's degree was in library science and she had five years' experience as an archivist, while my degree was in business administration. It made sense.

"Over time they started having to work in the vault fairly often. Both of them would be in there an hour or a little less. I started noticing that when a cute student would come around, Sally would get very friendly, pressing against him. Then she and the student would disappear into the archive for an hour or so. She was like a cat in heat.

"Then one day, Sally asked how I would like to join in a threesome with the boss. I told her I would rather throw up on myself."

In spite of her rigid professionalism, that made Pat laugh. She said, "I'm sorry. Please continue."

"That proposal was never mentioned again," Olga said. "So, no, I can't prove anything, but I'm pretty sure. Especially when you add the fact the Sally could come and go as she pleased, missed work all the time, and came in late and left early everyday without a word from Morra about it. I think it's pretty obvious."

Pat asked, "Wasn't it awfully risky for them to 'do their work' in the secure room? What if somebody would come in?"

"There are only two key cards that open the room, Mr. Morra's and Sally's. When they are in there, nobody can get in. It's a fairly rare thing that a patron even requests going in, so not much chance of a conflict anyway. The one time it did happen, I told the professor that the files were closed for an hour for maintenance. Actually 98 percent of the work in the department is done by me. Morra did meetings and presentations all the time, and Sally did what Sally wanted.

"I felt it was terribly unfair to me, but I couldn't make a complaint because there was no hard evidence of anything. It would be my word against my two bosses'. How would that work out?

"Actually, now I do have some evidence. I videoed the whole thing when Morra started raging yesterday "

"I'll need a copy of that."

"I'll give you one right now."

~

Bren met with Museum Director Dr. Philip Lazovich and explained that they were conducting an investigation at the museum stemming from Curator Morra's attempted murder of a Graham County deputy.

Dr. Lazovich was astounded that Morra would become involved in such a thing. "You are absolutely sure that the person you arrested is our curator, James R. Morra?"

"Yes. The deputy identified him, photo IDs, were in his wallet, and the truck he was driving was registered to him."

"Why would he do that?"

"Our deputy was investigating an artifact theft ring. Morra was using his unlimited access to the archival Private Collections Registry to fraudulently certify stolen artifacts as legitimate private property so they could be sold to high-end collectors, institutions, and museums."

Lazovich paled and seemed short of breath. "This is a horrible betrayal of trust. The man who is supposed to be insuring the scholarship and integrity of our accumulated knowledge has destroyed a trust that's taken us one hundred twenty-two years to build."

"There is some good news," Bren said. "But first let me tell you the other bad news—some of which could further damage the museum's reputation. Mr. Morra murdered a field archeologist who was supplying artifacts to him. We suspect the young man witnessed Morra shoot one of the young man's colleagues."

The director said, "This is a man that I have traveled with, sat in hundreds of hours of meetings, and saw on an almost daily basis. I just can't wrap my mind around it."

"We are also investigating Morra's assistant curator as a possible accomplice, though we have only the most tenuous suspicions at this point. Morra could have easily carried out his scheme without assistance. Probably by the end of today we will know if Miss Gaona was involved and whether we will file any charges against her.

"However, my deputy has uncovered some sordid details about the nature of the relationship between Morra and Miss Gaona, which will be of concern to you. It appears that they were not only in an after-hours relationship, but also engaged in such activities in the building during business hours. And she apparently did the same with a number of students. It's likely that Gaona was rewarded at the expense of Olga Jordan. So you have the potential of a harassment charge, lawsuits from both women, a major news scandal."

"That will be a public relations nightmare," the director moaned. "I'll need to put Miss Gaona on paid administrative leave while we conduct an HR investigation. That will deplete our professional staff in the library. We won't be able to deliver service to the university, which is part of our primary mission."

"Let me give you the good news. We will share our findings with you, which will allow you to handle much of this as discretely as possible. If Miss Gaona is not complicit in the criminal activities, we will not include any of the moral or HR issues in our report. They have no bearing on the criminal prosecution, and we will keep it quiet."

"I appreciate that but don't want a cover-up."

"There will be no cover-up. It is not our job to investigate workplace behavior problems. We will give you everything we have, and *we* will not release anything that doesn't have an effect on our case. How you handle it will be your prerogative.

"The deputy also mentioned something that might help a lot with interim operation of the library. Miss Jordan has handled practically the entire operation by herself. I suggest you consider naming her interim curator and providing two temps. The function of the library will probably improve. None of my business, but it might help you.

"Now for the *really* good news; Deputy Sanchez and an archeological researcher have discovered how to identify the fraudulent entries in the Private Collections Archives. I would be willing to allow those two to come down and work with Miss Jordan, and I believe all the fraudulent entries could be removed in less than one week. Having that accomplished would go a long way to restoring credibility.

"I need to get back to my investigation, and you have a lot of thinking to do, but one last thought before I go. I worked in internal affairs at a major police department and investigated a similar situation. It ended up in lawsuits and lots of news coverage and the chief losing his job. He just up and fired the male supervisor and the female willing participant, and left the aggrieved female employee in her job at her current pay. Both of the women filed lawsuits. The aggrieved was awarded back pay for loss of promotions, a nice chunk for emotional distress, and a half-million dollars in punitive damages. The participant won because the department did not protect her from the advances of her supervisor, and she needed the job so felt she was forced to participate. She didn't get her job back, but was awarded her legal costs plus three-hundred thousand dollars. So be careful how you handle both of those women."

"Yikes! Thanks for that. I'll start talking to legal right way about a settlement strategy to see if we can keep it out of court—and papers—altogether."

~

Officer Danes gave Al Victor a business card from Winona Victor, Human Resources Representative, Arizona Department of Administration, and pointed him toward her office. The office number was written on the back of the card. Al was interested in meeting her. It was not too often he met another Victor. Perhaps she was a long-distance cousin.

The office appeared to be a visitor office, and a young black student was the only occupant. Al looked around for an adult, but didn't see one. He hadn't noticed her watching him as he looked at the number written on the back of the card. He backed out and looked at the number above the door.

The woman said, "Sergeant Victor, I presume."

"Yes, are you Winona Victor?"

"Yes."

"Uh, you look much—"

"Darker?"

"Younger than I expected."

"You look not only like a San Carlos Apache Cop, but also like an Apache. Is that right?"

"Yes, ma'am . . . descended from Victorio."

"I figure I'm Zulu, descended from King Mpande."

"Well, I guess we aren't cousins, then."

Laughing, she asked, "What can I help you with, almost-cousin?"

"I have a search warrant asking for all museum and university personnel files on James R. Morra, Sally Gaona, and Olga Jordan. We want to see everything, including employment history, accolades, reprimands, evaluations, and grievances. We also need Morra's post-graduate academic records."

"What have they done that gets so much attention from the law?"

"I'm sorry. Here's your copy of the search warrant."

"Okay, let me see what we have." Winona pulled up their files on her desktop. "The two women have fairly small files, but Mr. Morra's file is large. He's an associate professor and the library curator and has been with the university or museum most of his life. His recent records and evaluations look very good, but when we go back into his teaching assistant and doctoral days, it's not so good. Do we have to print all this, or can you receive it electronically?"

Al handed her a flash drive. "What seems so bad?"

"His doctoral thesis was rejected, and which automatically eliminated him as a potential professor; his stated goal. His doctoral sponsor wrote, among other things, that he suspected Morra to be a sociopath. If you are looking for potential character problems, you found them."

Al thanked Winona for her help and walked back to the director's office, where Bren was still engaged in conversation. Al waited in the reception area with Officer Danes for fifteen minutes until Bren came out. While waiting, Al used his tablet to scan the files, study the notes that Winona had pointed out on Morra, and look at the resumes of the two women.

~

Dan Tomkins arrived at the Museum not really sure where he was supposed to go. He finally found a long, wide sidewalk to the front entry and was hurrying toward it when he heard his name called. He turned to see Bren, Al, and a female university officer walking toward him.

Dan apologized for being late and said he'd left the minute he got the authorization. Bren introduced Officer Danes, and told Dan they had been busy with preliminary things and were about to search the office and start the actual interrogation of witnesses.

When Bren and the officers arrived on the library floor, Pat met them and suggested they meet in the conference room for a few minutes. There were some things they needed to know. They sat at the table and Pat put the drive with Olga's video in the port "The statements I took from the two women this morning are essentially the same and seemed fairly accurate, though I felt Sally was being cautious and perhaps a little evasive. It turns out she omitted some things that touched on her relationship with Morra."

"So you give more credibility to Olga's statement?"

"I do. In fact at the end of her statement she handed me this video that captures most of what went on before Morra seemed to go berserk. I'll play it now."

They watched the tape.

"Wow!" Dan said.

Pat explained, "The tape shows that both of them substantially gave a true report, while Sally carefully edited out the part that shines a light on her activities. I think it clears Olga of any likelihood of knowledge of the crime, and doesn't implicate Sally."

Bren interjected, "One other thing about Sally is she spent a lot more time with Morra than Olga did. They worked closely, attended meetings and traveled together, and socialized. Olga seemed to have strictly a subordinate work relationship with him. Do you see a need to interrogate Olga?"

"No. Her statement was very detailed, and she gave her observations on the relationship of the others. If anything comes up we can just ask her and get a straight answer.

"Before we start the next step, one more thing needs mentioning. I looked at the security access reports. Morra's card shows that in the last four months he went into the "vault" only three times, all during working hours. The door was accessed 122 times by security, each time between 11:49 PM and 12:05 AM, so that is obviously a scheduled nightly check. It was accessed 141 times by Sally's card. Fifteen of those were after hours. When I checked the after-hours entry, neither Olga nor Sally's personal access card was used, but Morra's card accessed the front door within minutes of the secure room access each time."

Bren said, "That's great evidence against Morra, but it doesn't clear Sally. Someone could have been with him. I wonder if we can get the computer log-ins and phone calls for the three desks during those after-hours episodes. Could you check on that, Officer Danes?"

"Both logs are automated programs controlled by the IT department. I can call and get them."

Bren said, "I'd like to interview both women specifically about Morra. I want to know his habits, his friends or close associates, and how much on work he actually did with files.

"Pat and Officer Danes will participate with me as I interview Sally. When we finish that, I'll inform her of her rights, and we will interrogate her. Al and Dan, interview Olga, then search Sally's desk and work area for anything that might link her to artifact theft."

The two interviews specifically focusing on Morra found that neither of the women knew a lot about his personal life or history. Olga did a good job of describing his personality and character. He was brilliantly smart and could be funny and entertaining—even charming—when he wanted, but that was rare.

He was an egoist and vengeful. He would seek to payback even the most minor slight and would go to extremes to embarrass or slander anyone who challenged his statements or judgment.

He did not value people, but saw them only in light of what they could do for him. He valued Olga because she kept the place running and required no direction. He valued Sally because she provided physical comfort and occasional companionship.

They knew of only one person that he considered a friend, a fellow he attended university with named Mike Fulton. Morra had said that Fulton was the best conversationalist he knew and the only archeologist who knew the science as well as himself, but he thought Mike would never amount to much because he was too sentimental and not willing to make the hard decisions that brought success.

Morra enjoyed walking and hiking, liked to eat in good restaurants, and drank moderately. Neither woman had ever seen him inebriated. Morra enjoyed professional platitudes and exposure. The only thing he liked more was his success in the shooting competitions. Sally said that was all he would want to talk about after an event. He had never invited her to any of those competitions.

Sally, as expected, had insights that Olga didn't. Morra didn't really care much about money, but had plenty of it. He bought what he wanted when he wanted, but his material wants were rather modest. He was a good tipper, and in a group he would often pick up the bill. She said he had never had a close relationship with a woman, though he had serial girlfriends. She was his longest female companion.

Sally said Morra became furious and sometimes physical if you disputed what he said. He had hit and shoved her several times until she learned not to challenge him. He was rough and sporadic during intimacy, which didn't really seem important to him.

When Pat asked Sally why she stayed with him, she answered, "The money, the situation at work, and the prestige were really, really good. I made more working for him than the rest of my life combined. He paid me near the top of my grade, $52,000, and gave me great evaluations so that I got good bonuses. Plus I had all the cute guys I could deal with."

Officer Danes asked, "So he never had to force you or coerce you?"

Sally thought about that for a minute. "Not in the way you are thinking. I went to some event with an Anthro grad student who got smashed and passed out. Morra spotted my frustration, hit on me. He called himself Dr. Morra and he was free and easy with his money, so I was duly impressed and let him come home with me.

"Afterward he told me he was going to hire an assistant and asked how much I made. I lied and said twenty-five thousand. He said he could get me nearly double that with benefits and asked if I was interested? Of course, I was. So he laid it on the line: If I would provide benefits to him up to three times a week, he would hire me. So the coercion was get a great job or not. But I agreed to the arrangement without any other threat.

"The coercion came later. When you do something like that, you no longer have any control of your life. The first time he smacked me in the face, I told him I was going to report him. He said my job would disappear along with my professional reputation, so I could never get one like that again. Then he told me that I wouldn't have to worry about another job, because if I betrayed him he would kill me. I knew that he really meant it and that he could do it, so I had to stay and to keep quiet. That's why I was so scared when Olga told me he had a gun. I knew he would do it."

Pat asked, "How many times did he hit you?"

"Early in the relationship he hit me five or six times, but not at all for the last eighteen months . . . until yesterday in his office when he slapped me."

During Sally's interrogation it became clear that she knew nothing about the artifact theft. Al stepped into the room and handed a note to

Bren. It read: *Her work area and computer had nothing remotely related to the crimes. The phone and computer tracking report shows none of the three phones were used when Morra came in late, and the only computer that was logged into was his.*

Bren decided that they would find no evidence against Sally because there was none. He texted Director Lazovich: *No charges for Sally. Info to follow.*

He ended the interview by saying, "I appreciate you being open and honest with us. We will not be charging you, but if something comes up in the course of the investigation, we may reconsider."

Officer Danes took a letter out of her notebook. She handed it to Sally and said, "The museum has placed you on paid administrative leave pending ongoing police and museum investigations. Your pay and benefits will remain unchanged until both investigations are completed and you are given a hearing before the director. Box up your personal belongings, and you'll be escorted to your car."

Officer Dane's observed as Sally put her stuff in two small cardboard boxes, they each took a box and started out of the office. Olga stood and went over to Sally. "I'm sorry you have to go through all of this."

Sally replied, "Thank you. I'm lucky you were here to do the work. I wouldn't have known how." Then she hugged Olga, who said quietly, "You had to know that couldn't last forever and that this day would eventually come."

"Yes, I did, but at least I'm getting out alive."

The phone rang on Olga's desk. Heading to answer the phone, she said, "Good luck."

Director Lazovich was on the phone. He promoted her to assistant curator with a generous increase in pay, starting immediately; and that until a new curator was found she was acting curator. He explained that two temps would report to her the next day, so she could get operations back to normal as quickly as possible.

Chapter 17

A cursory look at Morra's computer provided all the evidence they needed to prove forethought and planning in the attack on Manny. It also provided various documents bearing the alias "Middleman." The trophy proving his expertise in pistol shooting sat on the cabinet.

Strangely enough, there was a diploma on the wall next to his master's degree from Saint Regis University, awarding James R. Morra a PhD in Anthropology with high honors. in 2004. There was nothing about that in his resume. A Google search found that Saint Regis was a fraudulent diploma mill that sold PhDs for $400 and high honors for an additional $100 dollars.

In a box stowed in the right lower desk drawer were a hundred or so business cards for Dr. Robert Middleman, each with a blank space where the phone number could be printed by a computer.

All of these would help build a solid case of attempted first degree murder against Morra and would help convict him for the felony murder of Jack Hager and attempted murder of Lester Kenton.

One key piece was still to be found—the program that printed the fake registry cards. They saw nothing of it on Morra's computer, but thought maybe the State IT Forensics Lab people would yet find it there.

The museum IT guy brought a device for quickly copying hard drives, which he had set up with Olga's new Curator profile and, guided by Olga, copied select files from Morra's drive to the new drive. Once she had all Morra's files she needed, he removed the hard drive from the computer and replaced it with the new drive. Morra's drive was marked as evidence, bagged, and boxed with the other evidence.

As the antiquities team was leaving, a maintenance man brought a new sign in for the office: *Olga Jordan, Acting Curator, Library and Archives*.

~

The team drove to Morra's home in Oro Valley. There they found dozens of shooting trophies on shelves in the living room and garage and took photos as further evidence to his shooting skills. He had several handguns, two rifles, a shotgun, and a good supply of ammo. They had the guns used in the crimes, so they left these to be impounded later.

In Morra's office they found a file folder with copies he had made of his Middleman Consulting invoices and payment records. They took two files of financial, banking, and tax records. He had a card under the base of his computer display with a list of passwords for various applications. They took the computer for analysis by IT Forensics.

By the time they added these new boxes of evidence to the cargo area of the SUV, it was filled to capacity. The box that contained the financial records and password list would not fit, so they strapped it in the passenger seat behind the driver.

Bren said, "Let's head for the office. We might have a long night sorting through this evidence."

Al said, "I'd like to take a look at the financial records while we drive, so I'll sit in the back and Pat can take shotgun."

"So, Pat," Bren said. "Now you have experience with several of the important aspects of investigation: scene preservation and documentation, photography, sketching, preserving, recording, tagging, bagging, and capturing the context . . . interviewing witnesses, interrogation, and gathering non-crime scene evidence. What are your thoughts on your work the last couple of days?"

"I really like it. I can't say it's fun because it's so intense making sure you don't miss something. But it feels good to be doing something that critical.

"It's a lot harder than I thought it would be. I learned so much watching you guys work. It made sense of the stuff I've studied. I truly appreciate the chance to do this. Put me on your mental file as being willing to do this as much as possible."

They were going west on Ina Road to I-10 south, and the rush hour was just getting started, so they were only making about forty miles per hour.

Bren chuckled, "You're hoping for a lot of murder scenes? Just kidding, I know what you mean. When I worked at Mesa I was a homicide detective and this is all I did every day. It gets tough after a while. What I really like about working for the sheriff is we have tremendous variety. We do a little bit of every kind of police work in the book. Times like this make you appreciate the calm quiet days and the calm quiet days make you appreciate the exciting days. The work is different than in a city, but it has its charms."

"That's true. I enjoy the patrols and minor crime too—not so much the drunks and druggies." They were nearing the I-10 and I-19 split and traffic was getting bad, so the conversation dropped off until they got around the bend and past Kino Parkway when the traffic thinned a bit.

Al said, "I just saw something that might be more important than we thought. I don't think two of these passwords are for the museum PC like we thought. I think they both are for different applications on the same computer, and I think that computer is in Ed Hale's anthropology lab in Safford. The first application is Hale Online Marketplace and the other application isn't a UofA personal computer, but an application called U of A Private Collections. Both of the passwords seem to reference their app. For the marketplace, it's "buy and sell," and for the Private Collections it's Doctor Morra number one."

Bren said, "That makes sense. We need to go to that lab and get into that computer. I'm going to pull off and call Pete Villa." He exited at Houghton Road and came to a stop in a wide spot. He found Pete in his directory and hit call.

Bren explained what they were thinking and said, "We are just leaving Tucson, and I understand the lab is somewhere close to Artesia, so we can stop on our way through. Can you give us directions to the lab and could we get into it?"

Pete answered, "No and no. I have been to the lab once but can't tell you how to get there because it's way out in the sticks. It has double security—a key pad and a thumbprint reader, but I don't know the code and you don't have Ed's thumb. So you are what, about an hour from there?"

"More like an hour and a half."

Pete said, "We can fly to Safford, but renting a car there at this time of day might be a problem."

"I'll have you picked up in a sheriff's vehicle."

"Okay, and I'll get the boss on the plane. He'll call you with directions, and we'll see you at the ranch."

Bren called dispatch and told them to provide the transportation in something kind of nice. He pulled back on the freeway and set his speed at 85. When he saw traffic clogs ahead, he would turn on the lights. When Ed's call came, Pat answered and wrote down the instructions.

She said, "I know exactly where the place is. We patrol by it regularly. It is a very, very nice ranch."

~

They got to the ranch a before the others. The ranch foreman, Clyde Jeffords, met them at the gate and told them he would lead them to the lab. He had them park in front of one of six garage doors.

Clyde came over and said, "The boss landed about ten minutes ago and the sheriff was there to pick them up. It will be about half hour before they're here. I don't have access to the lab, but Ed said to have you wait in the house, so come on in."

He showed them a wet bar adjacent to the living room. "There's ice and cold sodas, juice, water, and other beverages in the fridge. There are two bathrooms you gents can use down this hall, one right and one left, and one right behind the bar here the lady can use. Ed wants you to make yourself comfortable. If you need me for anything, just push the intercom and talk. It'll come over this radio on my hip. Make yourselves to home."

"Thanks, Clyde," Bren said. "I had no idea this place was out here. What is this, a guest ranch?"

"No, it's a working cattle and horse ranch. The old house, stables, and barns and such are about a mile away to the east. Ed bought the ranch quite a while ago and fixed the ranch house up really nice for him to use as a getaway. Later he built this mansion and also built a nice place for a caretaker.

"He suggested that since the caretaker house was bigger and nicer than the old ranch house, I should live in it and keep an eye on his place, so my family moved over here. The head wrangler and his family are in the old ranch house now, and the lead cowboy is in my old place, which is pretty nice too. The stableman's family lives in the third house at the old place.

"So four families live on the ranch fulltime and Ed or some of his friends are in the big house once in a while. There's also a guest house, which gets used some. The family really likes living over here because we get full use of the pool and recreational facilities."

"How big is the ranch?"

"It's almost two sections of owned land and fifty sections of leased range."

Bren nodded. "Good sized place, thirty-three thousand acres."

We ship about six hundred head of cattle a year is all, but the horse sales are our biggest source of revenue. We grow our own hay and sell the excess. We have Morgans and quarter horses. We sell some as colts, do some stud service, but mostly we sell trained working range or show horses. We ship horses all over the world."

"This is all done by four guys?"

"No, we've got a bunch of kids who are big enough to work and three men who work pretty much every day for us. We bring on extra hands for round ups, shipping, and big jobs. The farming is handled by a neighboring farmer for a set fee per acre plus his expenses, so we don't have to hire farm workers or buy any farm equipment."

"I better be on my way. The boss should be here any time now . . . don't want him to catch me loafing. It's nice to meet all of you."

The living room faced west with a glass wall that provided a nice view of the east end of Mt. Graham, Stockton Pass, and the southern Pinaleno Mountains. They sat in comfort and enjoyed the view as they waited for their host to show up.

~

Ed and Pete arrived at the ranch in Sheriff Bobby Bitters' big Expedition with the sheriff himself driving. They drove to a spot near the front door and walked into the house. They shook hands and were introduced by Bren to Deputy Pat Haley. Then the sheriff took charge.

"Okay, Bren, tell us what the plan is. I understand there's a key clue to solving how this Morra fellow was making his scam work."

"As we were leaving Tucson, Sergeant Victor was glancing through the papers we removed from Morra's home office when he made some sense of the list of passwords on a card.

"Basically, what we think is that Morra not only installed the Indian Trader Marketplace software on the lab computer, but also a bit of software that let him produce fraudulent Private Collections Registry cards that are visually indistinguishable from the real thing." Bren then explained the details of how the fraudulent cards were produce.

"So the card Manny Sanchez found first, with the help of Ed's researcher Lester Kenton, was for the owl effigy pot we believe was taken from the Queen Creek dig. Manny held the card in his hand and compared it to the ones in the file. There was nothing about it that looked different from the real cards."

Bren finished,"We believe that application is installed on the lab computer, and that's what we want to look for. Finding that will tie everything together."

"That's astounding," Ed said. "The guy figured out Marie's fraud using the Private Collections Registry, then he turned around and salted the registry to take away that method of detecting the crime. He came across as a smart guy, but this is amazing. Shall we go find this mystery app?"

They went to the computer and Bren said, "Ed, log in to the marketplace, and let's look around for an icon or function that would take us to the U of A app." They spent forty minutes opening every function but didn't find anything.

Bren said, "Al, do you have the password card?"

Al headed for the door. "No, but I know where it is . . . be right back!"

Ed logged out of his screen and logged back in with Morra's password. "Everything looks the same to me."

Pat said, "No, on your screen *Print* was an icon of a printer; on this one it says *Print*. Try clicking on that."

A print dialog box opened up. At the bottom was a red, white, and blue letter A.

"That UofA icon wasn't on your version. Click it."

It opened a new tab with a password field. Al read the password, which Ed entered. An app called *Typewriter Simulator* opened. Everybody cheered.

Pat, being more computer-savvy than the others, had become the de facto leader. She said, "I'm going to assume that he has set the defaults to produce the cards the way he wants them, so let's just click on *New Document* and let's see what happens."

It opened as a 3x5 card.

"Okay, just start typing."

Because of the surprise, everybody laughed. Each time a key was hit, it made the sound of an old manual typewriter. Pat said, "Don't say crooks have no sense of humor. Go ahead and type several lines . . . maybe five or six lines."

Ed repeatedly typed. "Now is the time for all good men to come to the aid of their country."

"Well, look at that," Bren said. "It looks like the real thing."

Pat said, "I don't think so. It's awful—uneven letters, some are darker than others. It's a very bad bunch of text."

Sheriff Bitters drawled, "What we have here is a generation gap. You just put us to shame with your computer talent, but now it's our turn.

"When I was young, this is the way most documents looked. Professional typists with a good ribbon could produce a beautiful text, but these were done on primitive typewriters from the twenties to about 1960 by a bunch of scientists. This, Deputy Haley, is how an authentic card should look."

"You're my executive boss, so I guess I have to believe you," Pat laughed.

Bren said, "Before we check to see if there is a card in the printer, we better put on gloves. We don't want to obliterate any fingerprints."

They all gloved up. It seemed nobody knew where to look, so Deputy Haley checked all the printer feed bins. She found one adjusted for 3x5 cards, but it was empty. They looked in drawers, where they found a very old brownish package of cards.

Al said, "Wait, before we print, how do we get an authentic signature on the card?"

Pat said, "Let's look at the *Insert* tab, then *Picture*."

The default was set to display a file containing a list of seven prominent deceased archeologists, among them Emile Haury, Gordon Vivian, and Ned Danson.

He clicked on Haury's name, and ten signatures of Emile Haury popped up, labeled by decade and ink type.

"Select one of them," Pat ordered. "Now select *Insert*."

The signature appeared in the center of the card on top of the text.

"Now click and drag the signature to the bottom right hand corner and drop it. Bingo! Signed by Dr. Haury himself, sometime in the 1950s with a dark blue fountain pen."

Ed printed the card. They now knew exactly how the forged registries were produced.

Bren said, "Let's try one more thing. I bet we can find a file of the forged cards. Save the card you just made, Ed, but don't click *Okay* right away. Let me make a note of that destination name."

Bren noted the destination and handed it to Ed. "Click *Okay* and go to this file." The file contained images of about a dozen forged cards.

Bren said, "We need to bag the package of old cards as evidence, as well as the test card we printed. We also need to take the computer as evidence."

Sheriff Bitters asked, "Does that mean that we will be shutting down Ed's online marketplace?"

Pete said, "It wouldn't matter. Ed is committed to whatever it takes to clear up the theft and fraud."

Ed answered Bitters' question, "No, the Marketplace resides on a commercial web server and predates Middleman by several years. It won't affect our market. Take the computer."

Bren asked, "Sheriff, would you mind hauling the computer back to the office? We have filled up all my space with evidence."

"Sure. Stick it in the back."

Ed said, "One more thing: Morra posted three items this week, and we bought them through our fake buyers. They haven't been delivered, and Morra has not billed for his services, so they may still be in the lab vault."

Ed walked to a normal-looking closet door and lifted the light switch cover to expose a key pad and thumbprint reader. He put in his code and held his thumb to the scanner, and the heavy steel door rolled open. The two pots and stone artifact were sitting on a shelf.

The team bagged, tagged, bubble wrapped, and placed the relics in a storage tub labeled as evidence and added it to the sheriff's cargo space alongside the computer.

Bren said, "If you travel to the sheriff's office with us, Al and Pat will switch to their cars, and we can put the computer in the back seat. We're going to my office in Central to organize the evidence and create the report."

"No problem. We're going right by it on the way to the airport," Sheriff Bitters said. "This is great work by your team, Bren."

Bren concurred. "They've done well. Ed and Pete, we appreciate your extraordinary support. Thanks for coming."

~

As they got on US 191 heading back to Safford, Bren said, "It's too late to work on this stuff tonight, so let's meet in the morning at my office after we've had time to get morning calls over with. Could we aim for nine o'clock?"

Both Al and Pat agreed to the time. Al said he would come and help move the evidence into the office.

At the Sheriff's office, Bren shook hands with Ed and Pete, and again thanked them for facilitating the search. He moved the computer and artifacts from the sheriff's car to the backseat of his car, using the seat belt to secure it. The sheriff took his passengers to the airport and Bren headed to Central with the others following in their vehicles.

Bren told Pat, "It was out of your way to come down here. I didn't expect you to come. Al and I will have it unloaded in no time."

"I know, but I helped make the mess. I want to help clean it up."

Bren chuckled and said, "Who can argue with that? But I thought you might have a date tonight."

"Not tonight. My dinner pal is on shift."

It only took about ten minutes to get everything inside. Just before they finished, Monica walked over with Layton and Lizzie.

Lizzie ran to Bren, and he squatted down for a hug and kiss. Then Lizzie greeted Al and ran to Pat. "Hi Patricia, I'm happy to see you." They became engaged in a conversation.

Al spoke for a moment with Monica, tickled Layton, who was now in his dad's arms, and took his leave.

Monica said, "I told the kids we could come meet you and ride home in the police car."

Lizzie held Pat's hand and tried to drag her to Monica. "Can I bring Patricia to dinner?"

Pat seemed surprised. "Oh, no. I need to get home."

Monica said, "I wish you would. I have a big pot of beef stew, a salad, and fresh homemade bread. It's not fancy, but it's nourishing. And you've had a long day. Wouldn't it be nice not have deal with getting up a dinner?"

Bren said, "I know you don't have plans, and you don't have dinner waiting. Come on over so Lizzie isn't disappointed."

She finally agreed, partly because it was a chance to get some more little kid training, and they all piled in the SUV for the one block trip home.

Pat enjoyed the dinner. She was tired and famished. The stew was robust and loaded with big chunks of chuck roast, potatoes, and carrots with a smattering of sweet onion and peas. The salad had a great vinaigrette dressing and the bread was terrific.

Before they were quite finished, Monica pulled a cookie tin out of the refrigerator. In about twelve minutes, she put a trivet on the table and covered it with the tin of cookies. She served them on napkins, and the entire tin disappeared rather quickly.

There was little conversation between the adults because Lizzie had decided Pat was there solely for her, and they engaged in a conversation that all the adults enjoyed. As they were eating the cookies, Layton made a delighted face and said, "Love it!"

Lizzie got a kick out of it. "My little brother is cute, and most of the time he is fun. Do you have a little brother?"

"As a matter of fact, I have three little brothers and a little sister. I never got to live with them, though, because they live far away. But I'm going to go see them in a few weeks. I have seen them on the computer, and I love them too."

"That's nice. I wish I had a little sister. But I'll be happy with whoever Heavenly Father sends to our family. I hope one is a sister."

"Well, I do too, Lizzie. My little sister is eight. I'm glad you're my friend because I never knew any little kids until now. Because of you, I kind of know how to talk to my little sister when I get to visit with her."

Pat stood and thanked her hosts and said, "That was a wonderful meal; it was just what I needed tonight."

Lizzie stood up in her chair and said, "Here's a kiss goodbye." She wrapped her arms around Pat's neck and smacked loudly on her cheek.

The whole family saw Pat to the door.

Bren said, "See you tomorrow."

"Yep. Nine o'clock."

~

After driving home from Tucson, Pinal County Deputy Dan Tomkins completed his report on the evidence from his investigation on Benson-Colley. He included the new evidence from the museum investigation. He was pleased with the strength of the case they had built against B-C. So far nothing had been said by them about not having any contact from Middleman/Morra. They may still get a stronger case when they hear about and discuss his arrest.

He sent his report to Bren's e-mail before he went to bed, exhausted, at ten. He arose at five and left at six for the work session in Central.

At seven thirty a.m. each morning, the Graham County sheriff's command and supervisory staff and sergeants participated in a roll call. Typically, the sheriff conducted, and the undersheriff, lieutenants, and department heads attended in the large conference room. The sergeants participated by conference call. Normally the constable and chief probation officer also participated to facilitate coordination between their offices, though they were independent of the sheriff's office.

The call usually lasted less than twenty minutes. The sergeants would then have a similar roll call via conference call with the deputies they supervised, where daily orders were given and information was exchanged. By eight, the night officers were released and the day officers began their shift.

A similar daily meeting and communication took place in the San Carlos Tribal Police Department. At eight-thirty, Al Victor left the Bylas Substation for Bren's office in Central.

Deputy Pat Haley got to take it easy. She participated in the 7:50 roll call, reporting she would be working in the Central sub-office. She spent an extra half hour watching the morning news show. They had a short report from the University of Arizona Police that an associate professor has been shot by police and arrested for attempted murder.

The news report said, "The incident did not occur on campus and no students or university personnel were involved in the incident or endangered by it. The university police say they cannot release any other information pending an investigation. The Tucson Police and Pima County Sheriff deny any knowledge of the event. The station had no other information at that time, but we are working on the story. Catch this evening's news for more details."

Manny Sanchez also participated in the call and announced he had been cleared by the therapist to resume duties. He would also be working evidence at the Central sub-office. Two deputies normally in other jurisdictions were working overtime to cover the beats of the two on special assignment.

Manny, worried about how Jenny would feel being alone, asked her if she would like to ride in with him and spend the day in Safford. Jenny was enrolled as a posse member and had signed a standard form allowing her to ride with deputies. She said she would do a little shopping and visit with her mom and friends. He dropped her off at the sheriff's office, and she took the Stratus for the day.

The computer lab contractor, an IT instructor at Eastern Arizona College, picked up the two computers and the hard drive to do forensics and analysis on them. Bren had prepared instructions to find items that reference Edward Hale, Marie Artiste, Steven Benson, Oscar Colley, Jack Hager, Mike or Jill Fulton, Deputy Manuel Sanchez, Middleman, Queen Creek, Superior, Safford, and Lab, as well as any references to Private Collections or artifact theft or artifact sale.

Bren then checked his messages and e-mail and found the report by Dan Tomkins. It was excellent, and he decided to not only use it in the final report, but to use its general format and approach. The first section was simply a description of the evidence. It was subdivided into physical evidence, witness reports and interrogations, audio and video evidence, photographic evidence, expert opinion, and documents. Dan then made a section listing conclusions and the combined evidence from all sources for each conclusion. Bren printed the report and made a copy for each of the officers.

The evidence was stacked on or under a folding table against the wall. He brought in another chair and four more folding tables to use for sorting through and grouping the evidence. He had loaded his little refrigerator with water and sodas, and Monica had sent him off with a couple dozen freshly-baked cookies.

Pat arrived first and told him about the report on the Tucson TV news.

Bren asked, "They didn't know who, where, or why it happened, so there's probably nothing to alarm our theft suspects yet. Hopefully, we can postpone the release of that information until tomorrow morning, so we can be standing by to record Benson-Colley's reaction when they hear the rest of the story."

Al and Manny arrived at about the same time, Al from the west and Manny from the east. Dan arrived about five minutes to nine. He had been worried about finding the place, but the four police cars parked in front pretty well gave it away. He added his Pinal car to the mix.

Handing out copies of the report Dan prepared, Bren said, "Read this report. It will refresh your memory of what has occurred up through last night with the exception of our search of the Hale Lab computer. We will use this method to consolidate all our evidence into an accurate and understandable chronology of the crimes involved.

"For the information of Dan and Manny--Al, Pat, and I met at the Hale Ranch by Artesia with Ed Hale, Pete Villa, and the sheriff and found the program and old cards that Morra, as Middleman, was printing for insertion in the Private Collections file. He had saved copies of several of the fake cards, so we have almost closed the loop on his theft ring. The only question might be whether he was doing this with any of the Artiste artifacts. And, finally, we will soon make arrests at Benson-Colley.

"Every morning Benson-Colley turns the TV on to the Arizona Morning Show and keeps it on until it is over at ten. The AG's office is going to have a news conference at 9:45 detailing the Morra arrest. At the end of the conference, the spokesperson will add that Morra operated an archeological theft ring under the alias Middleman. The Antiquities Strike Force will be making multiple arrests in the near future.

"We will be able to hear the conversation between Benson and Colley, and we expect it to rattle them to make plans to avoid arrest. That will be tantamount to a confession. Dan will be monitoring and will give the signal to move in. In case they try to run, they will find a Ft. McDowell water department trailer load of pipe blocking the road by the water tanks. So now that everybody is caught up, let's get to work."

Bren explained how he wanted the work divided. "Dan will use my desktop PC to view the security tapes from the Klondyke crime scene and create a timeline index of each important phase of the event. Then he will go through the witness interviews of Manny and Jenny and match the events in the interview with the event shown on the tape. He will note any inconsistencies or questions that are raised by the comparison.

"Al will organize all the bagged physical evidence and identify where in the case it bears significance and whether it applies to only the Klondyke attempted murder, the Morra office crimes, the murder of Jack Hager, the theft ring, or a combination of those.

"Manny will use his laptop to make a time line of the video from Olga Jordan at the museum, map the interviews of Olga and Sally Gaona into the time line, and note inconsistencies and questions. He will also work up a time line for the planting of fake Private Collections cards. He will use the door-access reports, the information provided by Lester, and the marketplace posting and sales log provided by Ed Hale, and the date that each fake registry card was saved on the computer."

"Pat will start on the hardest job, making sense of all the documents we took as evidence we want to do primarily two things with them. First, find all the income and financial information on Morra and identify where he has placed his illegal earnings. Second, make a time line of income and deposits. Third, identify any documents of any kind that relate to any of the cases, identify which case or cases they related to, and get them on the appropriate time line. Anything that has no value to any of the cases will be winnowed out and stored in a separate box."

"I'll use my laptop to digitize the crime scene sketches and confirm the placement of physical evidence to the numbered evidence. As each of you finishes one of your tasks, I'll integrate it into the overall report. In between, I'll assist Pat with the document work. Once any of you finish your assigned task, join the document review. Maybe we can get this done all by early afternoon."

They were heavily into the work by twenty after eight.

One unexpected finding was that Morra did not need money. He had sixteen million dollars in mutual funds as his share of his inheritance from his father's estate. He made over two million from his illegal sales, but all he did with it was offshore it in a Cayman Bank.

Pat asked, "Why would he do that when he wasn't into a flashy lifestyle and had all the money he could need if he did want it?"

Manny said, "It was never about money. He wants to show that he's smarter than everyone else."

Al added, "I agree. He was denied his doctorate and thus a professorship and that assaulted his ego. He wants revenge on those who found him wanting, to prove he outwitted them."

"That's the reason I believe he will end up answering every unanswered question in the case," Bren stated. "He wants the world to know he put one over on the archeologists that snatched his dream of glory. He will want to brag about it."

Al nodded agreement. "The irony is that what he has done only proves that his doctoral sponsor was right."

They had the report compiled and reviewed and all evidence placed in marked boxes by noon. There would be a number of things to add to the report as the forensics came back on the computers and as they tied up the Benson-Colley case, but most additions would only strengthen the evidence they already had rather than add new facts.

Bren e-mailed the finished report to Barry Dirocco and sent one to Officer Danes. He asked her to print it and deliver it directly to Dr. Lazovich, for his eyes only.

The team loaded the evidence and delivered the report to the Sheriff's office, checked the evidence into the evidence vault, and went to La Casita for lunch. The feeling of accomplishment made it a most pleasant time.

When they finished their meal, Bren said, "Let's hope that B-C gives us even more of a reason to arrest them, but if not, they will do some prison time and will most likely have federal charges as well. So let's not celebrate too much yet. Let's keep our guard up, keep doing our jobs, and get this thing closed with no wiggle room and no one hurt.

"Great work, all of you. We want to be staged somewhere near the B-C yard by ten in the morning. Pat, meet me at quarter to seven, and we'll pick Manny up in Pima and Al at Bylas. We've arranged two unmarked cars. When we travel to The Valley, Al and I will ride together, and Manny and Pat will take the other car.

"We'll rendezvous with Dan somewhere in the East Valley and then deploy to strategic positions designated by him. Dan will have some Pima deputies. Later we'll be joined by Dirocco and one of the AG investigators, and we will have a couple of Ft. McDowell Officers. When Dan gives the signal, we will quietly move in and arrest Benson and Colley. See you all in the morning."

Chapter 18

On the flight from Safford to Scottsdale, Ed Hale asked his attorney "How could we pay the police agency and attorney general for their costs in this investigation?"

Pete answered, "I'm sure there's a way, but before we explore that, let's analyze your question. Why do you want to pay for the investigation?"

"If it weren't for me buying into Middleman's proposal, there would have been no need for the investigation. It was caused by my company getting involved with illegal artifacts."

"No, it was not. It was caused by Morra's deception and lack of integrity. You and the customers were duped by claims of providing a finding service that would supply only certified private collection artifacts."

"Yes, but if I had investigated him, I would have uncovered his deception."

"Nobody does that. How many suppliers of goods or services do you deal with in your business?"

"I don't know. Probably hundreds."

"In your accounts payable vendor file you have over 1000 vendors. How many of those have you run background checks on?"

"None."

"Exactly. They offer their product to you and you either order it or not, depending on your business need at the time. It is their responsibility to meet all legal and ethical requirements associated with the product, not yours. If for some reason you suspect they are not doing so, you simply do not buy from them."

"True. But this investigation is helping me to restore my business integrity and reputation. You know how valuable that is to me. I would like to ease the burden on the agencies and the taxpayers."

"I can respect that, and I think we can lead the way to help them without making it appear that you're paying penitence for wrongdoing when you have done nothing wrong. I suggest two actions. First, I see a need for better certification and auditing of artifact suppliers and dealers. Second, we could seek funds from the criminal to right the wrongs.

"We could set up a foundation with voluntary contribution of the dealers association members to support a full-time auditor/investigator and possibly moneys confiscated from illicit trade. We could organize a board consisting of appointed or elected association members and a representative from each of the attorneys general of the Four Corners states.

"The sheriff mentioned Morra had made millions from illegal sales, but he has more in his inheritance. We could go after Morra's accounts to compensate the victims, including those killed or physically injured by Morra, those whose reputation was damaged by him, such as the museum, and your customers. I'm assuming you would not seek compensation for your damage."

Ed said, "I like your ideas. We could assist in undoing as much damage as possible, financially assist the mother of the murdered student and the injured victims, set up an account to continue supporting Marie's sister's Amazonian medical clinic, and compensate customers for good name damage. The new organization would be improving the legal culture of the business and reducing the likelihood of a recurrence. It will give assistance in rooting out illegal trade. There's only one thing lacking, and that is the lawsuit should compensate the cost of the investigation to all the agencies involved."

Pete replied, "I'll examine the RICO law, legal precedents, and case law involved. In doing all the things we're talking about, some of the agency cost is covered in RICO, but it will probably take a lawsuit to get some of the other things covered. When I come up with a strategy, I'll run it by you and then take it to Barry to see if he will partner with us."

~

The Antiquities Strike Force bolstered by Ft. McDowell Tribal Police moved into position on the access road to the Benson-Colley construction yard. The tribal water works parked a trailer load of pipes on the access road northwest of the of the community water tanks, making it impossible to get a vehicle onto the access road or the north jeep trail connecting with it.

Because the locale was rather sparse desert brush, there were few stands of brush and cactus large enough to conceal a man, but some officers managed to find cover within fifty feet of the only gate in and out of the yard. Pat and a Pinal deputy were in a clump of brush just south of the yard, so they could block access to the jeep trail to the south and the canyon below. Manny and another officer were concealed behind the parked pipe trailer.

A Pinal deputy was guarding the drainage arroyo below the tank in case an escape was attempted there. Dan was situated near the tanks, controlling the action by watching and listening to the live feed on his tablet. Al, Manny, Barry, and the remainder of the team waited on the north side of the tanks out of view of the yard. All the officers wore tactical hands-free radio headsets to receive instructions from Dan. Detective Espinoza and the sheriff watched the action on the monitor in the sheriff's office.

Dan spoke, "The TV announcer just said they had a breaking news report, and they are reading our report. Standby until I give the signal to move in. The two suspects are arguing about what to do. Steve Benson wants to run. Colley says they should stay calm, because there's no proof the law is on to them. Benson says it sounds like Middleman is giving them up. Benson is heading for his car. Move in."

Ft. McDowell Officer Calvin Russell was the closest officer to the gate. He waited until Steve Benson turned toward his vehicle, then made a full-on tackle in the manner he had been taught as right tackle back in his high school days. Benson hit the ground hard and was knocked unconscious by three-hundred pounds of Yavapai smashing down on top of him. Russell pulled the unconscious man's arms to the back and cuffed him.

Another McDowell Officer said, "Check his pulse. He might be dead." Officer Russell made sure Benson had a pulse and was breathing. He had a bloody nose, so they turned him on his side. His face was abraised, bruised, and sported embedded pieces of gravel.

The rest of the team stormed the portable office, catching Oscar Colley by complete surprise.

He said, "Don't shoot, I surrender. I'll cooperate with you." He was handcuffed while standing. When he saw Steve, he was glad he hadn't tried to run.

The water department moved the pipe trailer back into the tank yard and the Ft. McDowell EMTs tended to Benson, cleaning his scrapes and removing the gravel from his face. After determining that Benson was not seriously injured, Barry Dirocco ordered the prisoners transported for booking on state charges.

Barry oversaw the execution of a search warrant on the office and other facilities but found nothing that would have bearing on the case. He and his associates left for their offices. Dan turned off the microphone on the remote monitor—no sense in catching the idle chitchat that would go on between the officers.

The members of the antiquities team and the supporting officers held a wrap-up where Bren thanked them all. Dan suggested they get a group photo. He had them stand in the gate facing the monitor across the canyon. Using his laptop to focus, he told everyone to smile and took a picture.

He handed out cards and said, "Send me your e-mail addresses, and I'll send all of you a copy."

As they were finishing up, a tribal car drove up and Wassaja Thomas, the Fort McDowell general manager, got out. He greeted his officers and guessed that Bren and Al were in charge based on their rank insignia.

Thomas introduced himself and Bren introduced the team members. "We really appreciate your police and water department for facilitating a successful arrest. It went without a hitch, and Officer Russell provided us with best open field tackle we've ever seen."

"Yes, Calvin was always a master of that," Thomas said. "We don't have a great deal of information about exactly what was going on here; other than apparently our contractor was stealing artifacts from the site. Could you fill me in?"

"Deputy Tomkins, our team member from Pinal County, has been in charge of this operation, so I'll let him explain it."

Dan gave a summary of what Benson-Colley had been doing, how the team became aware of it, and the way it had been investigated. He explained that it was related to the same theft ring that committed murder and attempted murder near Superior, though neither Benson or Colley were not involved in those.

Al added, "We have recovered some of the artifacts that were stolen and will return them back to the tribe once they are no longer needed for evidence."

"Thank you," Manager Thomas said. "We prefer to let the ruins remain undisturbed, but since this one has been opened, we may need to have it excavated. We will in turn give the funerary to our Pima neighbors on the Salt River Reservation for reburial. The only work of this type that has been done under my administration was done by Benson-Colley. Is there a trustworthy company you could suggest?"

Bren said, "Officially, we can't give you recommendations, but a member of the team might have an opinion in private." He glanced at Al.

Thomas said, "Sergeant Victor, I'd like to chat with you, but first could you show me the subject ruin? I don't have a record of one on this knoll."

Dan led the group to the section of the ruin that was inside the yard and showed them where they had been digging. He pointed out that the ruin continued outside the fence for at least one hundred feet. Everybody walked back over to the office, leaving Al and the manager in privacy.

Al said, "The best company I know is EcoAnthro, LLC. It's run by Mike and Jill Fulton. They are very good and very honest, plus they have a native archeologist. They have been helping us with our investigation."

Al took out his phone and gave the manager the Fultons number.

"Good, thank you. We have a meeting in the morning, and I'll discuss taking some emergency action to get our project back on line. I'll give them a call after the meeting."

Thomas shook hands with each of the remaining team members and thanked them, then headed back to work.

Al took out his phone and called Fultons. Jill answered and Al explained that Ft. McDowell was looking for a replacement for Benson-Colley. He suggested, "Since you have a general contractor's license, they may want you to take over the job. If EcoAnthro assumes the contract, you would have all the subs already in place. Think about it. The tribal general manager will call you tomorrow."

"What does it entail?"

"I don't know in detail, but it is a small rainwater recovery facility, and they will be adding the excavation of a small to medium sized Hohokam ruin. Like I said, the engineering is done, subs are already contracted, and the material already ordered, except for the added archeological work. It may be your toehold to expansion and would give all the archeological work of the tribe to you."

"Well, thanks for the heads up."

"One more thing. Elton Godwin is now out of a job. He was working on this one. I'd appreciate it if you might consider hiring him, whether you decide to take over that job or not."

"I will do that."

~

Bren got word from Mt. Graham Hospital that James Morra had been upgraded from critical to serious and moved from the ICU to a private room. The sheriff had been maintaining a watch on him around the clock, and they were keeping him shackled to the bed, a situation that would be maintained until he was moved to jail.

At first Morra thought it was absurd that they kept him locked to the bed, since he could barely move without causing excruciating pain. He could use his left hand as long as he didn't move the shoulder, which limited that opportunity severely. As he considered his situation, he decided that the tight security was an admission by the law that he was too intelligent to trust ordinary measures to secure him. He took some satisfaction from that.

Bren asked Deputy Haley to meet him at the hospital to assist him with getting a statement from Morra. He told her to wear nice street clothes and do her girly thing with the make-up and hair and to wear something with a belt so she could display her badge. Since Haley would be with him, he decided to use her attractiveness to soften Morra up.

Normally Manny, who was a member of the antiquities team, would accompany him, but since Manny was involved in the shooting of Morra, it was prudent to use another officer. Pat and Bren met in the lobby and sat in an isolated corner so Bren could explain his strategy.

"We are going to come off almost like admiring fans. We are going to emphasize his intelligence, cunning, brilliant plan, and that it was just pure luck that Manny blundered onto his plan. That is why I wanted you to do the glam thing . . . and you did it very nicely, too. Any man is complimented to have a pretty woman pay attention to him. The fact that you are a cop will add to that. You will be our secret weapon in stroking his all-important ego. Can you swallow your desire to punch him and do that?"

"Yes," she laughed. "It will be a big roll change for me. I've never seen myself as a Mata Hari."

"I don't know how much we will accomplish with this first interview. It may take a series of interrogations before we get him talking. I'll explain that we have arrested Benson and Colley, that we have them on record dealing with him, that we have put all the evidence together and know everything about his artifact-laundering master plan.

"The end strategy is to convince him that we can convict him without any confession from him; but if he tells his story his brilliance will become world famous, and those who have jealously sabotaged his career will be shown to be short-sighted fools. Our success depends on how well we feed his ego and play to his delusions of grandeur. Do you have any questions?"

"None. Let's go get this killer . . . I mean brilliant mastermind."

"Let the games begin, Mata."

Bren led the way into Morra's room, greeting the reserve deputy seated at the door. Bren introduced himself and Deputy Haley.

Morra said, "Yes, I remember seeing you, Sergeant, at the scene of the shooting. But I did not see your lovely detective there." Haley flashed a fetchingly shy smile at him.

Bren said, "Mr. Morra, because you have been either in surgery or too critical to speak with the last few days, I felt I should come and tell you the status of your case. You have been charged with the attempted murder of Deputy Manny Sanchez, and within the next few days will be charged with operating a criminal enterprise to steal, launder, and sell stolen artifacts.

"We are not seeking to interrogate you at this time, only to inform you on the status of your case."

Bren outlined the strong case against Morra, commenting a number of times on a brilliant move, an amazingly clever forgery, and even the unbelievable shot he had made.

Bren's tone was one of grudging admiration. He finished by saying, "This will go down as the most perfectly-executed fraud ever. The top archeologists in the world were fooled into buying illegal artifacts. They are on display at the Smithsonian and the Peabody, where the foremost experts were fooled. In your personnel files, I saw that a jealous doctoral sponsor blackballed you, sidetracking your career. Now he will have to recognize how short-sighted he was. It is an amazing crime."

Pat added, "The judge will not allow you to profit from it, but you should write a book detailing what you did. There will be movies made. I'm honored to be working on this case."

Bren said, "I can see you are tiring now, so we'll go. But we'll come back when you are more alert. Of course you will have to be interrogated, just as a matter of practice. We would love to hear the unknown details that we cannot find with investigation of evidence."

Morra spoke, "Thank you for visiting and letting me know where I stand. There is one thing I would like you to do for me. Deputy Sanchez saved my life when it would have been easier for him to let me bleed. Tell him thank you for that."

"I'll do that."

~

Benson and Colley were booked on state charges and kept in separate holding cells to be arraigned the next afternoon. Bren and Dan met Attorney Dirocco at the jail, where they separately discussed the charges and interrogated first Benson and then Colley. They had been separated and taken in different vehicles and had no opportunity to collaborate on their stories.

Benson looked pretty battered from his run-in with Yavapai Tribal Officer Russell. They explained the charges against him and presented the evidence they had, saying they would be able to get a conviction with or without any statement from him, but would appreciate his cooperation.

"I'm not saying anything until I talk to my lawyer."

Attorney Dirocco said, "If that's how you want it. Who is your lawyer and what is his phone number?"

"I don't know her phone number, but her name is Lily Korrick. She's with Bogdan and Mailer in Scottsdale."

Dirocco remembered her as the attorney who represented Benson-Colley in the federal violations a few years previous. "We will call her and ask her to come in time to prepare for your arraignment at three o'clock p.m."

"If after talking with her, you decide you want to make a voluntary statement, have her contact us."

Benson was taken back to his cell.

Oscar Colley was brought in and the same presentation was given to him. He said he was willing to give a voluntary statement, so Dirocco recited his Miranda rights, told him that the interview was being taped, and confirmed that he understood his rights and wished to give a voluntary statement.

Colley said, "About three years ago at a company Christmas party at Rustler's Roost, Steve was approached by a man who introduced himself as Dr. Middleman a consultant. Steve was—"

"Excuse me, Steve who?"

"My business partner, Steve Benson. He was drinking and so maybe not thinking too rationally, but Middleman explained that he had a surefire method to market artifacts through the dark net. He explained it in some detail, and Steve was impressed. The next day Steve showed me Middleman's card and explained that we could make a lot of cash by selling these commonplace artifacts to Middleman. I told him it could be pretty dangerous, and that we should just forget about it.

"About a week later, he came in the office and handed me an envelope with two-thousand dollars cash. He said it was from Middleman and there would be lots more to come. We started moving four to six items a week, and nobody was any the wiser.

"We have Elton, a laborer who is a little mentally handicapped, and we trained him to excavate and leave the stuff in a toolbox. Steve figured that if we were ever caught, we could claim it was Elton who was doing it without our knowledge. He said no one would blame Elton because he didn't understand. Middleman had a key and after hours would take the latest shipment and leave a package of money for the previous week's sales.

"At first it bothered me but as time went by, we were profiting nicely from it, and it didn't really seem that we were hurting anybody. I became comfortable with it. It was wrong and stupid, and I'm sorry I ever let myself get involved."

Bren asked, "So the exchange of artifacts and money happened this way every week?"

"For the first year or two, yes. About four or five months ago it changed. Middleman started calling and telling us when he wanted a delivery and it was done the same as before . . . but some weeks he didn't call, so we didn't have Elton put anything in the box. It also seemed like the pay for the artifacts went up quite a bit during that time. He said he found a better market."

"This Elton," Bren asked, "didn't really know that you were selling artifacts?"

"No. He just thought we were supplying them to the state archeologist, because that's what we told him. Steve was the first one in each morning, and he would remove the envelope with the money in it before Elton arrived. I'm glad you asked, because I'm half afraid Steve will try to shift the blame to Elton."

Bren made a note on his tablet and asked, "It sounds like Steve is the senior partner in your business."

"No. We are equal partners, and I consider myself equally responsible. Steve is much more of a business man than I am, so he handled bidding, taxes, ordering and paying bills, that kind of stuff. I handled the engineering, job planning and management, and contractor oversight."

Attorney Dirocco said, "I strongly recommend that you get an attorney before your arraignment this afternoon. Benson has called Lilly

Korrick. I also strongly recommend that you get your own attorney. I think it could really hurt you to use the same attorney as Benson."

"Can you recommend a good criminal attorney?"

"I'm sorry. I'm not allowed to do that."

Dirocco had to leave and handed finishing up over to Bren. Bren said, "Your statement and this discussion will be transcribed, and you will need to sign it."

Bren tore off a bit of his tablet and wrote *Layton & Galbraith, Mesa*. He took out one of his business cards and handed it to Colley with the note. "If you think of anything else you need to tell me, this is my contact information."

Before lunch, both attorneys were meeting with their respective clients.

Since Barry Dirocco had filed the charges against them individually, and planned to prosecute them separately, Benson was arraigned first.

As Colley had feared, Benson's strategy was to put the blame on Elton. His attorney was trying to bargain no contest to simple theft, and not guilty of criminal conspiracy. She also requested that Benson be released on his own recognizance pending trial.

Dirocco opposed lessening of the charges based on overwhelming evidence against Mr. Benson. The judge let the charges stand. Dirocco opposed release pending trial because Mr. Benson had tried to flee after the news story broke and was later physically apprehended as he was running for his vehicle. He asked permission to play a two-minute surveillance tape to prove his point. The request was granted.

He said, "The first voice you hear will be Steve Benson, talking to his partner Oscar Colley. Only the two of them were present. The other voices in the background are the television, which had just announced the arrest of the illegal artifact dealer going by the alias of Middleman."

Dirocco started the tape.

"Listen to me Oscar. We need to get out of here. I'm getting my cash and heading for the cabin, then out of the country."

"Steve calm down! Running will make it worse. Besides, there's no proof the law is even on to us."

"It sounds like Middleman is giving us up. I'm outa here."

Dirocco shut off the tape. "Mr. Benson then came running out the door to his vehicle. He was chased by a policeman and literally tackled and arrested. The injuries to his face happened when he hit the ground. The officer was also scraped a bit. Mr. Benson has stated that he would run and that he had a sum of cash and a cabin for a short-term hideout, while he waited to flee the country. He is clearly a flight risk."

The judge ruled Benson held without bail. He was taken back to his cell.

Attorney Chris Galbraith pleaded Colley guilty as charged, but asked for favorable consideration since his client had no criminal record, had fully cooperated at the time of arrest, had offered a voluntary admission when questioned, would cooperate on further investigation, and had expressed remorse for his part in the crimes.

Dirocco said, "Everything Mr. Colley states is true. He has been fully cooperative, and his voluntary statement is corroborated on every point by our body of evidence. He gave his statement without any promise of leniency. Further, the State would not oppose bail for Mr. Colley since he shows no inclination to flee. I suggest $200,000 bail, with the stipulation that Mr. Colley stay away from the construction yard and scenes of the crimes."

Galbraith looked at his client who nodded, then said, "We would not oppose that bail, but as his attorney, I think $200,000 is excessive given the low risk."

"Theft of artifacts and criminal conspiracy are serious charges," the judge said. "Bail is set at $200,000."

~

Pete Villa put together a plan to compensate both the cost of the investigation and prosecutions related to Morra's theft ring, and to compensate the victims. He also proposed an organization to assist dealers with assuring the legality of their purchases, and with investigation of possible fraudulent suppliers of artifacts. It included all the elements he and Ed had discussed on the plane trip from Safford. Ed reviewed it and suggested a couple of minor additions and changes. He approved it to be presented to Barry Dirocco for consideration.

Pete e-mailed the proposal to Barry and called him. He explained what they wanted to do and asked Barry to consider it and get back to him. He explained that his company was willing to make a major annual contribution to the organization and have Ed or himself serve on the Board. In addition to asking dealers and legitimate suppliers support it with contributions, he said they could also seek a portion of RICO proceeds to offset the organization's cost of investigations that are prosecuted.

Barry responded positively to the concept and said he would look it over and get back to Pete with any questions before he talked with the AG.

~

After the news broke that Benson and Colley had been arrested and were awaiting trial, Barry Dirocco got a call from FBI Special Agent Marvin Burger. Barry knew that Agent Burger was one of the agents in the Phoenix office who specialized in crime on the twenty-two Indian Reservations in Arizona, covering over a quarter of the state's land area. He also knew why Burger was calling.

"Barry, this is Marv Burger. I see you made an artifact theft arrest on the Ft. McDowell Reservation. I wish you had involved me in that."

"Actually, I would have been happy to have you involved. It just didn't occur to me because neither the supplier or the seller were Indians, and it was just one of the crime scenes involved in a larger off-reservation string of crimes.

"The investigation was by the State Antiquities Task Force, so those participating were from the AG, three county jurisdictions, the San Carlos Apache Police, and the Ft. McDowell Police. Because you are the ex officio FBI member of the force, I have been sending you the minutes of the weekly Task Force call. I assumed you were keeping current on what we have been doing and planning."

"Well, I'm going to be put on the spot today when I get to work on why I wasn't there."

"I'm sorry about that, but you can't say I didn't tell you. I know you are covering a huge area, spend a lot of long empty road miles, and have more to do than you should, but I'm also buried in case load. I can't call all the twenty-two task force members who aren't participating in a particular case and report to them individually. If you want to be involved in what we are doing, join the call . . . or at least read the minutes."

"Gee, thanks for the sympathy."

"Look, just tell them you are cognizant of the investigation and agree with the process that was used. Point out that no Indians were involved in the crime at all, and the arrest could have been made in numerous other places. The isolated spot on the rez provided the best opportunity for a clean arrest with reduced danger to officers and without danger to citizens. Also, the Ft. McDowell police facilitated the arrest. Say that you will analyze the final case reports to determine whether any federal charges need to be filed."

"That's about what I was planning. If this grows with the investigation into interstate crime, I want you to tell me prior to the release."

"I'll do that. As we work with the three suspects we've arrested, we will get more details. Check the minutes or call in, and you can have a heads up before anything happens."

"Three! Who's the third one?"

"Geez, Marvin! Go back and read the minutes. It's the buyer with the alias Middleman, real name Morra, who tried to murder a Graham County deputy and was shot himself. He's recovering in Safford. Use the search function for 'Morra' before you get blindsided on that."

Chapter 19

Mr. Haley had asked Pat whether she would rather fly out of Phoenix or Tucson. She said Phoenix because the drive is almost the same and most of the Tucson flights stop in Phoenix anyway. He told her that if she could take the early Friday morning flight she would be able to see her brothers play in the first round state playoff game that night. He offered to put her up on Thursday at the airport in Phoenix so she wouldn't have to drive early. She agreed.

Andy talked her into letting him drive her to the airport and pick her up when she returned. He pointed out that parking was really expensive, and her car might be broken into. They enjoyed visiting as they drove to Phoenix, stopping at the Red Lobster by Fiesta Mall for dinner.

Pat's dad had gotten her a room at the Crowne Plaza across the street from the light rail airport connection. Andy helped with her luggage, then they went to the patio and sat under a palm tree watching a family playing in the pool. They had a drink and enjoyed some of the free snacks as they talked.

Finally Pat said, "You have to leave. You have second watch tomorrow and need to get enough sleep. Plus, I don't want you to get sleepy on the long dark drive home."

"No fear. I work dark shifts so much I don't get sleepy at night. But just in case, when I get to Apache Junction, I'll stop and get a 44 ounce bladder-buster Pepsi. If the caffeine doesn't do the trick, the frequent bathroom stops will."

She laughed, "Good strategy! Tonight I'll walk you to your car and kiss *you* good night."

"Okay. Don't forget to put your sidearms, clips, and ammo in your lock box before you leave for the airport. You remember the process with baggage check?"

"Yep, no sweat; though I'll feel strange without it on me."

"Thank you for letting me bring you down. It's been a great evening."

"It has. It's so nice of you to do this for me, but it's nicer to be with you."

They were now comfortable with lingering embraces and kisses and no longer had to wonder about what to do. Both felt a profound sadness as they parted, he waving his hand out the window over the top of his car, and she standing by herself on the sidewalk.

She was tired enough and the room and bed were comfortable enough that she quickly fell asleep. She was jarred awake by the alarm six and a half hours later. She grabbed a quick breakfast at the express breakfast area. Then, with her luggage strapped on the wheeled bag, crossed the street and took the sky train.

The check-in went smoothly and the plane actually departed with a full cabin five minutes early. Pat considered how much her anxiety about her family had changed with the weekly phone calls. She felt loved and accepted and only a little worried about how they would feel when they saw her in person.

She brought all feminine clothes, including her nice dress because Daddy wanted her to attend church with them. He told her to bring warm clothes, so she had some sweaters and warm pants, and she bought a pair of fashionable boots. She did bring her big down jacket with a hood, because Blacksburg looked like the North Pole on the Weather Channel.

She made a connecting flight at Charlotte Franklin, landing on time in Roanoke, where her dad and Lois happily embraced her. In spite of having seen her dad on the computer screen as they visited, she was surprised that he wasn't taller. He was stocky and muscular and probably about six feet tall, but she had always visualized him as being *really* tall. Then she realized the last time she stood by him he was actually twice as tall as her.

The Haley's family car was a 2014 Explorer with four-wheel drive and snow tires. Pat thought it was probably a necessity here. There was snow here and there on the hills, but quite a few trees were still sporting their bright fall colors, and the temperature was only a little colder than

Safford. Blacksburg was even more charming than the pictures and descriptions in articles she had found online.

They arrived home to an empty house—a very nice, comfortable empty house. Dad helped lug her bags and showed her to the guest room, telling her she could freshen up in the adjacent bathroom, which she did.

Lois told her, "If you feel like taking a nap, we have about forty minutes until dinner. Carol will be home in about twenty minutes and then the madness will start and continue until we are all home from the game."

"Oh, it's not necessary. I had a good sleep last night and napped for an hour and a half on the plane. Maybe I can help you with something in the kitchen."

Ten minutes later Carol arrived home and rushed to Pat, hugging her and saying, "Come with me I want to show you my room."

"Oh, I need to help get dinner ready."

"Not really. Mom does it by herself all the time."

Mom laughed. "Go with her. She's been so excited to have you here. I'll call you when it's ready. Thanks for setting the table."

Carol was remarkably precocious and a natural conversationalist. She had a My Little Pony with a pink mane on her shelf. Pat had a single girlie toy when she was a kid—a pony like Carol's. She bought it herself and her mom had a fit when she saw it. She was going to throw it away, but Erma, the lady who at the time was mom's roommate, jumped to Pat's aid and said everybody had a right to their own taste. Pat still had it sitting on a shelf in her apartment.

"I bought a Little Pony like that when I was about seven," Pat said.

Carol explained, "I got mine when I was just little, but I really like it, so I kept it."

"Me too; I still have mine."

They talked about many things before dinner was called and had planted a sister bond that would only grow stronger. At the table they all held hands and offered grace. Then the food was passed around, and they all talked about their day. They talked about Pat's trip and then the big topic of the night was the looming playoff game.

Football was another thing her mother didn't approve of, but Pat had attended games at the university and enjoyed the craziness with her roommates even though she didn't get the nuances of the game.

It was different having two brothers on the field. Daddy was an excellent play-by-play man and knew when Paul made or missed a block and when Larry juggled a handoff. The game was tied as the third quarter was winding down. Larry took a handoff through the hole Paul had made, as Paul regained his feet and hit the linebacker, letting Larry run for a touchdown. The fourth quarter had only a field goal from each team with the Blacksburg Bruins winning the game and advancing to the semifinals. The coach named Larry and Paul as game co-MVP.

On Sunday morning they attended church and Sunday school at Tom's Creek Christian Church. Pat enjoyed the worship service, especially the music, and found the discussion in Sunday school interesting. The rest of the visit was mostly Lois or Dad showing Pat around during the day and the family doing things together in the evenings. Pat particularly enjoyed helping the kids with their homework.

Larry mentioned that he thought Pat was too small and cute to be a cop, that he worried some big guy would hurt her. Dad told him that female cops had the same training as the men and did just as well in bad situations.

Larry said, "Pat, if I grabbed you, you wouldn't be able to get away from me."

"Yes, I would."

He replied, "Okay, you try to stop me."

"No. I would have to seriously hurt you. It's not a game."

As Pat turned to walk away, he grabbed her by the arm with one hand and the neck with another. She slammed her elbow just under his ribcage, spun and back kicked him behind the knee. He went down with her sitting on him and his arm twisted behind his back.

Larry gasped, "Okay I believe you." The other kids enjoyed seeing the big guy humbled by his sister . . . especially Carol.

"You are lucky. She went easy on you," Dad said. "If she thought you were actually trying to hurt her, she would have made the kick to the side of your knee and you would not have any ligaments left and would be writhing in pain. You'd be out of football for a year, if not for good. Cops have to play for keeps; they don't get second chances."

Larry had no hard feelings and enjoyed the teasing and banter with his siblings. He had a bruise on his ribcage; he would tell his teammates it was from police brutality.

The week ended quickly, and as Pat flew home, she was looking forward to going back for Thanksgiving. Dad had asked her about Andy, and after talking for about an hour, he told her to bring him with her when she came. He made it clear Andy would have to room with Larry. She made it clear she and Andy weren't anywhere near sharing a room. She discussed it with Andy as they drove home from the airport, and he said he would see if he could work his schedule for it.

~

James Morra was improving in health and had begun working with an occupational therapist to improve the use of his left hand. He was still in leg shackles and under constant watch of a reserve deputy. His pain was controllable with Tylenol. He was now allowed bathroom privileges rather than having to use a bedpan. The prognoses on his right hand and shoulder were that he would regain partial use of his thumb and two fingers. Because he was no longer using strong pain meds and sedatives, he was awake most of the day and slept most of the night.

Sergeant Allred and Deputy Haley had made short visits to update Morra on the progress of his case. The real purpose was to determine when he would be capable of giving a statement without the defense that he was mentally incapacitated by drugs. Secondarily, the visits continued the ego stroking and rapport building. Bren talked with the doctor about the degree Morra's medications or treatment might be affecting his mental judgment.

The doctor supplied a document that stated Morra was mentally unaffected by his current hospitalization. He was taking a dosage of Tylenol equivalent to that routinely taken by arthritics without any effect on their mental capabilities. He had suffered no physical trauma to the brain and showed no symptoms of any post-traumatic stress. Further, his blood chemicals, nutrition, and hydration were all normal. So medically his mind function and judgment should be 100 percent.

Bren and Pat found Morra sitting at the table reading a Tom Clancy novel. They informed Morra that the doctor had given the clearance to interview or interrogate him as needed and that they would be recording their conversations with him. Bren turned on the digital recorder and placed it in the center of the table.

Morra said, "I believe the doctor is correct. I have certain reduced physical abilities, but my intellect is as bright as ever. However, you can put away your bright lamps and rubber hoses. You shall need no interrogation. I want my story recorded accurately, not pieced together into a less-than-perfect narrative based on interpretation of evidence."

Pat laughed, "Just so the record is clear, we have no bright lamps or rubber hoses."

Morra seemed pleased that she was charmed by his wit. "Yes, it is best we start now being as accurate as possible. How do you prefer we proceed?"

Bren recited the Miranda rights, and Morra confirmed that he understood them, that he waved his right to have an attorney present, and that he was voluntarily cooperating with the interrogation.

Bren answered Morra's question. "I prefer that you simply give a detailed chronological narrative. Begin with when, and perhaps even why, you decided to embark on a path that you knew was illegal and could cost you the high position and recognition you held in your profession. It obviously was not greed or money that motivated you, since you were already independently wealthy. So start at the beginning and tell your story as accurately as you can."

Morra cleared his throat and spoke in his professional voice. "The genesis of my 'going to the dark side' was at the end of my doctoral work. I had maintained a nearly perfect grade point average through the university and had done some fine fieldwork. I had been a teaching assistant as an upper classman and a graduate assistant while working on my doctorate.

"From the groundless criticism of my Chair, Doctor Will Arrington, I began to realize that he was trying to sabotage my career. This proved correct when he rejected my doctoral proposal, and persuaded the other members of my committee that I was unwilling to accept direction. He had so poisoned the opinion of the faculty that I became clear I would never get a doctorate. That has been the great disappointment of my life.

"For nearly twenty years I have been the Arizona State Museum Archives Curator and an adjunct associate professor at the University. My career was dead-ended. I don't know the exact date, but several years ago a national parks archeologist named Marie Artiste came to the museum for research and took a deep interest in the Private Collections files. She spent three days working in the vault taking photos of some of the cards, and taking copious notes on the file system.

"Years later I became curious about her, so I did some research and discovered that she was consulting to facilitate sales of private artifacts to dealers. In short, I discovered that she was fraudulently certifying objects as legitimate that were most likely stolen from her own digs. Then, using a cleaned up version of my Rot-gut Rupert character, I became Dr. Middleman.

"I gave her insider information—very specific samples of pottery that the museum was looking to buy. She sold six of her fraudulent Private Collections items to the museum where Doctor Arrington served as the chairman of collection purchases. It was most satisfying that he had been duped."

From that point, Morra began to compile a record of Artiste's fraudulent sales to museums, schools, and to numerous private dealers. He finally decided that it would be even more satisfying if he was the one selling the artifacts to them. He was in a unique position to actually record back-dated entries in the file so that anyone who wanted validation could hold the card in their hands and see for themselves that the item was from the legitimate private market.

Morra began by approaching Steve Benson because he knew he was dealing on the low-end market under the table. He established a relationship with Benson-Colley that proved to be quite profitable, and he managed to get Arrington to add more illegal items to the museum collections. All his direct dealing with Arrington was by business correspondence, because Arrington would not be fooled by his disguise.

Arrington even asked for confirmation that the items were cataloged in the Ellsworth Private Collection file. Morra assured the professor they were. "After all, I had put them there myself," he roared with delight.

When he saw the clientele and the prices that Hale was getting for Marie's weak frauds, he revealed the evidence to Hale and offered to straighten it out. Morra offered to help him break his buying arrangement with Marie, and he provided a finding service that would guarantee artifacts he found were in the catalog.

He again laughed. "Hale almost had a heart attack when I showed him my evidence. He had no idea his supplier had been stealing them from the national park and providing fraudulent assurance from a dishonest private collector."

He explained that Hale eagerly agreed to his offer of help, but he ran into problems with Marie. "In our conversation I found out where Marie was currently working, so I made a surprise visit to her dig. I even offered her a million dollars to let me take over her business with Hale. She went insane and grabbed a rather large sifting screen and threw it at me. It caused me to go down on one knee. She lunged at me, and I whacked her on the head with a boulder. She was dead, so I left her and the bloody rock where they lay, and went topside and kicked part of the wall down on her. I made sure the scene made sense for an accidental rock fall, swept away my tracks to and from the site, and drove home."

He explained that he found a printer font on the internet that matched the old pica font, then paid a computer science student to modify the program to add offset shifts randomly on capitals and varying color density, like an overused ribbon or a poor typist would produce. Morra installed the program on the computer at the Hale Lab in Safford, so it would never be found at the museum. He took a supply of aged cards from the collections file to the lab to use in creating authentic-looking entries. He followed his own rules and always handled the cards with gloves, so there were no prints.

Morra liked and respected Mike Fulton from their grad school days. He found out that they were working the Queen Creek dig. Mike mentioned that one of his students was working overtime to earn extra money, including working occasionally for Benson-Colley when Mike didn't have work. Morra discovered Benson was paying Jack Hager under the table, so as Dr. Middleton, he offered much more for him to provide Salado artifacts, which were more in demand.

All went well on several of their digs until the day they were interrupted at Queen Creek. His Rot-gut Rupert instincts kicked in, and he shot that Indian kid.

"Jack got kind of hysterical and said he was through and was going to report what happened. I hit him in the head and shot him to look like a suicide. I took my equipment and the pots, and drove to Safford where I created the registry cards for the collections file and put the pots up for sale. My only mistake was with that other kid. I should have let him come over, and maybe I could have recruited him as well. If not, I could have shot him then."

Morra explained how he placed items in the correct chronological place in the Private Collections file, how he always used Sally's key card so nothing could be tied back to him. He explained what happened when he realized Manny Sanchez had been looking at the Private Collections, had asked about his truck, and had seen his shooting championship trophy. Once he saw Sanchez was a law officer, he knew he had to stop him from reporting his new suspicions. He found Manny's property record, saw it was very isolated and that he was sole owner, and drove like a demon there with plans to shoot him when he drove up.

"Sanchez was smarter than expected and caught me off guard with the speed and dust, but once the dust cleared he didn't have a chance. Suddenly a girl inside the trailer shot me with a shotgun. I knew he was single and lived by himself, but I had checked the trailer anyway. The whole time I was there, not a sound or movement came from the trailer."

Pat said, "Since your statement constitutes a confession, is it your intention to plead guilty?"

"Yes, but I still want a jury trial. I want everything officially on record for history. Also since I've been completely cooperative, I'm hoping I'll get some consideration by the court. Marie, Jack, and the Indian kid were impromptu acts, not planned. The attempted murder of the deputy was premeditated, but thankfully he did not die as planned.

I admire him as an intelligent and valiant adversary and am grateful that he saved my life after I was shot."

Bren stated, "You have been advised two or three times now that you should get an attorney. I recommend that you do that, just in case you are contemplating representing yourself. You are not trained in the law, so it would be like a lawyer doing a dig—different skill sets."

"I have an attorney that handles financial things, but he doesn't do criminal law."

"Call him and ask him to recommend a good criminal lawyer."

When they got to the lobby, Bren said, "That is cold. He has no feelings at all about killing and injuring people. His only regret is he didn't do a better job of it."

"It is getting harder and harder to keeping being pleasant to that jerk."

"You are doing great. A seasoned professional could not have done any better than you have on this case."

Chapter 20

The trials of crimes connected with the theft of the Baleful Owl occupied considerable space in the news media for the next two years. It would have been a much longer process if Morra's priority had not been getting his story publicized.

It was the most frustrating case John Spence, renowned Tucson defense attorney, had ever taken. He could easily have gotten some charges dropped and others reduced. He could have cast doubt on some of the evidence. Unfortunately for Spence, but fortunately for justice, client Morra would have none of that. All he wanted was to tell his own story in as many venues as possible.

Spence had even gone to the judge and asked to be released as attorney, but Morra objected. He specifically wanted Spence, and the judge enjoyed making it clear that Spence was in it to the end. Spence tried to get the Queen Creek event tried as a single case with two victims, but Morra wanted separate trials, so he was tried in two trials in Pinal County.

Morra was tried in Graham County for attempted murder. He was tried for murder by the New Mexico Attorney General in State Court in Albuquerque. He was tried in Phoenix for criminal conspiracy, forgery, and artifact theft and for similar charges in San Juan County, New Mexico. He was bitterly disappointed that the US Attorneys in both Arizona and New Mexico decided that his case was not worth their attention, since he would already be in jail for the remainder of his life, if not executed. No interstate prosecutions took place.

Since he freely, almost gleefully, confessed to every charge against him, Morra was convicted of felony murder, two attempted murders, criminal conspiracy, fraud, and artifact theft in Arizona, yielding a life sentence, two consecutive twenty-year sentences, and sentences totaling thirty more years on the lesser charges. He was convicted of second degree murder and the lesser charges in New Mexico for a total of thirty years, to be served at the end of his Arizona incarceration.

Through use of the RICO laws in both states, all of Morra's Cayman Bank accounts and his personal and real property in Tucson were recovered. The funds were distributed as reimbursement to the various agencies involved in the investigation.

Lawsuits filed on behalf of the victims reduced Morra's trust accounts from over sixteen-million dollars to four million. Mrs. Hager received the largest amount, six-million dollars, half of which she paid to her medical providers or donated to the cancer center in name of her son. Lester Kenton received $500,000, and $300,000 went into a trust fund to provide interest income to Dr. Artiste's Amazonian medical center. A similar fund was established to support the auditing and investigation program of the new Four Corners State's Artifact Trade Board of Ethics.

Steve Benson ended up spending two years in minimum security at the ASP Globe, in addition to paying court costs and a $500,000 fine. Oscar Colley received a six-month suspended sentence with two years' probation, and a $200,000 fine. They were forbidden to conduct environmental or archeological surveys in their business, so they became landscape contractors.

~

After Nettie Kenton returned to her Peridot home, Ed stopped by Emily Hager's place each evening to see if she needed anything, and he often took her to dinner. Emily responded well to her therapy and after a total duration of fourteen months was given a clean bill of health. She went back to work through the nurse's registry. Ed's visits turned into dates as romance blossomed between them.

Following his discovery of Nettie's excellent basketry, Ed had Pete thoroughly check that no one was selling or had any license to Nettie's work. There was no record of any sales of her products by her or anyone else.

Ed explained the market for fine crafted Apache baskets and told Nettie that he would be willing to buy some of her baskets. "I usually pay 50 percent of what I think I can get for it. I could get at least $100,000 for the one at Emily's, so your share would be $50,000 or more. In fact, if you would make a contract to exclusively sell through me and put an artist's mark on each basket, I would give you 70 percent of the sale."

"What's an artist's mark?"

"It's a tiny little symbol that you would weave into the design of each basket to prove it was made by you. It could be like an NK or any other symbol, and would be hidden in the weave somewhere."

"My Apache name is *Biih Ligai*, so I will weave a small white deer for my mark. How do I get one of those contracts?"

"I had Pete make one and give it to Lester to read. Feel free to take some time to think about it or talk with an attorney. One of the terms of the contract is that you have the right to end the agreement any time you wish with no penalty."

Nettie asked, "Lester, did you read it? Is it a good thing?"

"Yes, Mother, I did. Ed and Pete are good men, and we can trust them. The contract lets you make baskets when you want. When they sell, you get 70 percent of the sale."

"I don't care about that. Ed is a good man and doesn't lie or cheat. I'll sign it."

~

Ed Hale provided a $300,000 grant to the Arizona State Museum to digitize, index, and cross reference the old Private Collections inventory and make it available for online research. Acting Curator Olga Jordan took great care in overseeing the work, and the end product was excellent. Shortly after the completion of the project, she was named Curator of the Library and Archives by the search committee.

~

Elton Godwin was hired by the Fultons on a monthly salary with benefits and overtime pay. The Fultons were successful in taking over the B-C general contract, resulting in a great increase in contracts on reservations in the Southwest. Jill Fulton accepted a three-year appointment to the new artifact board of ethics.

~

Manny and Jenny Sanchez decided to continue visits with Dr. Curtis. Of the two, Manny had more lingering nightmares about the shoot-out. He was terribly anxious about leaving Jenny alone so much. He dreamt of Morra returning to kill Jenny.

He modified his patrols, so that he was driving past their house every hour or less, and fairly often stopping for a minute to take a bathroom break. After about three months everything began to return to normal.

~

Manny volunteered extra shifts during Thanksgiving week, as did a couple of other deputies, to allow Pat and Andy to spend the holiday in Blacksburg.

A wonderful and a significant event occurred on their last night. Mr. Haley had a long talk with Pat and Andy about their relationship. It started with him saying, "I don't know if you two know it or not, but you are in love with each other. You need to face that fact."

It ended with, "Don't worry about how you will adjust, or if you can be 'normal.' Nobody is normal. We all have our individual attributes and experiences. Marriage is accepting that we are the same and different on many things. Accept those things and enjoy each other. Be honest and faithful and try to put up with more than the other person has to put up with. A couple's love is a treasure to be preserved and nourished."

When they were alone, Andy told Pat, "He's right you know . . . at least for me. I'm in love with you."

"I love you too. Now we have to decide what to do about it."

~

On the Sunday after Thanksgiving, the Allred family had their evening prayer and put the kids to bed. Bren sat in his favorite chair, and Monica came in and sat on his lap.

Monica smiled and said, "I've missed my period this month."

Bren pulled her close and kissed her.

"Easy does it, Bucko. That's how this stuff gets started."

~

The Baleful Owl was put on permanent exhibit prominently displayed in its own pedestal case in the Arizona State Museum. There he stands sentinel over the artifacts of the vanished culture that created him, back near his homeland in a place of beauty and appreciation. Perhaps he thinks, *'Idam 'o'odham 'o sñho'ige'id.* (These people are kind to me.)

You will also enjoy the new editions of the other books
in this prize-wiining series
forthcomng soon from Aakenbaaken & Kent:

The Wham Curse
Deputy Allred and Apache Officer Victor - Book 1

Deputy Allred and Apache Officer Victor - Book 1 An inexplicable murder of a young Apache boy draws Deputy Bren Allred and Apache Tribal Policeman Victor into a mystery that can be solved only when they tie the murder to a century-old robbery of Army Paymaster Major Wham. Set in both the old West and today's ranch country, the story explores the natural and cultural history, and people of the contemporary rural southwest.

Saints and Sinners
Deputy Allred and Apache Officer Victor - Book 2

Intrigue and murder along the US/Mexico Border. Seventeen-year-old Mariana Villalobos' mystic gift creates a sensation in northern Mexico as hundreds of people undergo a personal religious epiphany. Even gangsters reject crime. Seeing revenues tumble in the drug trade, the Liones cartel issues a hit order on the girl. The Mexican police hide Mariana in the Gila Valley of Arizona while they work with a defector and international law enforcement to dismantle the gang. Graham County Deputies Bren Allred and Manny Sanchez join forces with San Carlos Apache Tribal Policeman Al Victor to identify assassins and protect Mariana. It's a race against time for agents of the DEA, ICE, Spanish Policia National, and the Mexican Policia Judicial. Can they bring the Liones cartel to justice before the girl is harmed?

And a new book in the series forthcoming summer of 2018:

Murder in Copper
Deputy Allred and Apache Officer Victor - Book 4

Copper theft and suspected industrial espionage drag Deputies Bren Allred, Manny Sanchez, and Patricia Haley and Apache Policeman Al Victor into an undercover investigation of new copper mines near Sleeping Beauty Mountain in Globe-Miami and in the Gila Valley. They find great difficulty with how the copper is disappearing, and the espionage turns nasty when a tribal member is murdered and the main suspect has diplomatic immunity. The mystery is set in a background of old west ranchers and historic mines and also modern, even futuristic, mining technology.

Acknowledgements

My wife Lois is my "first editor" and my greatest support; in this book she was also a technical advisor, since in the late 1960's she worked at the Southwestern Monuments Association/Southwestern Archeological Center (SWAC) in Globe, Arizona, an institution that plays a role in this story. There she knew some of the archeologists mentioned in the story, most notably Emile Haury, Ned Danson (actor Ted Danson's dad), and Gordon Vivian, whose wife taught us at Miami High School. One clarification: The SWAC scientists did start a Private Collections Index, but it was never even close to a complete index of private collections as fictionally represented in the story.

Thanks for the great professional editing by Sandra Udall. Likewise I appreciate our friend and cultural editor Yvette Reynoso Barnes for helping me depict elements of Hispanic and Catholic culture accurately.

www.ingramcontent.com/pod-product-compliance
Lightning Source LLC
Chambersburg PA
CBHW022201261125
35888CB00010B/89